BLACK CHALK

Albert Alla

Garnet
PUBLISHING

BLACK CHALK

Published by
Garnet Publishing Limited
8 Southern Court
South Street
Reading
RG1 4QS
UK

www.garnetpublishing.co.uk
www.twitter.com/Garnetpub
www.facebook.com/Garnetpub
blog.garnetpublishing.co.uk

Copyright © Albert Alla, 2013

All rights reserved.
No part of this book may be reproduced in any form or by any electronic or mechanical means, including information storage and retrieval systems, without permission in writing from the publisher, except by a reviewer who may quote brief passages in a review.

First Edition

ISBN: 9781859643570

British Library Cataloguing-in-Publication Data
A catalogue record for this book is available from the British Library

Typeset by Samantha Barden
Jacket design by Garnet Publishing
Cover images Silhouette of man © Harsanyi Andras and Diffuse sexy woman silhouette, hands © Daniel M. Nagy, courtesy of Shutterstock.com

Printed and bound in Lebanon by International Press:
interpress@int-press.com

One

I guess this is the story everyone's been waiting for. The badges who expected me to bow and confess. The friends who kept quiet and hoped I'd let something out. The twenty-year-old I met in the Mediterranean, who heard my name, stroked his chin, and demanded my story as if it belonged to him. And most of all, the inspector who probed and probed, until all he had left was a challenge.

I've never wanted cameras brandished in my face or tape recorders thrust at my throat. And I've done as much as I could to avoid it. Not only did I leave the country, but I've also been calling myself Nathan, for Nate Dillingham evoked too much blood.

Now eight years on, I'm back in Oxford. I'm sitting in an attic room that contains all the things I owned before I went off. A room my mother put together to help me dispel my doubts. There's even a poster of The Verve above my bed. And, of course, she's done what she set out to do: after years on the road, this red-brick house off the Banbury Road feels like home. She's thrust me back into the world I fled, as convinced today as she was then that stability is what I need.

My laptop is set up on the one item which wasn't mine, a creaky walnut desk which, if I remember right, was in the guest room of our Hornsbury home. The blue of my old chair has faded, but my back still rests comfortably on its cushions. There's a photo board to my right full of old family pictures. A childhood pruned of all my school friends.

In one picture, I stand between my father and my brother. We are in our cricket whites, standing in front of the pavilion. My sixteen-year-old frame hasn't had time to fill out yet. My torso leans away as if I'm trying to escape through the edge of the picture. I wear an awkward smile: my thick lips show a fraction of my teeth, while my eyes look seriously at the camera. In comparison, my little brother seems natural, holding a sullen pose on one arched leg, while my father stands straight and content, a cricket bat balancing between the thumb and forefinger of his left hand. Seeing this picture reminds me of who took it: Jeffrey, on the day he clung on to a one-handed diving catch at gully, which he talked about for weeks afterwards. The same Jeffrey who should be pruned from my life. I shouldn't have to think about him and the others in this roundabout way. This is exactly why I'm sitting on this chair staring at a black cursor flashing against a white background.

I've made myself two cups of tea since I started this, and my legs are consorting with my mouth, itching for a third. I won't do it, not until I've started writing. From photographic reels to blurs and blanks, I should begin with the destruction itself.

* * *

The 10th of February 2000 was a rare bright day in a generally overcast winter. The sort of day that made me think that school was almost over. Along with the rest of my class, I was ambling along, convinced that there was always more time ahead, and that if all else failed, I could use the weeks leading up to the exams to cram everything I'd been taught over the last two years. I already had an offer and I felt confident I could get the marks. In eight months, if everything went well, I would start Physics and Philosophy eight miles away, in Oxford.

The first lesson of the day, history, was held in the red bricks of the main building. When it ended, Jeffrey and I headed for our physics class, along an outdoor archway that stopped halfway down the hill, its arches supported by columns, and the columns adorned with eroded crests. As our school's only shot at the grandiose, it featured heavily on all its propaganda, and in much of the coverage that followed that day. Beth, whose lipstick matched the scarf around her neck, walked with us up to the point where the archway leaves the building – it was a detour in the cold for her, but she'd taken it every Thursday since the New Year. Ever since she'd dragged Jeffrey and a bottle of whisky into a night of platonic debauchery.

When she left us, I noticed his backpack for the first time. It was new: its body was bright red, its base was leather tainted burgundy. The same colours as that thing she wore around her head. I pointed at it and laughed. He smiled but he sounded sad:

'Tuesday, we spent the whole night in bed.'

'Alone, just the two of you?'

'I don't know what's going on. Didn't even kiss or anything.'

'Did you try?'

'She was like, she didn't want to. I even gave her a massage.'

We went quiet, for we'd arrived at the Kemp Annexe, a 1960s addition overlooking the sports ground.

For many months after that day, my conversation with Jeffrey was a safe memory. My thoughts would start with him looking longingly at Beth, and if I felt strong enough, I'd stop them at Jeffrey's new bag. In those happy instances, I would be left with a smile. But there were plenty of others when I felt weak, when the redness of his bag collapsed in a gallop, and I started thinking of the way Mr Johnson looked at us.

We were late and he stared at us. The last row was empty, the chairs still on the table as he insisted we keep them. He already had both hands in his pockets, his arms framing his pot belly, as he tsk-tsked and shook his head. We took our seats. Jeffrey nudged me under the table, and I struggled to keep a straight face.

'Mr Dillingham, Mr Baker, welcome!' Mr Johnson was still shaking his head. 'I'm honoured that you managed to join us. But let's give you your due: you're not as late as Mr Knight and Mr Williams. I'll give them another thirty seconds.' He looked down and clicked his tongue in time with the second hand of his watch, before he raised his eyes to the class, a satisfied expression on his face. 'Can't say we didn't wait for them. Let's get going.'

We opened our books on page 212 – it had a picture of a teenager in bright green short shorts, a basketball inches from his fingers, black dashes arching between his hands and the basket – and started a problem set. Mr Johnson believed in teaching passively, asking us to try problems much like the ones we would encounter in our exams. While we sat and worked, he was at his desk marking copies, and when he had no copies to mark, he gazed through the window at the sports ground. There's a form of respect in acknowledging that he was a little lazy, that he wanted to use his teaching time to do his evening work. But his methods were successful. Some, like Eric, had changed schools so that they could take physics at Hornsbury School.

A few minutes into the class, Jeffrey tapped me on the hand and pointed at Jayvanti who was sitting one table in front of us. Arching my neck, I couldn't see very much. But then Jeffrey whispered her name, she turned around, and for a few seconds, while they traded answers, all I could see were four undone buttons and a braid tickling the top of her brown breasts. When she turned to face the front, Jeffrey nudged me under the table and we stifled a snigger. Then he wrote on my notebook:

'Is it true Eric fancies her?'

'Who wouldn't?' I wrote.

He put his pencil down and started whispering:

'Can you imagine? Him with a girl!' He nudged me again. 'Oh, come on, tell me. I'm sure he told you!'

At that moment, Mr Johnson noticed students chatting and cleared his throat. He asked whether everyone had finished.

When no one answered, he considered us all one at a time, as if his next decision required deep thoughts, until his eyes settled on Anna.

'Miss Walker, will you come to the board and show the rest of us how to solve the third problem?'

She was still sitting on the other side of the room from me, where she'd moved to after we split up. And just as she had done for the last month and a half, she looked at everyone but me while she made her way up the centre aisle.

As she stood up, a rattling sound came from the vestibule, the sound of thick metal sliding, links clanging against each other softened by a door or two. Anna turned her head towards the door and when no one said anything, she went up to the blackboard and started talking about the problem: acceleration and velocity in a frictionless world. Just as she started to differentiate a binomial, the door opened.

Eric walked in – a chain in his hand, a large blue sports bag slung over his shoulder – and shut the door, his back to us.

'Mr Knight, you are late! But it doesn't matter. It's your future. Take a seat' – Mr Johnson pointed – 'and listen to Miss Walker tackle this problem.'

Eric paid no attention to Mr Johnson. Instead, he turned his attention towards the door, and we watched him, bemused, as he uncoiled his chain and looped it between the door handle and the frame of a nearby shelf, looping once, looping twice, as he bolted it with a padlock and checked the whole mechanism with a firm tug.

'Mr Knight?' Mr Johnson said. 'Eric, what are you doing? Eric!'

Eric advanced towards a window opposite the door, the one with a green exit sign above it, checked it was locked, and turned towards us. He looked prophetic: his face starved, his usually floppy black hair stretched above his skull, and his ever-intense eyes now bloodshot, wide open, taking in everyone. Even Mr Johnson went quiet as we waited.

Perhaps I am imagining this, but I have a vague memory of Eric's eyes boring into my face during that silence. And if I'm not inventing this, he lowered his chin once in my direction. Still, I can't be sure this happened, for all I have are those two faint images, a close-up on his eyes, a slow nod.

Some things, I remember as if they happened last week. Eric reaching into his bag and grabbing two objects. And for an instant, my eyes seeing nothing but the barrels' glistening metal, and the matte texture of the grip through the gaps between his fingers. Placing one in each hand, his voice: 'This won't last long.' He said it as if his future had already taken place, as if his design came from more than himself. 'And,' he added, 'don't worry, that includes me too.'

Writing this, I find myself squirming, making up reasons to leave my desk. It seems I've been telling myself the pain was gone, when I really meant the memories had grown more distant. I have to push past the image of Eric standing armed in front of us while we watched and waited. It lasted but a moment, and then the stillness shattered.

At first, it was Anna screaming and then desks flipping and falling onto the floor, chairs and bags flapping along. There was a rush of bodies towards the door which did not give, and two deep voices trying to break through the cacophony. The girls sitting at the table behind me stayed put and whispered to one another, as if they were discussing the best way to leave an awful play. But their whispers were hoarse: they were stifled shouts, a restraint on madness. And two voices kept on trying to break through. Mr Johnson, in the same voice he always used, proclaiming that we were not in America, that this was ridiculous. And another voice asking for calm. It wasn't Eric – he was observing from his corner of the room, waiting for us, it seemed.

It was Tom Davies standing up and moving towards Eric. When he was two metres away, Eric took aim. Tom stopped and raised his arms, his lips still forming soothing sounds – sounds which I wish I could recall. But sadly, they have left nothing but conflicting echoes. And yet, as I picture him now, I reconstruct his likeness and see him speak, and I hear him too, saying words that I conjure up from the traces he left behind.

Tom turned and addressed us, those who were listening. 'Quiet, quiet,' I hear him say, 'we can work something out. There's no need to do anything silly. We just need to talk it out.'

Tom was splendid, his voice coaxing us into hope, his gentle movements and his statements still carrying the authority he deserved. He loomed large in my mind then, an everyday example risking centre stage when it might mean death. He was facing the front wall, Eric to his left, the door to his right, and the rest of us strewn across the classroom.

'Eric, there's no need to do this. Think about it. Please.' He tried to engage Eric's eyes.

'Sit down, Tom,' Eric said, still aiming at Tom's chest. 'Don't get in the way.'

Perhaps Tom thought Eric was listening, or perhaps he thought he'd appear less threatening sitting down. Whatever the reason, he obeyed him, taking down a chair from the last row and starting to talk again, his tones low and soothing: 'Think of everyone here, think of your friends. You've spent two years here with us. And think of our families, think of—'

'Shut up,' Eric said with quiet strength. 'If you say another word, I'll shoot you.'

Tom looked stunned only for an instant. He recovered and looked at us, two rows from him, and started coordinating a sally with small movements of his head. I believe Eric saw it all but decided to ignore it. Instead he addressed Laura, and, almost kindly, asked her to put her phone away.

'Thank you,' he told her and turned to the three students working on the chain. His voice remained even, each sentence pronounced with the same rehearsed emphasis. 'It won't budge, and the vestibule's locked too. Go back to your desks. I don't want to get in between you and your deaths. If you want to write something, or if you want to pray, I can wait one minute.'

One minute. All of my blood seemed to have drained to my feet. I looked across at Anna and saw her looking at me. Her right hand was clutching the backrest of a chair, and her left was clawing at her right forearm. Her eyes were moist, and I wanted to bridge the distance. One minute. There never was that minute. Had Tom and Mr Johnson held off a little longer, the few who considered writing – I remember Edward Moss and Jayvanti Patel in front of me grabbing their pens – would have had time to set something down.

Instead Tom leaped, and there was the first of many hollow cracks, and there was no more splendour, no more calls for calm. And there was a jolt starting in my chest and spreading down my limbs, and I was fast as a blur. And Eric looked around, arms raised, or perhaps he was shooting from the hip, and there was no more pretence. And we were ducking, crawling, crying, and most of all shouting. And we tried the windows but the windows could only open so as to let in the smallest of draughts, except for the one window which opened all the way, but that was where Eric stood.

I tasted metal. I had blood in my mouth, but I wasn't wounded. The thought crossed my mind that I might not feel a gunshot, that I would die too quickly to feel the bullet butcher my flesh, but that, in death, I could carry over something so trivial as the taste of blood in my mouth – the last input my brain would have been able to decipher. But I wasn't dead: I just had blood in my mouth.

Anna was crouching next to me, holding my hand, struggling with the onset of a panic attack. For a brief moment, as I squeezed her hand, a sudden sadness weighed on my shoulders. And it was gone with a grunt, one loud grunt at first, and then four more in decrescendo. Jeffrey was on the floor in pain. And Anna was crushing my hand, her breathing reduced to a rasping sound, air scraping into her lungs, her breasts jerking up and down ever faster. In the few seconds I spent stroking her arm and whispering so she would calm down, I was aware of a body I had loved, now fighting itself. I knew I ought to feel something, perhaps apprehension or dread. Ideally it would have been love and forgiveness but I would have taken simple lust. It didn't have to be beautiful. But I wanted it to be strong. Nothing came.

Jeffrey was no longer grunting. Eric wasn't by the window anymore, and pretty Jayvanti's curvy body straddled a fallen chair on the floor. I surveyed the scene. It was meticulous, yes: neat and precise. Even the chaos made sense. Don't listen to me, there was no honour in the chaos. One, two, three, crack. I'd survived. One, two, crack, crack, three, crack. Even now, I can't do the moment justice. Even now, I can't tell it right: the images are there, however smudged, but the words don't follow.

* * *

They were all still, except for Anna whom I could hear breathing, and Grace whose leg I could see twitching. How long had it been since Eric had come into the classroom? It felt like it had happened a long time ago and that it hadn't happened yet. But the classroom was quiet, except for the three of us breathing and bleeding. Grace made no sound, as quiet in agony as she had been in life. And I crawled back to Anna's side, who was silent now. I lay there wondering what to do about the bullet in my stomach.

If a part of me remembers the pain, another sees me disassociated, above the room, floating amongst ideas and images. My hands were covering my stomach, my back resting against two school bags and part of an overturned table, my knees as close to my midriff as I could bring them, blood slowly seeping out. Help was coming, I knew. Help: the word came to life. I imagined a swarm of doctors resuscitating our limp bodies, lifting us onto comfortable stretchers, airlifting us to a new hospital, removing and discarding the traces of the day from our bodies, and discharging us a day later after a long night's sleep. I needed sleep. And then school would declare a week-long recovery, which I would spend reading and watching cricket.

The picture was too hopeful. Help would be two policemen coming to investigate a routine call, wondering what to do outside the chained door, and deciding to kick it in and assess what was inside before asking for reinforcements. They would come in, see the carnage and then, it was almost worth a laugh, I would die before the ambulance turned up.

* * *

Help arrived as help is meant to arrive. The spectacle trod on, and I was draining away in its midst, curiously overtaken by a profound wonder. Wonder at the eclectic scene around me, and wonder at the commotion gathering outside. At first, it was the lonely sound of a siren blaring far from all traffic – I imagined its cold blue light flashing past the grey leafless trees up to the cold blue sky. As if it realised its incongruity, it stopped, giving way to a murmur of muddled voices. To the sound of metal on metal: they were cutting through the outside door, and then they were hammering their way through. These were harsh sounds but they had to be. And then a teacher led them to the fire exit on the side of the building, hidden in between two thorny bushes. It wasn't much of an exit, just a low-lying window with a foldable stile. And then they were in. Shock gently etched onto their faces, giving way to an uneasy determination, the scowls and pursed lips smoothing into a final flat mask. There were to be no smiles, no tears – just a job to do.

A woman was sitting by me.

'Let me see,' she asked. But I didn't want to show her. I told her to go and see to the others, I was fine and they needed help. 'Let me see,' she said. I told her to take a look at Anna. I asked her whether anyone else was alive. She didn't know. 'Let me see,' she said. I just had to lift my hand for a few instants.

I noticed sweat glistening on her forehead. She was a nice woman, I decided. 'Are you cold?' she asked. I was a little cold – she took off her jacket and laid it over me. She told me to stay in the position I was already in. I was doing just the right thing. 'I'm a natural,' I told her. She smiled and helped me get more comfortable. 'Is this your blood?' she asked. I explained to her that I didn't know, but I thought a lot of it was Jeffrey's, and a little was Anna's. She wedged a toppled chair between my toes and another table. I hadn't noticed how tense my legs were until I was able to relax them. She asked me what had happened. Such an innocent question, I thought; she didn't need to look guilty. 'Eric,' I started and stopped. She seemed to understand.

I asked her why she was helping me when so many others were worse off. 'I'm staying with you until we can take you to a hospital,' she said. I told her she should take care of the others, I was fine. She gave me a tight-lipped smile and said the others were being taken care of. I looked around: there were about ten people in the room, all paramedics except for two people in plain clothes with a bolt cutter having a go at the chain. I recognised the groundsman and an old maths teacher. Their names stuck on the tip of my tongue. A man was by Anna's side, back to back with the woman taking care of me. She told me her name was Liz. Just like my mother. They were about the same age. I couldn't think of any more similarities.

I wanted to tell her something. But I couldn't recall her name. Yes, of course. 'Liz.'

'I'm here. I'm still here. You'll be on your way to hospital in no time. Don't worry.'

I told her I wasn't worried, but I had to tell her something. 'Yes, I'm listening, don't worry.' I explained I wasn't worried, but I wanted her to tell my parents how much I appreciated what they'd done for me, and that I didn't want a grave. I thought graves were too grim. If they needed a monument, couldn't they plant a tree? Liz was nodding along, saying I shouldn't worry – I wasn't worried – and that I would be able to tell them myself. I smiled at her and thanked her.

They put me on a stretcher, stuck a few cushions underneath my knees, and covered me with a blanket. Outside, rain was approaching. A hint of mist was drifting through Hornsbury School but the sun kept on shining. Colours were stronger and warmer for it. The incandescence of the ambulances on the grass, the reflections of policemen's jackets standing guard, the contrasts in the resurgent crowd. I looked for Anna and saw Grace in an ambulance shutting its doors. Liz was still by my side. 'Where's Anna?' I asked her. They slid my stretcher into the ambulance and she asked me who Anna was. She was already ahead, she then explained. I imagined Anna in an ambulance asking the same questions about me. She'd gone by helicopter, Liz added. Anna would like that, I thought. 'Where's Jeffrey?' I asked. She said he was being taken care of. I asked whether he was in an ambulance. 'Not yet,' she answered. I understood what she wasn't telling me.

I needed to stay awake, to fight off the great weariness dulling my pain.

And I wanted to ask where Tom was. And I wanted to know where Mr Johnson was. And Jayvanti Patel, and Laura Clarkson, and Satish Choudary, and Edward Moss, and Paul Cumnor, and Harry Williams. But Harry Williams hadn't come to class today. And Eric Knight. I had to complete the litany.

Black Chalk

I looked around myself and wondered where I was, wondered why I wasn't in school. My answers were exotic, my logic capricious, my impressions oneiric. Odd yet normal, twisted yet clear. It had to be a dream, I told myself. But my lacerated stomach wouldn't let me escape. I tried anyway, sprinkling my wishes with realism. It was morning and I was on my way to school, another day except that physics had been cancelled.

The ambulance slowed suddenly. Something rattled, a soft sound of metal on metal, and the spell broke. It started to come to me, a swirl of sensations sweeping all in their way, gathering speed, shimmering outside a familiar building, materialising in anticipation, and entering brashly into an unwary classroom – I stopped the thought. There was no need to go any further, I knew it all so well.

'That's right, we're almost there. You only need to hold on a little longer. You're very brave, you know. We're in Marston already, yes, it's not far.' She was holding my arm. It seemed like she was whispering in my ear, keeping me from wasting into nothingness with her murmurs.

* * *

My memories of A&E are incoherent. Like a childhood condensed, I remember things I didn't do and events I wasn't at. Liz had left me, or I had left her. And perhaps necessity unlocked an awareness that let me see my mother drive towards the hospital, or perhaps the vivid details that come to my mind are nothing but the product of a pronounced delirium. Yet there she is, coming out of a lecture and hearing of the shooting. Immediately deciding to drive to the John Radcliffe Hospital instead of my school.

Meanwhile, my flesh was in a large rectangular room on a table that paraded as a bed, surrounded by a team of doctors in garbs. I see them all wearing the same loose sober greens, asexual and indistinguishable. As I was wheeled in, I noticed two teams waiting and one already at work. Grace being brought in ahead of me; I had time to see her unit set up before the curtains were drawn shut. Her team seemed military: a stout man – his silhouette rises out of the fog – delivering curt orders, everyone following them, his soldiers either moving purposefully or standing at attention.

They ignored the shout-fest coming from the team on the other side of the room, but I couldn't. There, looking past two blurry greens, I glimpsed a foreign face: pale and drawn. It was her hair, ash darkened by damp, which I recognised.

A doctor gave me something for the pain: this will make you feel like you've had five pints, I heard. My carcass stopped mattering as its suffering washed away. What was left of my attention, the spirals which had survived the doctors' concoctions, listened to the enumeration of expletives coming from my left. And then I heard her staunch the profane. Was she speaking? My limbs weren't responding, surgeons were at me, I couldn't get closer and decipher her groans. I started to empathise with her pain, but too soon they were barking over her, and I was left to myself. Alive. Alone.

Loneliness was sweeping me towards a hollow, defeated and drained, when I saw my mother by my side. It's the last memory I have of that decisive day, the last memory before I gave in to the inevitable slide. She had followed someone through the electronically locked doors, bravado carrying her past hospital protocol. She stood and looked at me a full minute before anyone saw her. When asked to leave, she approached me. Her fingers covered mine. She squeezed them until she knew I could feel her.

Two

The memories of my early convalescence are of ash and soot. My eyelids too heavy to respond, I was at the mercy of a slow current. My consciousness dragged me through greys and blacks. Through the ash, I glimpsed a small house with no door. I tried to get closer but we were floating in the same river. For all I knew, the house could have been a pile of granite and burned wood. It left me behind when the soot settled.

Respite came when sleepless dreams congealed into dreamless sleep. There were voices around me and then they were gone. I did not have the will to understand them. All my strength veiled the blunt pain that spread through me with every throb.

The soot was more violent than the ash. It took me to a great windswept plain. I was surrounded by an ocean of yellowed grass. And the clouds promised blood. I turned and turned, afraid to look up, searching for shelter, a trench, a furrow.

Dreams went but the pain persisted.

As the slumber thinned, voices became people. There were nurses talking over me, and there were nurses talking over others. A new strand brought me relief: its warm lilt, its limpid diction, its calm command, and the courtesy it elicited. My mother was asking the nurses about me. I could hear her breathing by my side, murmuring, paper rustling. I could feel her hand on my forehead, the familiar calluses, her fingertips lingering at my brow before rearranging my hair.

* * *

My first complete memory happened on the 12th of February, two days after I was rushed through A&E. I am told that my eyelids flickered and that my tongue gibbered before then. I put my body's twitches to the fever I was fighting, an infection I picked up somewhere between the classroom and surgery, which was draining me quicker than a punctured stomach.

It was the sound of both voices at the same time that pierced through the stupor. And her confessional tones, almost submissive, made the moment stand out.

'Someone needs to be here,' she was saying.

'What about James? He needs you too.'

'Now that you're back, can't you take care of him?'

'He needs his mother.'

Her words briefly unravelled into inaudible whispers, before her voice reasserted itself: '... Nate gets better, I'll spend more time at home.'

They were right by my bed, speaking in hushed tones. I had the sense of listening in to a private conversation, the sort they would have in their room, the door closed, before coming out to present my brother and me with a common front.

'I sat next to Grace's mother at the meeting this morning,' my mother was confessing. 'I didn't know what to say... But she understood. It's not what she said, she hardly speaks English.' She paused. 'Henry, she's so dignified! I wanted to hug her... But I didn't dare, it's not like we know each other. Still, moments like these bring people together.'

They stayed silent for a minute. I wanted to stretch my hand and touch them, but my fingers wouldn't heed my orders.

'Have you seen Eric's parents?' my father said.

'Do you think I should?'

'Well, they were good friends.'

'Nate's friends with everybody... But I've been thinking about it. His mother must be suffering more than any of us.'

'No, you're right.' My father's tones became more assertive. 'You don't have to go see anyone. The police will do all that, and you heard that Hill fellow, they'll let us know what they find. We just have to wait for their findings.'

My mother's voice weakened. 'But does he really understand? He's got no idea. He can't, he doesn't know what it means to be sitting here.'

My father had come back from overseas, Kenya, I think, where he'd been volunteering for one of his company's pro bono projects. To have them both! I basked in the thought. But the matter of the conversation gnawed through the glow.

I groaned, my eyes half open, light streaming in. They were both up on their feet. My mother stroking my cheek, my father's arm around her. I looked towards them and tried to smile.

'Is he?' my mother said looking towards my father. She cupped my forehead with her hand.

He went around the bed and laid his hand on my left wrist. 'Nate?' he asked.

'He feels cooler. They said he'd hear first.'

I wanted to say I could but my lips wouldn't part fully. I focused on my left hand, on the warmth of my father's skin, and straightened my index finger, a tendon cording out all the way to my elbow.

'Nate,' my father said, 'you're safe. We're here with you.'

I could hear my mother crying. 'Darling,' she said, fighting with her face. She looked to my father: 'Oh, I'm glad we're both here for this.' Checking a sob, she turned towards me again, studied my face, and smiled timidly: 'Nate, darling, your stomach, and then that fever... We love you so much, you know.'

I looked at the tears running down her face and felt helpless.

'We're very lucky...' She was wearing one of my father's old cardigans, the same green one she would take on road trips. 'And look here,' she moved aside and pointed at the window, 'isn't that a lovely view? You can even see Grandma's old house from here. We used to go there once a month when you were little. Do you remember? She lived very close to here. I'll show it to you when you get stronger.' She leaned towards me and kissed me on the cheek.

She stopped talking and stood rooted by me. My father's face was tanned for February. I tried to speak and nothing came out. I felt her hair brushing my lips.

'What about the others?' I whispered. Whispering was all I could manage.

She didn't answer straight away.

'What did he say?' my father asked.

'He asked about the others. Your brother was here yesterday, but he's scared of hospitals you know. He's staying with Stan today. I know you want to see him.'

She stopped as if there were nothing else to add.

'What about the others?' I whispered again.

She leaned back and breathed deeply. Looking at my father, she said: 'He wants to know about the others. Nate, the most important thing is that you're safe here with us. The doctors say you'll be alright, you just need time to build your strength.'

I tried to speak again, but she didn't lean forward to hear what I had to say. She exchanged a look with my father.

'Darling, Nate. The others...' When it seemed like she wouldn't say any more, my father said:

'They told us to let him rest.'

For a moment, I thought my mother would agree with 'they', the control-men, but she shook her head several times. 'No, no, that's not how we raised them. Nate, it's not good news...' One hand on my cheek, another stroking the fingers of my right hand, she looked for the right words. I could feel it coming from the coldness of her fingers.

'It's tragic, Nate, it's so sad, I don't know how to put it. All I know is that you're here, and that's a gift, and we should be thankful for it.' She looked up towards the ceiling, tears illuminating her eyes.

I looked for the right word. It didn't come. 'Everyone?' I said.

She hesitated. 'No one outside your physics class.'

'And Anna?' I asked.

'What did he say?' asked my father.

'He asked about Anna.'

'Ah, yes.'

'Anna's very weak. And even if she makes it, she won't be the same.'

My father spoke: 'You'll get better in no time, Nate.'

I closed my eyes and searched for the house again, willing the current back into motion.

* * *

This morning, I went looking for my old drawing case. My mother thought I'd find it in the storage room under the stairs. The room was full of boxes, crates, and paintings that this new house has no space for. I didn't find it – I may well come across it tomorrow if I rummage through the back section of the room.

My search stopped when I came across a dusty blue chest. It was just as I had left it all those years ago, the rusty padlock testifying that it had stayed closed over the years. I felt relieved. Her son gone for eight years, silent for seven, I would have understood my mother breaking the lock and looking inside. Knowing her curiosity, I'm surprised she left the chest alone. Perhaps she always expected me to come back, or perhaps she preferred ignorance in this one regard. Whatever its source,

I appreciate her restraint – I don't think I would be able to face her over dinner tonight if she were armed with my hospital thoughts.

I couldn't remember where I'd hidden the key, so I fetched a large screwdriver from the kitchen and wedged it in the padlock and pushed. I could hear movements within its mechanism but it held together. There was a bigger toolkit in the garage: I found a handheld metal saw. I sharpened the blade and took it to the padlock. Once I managed to nick the shackle, the saw tore through the lock and the chest pried open.

The boy who locked the chest would have been too shy to tackle a reticent padlock. He would have scratched his head and moved on to something else. Or he would have asked someone else for help. Menial jobs, fluctuating finances, and wading through mud must have done their bit.

I've spent the best part of the day sprawled over my bed, immersed in my hospital diaries. In between tentative sketches, I found a medley of spare thoughts and painstaking descriptions. Nine words on Anna, followed by a sketch of my foot, and three pages on the nurses' interactions. A paragraph on Jeffrey, another sketch of my foot, a still life, six words (no verb) on Eric, a page and a half on Inspector Hill's mannerisms.

I'm starting to think that my psychiatrist was right, that I was fleeing it all. And yet, such things affect us differently. My reactions were just as right as those of snarling mothers and pontificating principals.

* * *

My parents moved to Hornsbury when I was four. A year before I was born, my father had left London and, teaming up with two colleagues, started a management consultancy. As luck had it, my mother was made a fellow of her college just as his business was becoming viable. Tired of their small Jericho flat,

Black Chalk

they decided to move out of the city and into the country. The way she tells the story, it sounds like it was my father who wanted to raise his children the way he was raised. But when I asked him about it, he explained in his careful, measured voice that he'd had a slight preference towards staying in Oxford, while my mother had had a strong preference for a garden: hence, as couples ought to do, they'd looked for a house in the country, and found what they were looking for in Hornsbury.

Now that I've heard stories of others' childhoods, I realise how good mine was: I had a spacious garden, and up until my brother was old enough to play with me, a father who happily taught me how to juggle a football, catch a cricket ball, swing a racket. During the winter season, my mother drove me to football games, and my father took me along to his squash tournaments. In the summer, I followed him around the county's cricket fields, at first cheering his every run, and then playing alongside him.

I still remember the day I first came on the field. I was eight, and it was only as a substitute fielder, but to me that didn't take anything away from the moment: I was all of a sudden in the middle of everything. Every time a bowler ambled to the crease, I expected the ball to come my way. I walked in as I'd seen internationals do on television: my hands on my knees, a smile betraying my otherwise focused face. Thinking about it now, I realise they'd put me at short forty-five, where the ball would never come fast, especially given the pace of our attack. I still see Garry, the wicketkeeper, crouching over his large belly, and turning to me every third ball to check that I hadn't moved, and happy I'd stayed where he wanted me, giving me one of his cavernous smiles before smacking his gloves together, and telling the bowler to bowl full and straight. And Garry calling to my father, telling him to warm up, and my excitement at the prospect – even then, my father didn't bowl much. And I still remember my father's off-cutter – it was in either his first or second over – and the burly batsman's wild swish, the ball looping ever so high (to my eight-year-old eyes) in my direction, Garry's call of 'Catch it, mate!', the fear that gripped me, my legs suddenly unsteady, and the ball arching down towards me. The sting of leather hitting my palms, the ball rebounding, and my desperate lunge to grasp it before it hit the floor. I'd made the simplest of catches look difficult, but that didn't matter. It seemed that the whole team was as happy as I was – they were shaking my hand just as they did when adults took a good catch. Even my father offered his hand, gripping mine harder than any of the others, so that I had to massage my palm when no one was looking. I fell asleep reliving the moment for weeks afterwards.

Perhaps I am looking back on my life through rose-tinted glasses, for school also seemed to have gone well. My mother tells me I was a sweet child, content to stay silent when left alone, but ready to break out of my reverie with a wide smile whenever someone talked to me. I found the first few days of school difficult, but I never locked myself in the toilets at home the way my brother did, and I don't remember any problems with the other students until the third grade, when Andrew joined our class.

To the teacher, he was a bright, jovial child with a penchant for practical jokes. To me, he was a selfish brat who wanted to be the centre of everyone's attention. When he walked in one day and, taking on a deep voice, pretended to be the principal, I didn't laugh the way my teacher did. I'm not sure why, but I decided that what he was doing was wrong, and that he needed to be punished. With Jeffrey, I chased him across our primary school's courtyard, caught him, pinned him down and spat in his face. It was a fitting lesson, I thought.

My mother had other ideas: never have I seen her so angry as she listened to my teacher over the phone. She hung up, walked over to where I was sitting, and slapped me. The pain shocked me; the shame had me in tears. She pointed at my room, and in a tone that expected no argument, told me to go and wait for her.

During the hour it took her before she came and spoke to me, I stayed glued to my bed and cried into my pillow. Whenever I tried to stoke my anger, to tell myself that I'd done nothing wrong and she was very mean to slap me, I remembered the paleness of her face and started crying again, feeling as though I deserved the shame. I'd almost exhausted my tears when she knocked on the door. She walked in with a solemn expression and sat next to me. Wanting to avoid her, I once again dug my head into my pillow. The smell of my tears on the cloth had me sobbing once again. I told myself that was a good thing, for it would make her feel guilty. But she didn't seem aware of my pain as she spoke.

'Do you know that Andrew lost his dad last year?' she asked me. Her voice that evening, as she carefully explained what it meant, and her tender gestures – stroking my hair, or holding my hand, which to me implied that I was as much a victim as Andrew – left a lasting impression. For many years, whenever I didn't like someone, I recalled a shadow of the Andrew episode and repressed my feelings. After my mother's intervention, I sought Andrew out, invited him to my house, and set out to make him my friend. I remember thinking hard about what present to get him for his birthday, and settling on the very one I wanted most: a gold and black football that had been used at the previous European Championships.

Andrew left Hornsbury the following year, but he was an exception. Most of the people who started primary school in my year stayed in the same track I was following, so that by the time I was in sixth form, I'd known many of my friends for over ten years.

Jeffrey was foremost amongst them. We'd first met as preschoolers on the cricket field, haggling about which of our fathers was the better player. When the cricket season threw us together, we seemed to spend every weekend with one another. He even came to Sicily with us one summer, the year after I went to the French Alps with his family. The winters saw us drift away from each other, as I had squash and football, and he played rugby, but even if I didn't see him outside school for a month, I always felt like I could call him and be at his house the next day, kicking a ball against the yellow-bricked wall at the back of his garden.

Jeffrey never disliked Eric as some of the others did, but he never understood why I was friends with him either. One day soon after Eric arrived at our school, as Paul Cumnor was relating an anecdote about him – the startled look he'd had when a teacher addressed him, his stumbling answer – Jeffrey turned to me and, in his usual tone, told the others that I'd been to Eric's the previous weekend.

'What's he like?' he asked me. 'What do you like about him anyway?'

At that instant in time, Eric's social standing was in the balance. He hadn't come across as likeable. Had he been awkward, we would have happily cast him aside, but his case seemed more complicated. Only a week earlier, at lunch break, I'd been chatting with Jeffrey, Tom and the usual crew, when I saw Eric pace around the building, his head down, his floppy black hair covering his eyes. The second time he walked by, I tried calling him over to our group, but he walked on as though he hadn't heard me, his eyes fixed on the pavement. Tom noticed and made a joke, but no one followed his lead.

Opinions were still divided. One camp condemned him – Paul and Tom Davies were in that camp. If he hadn't made it yet, he wasn't worth the effort. And another, to which it seemed most people subscribed, Jeffrey among them, still hadn't formed an opinion. Eric had just arrived and, despite his oddness, hadn't done anything that deserved to be condemned yet.

And in that moment, as Paul and Tom Davies smirked, hoping I'd give them some ammunition, as Jeffrey looked at me, sincerely wanting to know what I thought, all I could do was shrug and smile.

'I don't know. He seems alright to me,' I said.

Paul looked at Tom and sniggered. And I laughed along, genuinely happy to share in the joke.

* * *

The day after I first woke up, when the house and soot felt most distant, my mother grabbed my hand and talked to me. Her fingers squeezing mine comforted me more than her worried smile and the kindness in her moist eyes. She asked me how I was. Finding my voice strengthened, I told her the fever was gone. It had left me with an intense tiredness, deep enough that my lacerated stomach kept quiet.

'That's good, Nate. Good.' She let go of my hand and leaned back far enough that I could no longer make out her familiar perfume.

'Think happy thoughts. Are you seeing yourself on the cricket field?'

'No, but you're right,' I smiled. 'I should.'

'Yes, think about playing cricket with your brother and your father…' Her voice trailed off as she edged a little further away. 'Did you manage to fix your bat?' she asked, her voice almost steady.

'I think so. It took a few goes but it looked good in the end…' The roundness of her eyes and the cock of her eyebrow made me feel as though I were lying.

'Oh… I hope you didn't spend too much time working on it. Dad can buy you a new one if you need.'

'No, it's alright. It only took a few minutes, but it didn't work the first time, that's all.'

'Good,' she said, nodding while her eyes looked at my feet.

I extended my hand palm up hoping she would take it again, but she couldn't have noticed for she turned around and made her way back to her chair.

* * *

The world around me seemed to gather definition. Or perhaps I was now staying awake long enough to appreciate it, to expect its contours every time I broke through the lethargy.

I was in a large room with yellow walls and no doors. Badges roamed along a corridor to my right. And a window spanned the entire length of the room to my left. When I crooked my neck, I could take in the whole of south-east Oxford. I could lose myself in Headington's parks, and if I squinted hard enough, I could imagine my grandmother's old house, the one she had before she moved to Cambridge, my grandfather died, and my mother found her a nursing home. It stood off a main road at the end of a hazy cul-de-sac. I remembered the Sundays we spent there well: in the winters, I would only breathe through my mouth, because there was something wrong with the sofas and it wasn't just their flower print – no, if I breathed through my nose, their musky dampness would settle in my stomach and start breeding mould. Our summer visits were much safer: then, I could spend hours hiding with my cousins in the labyrinthine hedge that ran along the garden walls.

To the right of my grandmother's house, I could watch the traffic crawling on Cowley Road, and further right still, I could glimpse far-off Iffley and its lock. But I hardly ever looked. I preferred observing the people around me. When my mother was not sitting on a chair near me, when she wasn't watching over me, reading through academic papers, jotting down her esteemed thoughts, I was left with three other silent patients, perennially waiting for something: nurses, meals, examinations, or the omnipotent team of doctors.

I was luckier than most: my mother was with me throughout the entire visiting hours. She'd been spoken to – your son needs rest, he needs sleep, he needs calm. She'd nodded her head and made up her own mind. Her lab, her students, her colleagues, she told me, could go on without her, and plus, she pointed at her papers, she could work by my side too. A professor of experimental psychology. When I was little, I'd imagined patients reclining on a leather *chaise longue* while she fitted a flashing helmet on their skulls and jotted down the value of each dial. Even when she started taking me to her lab after school, on the first floor of a building that looked like an overgrown concrete bunker, I kept on believing there was something vaguely sinister about her work. It took me years to dispel that idea. Whenever I'd ask her about her work, she'd either give me an answer that was too broad or one that was too detailed – so that all I remembered was that she, and her lab, ran experiments on memory, biases, encoding.

Once, as she sat by my hospital bed, I put down one of the books she'd brought me, Dostoevsky's *The Idiot*, and I asked her what she was reading. She put her papers aside, stretched her arms out and, leaning towards me, asked me whether I really wanted to know. I hesitated but only for an instant: I hadn't seen her so engaged for some time. She read out the title of the article she'd been reading: 'Homocysteine and Cognitive Performance…' She stopped halfway through the subtitle. 'You don't know what homocysteine is, do you?' I could pretend to know what cognitive performance meant, but homocysteine was beyond me. 'It's an amino acid.' She waited for a sign. 'You don't know what that is, do you?'

The same day, after I'd lost her to her pile of papers, I asked her why she sat with her head resting against the window, when she could sit against the wall and enjoy the view over the town. I pointed at a spot right next to my bed, and I turned the cover of *The Idiot* towards her. We would discuss this book like we'd discussed most of the books I'd plucked from our collection at home – the rows of classic and modern novels that had left the upstairs bookshelves and littered my floor until they'd earned fresh creases. She would ask me what I thought, what I felt, and, talking to her, I'd work this book out like I'd pieced together the others.

She waved at the door:

'I like to be able to see who's coming in and out,' she said.

It was a sensible reason in theory, but in practice she rarely looked up from her reading stack.

'It'd be easier to talk if you were sitting here,' I said.

She smiled, moved to a chair by my bed, and plunged right back into her papers.

'Have you read this?' I asked her.

She took a few seconds to look up.

'A long time ago,' she said, and she looked down again, squinting.

From the way she was reading her papers, I realised that her usual prompts – How far along are you? Are you enjoying it? – wouldn't come. I lowered my voice until I felt sure that no one else would hear me. My words were travelling in a space that belonged to no one else but us:

'Everyone loves him, but I'm not sure why.'

She looked up sharply.

'In the book, I mean,' I said, lowering my voice further, so that she had to lean forward to catch my words. 'They all pretend that he's a fool, but they all love him. Don't you remember?'

'No, I don't.' She leaned back on her chair, glanced at the window, and plunged back into her papers, squinting hard this time.

The lines of my book went blurry, and the house shone through the ash. I heard her chair squeal. Standing up, she squinted and pointed at the window.

Black Chalk

'Natural light's better for my eyes.' She moved her things to her old chair, and I didn't mention it again.

There were many hours when she was away and my body wouldn't slip past slumber. My eyes ajar, I spent time looking at my three companions. There were curtains to divide the room into four but they were only ever drawn when nurses needed to undress patients. The rest of the time we were together because there was nothing to separate us.

The man in front of me fascinated me – my diaries include three long entries on his actions. From the safety of my cot, I spied on him in his bed, on his feet, in his chair. But spying isn't the word I'm looking for. I wasn't impinging on his privacy and no one wanted to know what I saw. It would be more accurate to say that I watched him like one watches a street performer. Except that his was the only act. While the two women to my right were staying still for days on end, this man was taking control of his space. He was younger than they were, in his late sixties I would guess, still infused with the energy to rise out of his bed.

The old man was a starer. He would lie down and stare. And then he would move to his chair and stare. And he would stand up and stare – sometimes out of the window down at the city. I could see something of Mr Johnson in him. He would rest the back of his hand on his lower back and gaze out of the window quietly, just like Mr Johnson liked to do. But whereas Mr Johnson would look at the field for a few minutes and then turn back to us, the old man could stare for five minutes, ten minutes, half an hour, without registering an emotion. And then he'd sit and stare. He stared at nothing in particular – his eyes were open and they needed to rest on something. I can only presume that he didn't need stark reminders to recall episodes of his life, that our mundane ward was enough inspiration. But he was certainly aware of what was going on around him. He knew I was looking at him – once, just as I was starting to think he'd lost contact with those around him, he looked into my curious eyes, batted his eyelid, and looked away. I felt an initial pang of shame, but that was misinterpreting the look he'd given me. There had been no judgement there, just acknowledgement.

* * *

Eight years later, I can finally acknowledge it. While I was in hospital, my relationship with my mother changed in ways I still don't fully understand. When I was lying in bed, and she was sitting by the window, I preferred to leave my raw emotions undefined. Every time pain made me wince, every time a memory had me slack-eyed, she was by my side, ready to adjust a pillow, squeeze my hand. But whenever my words circled around Eric and my physics class, I felt her grip loosen, her eyes shift, as if my allusions were making her uneasy, and I tried changing my train of thoughts until I had her comforting smile back.

Now that I see her every day around the house, aged and mollified, I yearn for a time before the shooting. I would like to see her in her long green dress sitting on her grandmother's old velvet armchair, shuffling through her papers, gold-plated pen in hand, pursing her lips and frowning in concentration, a soft 'no' or 'yes, that's true' humming past her lips, her hair draping down to her chin before gathering on the nape of her neck in an unruly ponytail. I would like her to look up at James or me, and to see her eyes swim for half a second as she'd decide whether to give us instructions. I would like her to call me to her side so that she could explain what my big-brother role entailed, to hear her say that James looked up to me, only for me to turn around and see him plucking away at his guitar, oblivious to anything around him.

Before it all happened, she was very certain of her role, and she wasn't afraid of pushing hard to get to her ends, since she also saw them as my ends. I remember my mother walking into my room every night for two weeks in a row and asking me how my work was going, knowing full well that I hadn't done anything since I'd discovered Tolkien.

'It's going well, don't worry,' I told her without putting down my book.

'You're reading too much. You've got your exams at the end of the year. You should be working every night. That's the only way you're going to do well.'

I ignored her, and she ignored my non-response. I don't think she was ever worried – she knew I was a good student – but she felt it was her duty to come and prod me. I could understand that. Even if I sometimes snapped back an answer, I was on the whole rather fond of her nagging. It'd been the first chink I'd pinpointed in her character, its discovery suddenly making her seem vulnerable, so that whenever she repeated something for the fourth time, I'd be caught between telling her off, and smiling at her.

After a cricket match one summer evening, Jeffrey came back to stay at my place. We were out in the garden re-enacting one crucial moment of the match, just as my mother called me to set the table.

Jeffrey was explaining why it wasn't his fault that he'd got out and left me stranded just short of my half-century, and I was trying to show him there were perfectly sensible ways of playing thigh-high full tosses. As I was tossing tennis balls at his legs, he was telling me why what I was throwing him had nothing in common with what he'd faced.

'Nate!' her voice cut across our play louder than before.

Jeffrey patted back a tennis ball, and said: 'My mum's even worse sometimes.'

Already a little frustrated with him, I took him up on that statement and grabbed a hard ball.

'Here, that's what you faced,' I said, and hurled the ball at his legs. He managed to absorb some of the ball's momentum with his bat, deflecting it onto the inside of his groin. When he folded in pain, I laughed hard so as not to feel embarrassed. He grimaced back, but by the end of the evening, I'd convinced him it had been a good joke, and that he'd deserved it for getting out when he shouldn't. He was too happy a person not to believe me. Still, after that day, he never made a disparaging comment about my mother again.

* * *

This morning, I opened my first hospital diary, the one with most of the sketches, and looked at an early entry. 'Eric: private mother moment after shed.' Short as it is, it's enough to make me remember how I felt then.

It also helps me challenge the revisionist approach I took to my convalescence. A psychiatrist and two psychologists were always going to be too strong for me. Believing their scheme fitted my condition, I wrote over my early convalescence, accepting their jargon, fitting it over my experiences, wrapping my reality. But their picture was always too simple. And now, years gone since they had me in their grasp, I prefer my thoughts complex.

Certainly, these thoughts show me that I was never in denial over the whole episode. Rather, mere days after the incident, I was already reaching for reason, pondering over the master of all questions, why, and all its guises. My thoughts were focused on Eric's interaction with his mother, on a moment that had left me puzzled as it happened.

It was in the spring of 1999. I was sitting down in Eric's living room when his mother walked in with her husband. He was polite but didn't linger, while she came towards us as if to start a conversation. Eric rose from his armchair and walked out into the garden, leaving me stranded behind. Rather awkwardly, I stood up and spoke with his mother about the weather, about school. When it became clear Eric wasn't coming back, I left her and found him in his shed, absorbed by woodwork.

'Why did you leave?' I asked him.

'I abhor him,' he said. 'Fuck her.' Abhor and fuck; they still stand out today as they did then. 'Of course, you've got no problems with them.'

I said nothing. He wasn't the only one of my friends fighting his mother. But that very afternoon, I had to rethink their relationship. His stepfather was out, and I was meant to be down in the shed clamping two pieces of wood together. I'd come up to ask Eric a question, and I was standing outside the kitchen window, peering in, afraid to walk in on them. I could see their shapes swaying back and forth, embracing each other almost violently, both his arms holding her head tight against his chest. When he eventually released her, I counted to thirty and opened the door. He was peeling vegetables, she was kneading dough. I looked at the space between them. But all I had was her gentle smile and his defiant look.

* * *

On the fourth day, my mother walked in late, after lunch had been served and cleared, and stopped by the foot of my bed as if she could go no further. I'd raised the top half of my bed so that I could better lose myself in my ward's dynamics. The first thing I noticed was that her eyes were bloated red. The rest of her appearance, the scarf hanging dishevelled from her neck, the coat drooping over her arm, had my fingers clutching hard at the sheets.

For what can't have been more than twenty seconds, she looked at me through a veil of welled-in tears. I could never handle my mother crying. I wanted to get up and throw my arm around her, but she was too far and I was too weak. It must have been my growing anguish that finally made her act.

'Anna...' she said before a sob took over. The tears breaking through, she crossed the space between us and took my hand, almost crushing my fingers.

It took her a minute to calm down, by which time I'd already guessed that Anna had died. I listened to my mother through a loud dullness. Shock was weighing on all my limbs.

Thinking of this moment now brings me a shadow of the pain it did then. I can still feel its contours, the shock bursting in to stay, its tentacles climbing down my arteries and up my veins, but it no longer has the power to stop my breath as it did then. Now I can think of the context surrounding my mother's revelation, and I can think of her early tentativeness. She seemed to hesitate in breaking news that belonged more to me than to her, and then, on seeing me struggle, she seemed to revert to her maternal role. Perhaps I'm imagining this, but now that I'm thinking of my mother, my thoughts keep on turning back to this moment, as if it was then that our relationship started changing.

'...She had both her sisters there...'

Through sobs and tears, my mother's story came together. I was feeling too slow to say anything. The only thoughts that came up had me wanting to tell her it wasn't true, but I'd held Anna's hand as she bled. However much I wanted to, I couldn't believe that lie.

My mother was adding more and more fragments to fill in my silence. She had been to see Anna many times since we were admitted to hospital. She hadn't told me about it because Anna had been in such a bad way. This morning, as chance had it, Anna had her whole family around her when my mother dropped in on her room. Sensing the end, my mother had tried to leave quietly, but Anna addressed her directly.

'...Her mother pulled me into their circle...'

She painted an idyllic scene: drifting in and out of consciousness, Anna had emerged minutes before the end, said what she had to say, closed her eyes, exhaled, and moved to another world. She almost made it seem like a natural death: Anna ageing peacefully and passing away surrounded by her loved ones. Something about the picture, its artifice and its charm, repulsed me. I didn't want any beauty in death. I tried to jerk my hand away, but her fingers were holding on strong. She immediately loosened her grip, as if she'd been unaware of her hand, and I felt shame. To make up for it, I mustered my strength and gripped tighter on my end.

'... She asked her parents to take care of her cat...'

Her voice was losing its shape as if she were hoping I would say something. Part of me wanted to stay quiet for fear it would all come up, but another part wanted to answer the call and cry, grunt, shout. When I spoke, it was in a whisper:

'We could take her cat if they don't want it. It used to snuggle up to me, and I'm sure Sloppy will like the company.'

It was a silly thing to say, and I knew that as I was saying it, but I thought about the long white fur that came off its back whenever I petted it, the way it floated gently down to the floor, and I wanted to have it purring against my leg now – warmth seeping from its slow stretches, a ball of germs in a sanitised world.

'We'll put a basket with a few cushions by the phone,' I said. 'That way it'll be able to see the whole of the living room.'

I talked more about how it would fit into our home, and how our dog wouldn't mind it. While I talked, my mother's tears dried up, and her eyes, trailing over my face, went out of focus. For a few seconds, the distant eyes, the tension around her mouth, made her look as though she was grappling with a great decision. Her expression made me think of the time I told her Jeffrey's family had invited me skiing and she decided she could put together the money to send me. And yet, it seemed far more than that. Her drying tears heightened her expression to something that made me go quiet. It continued for a few instants after I fell silent, before her gaze came back to me and found my eyes. Nodding, her long face tightened.

'Anna had something she wanted me to tell you.'

My legs tensed.

'Are you listening?' She yanked at my arm until I looked directly into her reddened eyes. 'She told me to tell you that it's okay, you tried.' My mother sighed, letting go of my arm. 'You know she would have liked to tell you herself. It's okay, you tried. Will you remember?'

'I'll remember.'

She rose, wiped something off her brow, and turned towards the window.

'We can't forget it. It's what she wanted you to feel,' she said.

In the ensuing silence, I tried to change the conversation and asked my mother where my father was. Her answer washed over me: part of my mind made sense of what she answered, while the rest left my ward and its tedious reality. Tiredness took over from sadness. It made sense, it all made sense. I felt old, omniscient, omnipotent. The world was clay waiting to be shaped and undone. And yet I had no desire to test my newfound powers. I wanted nothing. The world was as it was and I was content with it.

In that half-awake state, I started thinking about the sheets against my skin, and they were soft and comfortable, just as I wished them. I heard my mother moving away from me, and out of the ward, and I told myself that this was exactly as it should be. I smiled inside at the thought of how right everything was. Yes, I told myself, even what my mother just told me made sense. I had to struggle to remember what that was.

When it came back to my mind, it threatened to throw me out of my pleasant, knowing state. Anna was on the operating table, her hair darkened by damp, her pink skin gone grey. Behind Anna's drained cheeks, I could glimpse a host of other faces, basking in horror. Tensing up, I forced my mind back to my earlier image: the world was made of clay and her death was right. Yes, there was nothing sad about it. She was floating forever in the peaceful glow that I was merely touching. And the other faces weren't horrible but blissful. Ha, I laughed, there's such a thin line between beauty and horror.

From that thought came a burst of resolve: I was on the brink of something special, which I shouldn't forget, but which I couldn't remember either. I understood how dangerous the sort of thoughts I'd almost had were. My resolve was to Not, I told myself. I would not think such thoughts, and already they were out of my grasp, so that I didn't know exactly what I should not think. It didn't matter: I'd been so close that that one moment of truth could never leave me. Picturing the word 'Don't', I set it aflame and let its burning shape engrave itself in my mind.

* * *

Later that day, my mother brought me the ingredients of a forgotten pastime. An A4 drawing pad, four graphite pencils, four charcoal pencils, a soft black pencil, a blending stump, a vinyl eraser, and a sharpener. She'd assembled the different items inside a wooden case which she'd lined with a fleur-de-lys fabric. I brushed the paper, feeling its grain on the tip of my fingers.

I sat up, took the soft black pencil and drew three lines. My eyes following the swell of the curves, I reached for an object, an idea, leaving my hand to its own bidding. I revelled in the freedom of an uncorked imagination, the privacy of the page, the simplicity of pencil on paper.

I'd spent hours, days, even years drawing as a child. The walls of our house had been covered with my pictures, with the ones I'd copied and the ones I'd composed. My matchbox houses and green pastures had gone on the fridge door. As my drawings improved, they spread from the kitchen into other rooms. My parents would make a ceremony of the moment they hung them. At first, I spent a long time on each, but soon I started craving the pomp and attention, and I started to speed through the page. I still remember the day my mother told me a picture wasn't good enough to go on the wall. I ran outside, cried, and swore off drawing. But two days later I was back at it, working on a single drawing until I thought it perfect. The satisfaction! Seeing my mother come back from a shop with it framed! When it became clear that my brother wouldn't follow in my footsteps, my parents invoked equity and took most of my work down. I still kept at it, at least until puberty drove me to new distractions.

There were still three of my more elaborate pieces hanging in the kitchen. One was of our home bathed in a halcyon light. Another was after a picture of Hornsbury's Market Street. And the third was of my mother reading in an armchair. They were clichéd, simple, lifeless. That never stopped my mother from showing them off to my friends. How many times I cringed when she did that! I'd wait for my friends to leave, and then I would run her through my embarrassment, I would highlight the drawings' flaws, but my entreaties had no effect. Friends on their first visit still had to endure her beaming eulogies.

Four years after putting down my last sketch, two years after giving away my old kit, I sat in a hospital bed, pencil in hand, looking at the old man in front of me. He was sitting on a chair to the right of his bed, wearing a white and blue hospital robe, his brown legs naked, white slippers hanging off his feet, his head drooping towards the nurses' station.

Immobile. My subject.

I started with the head, with the curly white hair, short and barely receding. I moved to the neck and shoulders. The shoulders were key: they stooped but their strength was obvious. Dejected yet able. Atrophy settling in. Pencil in hand, I could understand the man in an instant. I ignored his loose torso and worked on the arms, smudging his right forearm around his tattoo, darkening sinews and bulges. His hands came together into a single fist. My touch lightened as I moved towards his legs. I didn't need his feet to ground him. He was a picture of stability.

Black Chalk

* * *

My brother looked back towards my mother. He stopped at the foot of my bed, his smile mirroring mine. A hand on his shoulder, words in his ear, she guided him closer.

'I like to see the two of you spending time together. In times like this, all we've got is family.' She looked at her watch: 'James, I have to make a few phone calls.'

We watched her leave and turned to each other. I reached for the controls of my bed and raised my torso so our eyes could be level. He seemed changed beyond the week we'd spent apart. He reminded me of the last time we'd come to blows, when I was twelve and he was eight. In Avoriaz, on the Thursday of a week-long ski trip, after three days of lessons, when I'd petitioned my parents to let me go and ski alone, on the slopes of course, and she'd told me that I could as long as I took my brother. I tried to negotiate a compromise – he wants to spend time with the two of you, not with me – but she didn't budge. James couldn't do a parallel turn, but he thought himself as good a skier as me. Whatever I went down, he could go down. Shutting his mouth, an obstinate look in his eyes, he pointed his skis right down the slope, and off he went, always trying to beat me to the bottom.

'Did you see that lady?' I told him. 'You made her fall. Look. Look!' I grabbed him by the shoulder and forced him to look a hundred yards up the slope. Dazed from her fall, one ski ten yards back, she slipped back on the other every time she tried to get up. 'Be careful!' I slapped him on the shoulder.

He pushed me back.

'It wasn't me,' he said, and he jumped down the slope, his thin skis trembling under him.

I rushed after him, howling as I overtook him. If he was going to be that way, I'd show him.

'We're not going up this chair this time. We're going up the big one. Are you scared?' I said.

He shook his head and followed me up to the top of the expert zone. There, looking at the first drop, he seemed a little hesitant.

'So easy,' I said and I went first. My instructor had taken my group down moguls for the first time this year. After the first fifty yards, my legs were burning but I'd managed not to fall. I looked up. James was stopped halfway down the slope, looking longingly at the safety of the chair.

'Come on!' I shouted. 'Hurry up.'

Hesitantly, he launched himself across the slope, rising and dropping with every bump, somehow keeping his balance, until he got too close to the trees and he realised that he'd eat bark if he didn't stop. Instinctively, he pointed his skis uphill until he came to a halt. There, facing the wrong way, he started to slip backwards, down the hill, gathering speed, until the top of a mogul flipped him the way he should have been, and he was rising and dropping with every bump, again somehow keeping his balance, towards the other line of trees.

He turned once more, this time the right way, and then he skied past me, bolder and faster. Thirty yards later, he was flying over a mogul, and his skis had come off, and his head was full of snow. He'd learned his lesson, I thought, and I went down to help. Juggling his skis in my arms, one of my poles slipped out of my hands before I reached him. It slid down until it hit him, face down in the snow.

'That'll teach you to be careful,' I said.

'Shut up,' he said, his head rising from the snow.

'Can't you be nice for once? I'm bringing you your skis. You could say thank you.'

He stood up, yanked the skis from my hands, and glared at me.

'Well, come on,' I said, 'put your skis on and give me my pole.'

'No,' he said.

'What! I just brought you your skis. The least you could do is give me back my pole.'

He turned away, hiding his face, and I knew it from experience: despite the day I'd spent nannying him, despite me picking up his skis for him, he'd decided that he had a right to be angry with me. My thoughts swam, and I shuffled up to push him down:

'Give me my pole!'

He staggered up and pushed me.

'I hate you.'

Pushing me, the little weasel! I couldn't believe it. I shoved and pushed until he was sprawled in the snow, lesson learned, and I had my pole back, and I left him alone with the moguls. When I reached the bottom of the black run, where it met the green slope ambling down to base, I pictured my mother, and I told myself I'd better wait for my brother. There, I plotted my revenge, looked at my watch, thought he'd hiked back up and chaired it down, that he'd broken something, until half an hour had passed, and he emerged over a crest, getting closer one slow mogul at a time.

When he came to the bottom of the run, he looked different. Up to that day, we'd fought often, twice a day it felt like sometimes, but we'd always made peace half an hour after he wanted to kill me. This time though, he kept his lips in a hard line for a whole day, and he looked distant for days afterwards. My mother sided with him as she always did – because he was younger, I was meant to be responsible, she said. But more than her reaction, it was his distance that stayed with me for years afterwards, that resurfaced and cooled me down whenever we were on the verge of a fight.

And it was this distance that I thought about when he stood by my hospital bed. He looked changed; it was in the way he held himself. But a week was too little time for change. The mere idea of it was ludicrous. If anyone had undergone change, it was meant to be me. I could hear experts say it: what I'd gone through, it was only natural. And yet, after days spent within myself, I could tell them that I was the same person I'd been a week before.

I decided to trust my first impression: he looked different. I was finding him awkward, almost shifty. I asked him about cricket training.

'We've got a new coach. He's making me change my grip.'

'Your grip was fine,' I said. 'What's he showing you? The Vs?' I parted my thumbs and index fingers into a V and held out both hands with the Vs aligned.

'Yeah.'

'They always want people to do that, but Atherton holds his bat the way you do, and didn't that serve him well? And you scored runs last season. He should just accept your way works.'

'He reckons it's better against the swinging ball.'

'Pff, don't worry about that. If the ball's swinging, you need to be able to play late and straight. And that's the key for all batting, swing, spin, all of it. If you can do that already, don't go changing your grip.'

He nodded and looked down.

'How's your bowling coming along?' I asked him.

'Good.'

'Is he changing anything there?'

'He's making me work on my left arm. Use it more.'

'That's good,' I said. 'I'm sure he's a good coach.' I paused. 'And how's school?'

'Fine.'

'Just fine?'

'Well… Yeah, I guess.'

'Okay. What are the other kids saying?'

'They… Nothing. Everyone's just, you know?'

'Yeah,' I said, because yeah was what I had to say. 'And home?'

'Fine,' he said, and he looked up, searching my face. 'Mum's being annoying.' He gazed at me for a second before he started to speak very quickly: 'Dad says it's because she's stressed, but she annoys him too. I know, I heard them fight.' He stopped and studied me again.

'What about?' I asked.

'You. Dad says Mum is spending too much time talking to everyone, and Mum says she has to, for you she says, but Dad thinks she should let the police do their job, and Mum says she doesn't want them to get it wrong.' He paused. 'And Dad's not happy,' he finished, looking satisfied.

I nodded for a few moments while I pictured the scene. Then, as I started to grimace, I changed the topic:

'Mum says Dad's taking care of you. What's he cooking? Eggs and beans on toast?'

James smiled.

* * *

My relationship with Anna ended strangely. I broke it off because it had come to that. Even though I still wanted to be with her, I had to bow to the inevitable.

It was a summer romance, strung through parties and gatherings, at first when we were drunk and high, strings weaving away from the public eye, with stolen moments in smaller outings, and then with just us two, alone and together. I approached her full of confidence. A month earlier, I'd had sex for the first time, at a friend of a friend's party in Oxford, and ever since, I'd eyed every woman with a newfound understanding: years of *Playboy*, pictures downloaded over dial-up, it suddenly made so much sense. When Anna started talking to me, my thoughts went beyond the mirage of my cock in her pussy. I wanted to put my nose in her navel, to count how many fingers I could put around her thigh.

She was coming out of an eight-month relationship with a nineteen-year-old boy – an aspiring plumber who was at a technical college on the outskirts of Oxford. After each of our first two booze-fuelled make-out sessions, I tried calling her, emailing her, all in vain. By the time of the party on Old Road, when thirty of us invaded the park that straddled the top of the hill, I'd had enough. Jeffrey agreed – she was acting like a spoiled brat. To avoid her, I shifted from one group to another until long after the sun had set, and we were all drifting into drunkenness.

'So,' she said, standing above me, 'how are you today?' She pushed my bag aside and sat next to me. Her arm accidentally touched my thigh, and I asked myself why I hadn't sought her out earlier. It brushed my thigh again, and it stayed there, and I felt happy.

Late one night, we looked back on our beginnings, and decided we'd started being a couple after our second drunken full night. Unlike the night up Old Road, we'd spent the morning together, as couples ought to do. It was as sensible a guess of a starting date as we could come up with.

Part of me, the romantic part, wanted her to say the relationship had started earlier, in our GCSE history class, when I'd spent all my spare time turning back and talking to her. But when I mentioned those months, she told me she'd been in love with Jeffrey then, much like half the girls of my class. She said it like she was sharing an old joke: all the girls had been in love with him then, and now they all wondered why.

Over a year later, we were safely out of Jeffrey's shadow and together. And we went on bike rides, and we watched movies, and she came to mine, and I went to hers. I liked to think of her, to call her, to talk about her – in all, love made me rather content. And yet, it was never an intense relationship. It never felt like it had to be. When school resumed, we spent most of our time with each other in and around class, perhaps meeting out of school once a week. I didn't own a mobile phone at the time; there were no late night calls, no texting flurries.

It was emails that brought it down. I'd gone to Cornwall with my family for the first week of the holidays, to visit my father's parents, as we'd done for many years. There was no internet there, and my grandfather had no intention to install it, even a dial-up modem. For six days then, I read novels into the afternoons, went for short walks in the countryside, and came back to Grandma's mulled wine.

Back in Hornsbury, I didn't feel the need to check my emails until the second morning after my return. When I opened my inbox, I found five emails from Anna. I started with the most recent one, in which she asked me to ignore her earlier emails, hoped I'd had a great time with my grandparents, and told me not to break up with her. Puzzled, I went back through the earlier messages. I don't think I ever read the third and fourth in their entirety. It was too much, the outpour. She was asking me to stay with her, and she was repeating it, and I was reading it again and again, and I was no longer paying attention, and I was thinking of us broken up. I closed the browser, left my desk and went for a walk. And I went to bed with my sword and sorcerer book, finishing it the next morning. Then I watched a movie, called Jeffrey and talked about nothing in particular. It was the next day I called her: our conversation didn't flow. We met in a park – I had no plan in mind, but when I saw her, it was there, in her already wide eyes, in the head she didn't dare raise, in the way she flinched when I asked her how she was. With a misplaced sort of sympathy, I understood that, to her, the relationship was already dead. Much like I'd accepted her hand on my thigh, I accepted her expression then.

'It's a pity,' I told her, and she seemed relieved. Everything we said after that took the break-up as a given, and I felt like we'd done the right thing.

It didn't have to make sense.

My days split between video games and a series of novels, the holidays dragged on. When school resumed, I was expecting a return to normal, if not in our intimacy, at least in our preceding friendship. Instead, she ignored me in the halls. She organised gatherings with my friends without inviting me. She went as far as to install her friend Laura in my old physics seat. When I challenged her over it, she looked away, pointing me towards Laura. Telling me I could take her seat, Laura's mannerisms mimicked Anna's in their disdain.

I don't want to judge her for it. I don't want to judge myself. We were both young. But whereas I can now separate the break-up from her subsequent behaviour, I then saw the one as vindicating the other: her coldness was ridding me of any lingering doubt.

It took bullets to break the barrier we'd erected. Bullets flying over me, past me, around me, while she hyperventilated and bled.

* * *

My mother put down her papers, got up from her chair and stood tall next to me, her shape darkened by the light coming from the window. I shut my notebook, keeping my writings and drawings to myself.

'I went to see Eric's mother this morning.'

The weight she put into those words made me want to stop her then and there, but I took a closer look at the stillness of her eyes and the line of her lips, and realised it was already too late.

'I know you like her, the poor woman. So I wanted to see her, and tell you what's happening outside this place. Hospitals, they can…'

'I know,' I said to fill in her pause. I didn't need to look around me to understand her: I knew my hospital corner all too well.

Feeling she hadn't finished, I ignored my misgivings and prompted her on: 'How was Eric's mother?'

My mother's smooth face hardened for an instant. She held her hand up as if to tell me to be patient.

'I went to see her after our morning meetings. That's a support group we started right away, but we can't invite her along. Some parents are blaming her, and that's easy to understand. Still, I thought she'd appreciate a friendly face. Do you understand?'

She looked at me expectantly, as Eric's mother and her pained smile came into my mind. I turned away.

'It's not her fault,' I said. I could see my mother raising her hand again from the corner of my eyes, but the words out of my mouth triggered more. 'It could have been any of the other mothers. The ones who are crying now, they could be the ones feeling guilty.'

'Don't say that!'

'It's true!' My voice rose, and the old man turned to look at us. He didn't matter; what I was talking about was more important. 'Why blame her? It could have been anyone, imagine if it was you—'

'Don't say that!' she hissed. A deep line spread down her forehead, her cheeks creased, and wrinkles quivered around her mouth. 'I don't want to hear anything like that.'

Her sudden intensity cut my thoughts short. When I got over the shock, I looked at her and chose to keep quiet: I could see the anger draining from her face with every word she uttered.

'But you're right,' she continued, 'we should forgive her. Not all families are as strong as ours. And she's lost a son too…' On that thought, her voice found the softness I craved. 'I knocked on her door this morning. No one came to open it, so I went around the back and found her sitting on the terrace, out in the cold. She wasn't even wearing a coat. She didn't recognise me at first; she shouted at me to go away. I think she gets a lot of media people, more than we do. She eventually let me in, but that's after I told her who I was three times.' My mother shook her head and stopped for a second. 'She remembered you; she said, "Nate, the cricket player", and that's all she had to say about you.'

She looked calmed: her lips had dropped open, and her brow was now smooth.

'Maybe she needs to be alone,' I whispered.

'Sometimes we feel like that even though that's not what we need. We're lucky, Nate, because, whatever we do, we have each other. I know you don't want to think about it, but I have to tell you that there are a lot of people out there,' she waved her arm at the window, 'who won't leave us alone, and who don't care at all how we feel.' She dropped her arms by her side. 'You're getting better slowly, and those people want answers. Don't you think we should be ready for them?'

She stopped on that question, waiting for me to take her up on her challenge, before she went back to her chair. But if I looked deep in thought, it was because I was starting to realise that there were topics my mother considered out of bounds, and I needed to grasp where those boundaries lay.

After my mother left and the caterers gathered our dinner trays, I thought of Eric's mother. I couldn't remember her name, and yet she was always kind to me. She was away working for the most part. When at home, she left Eric to himself. But she always did all she could to make me at ease when I saw her. A week before the 10th of February, I'd brought my bat to Eric, to see whether he could help me repair it. It was an old bat, a bat I'd used in the middle many times, over many seasons. Its weight and its pickup were too familiar to give up. With it, I could dig out yorkers, read shooters, attack googlies.

Eric had carved a chunk out of the toe, replaced it with part of another bat, sanded down the result, and was applying glue when I heard his mother calling us. I knew she'd never walk down to the shed. As I expected, Eric didn't react, his whole attention turned to applying glue. I took it upon myself to walk out of the shed, up the hill, and ask her what I could do for her.

'I made you boys orange juice,' she said, pouring me a glass.

The fresh pressed juice tasted sweeter than the bottled juice I usually drank. I told her it reminded me of half-time orange slices during the football season.

'I like it when you come over,' she said, holding on to the jug.

Feeling she wanted to talk, I sat down.

'It's nice here,' I said.

'You like it?' she asked, doubts in her voice. She always had doubts in her voice. Of all the mothers I knew, she struck me as the most resigned. Everything that happened to her seemed to be another piece of evidence against fate. It was the way things were, she would say, with a sigh and a shake of her head. Like the three times she couldn't take me home, all in the same month, and she told me, each time in the same voice, that that sort of thing only happened to her. Just when she needed a car, her husband was late, and the other car wasn't working.

'I can make you something to eat if you want,' she said on all three occasions, putting her keys down and looking through her cupboard. 'Pasta?'

But Eric was never hungry, so I waited until my mother came to pick me up. For Eric's mother – I know her name wasn't Mrs Knight – the only thing she could do was suffer gracefully until her husband came home.

'I like the field,' I said the time she made us orange juice.

'It's a field because Eric won't mow it. I keep on telling him to do it, it's his job, but he doesn't listen, no. He just stays in his shed and ignores me...' She trailed off and I felt uncomfortable. 'But I'm glad that you're his friend. It's good for him.'

I wanted to grab the jug and bring it down, but she held on to its handle.

'How do you think he is?' she said.

'What do you mean?'

'Is he doing well at school? Is he happy? I know he's not happy here, but a few more months and he'll have his own place. So, what do you think?'

I waited for a second, hoping she'd add something and I wouldn't have to answer her, but she looked at me expectantly.

'He's fine,' I said. 'Maybe a bit stressed, but he's fine. Why do you ask?'

'He doesn't tell me these things anymore. It's always the same. He used to when he was little but then he grew up and now he doesn't tell me anything anymore,' she sighed, letting go of the juice.

I brought it back down and drank most of it, Eric being too busy with the bat.

* * *

My ward waited for the doctors. Patients drifted through the days and into the nights together. Teams of nurses watched over our beds and left at the end of their shifts. On the stroke of mealtime, caterers wheeled meals in and wheeled trays out. Janitors pushed their buckets around the halls, and slopped their solutions on our floors. At the appointed hour, rule-abiding visitors stormed in and snuck out. And my mother outlasted them all.

Doctors swept through in the mornings. In packs, they discussed our bodies. Orders passed from old to young, from young to nurses, from nurses to patients. And we obeyed everyone: doctors, young and old, nurses, caterers, janitors.

And once more, we were left waiting.

The nurses fascinated me. I watched them, listened to them, and jotted down thought after thought. At first, I was amazed by their professionalism. They were dancers gliding through a routine. When, every quarter of an hour for a whole morning, the old lady to my left called her nurse to ask her the same question (where is Henry?), I was a little awed to see her nurse, a red-haired woman with a Polish accent, respond to each call with the same mixture of competence and care. It was in the way they never needed to run; they knew exactly how to do their job.

Then I noted that my quiet little ward didn't have a single male nurse, and I asked myself whether that changed their reaction to doctors. There were many female doctors walking around the hospital, but most of the doctors who came to our ward were men, and all of them were given an odd sort of impunity. When they weren't there, the space firmly belonged to the nurses. But as soon as a man in slacks and a shirt appeared, a badge hanging from his neck, the place changed; even a student carrying his books under his arm could sidestep around three nurses, walk behind their station and consult a wad of confidential papers.

The more I watched them, the less I noticed their work. I was certain of it: they were all avoiding Pauline, the cropped-haired, perpetually burned nurse, who talked loud enough that, deep in my corner, her voice still broke through the background whirl. They had a way of gathering in groups when she wasn't there and splitting as soon as she came back, of sniggering, whispering and laughing that reminded me of Anna and Laura, of Jordan and Rebecca, and of all the other social queens I'd come across. Pauline, on her side, threw herself into her work. She was consciously conscientious, always commenting on how good her work was, how sloppy others' was.

From my bed, I tried to come to Pauline's defence. One morning, when they were short a nurse and she was covering my bed, I called her over and told her I felt hot.

'Hot, darling, of course you are. Look at how tight those blankets are! Who did that to you? You need to breathe. Here, let me get this right for you.' She busied herself, shuffling my bedding, all the while telling me how much better it was going to be. 'Some people don't realise, but these blankets are heavy. You have to ask yourself what they're thinking.' She shook her head and tsk-tsked. 'How's it now?'

'Much better,' I lied.

She put her hands on her hips:

'Of course it is.'

At the end of her shift, she was still mumbling sheets and blankets and her colleagues looked annoyed. My notebook on my lap, I gave each nurse a line and I followed their movements until I had a pattern in front of my eyes. Then, holding the paper at arm's length, I searched the page. There was an eye and a nose here, an arm punching a wall there.

* * *

Two weeks after I turned fifteen, I told my mother I was going to get a tattoo.

'Don't you need my permission for that?' she asked.

'Normally, but Tom knows a tattoo parlour where they don't ask for your age.'

'Is Tom getting one too?'

'Paul, Tom, and me.'

'And what sort are they getting?'

'Tom's getting a Maori design. And Paul's getting the same thing.'

'What are you getting?'

'An eagle. Here.' I tapped my shoulder. 'I saw one I liked in the shop, but then I changed it. It's better, I think. Do you want to see?'

She studied my face. Then she turned away and I saw tears coming.

'Nate, you don't have to get one because Tom and Paul are getting one.'

'I'm not! I want to get one for myself.'

I watched her crying, and I felt like crying too, but the tears wouldn't come.

'What am I going to tell your father?' she said.

'I can talk to him.'

She grabbed my hand:

'Think about it first. Tattoos, they don't go anywhere. You grow old, they grow old. Do you want the same tattoo when you're sixteen, when you're thirty, when you're sixty? And you want to go to some tattoo parlour where they don't check how old you are… How good are they going to be? What if they make a mess of it?'

That night, I did as I promised her I would do: I thought about it. Every time I looked at my design (an eagle's neck, head, and beak in as few strokes as I could manage), I yearned to have it on my shoulder. But then I remembered my mother's words, and I told myself that she was right – it would wrinkle with age. By the morning, I couldn't remember why I'd wanted one in the first place.

'So you don't want one anymore?' she said.

'No. I'm only fifteen. Who knows what I'll like by the time I'm eighteen?'

'Yes, exactly what I was thinking,' she said quickly, but then she started again, a questioning, almost disappointed touch in her voice. 'Are you sure now? You told me you were sure you wanted one last night.'

'Oh, you know, that's just Tom and Paul.'

'Right, yes. You're right, of course, tattoos look silly anyway.' She glanced at me. When I nodded, she added: 'You could get your ear pierced if you want.'

* * *

I wasn't a week in hospital by the time my mother made me watch television. She came to me, found an articulated arm tucked under the bed, and rotated it until a screen appeared in front of our eyes. Plugging in some earphones, she gave me the right, took the left, and turned the television on. It was all happening before I had time to say anything.

'Daytime television,' she said switching through the few channels available. 'You might have to start watching *Neighbours*, or cooking shows even.'

I thought of protesting but from the tense resolve in her face, I knew what she would say – this is very important, Nate, please do what I tell you, don't argue now – at first with the same artificial ease, but as I pled my case, her words, her face would only harden up before they would budge. There was only one reasonable option: I turned away.

We didn't have a television at home. We'd never had one. As a child, I'd loved to visit friends' places and sit in front of the flashing colours and brash songs. Very young, I felt left out and clamoured for our own, of course. My mother still laughs at some of the scenes I made then: the tears I shed squirming on the floor but only when my mother could see me. But I wasn't very good at brooding. And soon I was rather proud of our lack of television. Friends would give me incredulous looks and I'd have offhand answers at the ready. Finding other things to do was easy enough: I read a lot, I drew, I played squash, tennis, cricket, football, I spent time with my brother and my friends.

'There's a special starting at 3 p.m. we should watch.' My pulse quickened. 'Is there anything you want to see beforehand?'

I said nothing. Reading the dial of her dangling watch, I saw I had ten minutes to stave it off. A lot could happen in ten minutes – yes, the doctor would come and check on me. The television was showing an old American crime series, the dusty cars of my childhood shiny new on the screen, an old man inspecting a dead body, his face wrinkled in concentration.

There was no doctor in sight; I decided to feign sleep and closed my eyes, letting my head sink into the pillow, hoping that my mother would leave. There was the sound of a car driving off, police sirens blared through, men shouted, a minute of theme music drew the show to its end. I turned my head away from my mother and caught my breath, as if my nose were a little blocked, and the earphone tugged at my ear before falling off onto my pillow. I couldn't make out voices anymore but I could still hear music.

I recognised the beat-raising tempo, the uplifting violins, the repetition and build-up. The news was on, and my heart was beating hard.

I heard her voice: 'Nate.' At first it was quiet, but then it was more insistent: 'Nate!' She knew I could hear her. 'They had the same special yesterday. Don't worry, it's done tastefully. I know it's not nice, but you need to watch it.'

I opened my eyes.

'Here, put this on.' She handed me the earphone. 'I didn't like it the first time either. Don't worry, it'll be alright.'

It was the note of hope in her voice which made me take the earphone. As if I could hear all her care and love in that note. She too feared for me, just like I did – of course, she was right, I decided; of course, she knew best. And it's that same hope I ponder over now, as far from understanding it today as I was then. How I wish that my mother would have asked for my story outright instead of forcing me to watch it on television! I can only presume that the days she watched me with my eyes half open, staring at the ceiling, were to her a proof of my distance. Or that the hospital psychiatrist told her I wouldn't open up to him, and that she assumed I'd behave the same way with her. But perhaps she was right to do as she did; perhaps I would have backed away had she extended an ear, in just the same way I yearned for the hand she wasn't willing to share.

All I know for certain is that I was caught in my desire for time and more time. I wanted to eat, draw, and close my eyes. The days to pass and the hospital to fade away. I wanted to stay in bed and go to school. Shut my eyes and hit my brother's leg-cutter over his head. I wanted time to stretch and protect me. I wanted the pendulum to swing into ash.

Instead, I got a newsreader's voice in my ear. Around me, the old ladies were fast asleep, the old man was looking out of the window, and two nurses were talking to each other. I could see no way out.

And it started.

A sandy-blonde woman announced the start of an in-depth segment on the Hornsbury School Shooting. The words jumped off her tongue and rolled off the screen. Hornsbury School Shooting. I knew that the words ought to have some meaning, that they should trigger something: ideas, emotions, sounds and smells. But perhaps because not enough time had lapsed, or perhaps because the name of my school already carried so much meaning for me, I dismissed the construction as preposterous. I wanted to scoff at the newsreader, to scorn her lazy journalism.

The newsreader ignored me and a man appeared on the screen, a suit standing in front of my school, right between the bus stop and the bike racks. His creamy skin and pastel tie obscured the red-brick façade, the doors I'd entered hundreds of times, the steps on which I'd eaten two years of lunches. He finished his introduction and a clip took over with its own voice-over. It panned across a horde of police cars, some with their lights still flashing, television crews dragging black cables across the lawn, and a hastily erected police line, half enforced by officers, half by reticent onlookers unwilling to get closer. Past the line, there were ambulances and working uniforms. The camera zoomed in on the entrance to the annexe: the back of a paramedic was coming out, his hands holding a stretcher carrying a covered lump. The camera zoomed out, seeking civilians, and found three teachers looking at the bodies coming out of the annexe, their faces limp with shock. And a crying man, his bald head red and bent.

Over it all, a man spoke:

'...since Dunblane...'

The reference to other massacres stood out but I wasn't really listening. His even and correct voice was punctuating the remoteness of the coverage. I'd come out on one of those stretchers and I didn't remember seeing any cameras. The crowd had been smaller. The images had to have been taken when I was already on my way to the JR. I was witnessing events I hadn't been a part of, I told myself. Events that didn't concern me.

The feeling was reassuring. The film cut indoors, to a classroom I'd never been taught in, one of the large rooms on the ground floor of the main building. A man gave a news conference. He wore a dark suit and a sober tie. His large square glasses climbed up towards his forehead, which creased up and down as he answered a swarm of journalists. Someone asked a tough question. He turned towards him, twitched his thick eyebrows, and reached for his glasses with his right hand. For a second, he stood in front of the cameras, in front of the flashes, silent and tweaking the frame of his glasses. Then he took them off, and twirled them between thumb and forefinger in time with his answer. Det Ch Insp Andrew Hill, the caption read alongside a time stamp: 18/02/2000.

The film cut his answer short and moved back outside, to the frosty grass and bare trees of our sports ground. The camera shot was still: in the distance, the Kemp Annexe loomed over the ground, framed by grey branches and dark bushes, two levels tall from this angle. The groundsman's workshop occupied the ground floor, its metal shutters drawn down, red and blue patterns painted by a long-gone class. The top floor still counted three windows, one for each classroom, and another for a mysterious cupboard I'd never seen anyone use. There was no one on the field – I could imagine the groundsman barking at anyone daring to set foot on his turf.

The picture looked right. When every shot before had been glaringly foreign, this one looked just as it should. On the right of the shot, I could glimpse freshly painted football posts. I wouldn't have been surprised if the camera had turned around to show two football teams passing balls around in their warm-ups.

I felt a surge of memories coming up, my eyes drawn to one of the windows, images flashing through my mind. Bangs, wafts. Tom's soothing gestures. The taste of metal in my mouth. The sound of a chair falling behind me. Eric's puzzled look. The memories rushed in; I tried to cut them short, remembering the shape of the command I'd burned into my mind: 'Don't'. The grass, the trees, the workshop, I'd played many a football game out there. Better, I imagined the sun shining on the field, Jeffrey running in, and me standing at gully, the very same scene behind the wary batsman, an edge flying my way, a successful dive, teammates surrounding me.

I could breathe again. My thoughts temporarily tamed, I diverted them to the journalist's concluding statement, to his open-ended remarks.

'Let's talk about some of these questions,' the newsreader said from her studio, half the screen devoted to her correspondent, the man in the suit in front of bricks, doors and steps. 'It's been nine days. Why don't we have a better understanding of what happened inside the Kemp Annexe?'

'Sarah, we simply don't have enough witnesses,' his voice flowed, clear and concise. 'Two students saw Eric Knight walk through the grounds with a blue sports bag, the same bag in which police found close to fifty unused bullets, and a teacher saw him enter the Kemp Annexe. The only survivor, Nate Dillingham, is in hospital, stable, but still too feverish to speak to the police. And we know that forensic evidence was compromised when paramedics came to the survivors' rescue.'

'That's all well and good,' said the newsreader, 'but what about the police? Surely, they can tell us more.'

My lower lip hanging loose, the words trickled into my mind.

'Sarah, the least we can say is that the police are being tight-lipped. Inspector Hill, who is in charge, is holding press conferences every day, but he's not telling us anything we didn't already know a week ago. We understand that he wants to speak with Nate Dillingham before he releases any new information.' He looked down at something off-screen. 'We are learning more about Eric Knight, the presumed shooter. His peers describe him as a loner prone to violent outbursts. He didn't take well to his mother's recent divorce. And he was sanctioned for instigating two fights last year. But no one saw this coming.'

'Yes,' the newsreader said. 'The least we can say is that Hornsbury is a community in shock.'

A new clip started on the screen. It started with pictures of Market Street, of the Rose and Crown, of green hills and Cotswold cottages. A door slammed shut on a journalist.

I was about to remove my earphone but something rigid in my mother's stance stopped me. Her hardness felt brittle all of a sudden. It was all in that hopeful quiver. Disappoint her then, when we were so close to her goal, and I'd be dealing her a wounding blow. So I listened to strangers dissecting my life, talking about an incident they knew nothing about and people they hardly understood.

The clip moved to the front of Eric's home, a sixties house a mile out of Hornsbury. To an aerial view of the house and gardens, zooming in to the shed at the bottom of the hill. And then we were looking at Harry Williams, at Harry's petulant mouth, Harry's spanky hair, Harry's tidy eyes. Harry who'd missed class for an orthodontist appointment. He was relaying a conversation he claimed to have had with Eric. Harry spoke with obvious relish, spitting the words to the camera.

'He said, "Just watch, they've had it coming". He was well angry, so I thought it means nothing. He'll calm down. But no, he said it. "I'm going to get them all, they f—."'

Harry held his 'f' for half a second.

'Sorry, I don't mean to swear on TV, but that's what he said. "I'm going to get them all, they eff-ing deserve it." He was really angry. But, you know, he was angry all the time.'

'When did this happen?' the journalist asked.

'Two weeks ago, during lunch.' His answer was quick, as if he'd rehearsed it.

'And did you think of reporting it?'

Harry stumbled: 'Well, no, you know, I thought he was just angry. I didn't think he'd do anything about it. Didn't think he was that crazy. Always knew he was crazy, everyone did. But I thought he was just weird crazy, not killing people crazy.'

And as the clip cut away to the shot of two guns, the journalist sympathised with Harry, with what 'no student could have seen coming'.

I couldn't focus anymore. The thought of Harry washed away all reason. If he'd been in the room, I'd have got up and punched him – I would have tried. He deserved that and more, the bastard. Trying to be famous, what right did he have! He hadn't even been there when Eric walked in starved and mad. What would he have done? Nothing. He would have crawled towards a corner and died there, drowning in a pool of blood and piss.

I yanked the earphone out of my ear and looked for the remote. It was in my mother's hand.

'Turn it off.'

'It's almost over,' she said.

'Turn it off!' I reached through the cloud for one more word: 'Please.'

She turned it off. 'It was almost over,' she said. I was striving to control myself. 'They'll probably show it again tomorrow,' she said.

The thought of Harry on screen one more time did it. I couldn't keep it in any longer.

'I can't believe he told them that,' I said. The words slowed. I was sputtering: 'He's lying. He's doing it on purpose, just so he can be on TV—'

My mother grabbed my arm. 'Nate, take it easy, don't get angry! He's only telling them what he remembers—'

'No, he's not, he's lying. I was there when Eric got angry and he didn't say anything like that. He was angry, yes, he was, but he didn't tell us he was going to go and shoot everybody, or whatever lie Harry came up with so he could be on TV!'

I felt my mother's arm around my shoulder, her soft voice hushing me, her hand pulling me towards her.

'Just because Eric wouldn't be his friend, that's why he's got to go and tell lies! He's a...' I caught myself, more aware of my mother's presence. 'He's a turd, that's what he is. I was there and Eric didn't say anything like that. He was just ranting, that's all... He just felt it that day... It got to him sometimes, you know.' I rested my forehead on my mother's shoulder and stared at a fold in the bed sheets.

My mind had gone blank and I felt drained. Her hushes stroking my ears, she held me for a minute without saying anything.

'Don't worry,' she said. 'Don't worry about other people. Harry, he's got to deal with it too. Some people, they rewrite the past, that's how they grieve. It's normal. Don't worry about him.'

She was crying, I thought. I couldn't be sure. She smelled like she was crying.

'Thank you, Nate, you were very brave.'

* * *

In hindsight, I realise I overreacted. My mother was right: Harry's lies were only natural. I can't recall Eric's outburst precisely. All I can say was that it was during our lunch break, in an outdoor hallway on the backside of the main buildings. I can still picture the rusty lockers, and the thick layers of white paint on the steel columns. If I'm still sure that Harry lied, it's because I wouldn't have got so angry otherwise.

I needed three hours of sleep to recover from my adrenaline rush. I woke up to find my mother reading on a chair by the window. Next to her were an apple and a small piece of bread.

'Did I miss dinner?'

She looked up and assessed me for a few seconds before answering. 'They just came back for the trays. But it's alright, I hid these just in case you were hungry.'

The sight of the pale apple and pasty piece of bread had my lips curling into a grimace.

'They had palak paneer tonight,' I said. 'You know I like that. Couldn't you have kept some for me?'

'You know they won't let me,' she said, as if she hadn't already disregarded half of their rules. A picture of Harry spitting saliva into a microphone came into my head, and all of a sudden I knew that I had to have cream, cheese and spinach on my tongue, or I'd stay welded to my bed and shiver until there were three more tubes pumping liquids into my body.

'Mum,' I spoke each word very clearly, 'I want some palak paneer.'

'Nate, it's health and safety. You know how they are.'

Her gentle words only made me more frustrated.

'Mum! It's not hard, you go after them, and you ask them for a dish that wasn't opened. There's got to be plenty of them.'

'They won't do it. They're not allowed to.'

'Then go to the cafeteria and buy some.' She took a deep breath, and I knew it: she thought that all she had to do was wait a bit and I'd start being reasonable. I raised my voice: 'Mum! I'm stuck in hospital, I've got a hole in my stomach, and all I'm asking for is some palak paneer. Just get me some!'

She stood up hesitantly, her right hand trailing over her bag.

'They probably don't have any, but I'll ask.'

'Mum!' I shouted. The burst startled her, and for the first time, she looked at me like she was ready to listen. I continued in a calmer voice: 'If they don't have any, there are plenty of Indian restaurants close by. I promise I won't move.'

Her long face took a moment to settle; then she smiled and squeezed my arm.

'Yes, of course I'll find you some. I'll be back soon.' She paused. 'Don't talk to any strangers.'

When she walked away, I closed my eyes and drifted towards sleep with a strangely satisfied smile – for half an hour, while the sensation lasted, I felt that the day hadn't gone so badly after all.

She was back with a paper bag in hand. Heat radiated from the dish's aluminium cover and I felt weaker, happier. Needing the warmth, I burned my tongue with the creamy spinach. With that taste in my mouth, I'd be alright in no time.

'Tell me, Nate,' my mother said, two fingers holding her head tilted back, 'what sort of things had Eric been saying lately?'

I stopped eating and looked at her. It was the first direct question she'd asked me about Eric, and yet she behaved as if she'd asked me whether I needed more blankets. The triviality of it all rubbed off on me, and I relaxed into an answer.

'You mean, regarding the…' I thought of the way they put it on television, but I couldn't bring myself to say it.

'If he said anything about that, yes. But anything you found strange, really.'

I looked down at my tray. A painting of a patch of earth on a mountain side: the spinach lightened by the cream, its strands flattened with my fork, the paneer floating white – they were blades of grass pushed by the winds, fighting for sunlight on a rocky soil. My mind held a long blank. I started speaking, hoping memories would follow.

'Well, there was that time with Harry, but… He didn't like some of the others, you know. He kept on saying they were getting in the way. I don't think anyone could have stopped him from doing anything, but that's what he'd been saying in the last few weeks.'

I looked at her. She was nodding with a faraway smile. She stood up and came closer.

'Just like I thought,' she whispered.

'Yeah, he was busy in the last few weeks. I didn't see as much of him as usual, except for my bat. He showed me a thing or two, but that's about it, you know.' She was still nodding, her smile shifting to me.

'Yes, that's good, Nate. That's—'

Her voice was as soft as my tiredness, and I felt I could share more.

'Just a few things, like interesting stuff he was working on. I told you he was good at repairing and making things, didn't I?'

'Yes, you said that. That's alright, you've answered my question already. Eat your dinner. You've done very well, of course, you've done well.'

Her hand circled up and down. I imitated her: my fork picked out a chunk of cheese, brought it to my mouth, and went back for more food.

'That's good. The more you eat, the quicker you'll get better. It's very easy to look back at everything that happened in the last few weeks, and knowing what you know now, to think that you could have done something to prevent it. That's called hindsight bias. Don't start thinking that way, Nate. You did everything right.'

Black Chalk

* * *

My diary includes three tightly spaced pages on a fleeting moment that happened the next morning. Before visiting hours, a young man walked into my ward and stopped by the nurses' station. A sling tucked his right wrist onto his left collar-bone. He turned his back to the desk and, resting on it, looked out towards the window. Two nurses walked around him to get behind the desk. His gaze moved from patient to patient until it came to me. He seemed to take me in longer than the others, and yet he barely acknowledged that I was aware of him. For my part, I stared at him and at his youth. Something else caught his attention and he ambled away down the corridor. I saw him stop once, at the edge of my world, before he moved on, out of my reach.

My diary entry seems bent on capturing every detail, from the clothes he wore, to his hairstyle, and his body language. I'd forgotten the moment, but reading about it, his blue sling and town clothes come back to mind. The entry's pages are out of order, further into the notebook than events that happened later. Perhaps I wrote about the young man days after he passed through, recalling the moment then as I am recalling it now. Or perhaps I just wrote my descriptions on the first blank page I found. Still, I wonder at the hour I must have spent on the entry. And much like the rest of my time in hospital, I doubt I can piece it back together seamlessly.

* * *

That afternoon, my mother arrived with a man in her tow. He waited by the nurses' station as she approached me. It took me a few seconds to recognise Andrew Hill, the policeman who'd answered questions on the news. He looked smaller in person than on screen. Faced with a deflated version, I found him short and stout, when I could see that he was about as tall as me. For a moment, the impression put me at ease.

'It's alright,' she whispered with a smile, 'he won't stay long.'

Even though my mother hadn't warned me, his sudden appearance didn't surprise me. That, together with the nervous expectation on my mother's face, had me nodding.

She signalled him to my bedside. He came closer, holding his hands behind his back. His navy suit opened to show a white shirt, a gold buckle, and a blue tie. He led with his head down as if he were caught in thought. When he looked at me, his chin rose level, and his bushy eyebrows lifted his heavy glasses for a second. Then they came down and his face was settled.

It was that general expression of a man who knows and understands that made me want to close my eyes and will him away.

He made as if to speak, but my mother started before him.

'Nate,' she said, 'Mr Hill would like to ask you a few questions. He knows you're making an effort for him.' She whispered the last part and turned to the inspector. 'Nathaniel very much wants to help.' She looked as if she was about to say more but she stopped herself. After a short pause, she added: 'Don't forget that he is just starting to deal with the whole situation.' And with a hand gesture, she told the policeman to proceed.

He breathed in deeply as he gathered his words. When he opened his mouth, I expected his voice to boom across the room, but the slow sounds barely reached me.

'Nate – can I call you Nate?' he asked.

I nodded.

'Thank you, Nate,' he continued, a bluntness clotting his West Country accent. 'My name is Andrew Hill. Call me Andrew. This is an informal chat. We'll take your statement at a later stage... When the doctors declare you well enough to go through the process. Today I would like to ask you a few questions. Can you answer them for me?'

I expected him to continue but he seemed to wait for my response.

'I can try.'

'Good.' He pulled out a notebook and was clearing his throat when my mother groaned. His eyes looked her way for an instant before going back to his notebook.

'Mr Hill!' she said. The urgency in her voice tore him away from his task. With a wave of her chin, she took him aside to the nurses' station. Their conversation looked animated, but they were far enough that I couldn't make out what they were saying. He came back with his notebook tucked in his pocket. Acknowledging my mother on the other side of the bed, he started again.

'I know how difficult it must be for you at the moment—' He caught himself, a finger reaching up to his right temple, stroking frame and skin. In that moment, I started hoping: perhaps I could say no, shut my mouth and stare him down. But I lay still, waiting for him to speak, my arms limp by my sides.

'Do you know why I'm here, Nate?'

I held silent for an instant, hoping he'd answer his own question. I wanted to beat him at his own game, but he waited for me and I had to speak: 'You're in charge of the investigation.'

'Yes, I am. Did your mother tell you this?'

'I saw you on TV.'

'On TV?' He raised a hand to his glasses and pushed them down his nose. 'Is there a TV in this room?' he asked, looking around.

I pointed at the articulated arm on the side of my bed.

'Of course,' he said, pushing his glasses back up, dismissing the matter. 'Do you know what it means to be in charge of the investigation?'

'I...' I held the single vowel for a long time, hoping that he would take over and get on with it. But he waited. 'It means that you've got to find out what happened,' I said.

His lips curved into the shadow of a smile.

'Yes, I need to find out what happened. This is where I need your cooperation.'

As he finished his sentence, he reached for his notebook and a pen. He shuffled pages until he came across the right one. Then, his eyes jumping between his notebook and my face, ignoring my mother's frown, he started the interview process.

Answers were easy at first. My mother had dropped me off at school; I'd bumped into Jeffrey before going to my history class; there, the teacher had handed essays back, which we'd discussed for half the lesson, before looking at new material. With every question, my answers lengthened. He nodded slowly as I spoke, taking note of every detail I gave him. When I told him I'd arrived a little late for physics, he raised his eyebrows in appreciation, the thick coarse hair climbing above his glasses' frame.

To my right, my mother was grabbing the railing at the edge of my bed. She had the window to her back, and the shadows stressed her glare.

She addressed me at first: 'You look exhausted,' and, turning to the inspector, 'He should be resting now.'

'A few more questions, Mrs Dillingham. I'll be quick.'

She was standing close to me but she was facing Hill, her shoulders square, her legs still, a hint of a forward lean to her posture so that she seemed ready to leap at him for me, but not to take my hand and smile.

He wanted to know whether I was the last student to come in. I told him of Eric and his chains, of the madness in his eyes and his aloofness. And when I paused, he hummed. 'What happened next?' My tongue loosened, I started answering before I had time to think. At first, everything I said seemed distant, as though it had happened to someone else. Three thin lines divided his forehead evenly, while his nods slowed.

'Eric shot Tom and everyone backed away.' He scribbled faster, keeping pace with my words. 'He was saying sorry.'

'To everyone?'

'I don't know. No, I don't think so.' He wrote two lines. 'I don't remember much.'

'You're doing fine.'

I spoke of the noise, I described Jeffrey falling, and Jayvanti and Anna, and I added more names, the ones I saw die. Name after name, the recollections slowed.

My voice trailing off, he asked me the question I'd been avoiding, the question I'm still avoiding. Looking back at what I wrote earlier, I can see that I included the moment, but how hidden have I put it! A series of cracks and no context. I'm battling the white page, writhing in front of my computer, but why? I was lauded for it eight years ago, and yet the shame still throws me into a pit.

'How did Eric die?'

My muscles stiffened, and suddenly I no longer felt in control. I looked at my mother in panic, dry sobs springing up my throat. Her whole body shifted towards me, her hands holding the bed's railing even harder, her fingers tantalisingly close.

'Eric and you were friends?' He carried on with the same calm expression.

I kept silent.

'What was the extent of your relationship with Eric Knight?' he asked.

'Nate is friends with everyone!' my mother said, loud enough that the whole ward looked at us. 'Nate's tired! Look at him, look at what you've done!'

But I was still absorbed by the inspector. He held his notebook at the ready, his pen resting on the paper. The thick rims of his glasses seemed to soar up, precariously resting on his brow, as if they were waiting for my answer to drop back down to the bridge of his nose.

'It's me. I shot him—'

My mother barked over the rest of my words. Mr Hill took off his glasses, and played with them as he stared at the bed's headboard. He tweaked them between his fingers as I'd seen him do on television.

'Yes, I thought so,' he said.

'Inspector!' She moved around to the other side of the bed. 'That's quite enough. You told me you'd be careful!' She grabbed him by the arm and snarled: 'Out, out!'

* * *

She lingered in the ward's corridor before coming back. 'Get some sleep,' she said. Her lips drifted open and the fingers of her right hand were slipping down her face. Suddenly, she pulled out her mobile phone, told me she'd be back later, and walked out.

The tears had retreated without ever bursting through. But they'd left me with a great sense of unresolved sadness. I wished I could have cried the sadness away or talked it out with her. Instead I was alone. The doctors had ordered nothing but rest for me that day, and I couldn't think up a ploy to attract the nurses' attention. One of the old ladies had a quiet visitor. Mother and son, I thought. It was the first time I'd seen him. He'd barely arrived that he'd opened his book. I looked at them for a few seconds, but their mutual silence seemed to hide even more sadness. I toyed with that sadness for a moment, hoping it would bring the tears up, but they were too far gone.

The other old lady was asleep, a wisp of white hair covering part of her forehead, the translucent skin glowing in the afternoon light. I looked towards the old man. He was in bed, sitting up, the sheets pulled down so they covered his legs from his thighs down. He was turned towards the old lady and her son – it had to be her son. The old man's face seemed like it had been creased by years of laughter. I stared at him resolutely, my chest facing him, my head pointing towards his bed, my eyes fixed on the contours of his face. I wanted him to notice me, turn my way and respond to my smile. He would come over and we would speak. I knew he could walk, I'd seen him.

I waited for a minute, but he didn't move. I focused all my thoughts on him, broadcasting them silently across the room. I waited for five minutes, but he was a patient man. I grew calmer, the emotions in my chest weaker. I waited for half an hour. At one stage, he shifted his stare from the old lady's son to a janitor coming through the ward. Then the son left, and his eyes moved to the window, turning from one side of the room to the other. He passed over me without acknowledging my efforts.

'Nate?' I looked up. Two nurses, both men, were by my bedside. The sight of two young men in nurses' clothes puzzled me. Perhaps Hill had ordered me transferred to a prison hospital. Or perhaps they'd decided I was crazy, and they were going to take me to a psychiatric ward. Either way, they'd sent two men because they were afraid I was going to fight.

'Nate, we're going to move you to another ward. You're going to get a single room, lucky you.'

I looked around me trying to think of a way to prevent this. The old man was now looking at me, but it was too late. The nurse in charge of my bed was nowhere to be seen. I looked at the ward's entrance, but my mother wasn't showing up.

'Why? I didn't hear anything about this.'

The bulkier of the two answered me: 'Don't know. We just got told to move you.' Seeing my worried expression, he smiled gently. 'One floor down. Your own private room and the same view, lucky you.'

The thin nurse gathered my things and they started wheeling me out.

'Don't you have some idea?'

They shrugged.

They took me to a large empty corner room and set up my bed so that I wasn't quite in line with the door. I didn't have the same view: there were windows on two walls, but from my position I could only see out of one, towards Headington. And I was too far from the window to look down at the town. I could see a few trees and houses, but they were hazy.

As they were leaving me, I asked the nurses to keep the door open. They left it so that I could only see a thin strip of the outside world; from my angle, it was a yard-long stretch of the corridor going around the corner of the building. It was a busy stretch: legs flashed through, clad in green, slacks, or town clothes. I never had time to see who was walking by. No one seemed to stop and talk as they had done in my old ward.

My mother found me an hour later. She bustled through the door and strode to my bed. She stopped to take in her surroundings, and with a satisfied look reached for a chair. Her hair was tied back, folded into a neat ponytail. I looked at her face, searching for a sign. When she faced me, it was with a decisive expression.

'Hill wants you isolated,' she said, launching into his reasons: he didn't want me watching television, he didn't want just anyone to speak to me. I lost interest in the subject as soon as I understood his reasons. I held silent, waiting for an opening, wanting to tell her more about Eric. But once she exhausted this first topic, she started on another without marking a pause.

* * *

Eric could spend days working away in his shed. All he needed was a good project.

The first time I visited his place, he showed me a tree-house he'd spent a year building when he was fourteen. When he'd first mentioned it, I'd imagined a couple of planks nailed to a tree. Instead, I saw something that would have fitted in Neverland.

We went down to a copse that separated his garden from the field it backed onto. He stopped in front of two ancient oaks, and with a broad sweep of his arms, he invited me to look up. It took me a few seconds to make out the tree-house through the green spring leaves. When I did, it all came into focus: the porches, the terraces, the ropes, the steps, the walls, the ladders, the bridge. They webbed across the branches gently, using and adding to what the trees offered, as if they were embracing the canopy.

I followed him around a smooth trunk, where he unfurled a short ladder tucked in between two branches. We climbed to a platform covered with a PVC sheet, which he'd built first, he told me, and on which he'd stored his tools as he worked. Steps, some carved into existing branches, others nailed into the trunk, weaved past a lookout and a space he'd styled as his desk, and led to the sturdiest part of his refuge: a walled-up room five yards above the ground, large enough to hold a camping bed and a coffee table. Waving his hands around, he showed me the room's features: it had an impermeable roof, straw to insulate the floor, and windows he could seal with clear plastic when it rained. Another door opened on to a long and sturdy branch. Fastened to the room's outside wall, two ropes followed the branch at hand-height, before meeting a third rope, tying up into a frail bridge, and plunging across the void to the other tree. He'd spent two weeks making the bridge, he explained.

The taller tree was his sanctuary. My feet dangling from a platform, his long limbs stretched across a hammock, we looked out across the neighbour's field and smoked a cigarette in silence. It was the only place I ever saw him smoke.

It was in his shed that he'd conceived the tree-house. And it was in the shed that he'd worked on all his other projects. Some of his more ornamental ideas ended up on the shelves of his room. Lying on his bed, I could see a sample of his ingenuity: toy cars made out of aluminium cans, a bow and a quiver full of arrows, stones carved into paperweights, even a nativity set – he wasn't religious, but he found the concept challenging.

It was his determination that I admired. He'd decide something and he'd carry it through, like the shelves he'd fitted into his tree-house. They were going to be made from wood he'd recycled himself. Buying freshly cut planks was too easy. He wanted to work with existing forms, to make something new from what people had discarded. For two whole months, he scoured through pits, scrutinised rubbish piles outside houses, until he had a heap of material spilling out of his shed. He studied each item: the headboard, the splintered table, the Ikea bedside table. He played with them all, unscrewing, sawing, gluing, until he had enough sketches to fill a whole notebook, until he had a design. For months, I'd seen planks like limbs shifting puffs of sawdust in his shed. And then, one day, he took me straight to the little cabin up his tree. Against an outside wall, covered with a small awning, his bookshelf was finished: from the bottom to the top, it narrowed in width, in breadth, and its wood lightened until a short and thin plywood piece, coated in white paint, capped the whole assembly.

He'd said he'd do it and he'd done it. Unlike me. I could hold a hammer, I could tie a knot, but I'd never set up a pulley system thirty feet up a tree. It was his determination that drew me into his world.

And how sullied it had been on the news! While the grainy images were bouncing off the shed's tin roof, the newsmen dissected Eric's relationship with his stepfather, his behavioural record, his broken mother. In malignant detail, they talked of the replicas Eric had turned into live guns. And not once did they ask how a seventeen-year-old could have achieved so much.

* * *

My body was recovering. The pain had gone, its departure unnoticed. It was taking me longer to fall asleep. Hoping the house would slump into the soot, I was spending hours caught outside a dream. My thoughts roamed unhindered by carnal impulses. They swirled into my past, rushing across vast plains, amassing at my defences. They started with the day just gone, scratching around one moment until it bled. Satisfied, they jumped further and landed on an image. Sometimes, the image yielded a rush of impressions. Sometimes, I fended it off, and my thoughts, undeterred, flowed on to another vision. But they were soon darting back, their question rephrased.

Was someone trying to get into my room? My mind jolted back to the sound of shuffling steps outside my door. I held my breath and listened, waiting for a hand on the door handle, for a muffled footstep across the lino floor. Nothing came. Two people moved down the corridor past my door, whispering to each other. I let air swell into my lungs, tension washing away as I breathed out.

No one was trying to get in. I smiled as my thoughts leaned into a safe topic. I was waiting for the soot to settle.

* * *

When my aunt came to visit, I found myself more engrossed with her toddler of a daughter than in what she had to say. For once, I wasn't the youngest person in the room. Nicole was the second of my father's sisters, and also the one who lived closest to us. For years, when I was little, our fridge had been adorned with her postcards: temples in Laos, the Sydney Opera House, Polynesian dancers, the Golden Gate Bridge – there seemed to be one coming every six months. On their back, a two-line description of what she was doing littered with exclamation marks. 'Just climbed Kilimanjaro! Next stop: K2!' came with a cloudy peak. 'I love Aussie men and I love surfing lessons!' she wrote on the back of a surfing kangaroo.

When she'd met an Englishman in Boston four years ago now, she plunged into a relationship with the same enthusiasm:

within months, she was married, pregnant, and ecstatic to be back home.

Green-eyed Tori was her second, and she was making sure that her mother didn't look at anyone but her:

'What's that?' she said.

'That's a window, dear. Now let Mummy speak.'

Tori gathered her teddy bear close, and pointed a plump finger in my direction.

'What's that?'

'Not what's that, but who's that. That's your cousin, dear. Where's your teddy bear? What was I saying, Nate?' She looked at me, but I shrugged the question towards my mother.

'Tori, Tori,' my mother was saying, her voice an octave higher than usual. 'Where's your teddy bear? Come and show Aunty Liz your teddy bear!'

Tori pouted, holding her teddy bear behind her back, as if to protect it from my mother's outstretched hands.

'Yes, that's what I was saying.' My aunt jabbed her index finger at the ceiling. 'It's so typical of your father to take on more work just when you need him the most. Don't give me that look, Liz. I've known him for a lot longer than you.' Tori was sitting in my mother's arms, fiddling with my mother's collar. 'When he was young, he was just the same. When our mother got her first tumour, the benign one, Henry went and spent his days in the library—'

Spending time with my aunt was both frightening and refreshing. She could hammer her truth in just as easily as she could delight us all with a story. On this visit, she opted for her genial self. After telling me about her brother's faults – I always liked the perspective she gave me on my father – she started recounting her own hospital adventures, the gash on her head when she was seven, the burst appendix when she was eleven, and I laughed along to the beat of her stories.

'Who's ever dislocated a shoulder on Christmas Day? And going surfing too! Now that's my luck, isn't it? A hot surfer, washboard abs to go with the stubble, picks me up and I'm thinking that it's not so bad after all, but that's as good a Christmas present as I got that day. Fifteen minutes later, two seventy-year-olds, each with a moustache, and I'll tell you what: one of them wasn't a man – so there they are, slicing through my brand new swimsuit, and then wheeling me off to hospital – hold on, Tori, let Mummy speak – and I look around the emergency room: from this wall to that wall, people lying around waiting, holding a bit of ice on their head, knee, you name it; they like to play sports in Australia and they like to drink, not an easy mix. And for all these people, three poor doctors asking themselves why they didn't take Christmas off!'

* * *

Andrew Hill's people came to take my statement two days after his visit. They knocked on the door and pushed it open before I could invite them in. My mother had gone to another ward's corridor to make a phone call. Ever since the inspector's visit, she'd become more dependent on her phone. She'd started using it apologetically; she'd come back to my side and tell me how much she hated mobile phones; but now that ritual had shrunk to a shrug.

Hill had sent me two people, both alluringly young. The more junior of the two must have been in his early twenties. His droopy eyes appeared fixed on the floor for the whole interview. After a cursory nod, he pulled a tape recorder out of a satchel he carried slung across his shoulders, and went about setting it up.

His partner entranced me, and entrances me still. I can still picture her today in a fitted grey suit, its lines following the curve of her hips down and around her arse, before dropping in one clean line to her feet. She was arching her back and holding her head tilted down as if she were looking up to me. I'm ashamed to put it down on paper, but the thought of her has kept on resurfacing over the years, even though I only ever met her twice. Now I can recognise in her allure the shape that some women reach around the age of thirty, but then I was caught unaware, and desire was stirring me into submission.

Her introductions almost made me hers. I was leaning back on my bed with a dumb smile and half-opened eyes, nodding to everything she said. It wasn't what she said: she was resorting to standard turns of phrase. But it was a quality in her voice which changed the meaning of her every word. A quietness. Quiet as a late-night whisper, her breath tickling my ear, one lazy finger stroking the hollow of her waist. It was halfway through her introduction, as lust was tightening its stranglehold, that my mother walked into the room.

'What are you doing here? I told your inspector you couldn't interview him without me.'

The woman's voice floated across the room, brushing my skin: 'We haven't started.'

'Well, you can't start until I give you permission. Do you have my permission?' She paused, daring a response. 'Give me a moment alone with my son.' She flicked her fingers towards the door. When they didn't move fast enough, she scowled: 'Now!'

She shut the door behind them and came to my side, her face transformed. Its vivacity gone, she looked aged.

'Are you ready?'

'I guess.'

'Remember one thing, Nate. Whatever you think you've done, shooting Eric saved lives. Think of the room next door. They were locked in too.'

'I guess.'

She held herself in silence, her eyes still locked with mine, her hand rising mechanically to her temple. Her eyes lost their focus and she turned away. She seemed to stagger on her way to the door – I couldn't be sure.

They were meeker the second time they entered my room. The woman came in behind my mother and stopped a yard from my bed as if she were waiting to be shown where to stand. She turned back to the droopy-eyed man, who'd stopped at the door. Her glance seemed to embolden him: he crossed the doorsill and went back to his equipment. That in turn strengthened her position: she edged closer to me, to where she wanted to conduct the interview from. For a few seconds, she stood with her hands crossed over her stomach, one thumb massaging the other hand's knuckles. My attention slipped from her hands to the turn of her jacket, and, once again, I saw what had troubled me before my mother came into the room.

Then, with a sign from my mother, she started speaking. If it hadn't been for my mother's upright posture, the tension in her jaw, the stillness of her eyes, I would have been lost to the woman as a child to a lullaby. I would have been fooled into thinking that she listened because she cared, and that she cared about even the most minor of details. The warmth of an undivided ear, and in a woman like her!

But my mother was vigilant. She cut the woman early in her spiel.

'So you're doing cognitive interviews now. And do they work?'

The woman looked startled when she answered my mother.

'Yes, we are. DCI Hill insists on them.'

'A modern man in the police force, who would have thought? Well, you're doing a good enough job… Keep at it.'

It took a few seconds for the unease to leave the woman's face. My mother had achieved her purpose: the woman's questions now seemed like they were coming out of an instruction book.

She asked me to tell her my story, and when I stalled she asked me to tell her more. 'Tell me more…' It could have been a lover's command. Instead, it was a ploy. I told her the story

I've already put down. Haltingly. Mr Johnson and his problem set, Eric and his chains, Tom and his sally, Jeffrey and his grunts, Anna and her blood, paramedics and their stretchers, the swelling crowd and ambulances. Tell me more… She asked me how I felt. Despair and acceptance. Fear and adrenaline. Pain and shame. Awe and calm. Tell me more… She asked me to go through events backwards. Arriving in hospital. Liz by my side. Anna's chest whizzing. Shots, shots and more shots. I struggled. Tell me more… She asked me to go through events from another person's eyes. I asked who, they all died. Tell me more… I balked, she retreated.

And yes, I told her what I haven't yet told the white page. Standing up as bullets wailed around me. Walking towards Eric, hands outstretched, coaxing a gun out of his hands, for him and against him, making and breaking a promise. One, two, three.

I told her what I felt: the burn the barrel left on my fingertips, the gun's weight and easy balance, the shock through my hand as my bullet left its chamber, and the overriding pain as his bullet missed my head and plunged into my stomach.

I told it to her backwards: dropping the gun and staggering back, pain gone blind on the count of three, my escape on the count of two, the trust in his eyes on the count of one, the implicit promise, my fingers curling around the handle.

I couldn't tell the story from his eyes. He wouldn't have understood – to him, I was a brother. Such things are better left untold.

* * *

The nights were slow, I remained stuck in bed, and I was growing restless. I'd been going to the bathroom on my own for some time. Doctors had advised me to consult the physiotherapist before getting back on my feet. But as it was merely advice, I could ignore it: I started by walking around my room. It was more of a slow shuffle than a purposeful walk, but it was a steady sort of movement. My legs were still faithful even if weariness piled down my spine. The ache in my stomach remained dull, but for certain movement that sharpened the pain, jolts radiating from the wound until my jaw clenched and my lips curled. I couldn't stretch my back or lean to the side, for example. But I could, a hand pushing along the IV stand still plugged into my arm, the other clutching my drawing pad and a pencil, keep my midriff steady and shuffle through my hospital wing.

My new ward looked much like my old one. The walls were painted green rather than yellow, but the patients looked just as wrinkled, and the nurses just as occupied. There was a gate at the end of the corridor, which opened silently onto the heavy grey doors of an elevator. I remembered the nurses who'd moved me: one floor, they'd said. The weight of the pad in my hand had me thinking of the old man upstairs. Pressing a few buttons, the elevator swallowed me in and spat me out. A nurse helped me through the door to my old ward: pulling was trickier than pushing.

When I came to the open room that used to be my own, I stood by the nurses' desk, as the young man and his blue sling had done, and looked at the great window. The ward looked ordered from afar, beds symmetrically arranged, the floor uncluttered. The city's lights broke through the distance, dimming points in the room's reflection. I was there too, in my pale hospital robe, spotty stubble darkening my chin, my back bent forward. The sight held me for a moment.

I recognised a nurse walking by.

'What happened to the old man who used to be in that bed?' I pointed.

She pursed her lips.

'The dark-skinned one,' I said.

'Oh yes, he's gone.'

'Dead?'

'No, gone home.'

Relief mingled with disappointment. We had spent days facing each other. Days of boredom, introspection, and solitude. And somehow, despite our proximity, we'd erected a barrier we never dared break.

I took the elevator down to a cafeteria I'd seen signposted. People were scattered in clusters across the expanse of tables. Opening my sketchbook, I sat in between two groups. A greying man talking to a woman with a creased pink shirt. And an Asian family: two sons sleeping over beds made of chairs, an attentive daughter tucking her mother's arm, a father typing away on his phone. I sat and sketched and then I had enough. I preferred walking.

As I weaved my way back, two floors below my own ward, I heard a patient grunt. The sound stopped me. A guttural burst breaking down into a howl. I peered into a room at the man's pain, but my mind was going elsewhere. I was back inside the classroom and Jeffrey had fallen to the ground with a loud grunt. He was on the floor, leg twitching, a new grunt rising muted past his rasping breath.

My body was going rigid – I had to think of something else. Grunts and Jeffrey... My brain parsed through hundreds of mornings, afternoons and evenings I'd spent with him over the years, until, as the seconds passed and the classroom threatened its return, I remembered that Jeffrey used to grunt on the cricket field. Gentle men in floppy whites, glare reflecting off the wicket, freshly mowed grass, the images came together and the classroom was banished out of my mind.

Jeffrey used to roll his arm over and hope the ball would swing, seam and spit. He called himself a fast bowler – when I made fun of his speed, he told me he bowled a heavy ball.

'Ask the three batsmen who couldn't play me last week. I'm quicker than I look.'

They'd been swinging across the line with their eyes closed, and one of them had connected five times before finding a safe pair of hands on the boundary. But that hardly bothered Jeffrey.

When I told him he was slow in the nets, he'd rise to the banter and scoff back an answer. One day he'd say that he reserved his best for matches. On another, he'd tell me that I wasn't worth the effort. This isn't to say he fooled himself. He was well aware that he was on the slow side of medium. But he preferred to think of himself as a fast bowler. When I told him that he should take a closer look at Ashley Giles, he laughed dismissively. It would be Brett Lee and Shoaib Akhtar for him.

If my advice had no effect, he was willing to listen to my father. For years, we'd seen him score a hundred every third match. His quietness at the crease, the restrained backlift, his backfoot punches, we'd spent years trying to emulate him. One day, my father took Jeffrey aside and said:

'Forget about speed. It's all in here.' He tapped his skull. 'Fool me and you'll get me out.'

Jeffrey took that to mean he should start grunting. He would start with three standard deliveries, respectable stuff on and around the off stump. On the fourth, we all expected it, he would sprint in, grunt, and bowl a slower one. The grunt would come early in his delivery stride, as if he was coiling so far that it was straining his back. He would land with a roar, release with a snarl, only for the ball to lob gently towards the batsman. Wary of losing their wicket, batsmen would generally pat the ball back, and smile at the laughing wicketkeeper.

Jeffrey's tactic worked once. A spiky-haired twelve-year-old blocked Jeffrey's first two deliveries, cut the third for four, and then tried the same shot on Jeffrey's slower ball, only to see the ball go over his slanted bat and dislodge a bail. Never one to miss a celebration, Jeffrey planted both feet on the ground and looked up to the sky, his arms outstretched. When he looked down, we were all around him, cheering him on. Ignoring the rest of us, he found my father and embraced him.

The image of my father and Jeffrey, arm in arm, brought up an overpowering melancholy. Drained, I made my way back to my room. The next day I told my mother I wished my father would visit more often.

'He wants to. He does. But he's busy, you know how it is. And he's got to take care of James.'

There was a sadness in her voice that stopped me from asking any more questions.

* * *

It was a day before Hill's last visit that my mother seemed to break the distance that had grown between us. Despite my best efforts, I could ignore it no longer. She'd never made me feel so caught up in my own silence. Whenever she entered the room, I'd pull out a novel and bury myself behind its cover. Even when she sat quietly, I dared not interrupt her for a slight furrow across her brow.

But that day, her phone clutched in her hand, she walked into my room with a smile I hadn't seen for many years. It was the same smile she'd had when her lab received a large grant. Or when she'd ensured her favourite doctoral student was offered a fellowship.

I was sitting on a chair, my forehead glued to the window, staring at the town below. Arching my neck, I immediately felt myself drawn towards her. She was pulling up a chair next to mine, her voice carrying the warmth of fresh gossip.

'There's a rumour going around,' she said, lingering over the word 'rumour', 'that they're going to replace Andrew Hill.' On that, she leaned back and stared up at the ceiling. 'Ah!'

'Why? What's he done?'

Her smile grew to include me. She tapped her phone absentmindedly.

'It's what he hasn't done that people worry about. Every morning, there's fifty journalists waiting outside his door for a coherent story, and he can't give it to them. He has twenty officers working late into the evenings and he can't give it to them! That's what he's done. That's what he hasn't done.'

Her enthusiasm was overpowering my confusion. I grinned as I spoke.

'But he knows what happened. I told him.'

'Exactly.' She kissed my head and got up. I turned around, waiting for her to say more. She was pacing, two fingers playing with her lower lip.

'Nate, he's just a policeman. He doesn't get how it works.'

As she walked around, unaware of my presence, I felt like a fool. I'd let myself hope too much, but she'd only come in so she could boast over one of her schemes. I suppressed the feeling as soon as it happened, but it had already coated my mind with a sticky dirt.

As she left the room, I tried to forget the smile she'd had when she'd walked in, and told myself to focus on practicalities. My mother was not being herself, I decided. But there was a weight on the insides of my stomach, as though I were falling, that stopped me from taking that line of thought any further. The only idea that seemed to fit was that I should take matters into my own hands. Whenever it came up, I nodded to myself and, for an instant, forgot the feeling in my gut.

* * *

In many ways, Eric had been unlucky when he first arrived at Hornsbury School. He'd spent his first weeks balancing the changes occurring within his home with his desire to fit in and make friends in a new school. There were days when he would be twitching around at his desk, hoping to start a conversation with his neighbours. I still remember him taking Jeffrey's seat next to me. Unhappy to see my friend relegated to the back, I spent the entire lesson ignoring Eric, just as he was trying to catch my eyes and smile. I feigned utter focus on my book, and when my attention wavered, I held my hand over my left eye so that our gazes wouldn't cross.

And there were days when he would trudge in, choose an empty table, and slump back, unaware of anyone around him. The strangeness of his behaviour could have worked for him. If Tom Davies or Anna, two popular students, had talked to him on one of his good days, they might have been inclined to feel for him on one of his bad days. Perhaps they would have gone and asked him how he was, and, touched, as he was still willing to be back then, he might have told them.

Instead, it became a bit of a sport to ignore him. Never something we openly discussed – we were friendly for the most part – but something jokes would refer to in passing:

'I was struggling to stay awake, and then Eric sat next to me.'

But it could have blown over with everyone like it did with me. On one of his gloomy days, he tapped me on the shoulder and asked whether he could borrow my book for a second.

'You don't have your own?'

'Not anymore.'

I moved to his desk so we could share. We said hello to each other in the mornings after that, and I was soon enjoying the conversations we had on his better days. With a little luck, and I'm not asking for much, the same could have happened between Eric and the rest of the class.

The first I saw of the incident, Paul Cumnor was pushing Eric back onto a railing. It happened very quickly: Paul's head stuck into Eric's face, his finger jabbing Eric's cheek, and then Eric's head striking Paul, Paul collapsing to the floor with a thud and a

'Fuck!', blood pouring from his nose, while Eric towered above him, a shallow cut across his forehead.

Eric told me the story later: he'd been staring in the distance, caught in his own thoughts, when he'd heard Paul calling to him. 'Stop!' Unsure what Paul was referring to, Eric assumed he was telling him to stop brooding over his problems. He smiled at Paul, and soon slipped back into his world. At the end of the lesson, Paul drove into him: 'Don't look at her!'

'I could count the hairs on his chin,' he told me. 'I had to hit him.'

Fights often bring people closer: there's something in fearing pain. But not this time: Eric was too absorbed in his own world. To those who didn't know him, he was shifty because he was guilty. Perhaps because he'd overcome Paul, Eric never blamed him for being ostracised. To him, everything was Tom's fault.

'He's fake. He's always calculating. A smile here, a pretty speech there, and I'll get through! You saw him yesterday. He never talks to me and then he asks me if I want to be his lab partner. He just wants my help! So why does he go laughing behind my back? Chatting up Jayvanti while I do all the work.'

Even though I always found Tom's barbs innocuous, I would find myself agreeing with every word of Eric's rants. And, as Eric well knew, I would bump into Tom the next day and find him just as likeable as before Eric's outburst.

* * *

When my mother warned me that Hill would be coming back for a final interview, she added a note of hope:

'It's almost over.'

Those three words became a mantra that I started to expect whenever I saw her coming out of a fog of thoughts. Pacing around the room, she said them as she saw me looking at her.

After my father called, she said them as she explained that, once again, he had too much work to come and visit me. My dinner cooling on my lap, she said them as she bid me goodnight. At first I thought she was trying to reassure me and the words annoyed me, but then I realised that she was talking to herself.

They seemed stronger as she buttoned her jacket and went to open the door.

The woman who'd conducted the last interview entered the room first. She wore the same grey suit that she had the last time I saw her, its lines still embracing her figure. My eyes lingered on her waist as she closed the door. If I still felt my throat tighten, I also knew that she'd leave as soon as I told her what she was after.

'Gina, will you get Mrs Dillingham some tea?' The inspector's voice came from the door.

Gina – this is the first time I remember her name – walked to my mother's side and whispered milk and sugar. She laid a hand on my mother's elbow.

'I'll stay here,' my mother hissed. 'Go and get it yourself.'

Exchanging a glance with her inspector, Gina swayed towards the door and left the room. That was the last I saw of her.

Andrew Hill loomed. The black wisps crowning his haggard face; the dark eyebrows settled at the bottom of his imposing forehead; the thick square glasses framing his brown eyes. He moved into the centre of the room with a ponderous walk, his feet settling a shoulder's length apart, his legs still as a plinth.

The inspector stood at the foot of the bed, while my mother stood to my right. A full minute elapsed from the moment he entered the room to the moment he started speaking. He removed his glasses.

'Nate, you are an important witness. We need you to answer a few more questions. Can you do that for me?'

Feeling more comfortable with the process the third time around, I nodded confidently.

'Good. Can you start by telling me about your friendship with Eric?'

As he mentioned 'friendship with Eric', I felt my mother tensing next to me. I composed my face, and gave her an assured nod.

'We were friends, but I was friends with everybody.'

The inspector's face had sallow skin lumped below his eyes. I looked closer and saw the same loose skin sagging from the lines of his jaw. Afraid to notice more, I let my eyes wander away.

'His mother mentioned you visiting. How often did you visit him?'

'How often?' The question brought up a string of visits all blending into one. 'Every now and again.'

'Well, let me rephrase the question. About how many times did you go to his house since, say, January?'

'Ah…' Summer visits crowded my mind. I was seeing his tree-house and our conversations high above ground. Narrowing my focus to the winter months, I tried to think of the cold, of damp January afternoons, hoping it would bring the right visits to mind.

'…Let me count, Nate,' my mother was saying, 'since I had to drive you. There was that time before James' football training, and that was it. Before that was in December. Once, inspector.'

I felt Hill's eyes on me as my mother spoke.

'Once, then?' he asked.

'Once,' I said.

'Alright. And do you remember seeing anything peculiar on that visit?'

My voice trailed off as my thoughts went back to Eric's shed. My bat was gripped in the vice on his workbench. He was bending forward and applying glue, creases spreading down his forehead. The smell of glue harrowed up my nostrils, but he didn't seem to mind it. I was glancing around, at the piles of sawn-off wood, at a canvas thrown over a heap, at a large metal box and a saw atop it.

'His shed was messier than usual. But not very messy either. Maybe there was something.' I could feel my mother's breath as she leaned closer. 'Maybe there wasn't. If I think about it long enough, I'm going to convince myself that there was.'

'Nothing caught your attention?'

'Nothing did then. But if I think about it long enough, I'll be telling you that I saw his guns and his bullets.'

Hill's hands rose to his head and stopped around his chin, wavering as he twirled his glasses.

'Alright. One final question, Nate.' Suddenly, he was looking directly into me. 'Why do you think Eric didn't shoot you like he shot everybody else?'

My mind reeled for a second. Through the white, I became aware of my hand cooped in my mother's, and I thought of my previous responses. I was ready to answer the question, even if haltingly.

'I guess…' I was looking at the inspector, hoping to pick up cues from his body language. He remained solemn. 'People either froze, or went for the door. I hid behind the teacher's desk. Thicker wood, and all that. And then I looked up, and I guess Eric was looking at me so I thought I'd go to him. He didn't want to die alone. That explains it, doesn't it?'

His eyes stayed fixed on mine, his mouth resolutely closed. It was when he put his glasses back on that I sensed he'd heard enough.

* * *

A squadron of suits was closing in on me. They were hiding behind the only column in the great cafeteria. I ran towards a slanted door, but it slipped ever further from my grasp. A blonde nurse in white bared her sharpened teeth and shook her head at me. When I asked her for help, she melted into the background. I could feel the men's moist breath on my neck. There was nowhere to run: I turned to face them.

It took me hours to fall back to sleep. The cold outside took its hold, my ward quietened, and the hospital crackled. With every thud, I imagined someone marching towards my door. With every crack, I imagined someone climbing up a window. Dawn came and went, and the hospital awakened. I let the bustle cradle me, nestling into its babble.

* * *

Beth was the only one of my remaining friends who visited me at the hospital. As we waited for my mother to bring us tea, she explained it all. Of course, she'd wanted to come earlier but one thing had led to another and she hadn't been able to. 'Don't worry,' I said. Of course, it was the same with John, with Josh, with Jeremy. And when she called my home, she heard I wasn't well enough to receive a visitor yet. It was only because she'd seen my mother at a service in the morning that she'd managed to arrange a visit.

Beth had never been a close friend. Our groups, originally separate, had merged after the summer of 1999. More from a lack of opportunity than of affinity, we'd never spent much time together. I knew her best from what Jeffrey had told me. For the three months leading to the shooting, it seemed like every time we had a quiet minute, he told me another story about Beth. Once, a few weeks before Anna and I broke up, I told Anna what was happening between them, and she took it upon herself to organise a double date.

'You invite Jeffrey, I'll take care of Beth,' she said.

She chose *The Sixth Sense* because it was meant to be scary.

'Dead people. She'll jump into his arms,' she smiled in anticipation.

But Beth went to the bathroom while we chose our seats, and by the time I saw her, she'd come down the wrong aisle. She sat next to Anna, as far away from Jeffrey as she could be. Thankfully, the movie was good enough that we had something to talk about afterwards. When we left the cinema, I tried to pull Anna to my side, but we had to squeeze through a crowd, and Beth ended up alongside Anna. Jeffrey shrugged at me, and I shrugged back. Still, Anna wasn't going to give up: she took us to the canal and pulled out a half-full bottle of vodka. Three shots later, I was kissing Anna, and Jeffrey was leaning close to Beth.

'It's going to happen,' Anna whispered in my ear. I looked at my friend and I thought the same.

The next day, Jeffrey and I were lounging in my room.

'No, mate,' he said, 'nothing. She left five minutes after you.'

'My guess is that she's a lesbian,' I said.

He chuckled louder than me. I made many other guesses – she's scared of you, she thinks you don't like her (Anna's theory), she doesn't fancy you – but whatever I said, he always brought it back to the same thought: 'No, it's more complicated than that. It's just…' he started and then, trying to work out what to say next, he trailed off, and then he smiled for he liked the way she made him suffer. He liked it even more when he felt that they were moving in the right direction – then he boasted about cricket, football, rugby, girls, about everything and anything that I could mention.

I was all smiles as Beth stood by my bed and explained her absence.

'Don't worry,' I echoed, as she told me of her older sister needing the car, of buses not coming back late enough, of the flat tyre on her bike. The apologies only stopped when my mother came back with our teas.

Beth fell silent. My mother left and we were alone and Beth stayed silent. Her stillness was contagious. It was louder than her apologies. It was tightening my smile, and I needed to smile. I had to go for its source.

'How is everyone doing?' I asked.

She looked startled, and, for a moment, I thought I was going to get back to Jeffrey's ebullient Beth. But then she smiled a sweet smile, an old smile.

'Everyone's fine,' she said.

'Fine?' The word came out as a challenge, surprising me as much as her.

She flinched and her smile disappeared. I found myself liking her face better without it, as if the smile I'd yearned for a few seconds earlier had suddenly acquired a meaning I couldn't bear.

'You can imagine how it is,' she said, yellowed merriness settling over her face once again. 'Everyone was shocked. Completely shocked. But we've got to move on.' She sized up the horror on my face, and added: 'Of course, it's not the same for everyone. I don't think that!'

I gulped.

'Are people moving on already?' I asked.

'No, I don't mean it like that. I just meant that when it happened, no one knew what to do. And now people are a bit more normal.' I stared into my cup. 'It was John's eighteenth on the 15th and he'd put together a big party. Well, he cancelled it of course. But he still wanted to do something, so we had a few drinks the other night, and it was nice to get together like we used to do. You'll have to come and hang out with us when you get out.'

I forced a smile. 'Thanks,' I said. 'It seems like everyone is moving on as you say. I'm not sure I can… just yet.' She cleared her forehead of the curls bouncing their way down to her eyebrows, and I noticed how solemn she had become. 'You said something about a service. I haven't heard anything about that. What was it?'

She sighed. 'It was a funeral.'

'Have there been many… services?'

She nodded.

'Have you been to all of them?'

She looked up and studied my face for a few seconds.

'No, I haven't. There were too many.'

'Who was it this morning?'

'Jeffrey.' And as she said that, I realised there was no more colour in her cheeks. She was tugging hard at one of her curls, swirling what was left of her tea with the other hand. 'Look,' she said, a quiver in her voice, 'let's talk about something else. What's it like being in hospital?'

As the conversation moved to safer grounds, I found myself looking around my room, wanting to shatter a lamp, snap the IV stand, throw a chair through the window. But I lay quietly and talked small stuff.

* * *

'There he is.'

The deep voice broke through my reverie. A tall man followed my mother in, his entrance dispelling all of my thoughts. Despite the size of the man, his movements seemed contained and measured.

'You must be Nate. I'm George Hume.'

I took his extended hand, and let the warm flesh engulf mine. He was the first person to shake my hand properly for a long time. The ritual, a relic of my past, put me at ease.

'Your mother was kind enough to invite me in, Nate. When she told me that no one had been to visit you, I had to come and see how you were. So tell me, how are you?'

'Mister…' I paused, looking at his pin-striped suit, at the gold wristwatch and the engraved cufflinks.

'Oh, I apologise, I forget how young you are... Hornsbury is part of my constituency, Nate. Now, when you turn eighteen, you will try to remember that, won't you?' he said with a sly smile. I almost laughed at his joke. 'Call me George, Nate. You've done so much you could call the Prime Minister Tony.'

This time I laughed, although I felt a little confused.

'How long must we wait until you're well enough to get back on your feet?'

'I can walk already, Mister... George. The doctors say I should be heading home by the end of the week.'

'That's good news,' he said, joining his hands up by his chin as if in prayer. 'Can I ask you something, Nate?'

I nodded instantly. His hands ran down his lapels before they met behind his back.

'There are many rumours going around, but one in particular has caught my attention. I feel hesitant to bring it up, but is it true that you shot Eric Knight?'

My eyes jolted towards my mother.

'I've heard,' the politician continued, 'that you bravely disarmed him, and that you shot him when you had to, when he was going to make his way to the other room in the annexe—'

'No,' I interrupted him. That first word had come out forcefully, but I didn't know what else to add. He gave me the chance to say more before he spoke on.

'You're reluctant to speak, and I can understand that. I was in the army for thirty years myself, and there were times when I was lauded for things I hated. That's normal, do you understand?'

When I didn't respond, he looked at my mother.

'I shot him but it wasn't like that,' I said.

He became very serious as he answered me, speaking as though his every word mattered:

'Nate, you're clearly an intelligent young man, and you have a bright future ahead. But listen to me, sometimes you do what you must, and you're left with a hollow feeling down your stomach. It won't do you any good. Steer well clear of that feeling!'

* * *

My last two days in hospital were spent largely alone. My mother came in twice on my penultimate afternoon, setting her things down as if she were going to stay, but then letting a message, an idea, whisk her away before her weight had had time to mould the foam of her chair. I barely looked up as she left the room.

By myself, I thought about Eric, despite all I had told the inspector. Particularly, I pondered over Eric's last month, thinking of the changes he must have gone through, and the symptoms I could have detected. There were incidents that happened at school. Raising his voice outside an exam hall, when he knew there were students inside taking their tests. And the moment Harry had so willingly recounted.

But my mind turned to the time we'd spent outside school. So much could happen at school that there could be a hundred explanations for every flicker or outburst. Ever analytical, Eric would have told me that such data points were noisy signals.

The times I'd seen him alone outside school were cleaner. There was the time his mother made us orange juice, and the uneasy silence that had pervaded the visit. The silence hadn't shocked me then. After all, we were teenagers, sweet one day and vile the next.

But now that I think of my subsequent visit, I can't help but think that his mood changed too much and too quickly. It was the following day. I had brought him another bat, an older piece which no one had used for years, but which was also made of Grade II English willow. The chunk he'd glued the previous day hadn't held because it was too coarse. I'd been the one to suggest using another bat, and I'd felt proud when he agreed.

When he finished clenching the newly-glued chunk to my bat, we put on our coats and headed down to the copse. He spoke as we walked, his voice calm and measured.

'You like them, but you're too easy on them. The system isn't efficient. A bunch of idiots dictate terms to everyone else, and because we're fragmented, we can't fight back. Tell me how that makes any sense.'

He picked up a bunch of pebbles and, one by one, he aimed them at an empty nest high up a bare branch. It was a harmless gesture, a liberating gesture, but how easy it is to see it as some sort of omen. I too joined in: I bent down to gather ammunition, and fired it at the still nest.

* * *

Each memory came innocent and left tainted. And once tainted, memories grew persistent. Their stench remained and coloured other thoughts, so that, like an infection, I was soon left with nothing but tainted memories. Even fields of heather and gorse hugging the Cornish coastline took an ominous turn. I started thinking of the shadows in the recesses between cliff faces, of the waves crashing into rocks at the bottom of the drop, of the birds plunging down to the dark sea for their prey.

With memories came dread, spreading and thickening but never rising to the surface. It skirted the politician's cufflinks, bounced off the police's tape recorder, and amassed at the inspector's eyebrows. I even grew afraid of the old black man who brought me my dinner on weekdays.

I don't want to exaggerate. The dread never had me shivering in a corner, but it settled snugly into the background. For weeks, I woke up with a mass the size of an olive stone pulsating in my stomach. It was in the shower that I remembered where it came from, and it was in the shower that, months later, I realised it was gone.

***

My pencil point balanced on the half-empty page, I smelled the flowers before I saw them. Their fragrance drifted over the sterile floor and opened my eyes like one throws off a heavy blanket. Two nurses had entered my room, each carrying a bouquet in hand. The small dark-haired one was my current day nurse, while the red-haired nurse with a Polish accent had been in charge of my bed in my old ward.

'We heard you were leaving today,' said the dark-haired one, half a step closer than her companion, 'so we all thought we should get you something.'

I had always interpreted her pale irresponsive features as a sign of distance. But I was now seeing them shaped into a genuine smile.

'Flowers for a young boy...' said the redhead. The way she tilted them, the words jarred less. 'Maybe you can give them to your mother?'

'Yes, she likes flowers...' I said before realising I was being rude. 'They look very nice! But... do you give them to everyone?'

'No-no-no,' said the dark-haired nurse. 'Can you imagine?' she laughed towards the red-haired nurse. 'Thank God!'

She reached behind her for the red-haired nurse's bouquet and laid both on a table by the window while she addressed me: 'We're not meant to talk to you about what happened. But now that that MP has gone and told everyone, we felt it'd be alright to come and thank you. What you did, it was very brave.' She mouthed a silent 'thank you'.

She started to fidget and her features tightened into a more familiar expression.

'Okay, we've got to get back to work. Is there anything you need?'

When I shook my head, she made her way towards the door with her colleague.

'Put them in water when you get home,' the red-haired nurse said as she shut the door.

They were probably too far down the corridor to hear my words of thanks. My diary includes both a written description and a drawing of this scene. I've stayed faithful to the description here. The drawing fills the rest of the page my pencil had rested on. The flowers in the foreground come through well enough, but the nurses' faces are flat. Just after they left, despite their kindness, despite the weeks they'd spent taking care of me, I could only recall two or three details and had to make up the rest.

* * *

I left my ward on one of those glorious crisp afternoons that make you forget winter's gloom and wish for spring to hold off a little longer. I was getting half the experience from my window: the sun was shining to all and sundry, and the few clouds running through the sky never seemed to obstruct its rays. I wanted to be part of it, to feel the winter wind on my skin, and a tingle of blood rising up my cheeks. I wanted to spin around and smile at the beauty of the world.

My mother was leading me out through a labyrinth of doors, elevators and corridors, carrying a bag with all of my things in one hand, and both bouquets in the other, when we passed an empty room with a television turned on to a 24-hour news channel. Had I walked on, I would have only caught a couple of isolated images. But the newsreader's steady cadence broke through, and my feet turned into the room of their own accord.

'And a reminder of today's top news. Police investigating the Hornsbury School Shooting have released the shooter's diary' – The screen showed a piece of paper, a cursor highlighting the words a voice was reading.

'Nothing will be the same when I'm done with them.'

The cursor skipped down the page, and the voice read out another section:

'People will wonder why. They'll wonder for eternity. The ones who don't get it are as guilty as the ones who will die today.'

From the corner of my eyes, I could see my mother's hand reaching for my arm. The prospect made me shiver. She didn't understand. I shoved her back.

'Fuck off!'

Anger was shaking its way through my limbs, frothing at my lips, gathering around my eyes. And then it was gone. With a glare at my mother, I sat on a chair and hid my head between my arms. On the chair's soft cushion, my spine buckled and my legs hung limp. The feeling spread. I was worth nothing.

I started crying, at first hiding the tears, but the sobs gathered, as if they'd been held back for weeks, and finally sensing an opening, they were all rushing forth together. On the one side of my mind, I heard Eric ranting, passion and hate coursing through his veins, holding him upright, warm and alive. On the other, there was nothing: a void, an absurd ending. I felt as though I belonged to that void; my life was an anomaly; there was no sense to my tears. But that didn't console me – on the contrary, it made me sadder.

My shoulders shook up and down; spit was dripping down my chin; I could hardly breathe. Gasping for breath, I wailed through my tears. The noise bounced off the wall and came back to my ears. It was too much: needing to control myself, I forced deep breaths into my chest. The sadness mellowed every time I exhaled, and the tears dried.

As I write this, I realise those were the first tears I shed since Eric had burst into the classroom. For weeks I'd managed to restrain my memories and wall my shock in. I'm still convinced it was the right way to go. The politician was correct: sometimes it's better to steer clear of a feeling. Had I spent days on end wallowing in my own tragedy, I would have come out depressed. My way just meant the occasional outburst.

When I felt calm enough, I looked at my mother through my fingers. She was sitting down with her bent head softly bobbing up and down, her hair hiding her face, the bouquets across her lap, the bag by her feet. I stood up and laid a hand on her shoulder.

As I came out of the hospital, a photographer took a picture of me. It is a sympathetic portrait: I'm walking with my shoulders slumped and my eyes puffed, the skin under my eyes illuminated by a trail of tears. I'm wearing a jacket which seems too big for my reduced frame, and I'm holding a bouquet of flowers tight against my chest. My mother stands behind me, car keys dangling from her fingers.

This picture still comes first when I do an image search of 'Nate Dillingham'.

Several years later, well after I thought my scars healed, I sought the rest of Eric's note online. I came across a report on the massacre. It described the notebook police found: its cover lined with dust, a thin powder settled in between every page. They found it neatly stacked on top of papers Eric kept by his workbench. The note follows countless pages of long divisions, object sketches, and measurements. I read it three times; then I closed my browser and never looked at it again. All these years later, I still remember it in its entirety.

We've had enough. It's time for the underground to come to the surface. Once again, it's my turn to start everything. The plan is simple and direct, it won't fail. Finally people will see my work.

I've endured a lot in my years. The weakest of punches leaves me with a bruise that never fades. This will change today. Nothing will be the same when I'm done with them. I know I'm young to die, but I feel so old old old. I could be seventy.

People will wonder why. They'll wonder for eternity. The ones who don't get it are as guilty as the ones who will die today.

Reading it, I imagined his voice trembling in anger, his fist clenching with every point he made, his rapid tones smoothening his logic. And to that, I had to add more, for I knew him better than most. A prolonged squint, his hand running over his face, his gaze jerking towards the door, and anguish dripping from every third word.

Three

My mother was taking me home. To my house of thirteen years, its weathered stone façade, its two wonky floors, its sloping garden. Every time she'd visited me in hospital, I'd known that she hadn't spent a night with three strangers and a rotating staff. No, she'd spent her nights next to my father on her king-sized bed, where I used to nestle after a nightmare. Next to the books she meant to read, piled under her bedside table, spilling to the doorsill. I'd thought of the smell of that room, her cooking, my father coming home late. These were brief thoughts – images, flashes – operating under the surface, but they'd made me long for my own sheets, for my dog, for home. In hospital, I hadn't been my normal self. I'd realised it: it'd started with the wound, draining me of all will, and it'd carried on when doctors, my mother, the inspector took every one of my decisions upon themselves. I'd become passive, but I hadn't worried about it, for, whenever I'd thought of home, I'd imagined myself flowing into my old mould and emerging a good man. Even the calendar agreed with me: March, that great time of change.

Yet, I felt it as soon as I walked into the dim vestibule, when my mother's voice was ringing through the house, the familiar echoes meeting me by the umbrella stand. Home had changed. It came across subtly. The light was duller than the warm glow of my memories. I walked in expectant, apprehensive.

'We're home!' my mother shouted.

Further into the house, past the coat rack, Sloppy was struggling to stand on his legs. His stiff legs still straightening, he turned to smell my knee, and, content he'd done his job, settled back into his blankets. I bent over to kiss the greying fur on his head.

'James, come down! Your brother's home!'

My fingertips grazed the wall's rough stone, stopping at a well-worn crevice just as my father walked through the living room's French windows, a stack of wood in his arms.

'Dad!'

It took him a second to adjust to the light. When he saw me, he put the wood down and came towards me, stopping to brush his hands on his trousers as he cleared his throat. That simple gesture made me nostalgic. Before he had time to recover his voice, I hugged him and held hard onto his chest. I was a few inches taller than him, but my head resting on the side of his shoulder, smelling his old leather jacket, I felt small.

A hug from my father was a precious thing. He'd never been an affectionate man. When he got me into cricket or squash, two sports he excelled at, he spent a few hours introducing me to the basic technique and then entrusted me to coaches. Every now and again, he'd see me in the nets and tell me to keep my head still, or he'd play a match just as I was practising next door, and if we happened to take a break at the same time, he'd tell me to force myself back to the T after every shot. I always followed his advice.

He let go of me when my mother walked into the room.

'Where's James?' he asked.

'He's upstairs, playing video games.'

'I'll get him,' he said and climbed the stairs.

I wanted more and I realised that it wasn't possible. His reasonable tones carried down the stairs. My brother had really started to get into video games just as I was losing interest in them. At first, he'd played the ones I'd spent all of my savings on. Strategy games in which I'd strived to conquer the world and the universe, or racing games in which I'd gone round and round to shave milliseconds off my time. But in the last year, he'd started buying his own games: first-person shooters mostly. Last I'd seen him play, he was hopping around and hacking at people, a crowbar in hand.

'Do you want a cup of tea?' my mother asked me. 'Sit down, I'll put the kettle on.' She pointed at the sofa. A cup of tea in the living room; coming home wasn't the loud bang I'd hoped for.

While the kettle was boiling, my brother stole down the stairs and stood in front of me, fidgeting.

'Hello, Nate. Welcome back.'

'Were you playing something?'

'I'm trying to get through the silo level in difficult. I'm at the machine gun boss.' His head jerked towards the stairs.

'Okay...'

He stayed silent.

'Do you want to play cricket in the garden later?' I said.

'It's cold... But okay.'

As he turned and ran back up the stairs, I told myself that at least there was still cricket. My mother walked my way from the kitchen, vapour swirling from my favourite mug. She handed it to me and sat on an armchair.

'If you go outside, you must be careful. If you run into anyone, don't answer any questions. There was a tall thin guy, grey hair, who tried your room a few times while you were in hospital. I had to have the police talk to him. He was lurking around the other day. But,' she added as she leaned back into the sofa, 'you should be safe in the garden. Go and play, enjoy yourself. You're home now!'

* * *

The house spilled over into the garage. Entering the space that nominally should have held two cars, I fought my way through half-empty cardboard boxes, around a ping-pong table, to reach the set of metal stumps that James and I had been using regularly not eight months before. Dusting it off, I looked for an old wrinkled shoebox, and found it inside the drawer of a chest we'd taken from my grandmother's house. I checked inside: there were still three taped tennis balls in good condition. A cricket bat and the stumps in one hand, the box in the other, I weaved my way back outside, the stumps crashing into metal, wood and cardboard until I emerged into the garden with a smile on my face.

'James!' I yelled.

Setting the wickets against the gate we used as a virtual wicketkeeper, I crouched down, bat in hand, and faced an imaginary delivery. The ball swung through the air, starting down the legside, coming back into my body. A stride forward, I met it with the full face of my bat, dispatching it all along the ground towards the bushes for four.

'James!'

My breath left a mark in the air as I shouted my brother's name. He was coming through the French doors, still putting his jacket on. I was minutes away from the feel of a ball on my bat, from the joy of a good shot. I smiled.

I reached into the shoebox and pulled a ball out. Cocking my wrist, I took two steps, and let my right arm whistle past my right ear and hit my left pocket. Two thin lines of pain spread from the hole in my stomach, and I winced. My brother was in front of me.

'Sorry, Mum was being annoying.'

'What?'

'She wanted me to move my stuff from the computer.'

'Ah... So what's going on with Mum and Dad?' I said.

'They're being weird… Mum started crying so they stopped fighting, but now that she's happy, Dad…'

'Is he giving her the silent treatment?'

'I guess.'

I nodded.

'Alright, it's cold, let's play. Bowling might be a little painful for me. You start bowling, I'll bat.'

He gave me a suspicious look, but took the shoebox from my hand and walked up to the bowling crease. His left arm raised, his jacket stretched, the ball dipped through the grey, while I waited with my bat held high.

We used to play for hours. This time, we played for fifteen minutes and I was exhausted.

* * *

My mother spent her afternoon in the kitchen kneading dough, dicing pumpkin and caramelising raisins, until the house was filled with the smell of all my favourite dishes. She called us to the table, a bead of sweat forming on her forehead, her apron smeared with flour and chocolate. Munching cumin seeds, soups suggesting saffron, curries seeped in ginger, oranges dipped in chocolate, the flavours tickled my palate. I could smell more ingredients than I could name, and I could taste more than I could smell. I pictured birthdays, Christmases, family, friends and girlfriends.

'You have your A-levels a few months away. You have to think about it.'

'But not now, I've just come back.' I felt immediately frustrated by the topic, even though it was the first time she'd brought it up.

'If I talk about it tomorrow, you're not going to like it either. Let's resolve it now that it's in the open.'

'Mum!' I looked at James for support but he was looking down at his plate. 'I'm enjoying my dinner, and now you're ruining it.'

She flinched, holding her eyes closed for a second. When she opened them, I saw they'd become moist. I was surprised. I'd thought that she would push on regardless of what I said, but seeing her on the brink of tears, I tried to master my frustration.

'But yes,' I said, 'now that it's in the open, we might as well get it over with.'

My voice came out harsher than I intended. She took an instant to assess me, before she spoke in a tentative tone:

'Everyone understands that you might not want to go back to school, and that it's a bit late to go to a new school. So your principal's put together a study package for you, and a few teachers have even volunteered to come here and help you in the evenings.'

I mumbled that it could work, surprised by the strength of my reaction. Finishing school had always been a given. Turning to my father, I asked him whether he was going to training this Thursday. I saw him nod at my mother, as if to tell her she'd said enough. For a second, I thought he understood me.

'No,' he said. That single word cut me down. 'Three reasons. First is that I have a heavy workload at the moment, Nate. I've had to take clients in Dorset, and that involves a lot of travelling, mainly on Thursdays… The second is that you need to rest. And the third is that the season's still a long way off.'

It was a little further into the conversation, after my mother had quizzed my brother over his homework, and after my father had complimented my mother over the food, that she turned to me and told me that journalists had been calling her, asking whether they could interview me. She'd already made a decision. Asking me was just good manners. But then I heard it, as she talked of how often the media had tried getting in touch with me, with her, with anyone in the family. There it was, the tentativeness in her voice. Tentativeness! More pronounced than when she'd discussed school – she didn't want me talking to the media. No, she wanted me safe, so why was she asking me? And I saw it, like a door opening onto a long corridor, the distance, the perspective, and above all, her great fears, the way she'd hammered them into the ground, until she could help me, save me. Yes, the hardness in her face as she'd forced me to watch television, the coldness by the side of my bed, symptoms of channelled emotions, tunnel vision. And I'd told her to fuck off! But before I could feel shame, I felt anger – she'd lied to me, lied, lied, lied; it was all a great falsehood – and that anger was more satisfying than any glimpse of compassion. I shut the door, and the corridor narrowed. My mother was speaking: there were some who were calling from magazines, but others wanted to record interviews for their television programmes. My mind leaped on the distinction: the thought of a journalist, pen in hand, notebook at the ready, asking me what had happened, while trying to trick me, repulsed me, while the thought of a television interview brought back the few memories I had of such things: relaxed hosts leaning back on their sofas, smiling and joking, their hair settled in improbable waves. There was a deep sense of the unknown, of a world I could explore.

I listened to my mother intently, my eyes wandering nonchalantly to hide my interest and make her say more. Then, my mouth pursed in caution, I told her I could try one or two.

'Are you sure?' she said. 'You don't have to.'

'No, I want to.'

'It'll be hard.'

'Mum! I want to,' I said.

She closed her eyes and took a deep breath.

'Alright,' she said, 'let's try it, but you let me know if there's a problem. Will you do that?'

* * *

The next day, I sat at my desk unable to focus. The large folder sat intact next to my pencil case, yellow and purple plastic sheets separating bundles of stapled paper, elastic bands and cardboard binding the whole thing together. My name was printed on a label pasted three-quarters of the way up, adorned with my lip-licking principal's ornate signature and a sentence in which every word was capitalised but of which I could only make out the first two: Get Well. I was meant to spend the day working but whenever I felt a pang of guilt and tried to bring my mind back to physics, history and maths, my thoughts slipped over the folder and narrowed on another idea: my principal's writing was as bad as a doctor's because it gave him doctoresque authority; *A Room with a View* ended as it did because Forster couldn't think of a proper ending; elastic bands more than doubled in resistance when they were doubled over. After an hour at my desk, guilt gave way to boredom, and I roamed the empty house.

My parents' room drew me first: I ran my hand over stacks of sweaters, shirts and trousers, looking for a bulge, a rustle, or any sign of the hidden. When I found an unopened box of condoms in my father's bedside table, I decided that I'd had enough and moved on to my brother's room. The smell emanating from the heaps of dirty clothes almost had me out before I could find the three A4 colour prints he'd hidden between his mattress and his bed base. I looked at the first: a blonde in the sun, ruffled hair framing her soft eyes, a chequered shirt ripped to show a nipple, her hand playing between her legs. With a jolt, I realised that my brother was almost thirteen. While the pictures had me excited, the thought of my little brother ogling them made me uncomfortable, and putting the photos back exactly from where I'd taken them, I left the room.

Bookshelves lined the lengths of the upstairs corridor and the back wall of the living room. Books had always drawn me to them. Starting in the better lit room, I perused the titles, largely non-fiction, that had made the bigger and darker downstairs bookshelves their own: William James' drunken jottings heralded a host of historical psychological titles, their bindings frail with age, before they gave way to Napoleon and nineteenth-century Europe. One late nineteenth-century travel narrative set in the Pacific caught my attention, but its part-patchy and part-grandiose language made me put it down before I could sit on the sofa. Coming to a collection of existential essays in French, German and English, I decided that I preferred fiction and walked upstairs.

My eyes found their way to a familiar sequence of worlds. Graham Greene's spies in smoky rooms, from the heat of Havana, to the humidity of Saigon; strolling down broad empty streets, a thousand eyes following my back. Joseph Conrad's gut-wrenching dilemmas, choosing between stern and bow in a sea of grey; I drifted down a brown river past logs bloated with meaning. At the end of the shelf lay Hemingway. I picked up *A Farewell to Arms*, and descended into the living room, my body slumped across the cold leather of the sofa. Soon, I was in wartime Italy and Catherine Barkley was straddling me, her face inches from mine, her blonde hair a curtain shielding me from the outside world. As the days passed, I kept on choosing books set in faraway destinations. At home, a man was bound, but in those distant places, a man could do things, and, more and more, the urge to do something was building inside of me.

I look back at those youthful readings with an ironic smile. To my dreams of the Italian front, Mexican provinces, and the Congo, I'd like to add the crusts of dust and dirt the road piled beneath my runny nose. I'd like to add corrupt border officials asking for bribes with a smile and a gun. And I'd like to add the hours I spent crouched over a Turkish toilet in the Sudan, as all the water in the Nile poured straight through me.

In those moments, my thoughts wandered back to the comforts of Hornsbury: the old sofas, the working chimney, the safe food, and, with a frown, I told myself how lucky I was to have seen so much of the world.

* * *

From the moment my mother told me she'd booked me in for my first interview, scheduled four days after I came out of hospital, I stopped telling myself that the hours I'd spent each day at my desk were in any way fruitful. Three pages of laboured notes didn't count as an achievement. And I started to picture myself walking on a sharp ridge: on the one side was home, its slow way of doing things, A-levels, and a scree that I needed to clear; the other side was hazy, but I was sure that it hid waterfalls, palaces, harems. The world of television belonged to the haze.

In the car on the way over, I tried to think of the glamour ahead, to piece a picture together from the few times I'd watched morning shows.

'What sort of questions are they going to ask me?' I asked my mother, when we were at a traffic light on the outskirts of London.

She glanced at me, her hand toying with the gear stick.

'They'll want to know about your experience. What you felt, what you saw, things like that,' she said. 'We don't have to go. I can call them now and cancel.'

'No, I want to go.'

The light turned green and her attention was back on the road. A little unease marred my excitement. I could feel her wanting to cancel and I wasn't going to give her an excuse. I kept on smiling excitedly. Half an hour later, we were there.

Four lanes of asphalt separated a broad span of concrete from a broad sweep of bricks. A tower loomed over the studio's revolving doors. I looked around the spacious lobby in awe:

this was where it all happened. Three minutes after giving the receptionist my name, a girl who looked about my age but who had to be older, introduced herself with a wide but short-lived smile:

'Hello, my name is Chloe. You must be Nate, and you must be Liz. I'll be taking care of you today.' Before she had time to finish, she walked to the reception desk, and scribbled on a piece of paper. Coming back to us, she asked: 'Is this your first time on TV?'

The question reminded me that I ought to be nervous, and my shoulders knotted up.

'Well, yes,' I said. Her voice grew even more excited.

'You'll love it!' she said. 'Come with me, we'll get you ready!'

We followed her through a maze of corridors.

'Chloe!' I called.

She turned, surprised to see me ten paces behind.

'I can't walk fast.' I waved at my stomach, a general expression of pain on my face.

'Oh, of course!' she said, and proceeded to walk only five steps ahead.

She zigzagged down grey corridors with PVC floors, her toes squeaking with every step, until we reached the right door. We walked into a wide vestibule, five red raincoats ranged against the wall to my left, and three large framed pictures of beautiful people laughing to my right. Chloe ushered us into a room directly opposite the entrance – she called it the green room, even though there was nothing green about it. Inside, strangers talked and laughed.

'Only minutes away, Nate! We'll call you when we're ready. Ask me if you need anything,' said Chloe before she hurried away into another room. My mother took a second to take in her surroundings, and, with a nod, she told me to wait while she went and talked to the hosts.

Feeling shy, I made my way towards a tray of neatly cut sandwiches artistically arranged around a pot of tzatziki and celery sticks. Trying not to upset the symmetry, I picked out four sandwiches, one from each corner of the plate, and scanned the room. A bald man with a double chin was sitting on the room's only sofa prattling to a white-haired man with a puffy nose. Something about their energy scared me towards the other side of the room. I chose a design chair, which managed to hold me despite the curvy holes in its wooden panels. Nibbling on my sandwiches, my eyes looking at everything but the people in the room, I eavesdropped on their conversations until my mother came back.

'I had a chat to them. They know how you feel. They want to do a practice run now,' she said. 'Don't forget to sit straight and articulate.'

The others gave me a sympathetic look as Chloe led us out. In the studio proper, my curiosity was first drawn to a messy wall of cameras and cables, looking clunky and dated, before I turned to what they faced: a red armchair, a Moroccan coffee table, and a lush two-seater. These images felt familiar: I'd watched the show once at Jeffrey's house, and the strongest memory I had of it was of a blue armchair. They'd changed the furniture, but they'd kept the cosy feel. The Thames shone through a long window behind the sofa set. For a second, I thought the window was a fake, but then I noticed that the wind was whipping water off the river's surface, and that three passers-by in thick coats were walking between the river and the studio. A fake would have looked more appealing.

Chris and Mary were sharing the sofa, leaning towards each other before they noticed me and smiled. He stood up and met me outside the furniture circle, while his wife smiled encouragingly.

'Hello, Nate. How are you?'

'Fine, thank you.'

'Thank you, Mrs Dillingham. You can stand there if you want.' He pointed at a spot behind the cameras. 'Sit down, Nate. Sit with us.'

He lounged back, threw a floppy arm over the seat's backrest, while his leg propped itself against the coffee table, and smiled at me as if we were old friends.

'We're going to run through the sort of questions we'll ask you on air. Are you excited?'

'Yeah.'

He nodded assuredly.

'We always start with a few friendly words to introduce our guests to our viewers. Let me try something for you,' he said and turned towards the unmanned camera. 'The Hornsbury School Shooting threw a chill over the nation, but as we struggle to understand what happened on the 10th of February,' he stumbled and immediately donned a thoughtful expression. Then, without anything changing that I could notice, he ran his hand through his hair, and started again as though he hadn't stopped. 'As we struggle to understand what happened, and we've had a few memorable guests here to talk about it, at least we can say that one glimmer of hope came out of the events. And that's the actions of Nate Dillingham, the only pupil who survived the actual shooting. Nate, we're very grateful that you could come and talk to us so soon after coming out of hospital.' He paused and looked at me. 'I'll say something like that on air. Is that alright with you?'

A vague unease started to take hold of me. Feeling he wasn't expecting an answer, I shrugged.

'Alright, let's ask you a few questions. You've spent weeks recovering. How was that?'

The question threw me: I hadn't given much thought to my time in hospital by then. The oddness of the weeks I'd spent sequestered, and the impact they had on me, struck me much later.

'It was... kind of boring.' They laughed at that. 'I spent all day in bed, I drank a lot of tea.' Again they laughed. They were affable hosts. 'I had to do a bit of rehab work, but not much.'

'Are you still in pain?' he asked.

'A little, but not anything like before.'

'Thinking of the whole tragedy, I find it difficult to imagine that you're barely seventeen. But of course, that's precisely how old you are. Before this happened, I suppose you were preparing for your A-levels.'

His unctuous voice had me wanting to agree with everything he said.

'Yes, exactly. We were all doing it. Just getting ready for our exams. Actually, I was thinking more about the cricket season than my exams.'

They laughed. Mary spoke for the first time.

'We had George Hume here last Monday telling us a bit more about what happened. Could you tell us a bit about that?'

'Well...' I trailed off, trying to get my thoughts around the question. They were nodding me on. 'I guess what he said...'

She leaned towards me:

'Your story is simply extraordinary. As the shooting was taking place, you stood up and walked to Eric Knight, and you managed to disarm him.'

'No, it wasn't like that,' I said before I had time to think. The uneasy laughter that had quietened was now gripping me tightly. A surge of memories was building inside me, and my mind was going blank in anticipation.

'But you managed to wrestle a gun from him,' said Chris in his easy tones, 'and then, and this must be very hard to think about, you had to shoot him so he wouldn't go and hurt more people. We were talking about this last night, weren't we?' he said to his wife. 'In the end, we had to admit that we probably didn't have the courage to do what you did. It's not often we can say this, but it truly was an act of heroism. What was going through your mind then?'

I stared at them, past her lacquered curls and his perfect parting, past my mother's lengthening face, at a camera aimed at my toes, at the black curtains hanging behind it. And the memories came: Anna panting, her lungs rattling every time she gasped for air; Jeffrey on the floor next to me grunting; and Eric's brief shock when I fired first, before pain wiped off his last emotion. There was no heroism in those memories. Nothing but horror.

'I…' I struggled to bring my voice under control. 'Nothing, I didn't have time to think. It just happened. I don't know how to explain it.'

'Anna Walker was your girlfriend, wasn't she?' asked Mary.

'Ex-girlfriend.'

'It was so sad. For some days, all of us here hoped she would make it, didn't we? But as she died, she had words for you, didn't she?'

I stared at her in silence, my eyes bulging out of my skull, my thoughts flaying my so-called heroism.

'She thanked you for trying, didn't she?'

There were no traces of a smile left on my lips. Chris broke in:

'This is all terribly hard for you, Nate. For weeks we've all been glued to our TV screens wanting to learn more, but this is far bigger than news. You've just been through hell. But you have a family, and they're all in it with you. You have a brother, don't you?'

At the end of the mock run, they leaned towards each other and whispered animatedly. My mother joined them. Feeling like I was intruding, I rose and moved towards the green room, hoping to see Chloe or the prattling man, but not daring to leave the studio until they'd told me I could. I saw myself in a mirror hidden in a nook – a toad, a cockroach, a bastard, a man who shouldn't have survived, who didn't deserve to be standing in this studio. A hero, I scoffed.

A man and a woman had joined Chris and Mary, and now I could hear parts of their conversation. It was about me. After a few minutes, the woman got up, and noticing me for the first time, came to me:

'We'd still like to do the interview live. But we'd like to practise a few more questions. Is that alright with you?'

Wanting it to be alright, I agreed. We were on air fifteen minutes later. I was emotionally drained, and their questions, gentler than they'd asked me in the practice run, felt like they were about someone else. I heard later that some viewers lodged complaints with the television regulator anyway. There is a popular clip of it divided into two pixelated segments online. I guess it will pass down the generations over the cloud, so that in a hundred years, those interested in as grim a moment as that which made me what I am, will be able to turn to their computers, and see me lounging back as I discussed the massacre.

It's not the only interview they'll be able to find. I was scheduled for two more before the television men probed past the novelty. One with an earnest lady who almost cried with me, and the other which lasted thirty gruelling minutes, and was cut down to five when it was shown on television. By the end of the second, I felt like I'd risen above a part of my memories, the part people were interested in. Television and its glamour had switched from one side of the ridge to the other. No longer part of the haze, it was dragging me down into a world of fixed images, fixed memories. I needed to move on.

'They all want to hear the same thing, but they expect me to tell them something new. What's the point?' I told my mother, before she called to cancel the other interviews.

* * *

As the days passed and I remained in the house, it became clear that I'd traded one confinement for another. In hospital, I'd been surrounded by a sea of strangers, directed by every uniform in sight, but at least there'd been the prospect of home. But now that I was home, I felt irremediably stuck. Everyone was tiptoeing around me. A mere weakling, I needed five inches of down padding me from the elements.

I'd seen it during Mrs Hitchcliffe's first visit. Her history books under one arm, honeyed sympathy all over her face, I'd made it through three-quarters of a lesson, nodding to everything she said, listening to nothing, until she shut her books and asked me whether everything was alright.

'What do you think?' I barked, and she gave me another of her compassionate smiles, the sort I'd never seen in class – there, true to her inner despot, she'd tolerated no dissent. We stopped the lesson for I clearly needed time. But what I really needed was Mrs Hitchcliffe as she'd been, for her to tell me to shut up and listen, to let me off with a warning this time, to punish me the next. When she left, she conferred with my mother, and together, without asking me a thing, they decided they'd start the lessons again when I felt better. Even my brother, who normally took a perverse pleasure in saying no to me, talked to me, played with me whenever I asked him to.

In my head at least, life went as I wanted it to go. I trekked up glaciers, I sailed around Cape Horn, I drove to Siberia. I lived a life of adventure, wild and getting wilder, because I knew that when my imagination ran out, my reason would take over, and once again, I'd find myself stuck.

The first person to call me was Harry Williams, the same Harry I'd consistently tried to sideline over the years, but who'd still weaselled his way into all of my friendship groups. The same Harry who'd reported a fictive conversation on television. And yet, when my mother called me towards the phone to talk to my 'friend' Harry, I had to remind myself that I didn't like him, so that my voice wouldn't sound too eager.

'How's it being a celebrity?'

'What are you talking about?'

'Well, you're a big man now. Going on TV and all, getting your fifteen minutes of fame.'

I could feel Harry's familiar struggle with a joke. I'd often seen him interrupt group conversations a beat and a half late, starting with a sharp opening only to flounder with all eyes on him.

'I've been on TV longer than fifteen minutes already.'

'Exactly,' he said, his tone tightening, 'you're not only a celebrity, you're a hero. It's all over the newspapers. Soon you'll be solving the Middle East crisis.'

I took a deep breath, harnessing my anger.

'Handing bread to Africans?' I said.

'Yes!'

'Why are you telling me all this, Harry?'

'Because everyone's saying it.'

'Who?'

'Everyone at school. Everyone.'

'So, you're just repeating what everyone else is saying. And, do you have anything of your own to tell me? Or are you only good at repeating what others said?'

He mumbled an answer and I hung up. I went back downstairs, set the phone in its base, and stood by the French windows, looking at the garden. There, where no one could see me, I smiled, proud of what I'd told him, happy that someone had been angry with me.

Later I would have ready answers for such comments. Most of the times, I'd laugh along: 'Fun, I went for a joyride last night but I must have flown too close to Krypton. I'm feeling knackered today.' Sometimes, I gave my meaner self more leeway: 'It takes a special talent. And now that I know it, I can tell you that I haven't met too many people with it. Well, maybe one. No, actually, zero.' Only once did I bark back. It was Beth's brother, and I called him a twat.

But most importantly, I learned to ignore the malice they disguised. I laughed, I retorted, and I forgot. *Veni, vidi, vici.* Nate-style.

That day, just like every day before it, my mother came and asked me how my work was going. For the first time, I told her the truth.

'It's not. I'm not doing any work.'

I was lying on my bed, my chin hanging down over the edge, my eyes staring at three threads coming undone from the carpet. She sat down on my desk chair and swivelled to face me.

'Yes, I've noticed. I went to see the Master of Balliol today. He said they'd accept you on your predicted scores alone. Which were fine. All you need is to pass your A-levels.'

I nudged my nail under one of the loose threads and pulled until she left the room. I couldn't speak to my mother: she was part of the world I needed to flee.

* * *

Rereading over what I've written, I realise it sounds like I was spending weeks alone. That wasn't the case. My life went beyond books and my brother. Once a week, my mother took me to hospital, where they monitored my progress and gave me instructions I ignored religiously.

And on most Friday nights, I met up with Beth and a few others, the ones I had left, to watch a movie and get drunk. Since I'd seen her at hospital, Beth had adopted a new style – bright red lipsticks to go with a red hat and red boots. One night on a bus, when we were both sitting drunk, we turned towards each other. It started with a peck, and then, for a minute, her tongue thrust deep against mine. We stopped just as abruptly as we started, and we never mentioned the moment again.

It's not that I was secluded, but that, however hard I tried, I always needed more. Alcohol, books, movies, they distracted me for a while, but in the end they only ever gave my thoughts further to fall. Some days, I looked around my room, saw everything I'd seen the day before, and I blamed myself, ramping up the insults, hoping it would spur me on. On others, I told myself that it was my mother's fault: if only she could understand how I felt, I'd be able to get my frustration out and move on. And on some others still, I lashed out at society. It was an easy target: I had friends who couldn't connect, journalists who hadn't listened, a policeman who'd stared down at me through his large square glasses. And when I needed more, I could focus on a broader culture that glorified something – I didn't know what – that made me sick.

In late March, my mother asked me to come and help her do the shopping. At first reluctant, I finally agreed when she said we'd be going all the way to Witney. She had to pick up a dress there. Whenever we went shopping, my mother divided up her list, kept two-thirds for herself, including all the fresh produce, and sent me around the aisles to get the rest.

While looking for washing powder, I saw the back of Jeffrey's mother's head. She was pushing a trolley towards the toiletries aisle, while one of her daughters, ponytail flailing, was holding an arabesque with one foot on the trolley's chassis and the other stretched far behind her. With a sudden pang of guilt, I doubled back and hid behind a canned olives stand, spying down two aisles until I felt sure the way was clear. I wouldn't know what to say if they asked me about Jeffrey. They deserved more than I could tell them. As I continued with my list, or with what I could decipher from my mother's scribbles, I almost bumped into them twice, but, both times, I heard the girl singing before it was too late.

'Nate, are you done?' my mother called. I turned around to see her pushing a full trolley my way. 'Let me see,' she said, grabbing my list. 'Good, good. Almost perfect. Can you go and get the aqua colour version of this, please? I'll be at the till.'

I came back with the right product in hand just as Jeffrey's sister was slotting in behind my mother, her gaze skipping over the rows of gum, chocolate, and gossip magazines. Pushing past her, apologising, I saw a faint flicker of recognition.

'Darling,' Mrs Baker said to her daughter absentmindedly before her voice caught and trailed on the 'ing'. My mother turned around.

'Amanda.'

'Liz.'

Something had to have happened between them, I thought, for them to speak so carefully. Mrs Baker smiled awkwardly at me, and all of a sudden I wanted to be anywhere but where I was. Her smile breaking down into a grimace, she addressed me:

'How are you, Nate?'

'Fine. I'm fine.'

'That's good.'

She stood behind us as silence weighed in. And then she talked to her daughter:

'We've forgotten the bread. Come.'

'Do you want me to hold our spot in the queue?' her daughter said.

'No, come and help me choose some nice bread for Dad.'

I watched them walk away: Mrs Baker steadily pushing the trolley, her daughter skipping every third step. When we left the supermarket, they still hadn't come back.

As we drove home, I thought of Amanda Baker's expression. She'd been so kind to me over the years – she always had a box of Coco Pops in a cupboard just in case I came over. If I couldn't face her, if I couldn't spend time with my mother, then it was clear, I had to leave. Another continent, another country, another language – some faraway corner of the world, where it took fifty deaths before an event made the news, some mountain inhabited by goat herders and a hermit in a cave, a long beach parading as an island. Turning up the music, I tapped my fingers along to its beat, and recalled Jeffrey's sister, the freedom with which she'd moved. Compared to her, I'd lost something. But I wouldn't despair. I could get it back.

Over the next month, until my eighteenth birthday, I made and unmade plans. Using my mother's computer, I found a website advertising for fruit pickers in Dorset from May to October. The money wasn't good but they offered cheap accommodation, cheap food. Five months up pear trees meant a year living on the cheap in India, or better, in Thailand. But money wasn't necessarily an issue: on my eighteenth birthday, I'd finally come into my grandfather's money, the three thousand pounds he'd left me. Not much, but enough to leave England and find my feet in a different country. I remembered a friend of my father who'd come over for dinner seven months earlier, and who'd talked about the money his son was making teaching English in Korea.

'Four hundred pounds a week and his flat's paid for,' he'd said. For half of my bank account, I could go to Korea and look for a job – a year there and I'd be rich. But the only thing I knew of Korea was a movie I'd watched once: men chopping each other's fingers off in the name of some arcane game. I didn't want to be in perpetual exile. I needed a place where I could fit in. In my imagination, I was spending my days working an easy job, my evenings surrounded by friends, my nights in the arms of a pretty girl, and I was buying everyone drinks. Korea wasn't that place.

As my eighteenth birthday neared, I grew restless. It was that night or never: sneak out one evening, or remain forever a Hornsbury boy. What I needed to do was to move, to see places. A week before my birthday, while I was at the local library, I browsed through their career stand. I ignored all the jobs that required a degree – they were what I'd expected I'd end up doing, but my situation had changed. Now I needed to find myself something, anything. Amidst all the leaflets, I found two that could take me overseas. One for the armed forces, but I put it down straightaway. I'd done guns, and I wasn't going to do them again. And another for merchant ships: toiling away at sea, visiting the next port. Picking fruits, working on a ship, teaching English, there were things I could do.

I kept on thinking until the morning of my birthday, when, packing my bags, hiding them in a cupboard, I told myself that I'd leave that night and work out the next step on the fly. What mattered most was that my mother didn't know I was leaving until I'd left.

* * *

After I put away my bag, when I was alone in the house, someone rang the bell. I didn't recognise him when I opened the door, but then I saw the big square glasses, the same glasses he'd scrutinised me through as if every one of my words were a lie, I saw the jeans and jumper he was wearing to trick me, and I wished I'd left the latch on the door.

'Hello, Nate. Can I come in?'

'My mother's not here.' I stayed in his path.

'According to my files, you're eighteen today. She doesn't have to be here.'

'I thought you already had my statement,' I said, a burly edge to my words. I wanted to shut the door in his face, and watch him amble back to his car, blood dripping from his nose.

'I'm not here to take your statement, Nate. I just want to talk to you.' He waited for my response, but I stayed silent, blocking his path. 'Your case is closed. Whatever you tell me now, I promise, I won't reopen it.'

I studied him, his plea so different to the questions he'd asked me in hospital, and I believed him.

'We can speak here.' I waved at the porch.

He nodded and took a step back.

'Would you mind coming out? I can't see you with the light.'

I closed the door behind me, and leaned back on one of the stone pillars.

'My case is closed?' I said.

'Don't you know it?' he asked. 'You're a national hero.' I winced. 'You don't like that word?' he said.

Fighting a grimace, I shook my head.

'You know what, Nate. All the people you'll meet, they'll know you as the one who tried to save the others. It doesn't matter that you failed. You're the only one who tried, and when something's as big as that, well, we'll latch on to any bit of goodness, you see?'

I avoided his gaze.

'Of course, you don't,' he continued, growing agitated. 'But me, I was there. I saw that classroom when there were still dead bodies in it. Dead bodies!' His words drew me, and I couldn't avoid looking at him anymore. 'Your friends, dead, dying, I saw them all. I went to speak to all the mothers. And I interviewed everyone. I spoke to them, I listened to their stories, I tried to make sense of it. Me, Nate, I know you're not a hero. I've seen your type before: you try to flee but inside you're all guilt. With me, you don't have to pretend.'

He looked at me expectantly. I could feel it deep down my throat – he had me in his grasp.

'What do you want?' I asked in a small voice.

'I want your story, the whole of it. Not your mother standing between us, whispering in your ear. Of course, I know what she did, how she leaked all that information! But now, it's just the two of us, Nate, man to man. Remember, I stood in that classroom, I had blood on my shoes. And I know that you didn't tell me everything. I need to know what you know. Not for my job. For myself.' He pulled at his jumper and I understood him: he'd come to me a civilian.

I looked at his ponderous forehead, more creased than I'd ever seen, at the rim of his glasses pushing his thick eyebrows into his waving brow, and I tried to reach for a memory, but I found a dark pit, and I shook my head, slowly at first. As I pictured telling him more, dread rose and my shake became more resolute, until I had my jaw clenched, and I finally spoke through gritted teeth:

'I told you everything.'

His head dropped for a second, and then it rose again, his eyes suddenly full of intent. He grabbed my shoulder and squeezed hard.

'You didn't and we both know it. But tomorrow, next month, or in ten years, you'll want to, and you won't find another person like me. And I promise you something: I'll still want to listen. So when you finally man up, come and find me.'

He let go of my shoulder, and studied me, a mournful look on his face. He took his keys out, and let them dangle from his fingers.

'I'm leaving,' I said.

'So you are,' he nodded.

'I won't come back.'

'I'll still be here,' he said, and he extended a hand. I shook it, and he left.

* * *

To the few people present, we were celebrating my birthday. To me, we were celebrating my departure. I spent the first hour of the party gliding in between guests, thinking of how I should break the news.

Her son already tugging at one hand, my aunt put down her flute so that her daughter could grab the other. Pulled from both sides, she listened to my descriptions of television studios.

'But what did you think of them?'

'What, the lights?'

'No, Chris and Mary.'

'Ah.' I raised my eyebrows. 'They seemed nice enough. Didn't you watch the show?'

'Yes, but I wasn't there.' She looked down at her daughter: 'What?'

I finished my glass. She crouched down to the level of her children, shooting me the odd encouraging smile while I rattled my memories for titbits she wouldn't have seen. I didn't know whether they were only pretending to be together for the cameras – my mind had been on other things. I spoke about the cameras, the green room, while she juggled her children and her nephew, until I felt the courage to point at my empty glass and move away.

There was too much room for the children to run and scream between the three groups people had flocked towards: my friends around a sofa, my grandparents talking to James and my mother, and my father speaking to his sister and her family. A champagne bottle in hand, I strolled past my grandparents and joined my friends. All four were giggling, squeezed together on a small sofa. I perched myself on the coffee table and, facing them, brandished the bottle.

'Yes, please!'

'Here, here.'

'Leave the bottle, will you?'

'What's so funny?' I asked, downing my flute.

'Nothing,' Beth said, her response muted. She seemed embarrassed when I looked at her.

'What?' I said.

She pointed her chin towards my aunt.

'What?'

'She just spilled her drink over your cousin.'

My aunt was waving a hand manically in her husband's direction while addressing my father. Clearly more used to his sister than me, my father left her with a smooth smile and made for the kitchen. Here was my father alone in the kitchen, I thought. It was time to act.

'Finish the bottle. I'll go see if there's more,' I told my friends. My father was pulling ice out of a bag onto a cutting board.

'Can I speak to you?' I asked him.

His head turned my way for a second.

'You are speaking to me.'

'Alone.'

'We are alone. What is it?'

'I'm leaving tonight,' I said, looking at the floor.

He put down the ice hammer, assembled the ice he'd just crushed, and, cupping it in his hand, transferred it to a bowl. Then he turned to face me.

'What do you mean?'

'I'm leaving. I'm not coming back. Tonight, I'll go to Oxford with my friends for my birthday. And then I'll leave.'

'How?' he asked, ever practical.

'Does it matter? I'd rather not say.'

He wiped his hands on a kitchen cloth and came close. He hadn't stood so close to me since I'd come home. He held his hands behind his back, in his heavy thoughts pose, the weight of his arms counterbalancing the rest of his frame.

'Your mother will want to know why. Have you talked to her?'

'No, Dad, I don't want to,' I said. The thought of facing my mother and seeing her break down was off-limits. Keeping my voice firm, as though I'd given what I was saying much thought, I spoke on: 'I thought you could do it. She'll understand better if it comes from you.'

He nodded slowly.

'And when should I tell her that you're coming back?'

I reached into my pocket and pulled out a bundle of documents.

'My passport's got three years on it. That's my birth certificate, my driving licence, and I've made copies.'

His head rose to take in the documents, and his hand made as if to touch them, but his arm dropped before he reached my passport. He leaned back against the sink.

'She would want to hear it from you.'

The champagne was making me harsher than I wanted to be.

'No, I can't. Tell her yourself. But promise me you won't until tomorrow night. Do you promise?' I looked directly into him, almost violently.

'Yes, Nate, if that's what you want.'

'Yes. I don't know what you should tell her. Say it's got nothing to do with her,' I said, grabbing his arm and releasing it instantly. My shoulders slumped. 'There's nothing for me here. And it's not my fault either,' my voice rose on the last syllable, as if I were asking a question.

'I won't tell her anything. You're an adult now.' Jerkily, he grabbed me and brought me closer into a hug. 'That might just break her. Go and spend the evening with her. Be nice, like old times.'

I left him and stumbled into the living room. Fighting the tension building around my shoulders, I walked towards my mother and grinned.

Black Chalk

* * *

Late that evening, as the coach pulled out of Gloucester Green, I didn't think of the friends I'd lied to. They would enjoy their night out in Oxford without me. No, to avoid the inspector's challenge, my thoughts were circling around my mother's opened mouth when I sneaked into her conversation, the crow's feet around her eyes when I praised her in front of my father's parents. Her broadening smiles, her fingers shyly tapping my arm, her spontaneous laughter – she'd looked happy and it was all because I'd lied to her. Still, I hoped that she would cling to these memories while I was abroad, that she'd know I didn't meant to hurt her, that I appreciated what she'd done for me. That she wouldn't ask herself why I'd spoken to my father and not to her. I closed my eyes. The coach drove over Magdalen Bridge, past the John Radcliffe, out of Oxfordshire.

Four

It's been eight years since the shooting. Four months since I came back to England and sat in my mother's little attic room to record what made me leave. And now, I'm balancing on an exercise ball in the spare bedroom of my Cowley flat, struggling to impose sense on the paths my life has taken. It's the knowledge that this journey is coming to an end that is once again driving me to the soft clicks and clacks of my keyboard, to the saccadic travel of a cursor over a blank document.

Every minute of my life has been a step across a mountainous landscape. Whenever I reach a pass, as I have just done, I turn back and look at the ground I've covered. In some places, I see my footsteps clearly etched into the snow, and I recall exactly my fears, my desires: how afraid I was of slipping towards the drop to my left, how I aimed for a knoll ahead, focusing all I had until I reached it. In others, my path has gone faint, perhaps because of a shadow thrown across it, or perhaps because I was walking on rocks. But in the majority of places, I can't see where I've been. My memories lie below an incline, in a damp hollow, or they hide behind a peak, and if I remember that a section was tricky, I still can't use my vantage point to see the land around it, the rocks perched above a tight turn, the crumbling cliff hidden underneath wild flowers.

From pass to pass, different sections of my life come into my line of sight, so that, when I ask myself how I got to where I am, I look back at the landscape, and think that, of course, it all had to do with that particularly treacherous stretch the sun is shining on at the moment. A stretch I can see now that I'm a few miles further down the road. And yet, six months ago, I was on the other side of the range, tracing my steps down a ridge which then seemed crucial, but has now become irrelevant. I'm forever looking back, and yet, what's behind me is forever changing.

Reaching this pass, I look at the charred stone ahead, and smell the coldness of the wind behind the drop. My legs burn as hard as my fears, forcing me to stop and contemplate what I've done. But, even if I give in to these impulses, I know that whatever I'm going to remember over the next four days is only part of the story.

This room around me hasn't changed much since I turned it into my studio. Thinking it'd be good for my back, I haven't swapped the exercise ball for a chair. The five sketches I've made since I took it up just about cover the walls, and the tiny window fogs up minutes after I lock the door. Besides two virgin canvases hiding a small stack of sleep-deprived doodles, there's nothing but this desk and my computer around me, but the room feels jammed full.

* * *

For five years, I drifted. Problems arose, and then they were gone. Anger and love washed off with the rains. And I drifted on, refreshed.

I left England in that time-proven way: as cheap labour on a cargo ship. My first was a black beast going by the name of *Hunter*. She was a thirty-year-old matriarch, lumbering into ports, her prow held high, staring down any who thought she was too slow to crisscross the tropics.

Aboard, my Conradesque ideas of life and honour on the ocean survived the best part of a year, despite the months I spent chipping rust and washing dishes. If anything, that sort of work fitted well with my desire to stop thinking. I woke up sore, ready to gaze at the horizon and dream of cannon balls crashing into ancient frigates, worked hard and finished the day exhausted, yet satisfied.

We stopped in ports for a few days at a time, during which I pulled out my notepad, and made sketches where others were taking pictures. Being idle didn't suit me and my duties were considerably lighter when we were dry, so that after a few days on land, I'd yearn to be back at sea. It was during a prolonged break in Vancouver, while our ship underwent minor repairs, that I received my mother's first email. I'd fished it out of the junk folder.

Subject line: test.
Body: Nate, this is a test. Tell me if you've received it. I'm still new to emails. Beth has been very kind. She's given me your address, and then she's set up this one. I'll send you more news once I hear back from you, Love, Mum.

I didn't reply, but I started to question what I was doing. I was certain that I'd done the right thing in leaving England, but I also had the feeling that my travels couldn't last forever and that spending them aboard *Hunter* wasn't as exciting as I'd first made it out to be. I started voicing my doubts to OJ, a man with a forward jaw, a full beard, and a rising count of tattoos, who came from one of the Home Counties. Ever since I'd come on board, he'd taken me under his wing in a rough fatherly way, alternating between stern instructions and hefty pats on the back. One drunken Canadian night, as he fed me cheap blended whisky, I started telling him about home. He stroked his beard and told me of his village green, of his father the butcher. I spoke of our cricket square, of the view from Stone Hill. And as he poured me another glass, as he told me about his mother's blackberry pudding, something in me moved. I caught the tears before they'd gone too far, and downed my glass, stinging myself back into shape.

'What's wrong, my boy?' he asked me, putting his hand on my shoulder.

And I didn't know. I had trouble speaking, but the only feeling I understood was a sense of wasted opportunity. So, without realising that he'd started his career doing what I was deriding, I told him that cleaning toilets and dishes didn't satisfy me. He was a good man, for he bent his head and listened, refilling my glass when it went empty. When my babble turned back into man's talk, he put a hand on my wrist, commanding my silence, and with a knowing look, told me what I needed:

'A pair of legs and a pretty cunt, that's what you need, my boy.'

He spoke to the captain, and arranged to have me transferred to a cruise ship. It happened in Brisbane. I was given a white uniform with sparse epaulettes, and I was ushered into a cabin with bunk beds. In my new job, I carried drinks, cleared plates, coached racket sports, smiling to all the old ladies I passed, strutting past rich men's daughters. Despite my rather dashing uniform (I must say), it was difficult to follow OJ's instructions and socialise with our guests. For one thing, there weren't many young people on board, and for another, they tended to band together and giggle in their closed groups. But the crew was a different prospect – more than half were young and looking for adventure. We partied hard, and soon I was in a stormy relationship with Sally, an Australian girl with hair more pink than red, who appeared shy only around people she didn't know. A few drinks in her, and she'd suddenly grab a chair, thrust it in the middle of a group, and sit on it as on a throne. It was the same thing when she took her clothes off. She once tied me to the railing of my bed while I was sleeping, and left me there until my roommate walked in and undid me. Word spread, but nothing came back my way that justified my own mortification.

Sally kept my mind off my mother's irregular emails.

Your father is working harder than ever. And your brother is turning into a full-blown teenager. He leaves the house for the whole day and he doesn't tell me where he's gone. You were never like this. I'm going to have to get him a mobile phone.

Beth had encouraged her and, despite my silence, she'd kept at it. On birthdays, around bank holidays, she'd send me short vignettes. Always truthful, always brushed clean of conflict, she needed me to think of them, to long for home. Her first few emails repulsed me. There was one I left unopened for three weeks so strong was the feeling. It stood bold like a great pulsating barrier, representing all I needed to flee. To live, I needed to be a thousand miles from their great hunt.

But as with all things, I grew used to her intrusions, pebbles aimed at a still pond.

* * *

Sally and I stayed together for over a year, somehow managing to work the same routes, and OJ was right, her legs engrossed me for that whole period. It all changed when we were shifted to the Mediterranean, and I met George. George was a twenty-something intellectual, the sort who knew his own genius and expected the world's universities to recognise it as soon as he'd decide to grace them with his presence. His bedside reading started with Freud and moved on to such exciting titles as *Core Reading in Psychiatry, an Annotated Guide to the Literature*. George's chief danger lay with his ability to hide his ideological fervour behind a normal, almost jovial appearance. When he was one among many, he could laugh just as hard as the rest of us, but taken alone, he would suddenly grow very serious, identify a barrier, and try to break past it.

'Nate,' he told me once at the end of a drunken romp in Crete, waving at the group that had walked ahead of us, 'look at them. Take Jung and Winnicott together, and you have it...' He marked a pause. 'The personas we adopt are walls to our true selves. They might be a social necessity, but don't you think we should go past them?'

He spoke as if he had no doubt that I would agree. Agreeing seemed easier, so I did, but if anything it proved to be a greater mistake. George was English, and on hearing my name had immediately worked out who I was. He'd kept silent about his knowledge, hoping to do a good deed quietly, as all good men should. He'd tried to speak to me alone many times, drawing me out into philosophical discussions, only to interrupt halfway through my answer and ask me about home. 'But take your dog, for example. What does thinking of your dog make you feel?' Unaware, I played along until I saw something better, perhaps Sally's outstretched hand, or a free bottle of booze, and I left him frowning thoughtfully, his lips delicately pursed.

It all came out one evening three weeks into his assault on my psyche.

'Nate,' he said while I watched Sally speak to a new guy, 'I have to confess something.'

And he confessed that I ought to confess. And with his words, my bubble seemed to collapse – the purity of drunkenness, the appeal of ever-changing shores, the joy of Sally's mouth over my cock. It was a simple world, built on a thirst for endorphins and new experiences. With his roundabout revelations, I harked back to Andrew Hill's thick glasses, to my hospital bed, and I heard screams and smelled smoke, and my mother was by my side and yet further than she'd ever been. It was as if I hadn't and couldn't ever run far enough.

'I have to be frank with you,' George said. 'Keeping this quiet is not healthy.'

I guess, Yeah, That's interesting, Each to his own – I said them all, but he drove on, his questions more direct – Have you spoken to anyone about it? To Sally, at least? – and I shrugged, but he wasn't going to let me go. As if I'd just heard Sally call me, as if that call were interrupting the best of conversation, I made an apologetic face, asked him to hold his thought for a second, and retreated towards the others. I spent the evening avoiding him, holding on to Sally as I'd never done before, shoving the new guy out of the way, fondling her in public one instant, downing half a beer the next. But even my beer tasted warm and leaden. The streets of Cairo, which a few minutes before had felt full of well-meaning strangers, suddenly seemed overflowing with clingy touts. I woke up the next morning with dried vomit stuck to my hair and the sticky blueness of one dirty memory. That memory rushed back, all at once, when I was convoked to my boss's office: slurred insults, wide bloodshot eyes, an aggressive lean, I could recall doing all that and more. Her formal manner, the careful words she chose, instantly sharpened my mind.

'I'm afraid that sorry isn't good enough,' she answered, in the same dry, rehearsed tones she'd used since the start of our interview.

'Well, it was more than that,' I started, and her expression changed as she listened to me, until she looked as if it was her who could never be sorry enough.

I left her office with my job safe and my honour sullied. For two days, I walked around feeling like nothing could wash away the layers of dirt I'd encrusted in the skin of my palms. Two nights after my antics, her roommate gone for a strategic walk, Sally called me to her room and faced me with tears in her eyes.

'After all we've done together,' she said, her voice breaking with every sob, 'sixteen months with me... and you never told me a thing... How could you do that to me?'

Two weeks later, I disembarked in Nice and holed up in a dirty hostel near the airport until I saw the cruise ship leave. It was the end of my sea career.

* * *

George wrote to my mother and my mother wrote to me. The nerve of the man, the sheer confidence – he hadn't spent a full twenty hours with me that he already knew how best to cure me.

> Nate, darling, your father informs me that emails should be short. Not like the long letters your father and I used to send each other when I was teaching in Newcastle. So let me get to it: I'm afraid I have bad news. We went to see the vet about Sloppy yesterday, and the prognostic is what you would expect for a sixteen-year-old dog. The vet recommended putting him to sleep now. The three of us talked about it, and James felt very strongly that Sloppy is your dog, and that you should be the one choosing. Do you think that perhaps you could let us know your wishes?
>
> On another note, your friend George emailed me on Tuesday. I was glad to receive first-hand news about you.

She signed: Your mum and your dad who love you very much.

* * *

It was the start of years drifting between the Mediterranean and the Alps, drifting with the seasons. I spent my first summer raking sand, my first winter shovelling snow. And there were friends, enemies, bosses, colleagues, jealousy and lovers, the sea and the slopes – but none of it ever reached deep, for I was always one season away from another move. In Antibes,

I worked at the Galapagos, a beach bar on a narrow strip of sand, where pink skin reddened during the day, and where, in the evenings, it came back, clothed in white, adorned with gold, to sip mojitos and watch black Ferraris roll past. In Chamonix, I started on the mountain, and when the constant glare, wind, and sun got the better of me, I switched to working in shops. Of all the places I lived in, Chamonix was the one I returned to the most – for its slopes, yes, but also because the valley soothed me. Weeks into my first season there, I'd learned to ignore the glitzy shops selling branded bags/jewellery/clothes, the mountains rising above the valley, where every day someone else seemed to die, until I had the town down to its essentials: three bars (one Scottish, one Irish, and one strange mixture: between its polar bears and fake stalactites, it was a haven for all things kitsch, but there was something there that had me coming back), two cafés (to read, to meet pretty tourists), Guilia's restaurant (with her homemade pasta and her fresh pesto), and one supermarket (grey but functional).

Still, if I thought I'd avoid people like George by leaving the cruise ship, I quickly found out how wrong I was. The crew had been full of ignorant Antipodeans, while south-east France was a haven for British accents. For people who'd been transfixed to their screens, to their newspapers, as Hornsbury drew the nation's news outlets. Whereas I'd gone for almost two years unrecognised, I now couldn't spend a week without seeing someone's eyes widen, and a month without someone asking me outright about it. That was when I started calling myself Nathan, instead of Nate, and although it worked to some extent, I also found that it wasn't the recognition itself that bothered me, but rather, it was the idea that I owed people my story. Not everyone behaved that way. In the way they turned words, in the way they squeezed my shoulder, I learned to identify the undesirables. They were the ones who pitted everything on my answers, as if I held the key to a puzzle that had become theirs.

'But why' – they'd start, and then they would ask me about Eric, about his parents, about the wrongs of our community, the certain evils it must have hidden, sexual, moral, or otherwise. At first, I looked at these people with refreshed horror. But soon I was as impervious to them as I was to an evening's first four pints, and I swatted them away with my sharpest contempt. When that didn't work, I feigned pain, letting my eyes go blurry and my mouth drop ajar.

Most of the people who remembered the shooting, and who linked my name to it, were kind enough not to care about what I had to say. A minute after they asked me what it'd been like to be there, after I answered with distant bravado ('Oh, you know, you just accept it, right?'), they harked back to our previous conversation, and five minutes later, we were drinking, dancing, and laughing as hard as before. The matter was handled so casually that soon they were pointing to me, and telling their friends that I was the man who'd survived, and the friends felt satisfied enough that they didn't come to ask me anymore.

Some people, and George was one of them, think that I handled things wrongly. Victims of PTSD needed to be followed. Followed and then cajoled, medicated, drugged, treated, even confined if their situation demanded it. Perhaps because it doesn't involve practitioners, no one speaks of the benefits of distance – and yet for me, it was the best of cures. In hospital, three specialists of the mind had lectured me on how I would feel, how I should think – and with them, my memories were only ever a stab away from breaking my calm. On the road, they were as distant as home.

Had I stayed, my life would have revolved around the one incident. I could have explained all of my weaknesses on one morning of my life. The love I couldn't give, the hate I couldn't source, the dullness I couldn't outflank. But away from those who knew me, banishing the past to a foreign land, avoiding those who wanted to talk, I soon learned to spend a day without thinking of it, and a day became a week. And I loved without looking over my shoulder, and I hated just as hard. And there were weeks spent fixing skis, and weeks spent serving martinis. And slow days behind a glass counter, and manic days on my feet, rushing up and down three flights of stairs, a phone on my ear. Now, as I face the greatest of calms, I realise that for close to six years, jobs, faces, flats all blended into a trail of warm-tinted pastels. I was drifting so fast that everything was possible, so fast that happiness was rushing past.

My mother's infrequent emails tried to ground me to my past, but I brushed most of her words away. Thinking of home no longer had blood pumping unease into my limbs. It was only in what she hid that I felt discomfort. 'Hornsbury's changed so much that we're thinking of moving.' 'Your father and I went on a holiday to Greece last year. It was the first time we'd taken a holiday together for three and a half years.' Or: 'I'm going on sabbatical for your brother's A-levels.'

Sometimes, the incident felt distant enough that such off-handed remarks made me doubt my reasons for leaving.

*\ *\ *

I enjoyed the transient nature of seasonal jobs. Love was free, and drugs weren't much more expensive. There was Naomi, with her generous breasts and loving thighs, Jennifer, with her eager mouth and droopy eyes, Maura, with her unshaved armpits and marijuana plants. There was also coke, speed, ecstasy, pills and powders, but while I was happy to dabble, I was too careful to plunge into their world.

As the weeks passed, as the seasons ticked over, I drifted towards a French crowd, drawn in by their authenticity and Marie's freckled nose. Marie was French as I'd expected the French: small, dark-haired, with a fiery brow, and a hatred of everything English.

'Pour toi, je fais une exception, mais seulement parce que je te trouve mignon.'

I was the exception which confirmed the rule – we never spoke English, since we were in France, and French was a superior language: clearer in its diction, prettier to the ear, free of the sort of shifty vowels she hated in English. As our relationship grew, I moved away from the expat community and into hers, a loose group of true Français. The men had goatees, the women smoked like Audrey Hepburn. The conversation often turned to the hordes of tourists who descended on our fief when the sun shone hard, when the snow piled high. It was easy enough to make fun of the Germans, since they were, after all, Germans. The English were another favourite target:

'There was an English stag party at my bar,' Marie would say, 'and they drank and they drank—' but instead of the usual reverence an Englishman would have in his voice while relating a big night out, disdain would drip from her every word, as if I'd never had to carry her drunk and stoned back to our place.

Early on in our relationship, I'd wanted to tell her that I loved her, but feeling she would laugh at me, I'd kept quiet. Even though I was still learning their boundaries, I already knew that French words were not made to express love. And if what I was feeling was not love, then it was something strong, and the key to understanding it was in the language. In the evenings, lying next to Marie, as smoke mingled with the smell of sex, I would repeat a sentence until it sounded French.

'You sound Belgian,' she said to me once. Holding my breath, I asked her whether I sounded Walloon or Flemish. 'Faut pas exagérer,' she said, 'you sound Walloon, but like a dairy farmer.' I felt proud for days afterwards.

Marie was beautiful, Marie was good in bed, Marie worked the seasons with me. I liked holding her tight against my chest, I liked the words she whispered in my ear, I liked bunching her blue miniskirt over her hips and taking her from behind. Our desires were simple enough that we kept on coming back to each other for two and a half years.

* * *

Denret was the one who brought me to a halt. Whenever he came into our group, he became its very centre. A reputed mountain climber, a daring windsurfer, he was a giver, whether it be of the story that everyone would be repeating the next day, or of the few spare pills he always found in the pocket of his sports jacket. He had a way of standing, lightly perched on the one straight leg, his hips cocked and his head titled to one side, which seemed to suggest ease and indifference. To Marie, he was aristocratic. But his parents were honest and loving accountants, and his demeanour went beyond affectation. I came to understand it as I spent more time with him: emotions ruled him. An image, a memory, an injustice, and we'd all fade from his sight, and he'd be wagging an imaginary finger at a long-dead general, and he'd remember his first love's scent, her promises of an unbreakable bond. My French was poor enough that I stayed quiet when a memory took hold, and he stood silent in that deceptively warm and off-handed way of his, a stance he'd developed to mask his emotions. It was perhaps for my reserve that Denret sought me out.

It started in Antibes. He picked me up in his red 2CV, and drove away before I had time to close the door.

'I'm taking you to a spot no Englishman knows about,' he said, refusing to answer any of my questions. We pulled away from the main road, and hugged the dented coastline. At one stage, he stopped in the middle of a tight turn, got out, and climbed on the parapet. His finger first indicating I should do the same, then pointed high up towards the red hills.

'Do you see her? That's where we're going.'

'Oh, yes,' I said, balancing on the parapet, ignoring the drop behind us, and not wanting to disappoint him. 'How do we get there?'

He went back into his car and waved me in urgently. At some stage, he turned into a road much like many we'd passed before. In first gear, his car struggled up the hill, its frame rattling with every bump. Denret looked straight ahead, first at the bitumen road, then at the clayish track.

'We have to walk now. Are you afraid of walking?'

He would challenge me with such statements whenever I started to feel comfortable. And an instant later, he'd be talking as if he hadn't noticed my startled look.

'This is forgotten history, Nathan,' he said as we neared the top of the hill. 'Notre-Dame d'Afrique. Look at her, and look at her closely. Ask yourself why you haven't heard about her before.'

I could see a weeping Madonna facing the sea, her arms outstretched. She was looking in the general direction of Africa. Around her, at her feet and all over a low wall, were hundreds of plaques. He kneeled down and tapped a plaque with his finger: 'Bertrand Denret, Algers'. He waved at a section of the wall:

'All of these were killed in a single massacre. You won't find it in the history books. Is that right, Nathan? Is that right?'

My mind went blank.

'No, that's not right,' I tried to say. To my relief, he started talking about the war.

The question of what was right seemed to preoccupy him only when he was around me. He lumped our lives as we were living them now, me with Marie and a comfortable flat, him with his mysteries, on the side of wrong. On the side of right was a leap towards a greater justice.

When I tried to piece his days together, I found that the hours he spent with me were by far the most contemplative. The rest were spent in action of one kind or another. He worked, but when I asked him more about the subject, he always answered vaguely. 'Let's talk about something else. Business isn't very exciting.' When we were on the French Riviera, he spent large parts of his days at sea, either on a boat, or if the winds were right, on a windsurf. Up in the Alps, he alternated between ice climbing and skiing. And every evening, he was out and about, sometimes with a girl in tow, but mostly alone. If spending time with him was exciting for me, it must have been a more sedate affair for him.

'There's no need to beat around the bush, Nathan. You're smart, and I'm smart. But look at us. Shouldn't we be doing better?' he told me once, when we were sipping rosé at his friend's bar.

'You worked sixty hours last week, and how much did you make?' he asked me another time, at another friend's bar.

'You're almost twenty-five,' he said once as he stopped his car on the side of a Nationale. 'I'm closer to thirty.' He put his car in neutral, and revved the engine. 'We're not meant to be slaves, you and me. What are you going to do in September?'

Denret infused his words with his own vitality, so that everything he said sounded like a challenge. His musings over the rights and wrongs of our lives were never mere complaints. He meant to do something about them, and while he worked out what, he was using me as a sounding board. Had they come from anyone else, I would have gladly ignored them. But there was a sense of impeding action surrounding Denret, so that, after having sex with Marie, I'd cover myself up with our duvet, stare at a mouldy spot on the ceiling, and think about my life.

Those were never productive thoughts. Rather, I was concocting a brew of past and present: thoughts of home and my years on the road mingling with the day's tiredness and the echoes of an orgasm. But for the first time, I started to think about what my life would be like had I stayed at home, my mind sticking to the sort of plans I had as a seventeen-year-old.

I imagined three raucous years at university ending in a 2:1 and a job in the City. Going by what my father had done, I imagined taking up a consulting job or a banking one, and earning a bonus as big as my salary.

Whenever Marie left me in my world for too long, I ended up staring at the stains on the carpet, at the dirt between the tiles. My fingers would feel the threads of our sheets and find them coarse. And every time I emerged from such depths, I looked at Marie's body in a new light: tobacco was darkening her teeth, loose skin dangled from her arm, dark veins were breaking through her hitherto smooth feet. In such moods, I found it difficult to speak to her: everything she did and said seemed tainted. My eyes were following her fingers, as they toyed with series of lit roll-ups, the cigarettes' paper drawing lines of red against the white wall, before turning ash grey and crumbling into a full tray. My ears were listening to the texture of her voice, as her words rubbed rough against the tender part of my ears. She stood between me and something out there. I didn't know what, but it gripped me tight, leaving behind only isolated images. Blackberries, honeysuckle, grass running down a hill, stone walls whitened with chalk – these appealed to the child buried deep within. A gold watch with three precise dials, a large clean room in a tidy house, leather seats and a smooth gearbox – though new, I felt these were the sort of desires a man should have.

Denret disappeared for the whole month of July 2006. In that time, I broke up with Marie. To my surprise, tears poured down her cheeks. She turned away, and covered her eyes with her palms. I came closer impulsively, but then, considering what had just happened, I stopped awkwardly and put my hands in my pocket. For a few seconds, she looked at me through her fingers, her shoulders oscillating between facing me and showing me her back. But then, just as I was becoming too tense to move, she seemed to make a decision, and using the momentum of a turn, she laced her arms around me. Holding tighter than she ever had, she dug her fingers in my shoulders, and told me she loved me. I was taken aback. In my mind, she was too smooth to let herself fall prey to her emotions. Feeling her warm body crying, I hesitated. My nose brushed her forehead, and falling back on habits, I sniffed hard. There was that faint acridity along her hair line, the trace of rose rising from her neck, and my nose skimming past her eyebrows, the muted lushness of her cheeks. Nearing her mouth, I first felt the dampness of her breath, soft on my skin, the broad, familiar spice of her cigarettes, and then, a fraction of a second later, coming from deep within her, I smelled a sharp pungent note. I inhaled again and again, letting it dispel my doubts.

When Denret came back, I sought him out, and with more strength than I'd used in a long time, I told him that we ought to do something. For the first time, I saw surprise etch two deep lines along his brow, but it only lasted an instant.

'Yes,' he told me with his usual force. 'I have a project you can help me with.'

Denret prized my English – with me as a translator, he could expand his operations to new markets. We weren't working within the law, but we weren't far from it either. Just like one would in a normal framework, we were buying and selling legal goods, putting people in touch for an introduction fee, and running errands for those who would pay. The only difference was that the goods we dealt had dropped off the normal circuit, that we weren't signing receipts. Still, I was so eager to do something well back then, that if Denret had told me we were going to trade cocaine, I would have asked him why we weren't adding crack to our inventory.

Unloading trucks at two in the morning, driving vans down little country roads, organising drops and collecting money, shadowing our competitors and ensuring they weren't shadowing us – for months, I enjoyed following Denret's lead.

I followed him until he went too far. On the 8th of April 2007, he deemed that we were betrayed, that he was betrayed, and decided to retaliate. When in the right, he was unstoppable. I skirted and evaded and he spent the night at the gendarmerie and they barely knew half the story – I couldn't help Denret, and in any case, he'd only ever used me for his own purposes – and I expected the gendarmes to come for me that night, or in the middle of the next, as they were wont to do, and I decided to leave. I narrowed my life down to a single suitcase, and made for Marseilles, where a friend had told me he could find me a job in the port.

* * *

My first two days in Marseilles, Julien put on a black t-shirt, clasped two gold chains around his neck, and went out to work. I spent both days researching the Foreign Legion: how to join, what being a legionnaire meant. This time, I could run away and come back with a new identity. On the evening of the second day, he told me he'd found me something. 'You spend a month working nights, and then you'll get day shifts.' I remembered our gloves, hats, precautions – had we really done so much harm? – and I put the Legion to the side.

Dividing my days between a job in the Port de Marseilles, and the one-bedroom flat I took near the Vélodrome, I started to feel dirty. The twenty-one-year-old boy who'd arrived in Chamonix was nothing like the twenty-five-year-old man watching sitcoms on a torn armchair. Dirt had seeped into the boy's bones and made him a man. Dirt in everything that ought to be beautiful. After Marie, I could never again believe in the purity of love. I would always second-guess it. After Denret, every man was out to use me. I still half expected a gendarme to come and knock on my door, and ask me where I'd been on the night of the 8th of April 2007.

In England, if only I could get over my apprehension, I could go to a good university, rely on a well-connected family, find myself a good job. The last few years had been so full that the shooting had become a distant memory. An item in my past, yes, but one that almost belonged to a different man.

* * *

After three months of night shifts, the stevedores moved me to day shifts, and I settled into a comfortable routine, split between work, my flat, and a bistro next to the port.

On the 19th of December 2007, my father rang the bell of my apartment. His auburn hair gone grey, a box of chocolates in hand, his skin duller than it used to be. The man who'd scored countless centuries for Hornsbury CC looked unable to swing a bat.

'I didn't think you'd want flowers, and there was a chocolaterie near my hotel.'

I kept my arm across the doorway. 'How did you find me?'

'Your mother,' he said. He appraised the situation. 'Will you let me in?'

The question shook the surprise out of me. I accepted the chocolates, and waved him through the door. He asked me how I was, and, settling into small talk, I listened intently to every single one of his words, his intonations. I imagined him relating the most minute of details to my mother, and for a fleeting moment, they were both in the room, in my space. But then my father's presence took over, his formal brevity, and with it, I fell back on my old comfort with his ways. Later, while he was sitting in the only sound armchair, he summed up the reason for his visit in a few words.

'It's your mother, you see. James has had some problems of late. They're over' – he knocked on the wood of his chair – 'we hope, but your mother… She's not as strong as she used to be.'

Seeing my aged father mentioning problems, the image I had of my family suddenly shifted, a depressed void in its stead. My mother was closing on sixty, I realised, and I tried to imagine what that meant. But the image that affected me most wasn't the one I expected: I'd left my brother just as he was hitting puberty, as an already rebellious thirteen-year-old. He was now twenty, the same age I had been when I was working with Sally in the Pacific. I couldn't picture him taller, broader, hairier.

'What problems is James having?' I asked my father.

He drew a deep breath, averted his eyes, but then, true to the man I had always known, he looked directly at me.

'James fell in with the wrong crowd early on, Nate. It was my fault. I should have realised, but I thought he was acting like a difficult sixteen-year-old boy—'

Seven years on, I was only going to listen to him if he gave it to me raw. I interrupted him:

'What sort of problems, Dad?'

He waited to see whether I had any more questions before he went on:

'Drugs. He smoked cannabis with his school friends. And then he went out with a girl who did heroin. Liz realised what was happening, and we pulled him out of that school before he had time to become fully addicted. She did everything she could to help him. For a while, it worked. He passed his A-levels and got into UCL.' He paused, and frowned. 'He didn't want to, but we thought it was too good an opportunity. For the first year, he was fine. But then he met the wrong sort of people again, and…'

My father's voice trailed off, and his chin dropped. I didn't ask any more questions. Before he left, he asked me whether I could write my mother a letter, if only a few lines. I hesitated out of habit. But then, faced with my father's rational presence, I asked myself why I wasn't answering her, and I couldn't settle on one sound reason. My hesitancy cast into absurdity, I took a piece of paper out, and writing big so the page would look full, I wrote:

'Hello Mum, Dad just brought me chocolates. I don't think he thought too much about it, because there are plenty with liqueur in them. Perhaps he will learn one day... I wish you a merry Christmas and a happy New Year.' I thought about signing Nathan, but I didn't think she would understand, so I gave her a big sprawling 'Nate'.

Two weeks later, my mother wrote me a letter:

> I received the best Christmas present I could have hoped for. I'm very grateful to have such an enterprising son as you, darling. Your father told me all about seeing you, and he mentioned your travels. You know the world better than us.

Later in the same letter, she wrote:

> James was in Oxford for Christmas. He spent the morning of the 25th with us. He looked very pale. He told us he wants to get better, but that he's not ready yet. Perhaps it would help if you wrote to him.

That letter moved something deep in me. Seventeen years of love and care and comfort. With each winter, I'd laid slabs of ice on all that had gone well before it had all gone bad, and now they'd tricked me, and I'd let myself be tricked, and we'd reopened a narrow treacherous channel across our distance.

Before responding to it, I took three days off work and went skiing in the Pyrenees. It was on a chairlift after a great powder run, as the sun's rays glanced off my shoulder, that I decided that I couldn't hide behind Nate the teenager forever, that whatever there was with my parents, I was now man enough to deal with.

Pen in hand, I felt as though I'd made a decision but I hadn't quite worked out what it entailed. I wrote that I was thinking of coming home, but that I was unsure of what I could do. My mother's response was more like the woman I knew: she'd researched the subject, and presented me with a list of options, nuancing her enthusiasm with sentences such as: 'If you still find physics interesting', or 'Perhaps you aren't interested in university anymore, in which case.'

For some months, we exchanged handwritten letters, never an email. My letters mentioned hazy ideas, and spoke of my father and my brother as if I had seen them the previous week. Hers, on the other hand, were far more concrete. I wondered whether I wasn't too old to go to university, and she was quoting studies on mature-age university students. I talked about living in London, and she spoke of opportunities and median house prices in Reading.

Just as I was becoming comfortably entrenched in the position of the soon-to-return son, she wrote about an incident between James and my father that happened the day after my brother came out of a Berkshire rehab clinic.

Your father went to speak to him before dinner. He normally listens to him, but not this time. They had a few words, James packed his bag, and then he left.

Later on, she added:

We're getting too old for James. He doesn't listen anymore. But you remember how he looks up to you. Perhaps he would listen to you.

Everything in the letter was veiled, but that only made it worse. The overall tone, the reference to James listening to his father and hence not to his mother, and the 'few words', which I knew to mean that they'd had a fight. I pictured my brother, stubble on his chin, hitting the man he'd once have never dared touch. Shocked, I looked online for plane tickets and bought them that night.

Two weeks later, in late May, I left France. She was waiting at the Heathrow arrivals, holding hard onto the railings. When she came to hug me, she didn't walk with the same purpose. There was a hesitancy as she shifted her weight from one leg to the other that made me want to protect her. She covered my cheeks with her palms, and traced the contours of my face with the tips of her fingers.

'This is new,' she said, as she brushed a crease on my forehead.

* * *

The first time she made a suggestion, she shrouded it deferentially. I'd imagined that I would have to rise up and tell her I couldn't be dealt with that way now that I was twenty-six. But instead, I realised how frail her hands looked and did what she said.

Coming home, even if we no longer lived in Hornsbury, brought the ghosts of the shooting to the fore of my consciousness. Now that I drove past streets in which Jeffrey and I used to play, now that I saw a shop in which I bought Anna a present and Eric a card, I realised I had to do something quickly. There was a dark grey mass radiating heat in a corner of my mind: every time I came close to it, I shrunk away like a hand getting too close to a hot plate. And it was growing a tongue: the sort that's normally rolled neatly in between two sets of fangs, but which jumps out further than an iguana is long when it darts at a firefly. The early hours of morning were the most dangerous: the tongue licked me with its stickiness, and they were shaping themselves around Mr Johnson's desk, the window he would look out of. They were gathering strength. I had to stop them. I'd heard the solution a hundred times before: bring them out into the light of day, and they will wither. And so, I decided to write the events that led to my departure as they happened.

The day I wrote about leaving Oxford, these visions had gone past Jeffrey's red bag, all the way to Eric's black button-up shirt.

And unlike the hazy memories I had when I wrote, they were vivid – I was in them like I'd been in the classroom eight years ago.

After a week of writing, my life changed. Now, four months on, everything that happened to the man who called himself Nate, and to the one who calls himself Nathan, seems like a sad joke. A dash in a history book – the sort that a good eraser can remove with a quick rub. Bye, bye, Nathaniel Dillingham.

Five

Almost four months ago, the day after I finished my account, I left my parents' North Oxford home and rode down the Banbury Road to meet a man my mother had called. After months of meandering letters, my mother had welcomed me home with a folder six inches thick, topped with a three-page handwritten summary. It took me a week of paper shuffling and jargon decoding to reach the same conclusion she'd laid out for me at the start – a condensed course the university's Department for Continuing Education offered over the summer, which would gain me a year in three months' work. There was one problem: I didn't match their requirements. 'Criteria are more flexible than you'd think,' she told me. And so, on a morning announcing summer, under white and wispy clouds, I locked my bike to a wrought iron fence, and I went to meet my mother's colleague to ask him whether I had a future beyond raking sand. A tall, thin man with a crane of a neck, he kept on crossing and uncrossing his legs.

'You look like Liz,' he said, and when I told him I hadn't even finished school, he held a single finger in the space between my eyes and his glasses.

'With what you've told me of your education,' he cleared his throat, 'and more importantly, with your life experience, it's my opinion that you should be able to put together a successful application.'

He opened a drawer and found just the folder he was looking for. While I perused through the structure of the course, three evenings a week, he told me what I needed to do to put together a strong application.

'It started this week, but don't worry, you can catch up.'

And with that, I realised that what I'd anticipated, the possibilities my country, my town, could give me, might just come true. As I came out of the meeting, I stopped on the sunny concrete steps and gathered my thoughts between two clouds. They were coming from all directions – a sense that I hadn't earned this opportunity, glee at its possibility, a fear of success. Rather than rush, I decided to clear my mind, and spend the afternoon in town.

* * *

To all intents and purposes, Oxford had stood still. These were the streets I'd walked as a child and roamed as a teenager. There was the first pub I'd been served at, when I was fifteen. And there, a bit further down Broad Street, was Blackwell's, the bookshop my mother used to usher me into whenever she needed more time in town. But I felt out of place. Peckish, I walked into a café outside of Balliol. The counters were full of cheesy paninis and meaty pies. There was a queue of eighteen-year-olds waiting for their turn, all eyeing the white white bread, the white white cheese, and the pale tomatoes as if they were a treat. I walked out.

A limousine pulled up outside Balliol and three black-clad bodyguards spilled onto the street, spreading out according to some mysterious design. Like them, I waited for an important man. Two minutes later, I decided that they were more patient than me, and I locked my bike outside the Trinity gates. A slick-haired man broadcasting to all and sundry: 'Go inside the colleges and see where they filmed Harry Potter.' Making my way down Turl Street, I walked around three separate groups of

American teenagers, all marching up the street four abreast, all sporting the same hoodie. My steps retraced those I'd taken as a boy, and I found myself in the Covered Market. Some of the shops I remembered had closed and been replaced by others just like them. And there, down one of the middle aisles, was Georgina's, the café in the market's eaves I used to take Anna to. Its door stood red and wonky, a wrapped gate.

Because it scared me, I climbed up the steep steps and peered through the wooden beams. New posters lined every inch of wall space. Amélie smiled her devilish smile between two James Deans. I waited at the counter behind two twenty-year-olds in pink trousers and tailored shirts, hesitating between the bean and Greek salads. When my turn came, a blonde girl with a kind face asked me what I wanted. I reached into my wallet and fumbled. She spread my coins over her flat palm and studied them. I'd given her euros.

'Have you been living in Europe?'

I looked at her. She was standing on the tip of her toes, a green bandana holding her hair back.

'In France,' I said, handing her the right amount in sterling.

I took my quiche and salad to my table, pushed two used mugs to the side, and sat so I could face the rest of the room. A couple was sitting at the table Anna and I used to sit at. He was picking food out of her plate. Their scene should have brought up a crowd of memories, but I found myself calm.

The folder I'd been given had a picture on its cover: three women, two black and one white, and an Asian man, laughing with their heads tilted back. I rested the point of my pen on the empty space to the right of the picture, and a swirl became a woman's face. Her hair flowed and rested at her feet, her chin drooped, and her mouth hung open.

Between mouthfuls of feta and olives, broccoli and stilton, I skimmed through the folder, annotating its pages with my sketches.

'Can I take these away?'

I looked up and saw the blonde girl by my table pointing at the used mugs. For the first time, I studied her properly: the curve of the hip hidden behind her apron, her t-shirt wrinkling as it clung to her skin, and her lips, puckered together and ever so slightly open. I had her face down to two master lines: one completing an oval before scribbling her hair into a ponytail, another following her mouth, closed with its edges blossoming into a grin.

'Of course,' I mumbled.

As she bent forward, I tried not to look at the line between her throat and the swell of her breasts. She noticed the folder:

'Are you an artist?'

I made sure she was serious.

'No, I just draw a little.'

'You're very good.'

I grimaced, a little embarrassed. Both mugs in her right hand, she traced the lip of the blue one with the fingers of the left.

'Do you draw?' I asked.

'A little but I'm not very good at it. I can't draw like that.' She pointed at my doodles.

The compliment seemed genuine, and I was all the more embarrassed for it.

'What are you good at?' I asked.

As if she were considering all of the question's implications, she cocked her head to the side, her eyes on the ceiling. While she thought, the tip of her tongue pushed out of the corner of her mouth, and a strand of her hair buckled slowly over her head until it landed on her right shoulder.

'I write poetry,' she finally said.

'Oh.'

She righted her head, smiled, and her seriousness was gone, making way for a merry warmth. She even laughed a little before she glanced back at the counter and saw someone waiting. As I finished my lunch, I spent more time observing her, and once or twice, our gazes crossed. I tried to draw without making it too obvious that she was my subject. Half of the times I stole a peek at her, she was laughing. The other half, as she reached for the salads with a large spoon, or as she walked back from the kitchen, a cup of hot chocolate in hand, her face was a picture of concentration.

She took her apron off just as I was gathering my things. If I slowed down enough, we'd leave the café together. Seeing her edge past the counter, I stuffed my folder in my bag and hurried towards the stairs. I looked over my shoulder: she was talking to a colleague, exchanging goodbyes, it seemed, but I couldn't be sure. Two customers were staring at me – yes, I was blocking the entrance and I had no reason to be there. Putting on a purposeful air, I made my way down the stairs. Outside, on the paved aisle, I felt a pang of regret and reached inside my bag as if I'd forgotten something, convincing myself that I really was searching for something, even though I didn't know what. Everyone walking past seemed to have their eyes on me.

The two pink trousers came down the steps to the sound of their light banter. I moved to let their questioning looks pass. Just as they reached Ben's Cookies, I heard the girl run down the steps, a duck of an umbrella in hand. Her face opened up for an instant when she smiled at me, and then she was looking right, looking left, calling out, hurrying towards them. Hurrying away from me. The pimply pink trousers clutched at his leg, as if to make sure it really was his umbrella. After she gave it to him, she turned around and walked back towards the café. My initial relief gave way to a touch of nerves.

'Hey,' I said, my hand still in my bag. 'Here it is.' I pulled out a pen.

She stopped next to me, studying my brandished pen.

'Are you finished for the day?' I asked.

'No, I'm going to buy vegetables. We ran out of tomatoes.'

She spoke with such enthusiasm that, for a second, a basket full of plump vine tomatoes sprung up in my mind. Then I realised that she was standing close, that her feet were facing me, and I once again felt that I couldn't speak properly.

'When do you finish work... normally?' I asked.

'Half past five, that's when the whole market closes.'

'And what do you do after that?' I rushed to ask before I could stumble.

'Well, it depends on the day. Sometimes I go for walks. There's a park I like to go to near my home. With a reservoir and some swans.'

Water glittered around a flock of swans, and dread weighed down my chest. Taking a quiet breath, fearing the step, I plunged in:

'What are you doing tonight?'

Once again, she cocked her head and looked up, puckering her lips together.

'Well... I was thinking—'

'Do you want to go for a drink?' I interrupted her.

She smiled instantly and I felt relieved. The rest of the conversation seemed so smooth compared to that start. We flowed from names to a time and a place.

'Nathan,' she said. She repeated it with more emphasis on the first syllable. 'Nathan.' She seemed to like it better that way. 'I'm Leona.'

'Leona,' I said, my tongue slipping slowly from my palate to the floor of my mouth. The name sounded both familiar and exotic.

As she searched her bag for her phone, a notebook popped up precariously. I grabbed it before it fell out, and looked at the eerie postcard she'd pinned to the brown leather. It was a reproduction of an otherworldly painting: in washed colours, a red poppy field by a grey sea, distant waves foaming against the sand, and a blonde girl in a white dress curled up on herself, sitting over the frame of a young man, dead and naked. I looked closer: he was a hairless giant lying limp over winter-green hills, enclosed in a coffin-shaped frame. A withering poppy in each hand, her eyes closed, she faced the ground with a look of ecstatic mourning.

'Nice, isn't it?' she said.

I looked at Leona's broad smile.

'So what's your number?' she asked.

She typed my number into her phone with the uttermost focus, her head not cocked as far as earlier, her tongue still sticking out. From the warmth of a smile to the focus of her cocked head – it had only taken an instant. In her, two contrasting emotions could coexist, I thought. And for some reason, that left me awed.

* * *

I remember the rest of the day in bursts. I know that I waited in town, strolling along the Isis, settling down over a cup of coffee in Blackwell's. From 6 p.m. onwards, Cornmarket was full of chubby white kids in Adidas trousers and England football shirts walking around with pimply faces and KFC paper bags. At the start, I felt rather proud of my upcoming date, but as the image I had of Leona faded, I started doubting whether I was in fact attracted to her.

I was anxious when I saw her loping down the High Street to meet me, a dress of reds and blacks shimmering in the dusk. She leaned towards me, her head going for a space by my shoulder. Unsure of what she was doing, I reverted to my French habits and kissed her cheek. She froze for an instant, and in that moment I realised she'd gone for a hug, but before I had time to apologise, she'd offered me the other cheek and leaned back as if that were what she'd intended to do all along.

I looked at her relaxed smile and, with a pang of nerves, I realised how lucky I was. Strolling over Magdalen Bridge, I noticed the way she moved and the pang tightened. Such flow: in her upright posture, in the suppleness of her limbs, like a cat patrolling its fief from the top of a wall. In the way she climbed on her toes as she walked, the easy swing of her arms – I wanted to stop one of those arms and put my hand in hers right there, while we were looking down at the Cherwell and talking about May Day, but I didn't dare.

The flow spread to the way she talked, to her bucolic descriptions of France. Yes, I found the words interesting, but now that I'm writing them down, I realise they didn't fascinate me of themselves. Rather, it was the way she seemed to put her whole self into every word, whether it be a passing joke or a key memory.

'—They had a house near Rouen. My grandfather used to mow the lawn, and we could ride his tractor. I loved sitting on his lap. He let me steer the wheel—' she said, and I was with her, smelling cut grass, imagining a creek and an old stone table covered with moss. With a girl as easy-going as that, I could share the strangest of my ideas.

When we entered the bar, she stopped talking, marched three paces in, and swivelled slowly, her gaze taking in the whole of her surroundings. Oblivious to anyone around her, she pivoted around her left foot, and for one instant, I had all her grace to myself. She was with the room and I was with her. Suddenly, I doubted that a girl floating happily through life could like the sort of man who'd been a ski bum in the mornings, a black market entrepreneur in the afternoons, a drunk in the evenings; a man who had trouble sleeping now that he'd gone clean.

Later, as we were finishing our first drink, I found out that she was nineteen, that she was studying French at Brookes, and that she had over four months of holidays before her second year started.

'I'm saving up for my third year. Paris is expensive. What about you?'

'Me? My age? What I'm doing? Holidays?' I lined up the questions, hoping for more time. At nineteen, she was already going into her second year of university, while I was seven years older and I hadn't even finished school.

'Let's start with the one question…' She played with her lower lip as she considered the questions. 'Alright: what are you doing?'

'Now? In life?'

'In life,' she said and looked at me, expecting an answer.

'Well, it's complicated. Things happened when I was at school. I was a good student and all, but sometimes you just need to leave. So I worked on ships for a while, and then I moved to France.' I saw her perk up on the mention of France. 'And now I'm going to start a bridging course so I can go to university,' I said. From the way she reacted, I thought I'd done well.

When I went to the bar to get us a second round, the barman and I looked at Leona. She was studying a wooden beam on the ceiling. For my part, I looked at the line that muscles and bones drew around her bare collar-bone.

'First date?' he asked.

'Yeah.' I turned towards him. 'She's a nice girl.'

'Is it going well?'

'I don't know.' I pinched the bridge of my nose. From the way he raised his eyebrows, I knew he understood my plight.

'You can have a bottle of wine for the price of two large glasses, if you want. If you need.'

Leona was delighted.

'Nathan and the barman,' she said. 'That could be the title of a poem.'

'How would it go?'

'Nathan and the barman, let me think.' She hummed as she thought. She took a sip of wine and started: 'Red as Jacob's creek, The finger pointed, And the bar whispered, Here's a bottle don't be meek.'

I laughed. 'It rhymes,' I said.

'Yes.' She paused. 'Do you like it?'

I studied her face. 'I like it,' I said.

She smiled. Her hands were gripping the edge of the cushion by her thighs. When she shrugged, her whole body seemed to fold together, and I wanted to kiss the tip of her nose.

'Can you draw me something?' she asked, her smile growing playful.

'Draw?'

'I made up a poem. It's only fair.'

'Alright.'

I tore a page out of my notebook and squinted.

'Look over there,' I said.

She followed my direction. 'Are you drawing me?' She tried to look serious.

I hushed her and donned an engrossed expression. Without doubling back, I let my pen find the lines I'd identified earlier that day. I added what they missed, the small tilt at the end of her nose, the wide eyes and the marked eyebrows, the sharp arch of throat and jaw.

'Oh,' she said. 'You see, I told you, you are very good. You're an artist. You were just being modest.'

I'd had enough wine to laugh, and I liked the look she gave me as she spoke.

'Do you paint?' she asked.

'A little.'

'Can you paint me?'

I laughed and let my hand drift next to hers, skin touching skin. Her hand didn't move one way or the other, and I started to hope – it was a gentle bond, that contact, steady and comfortable. Our hands stayed touching until she mentioned the Ashes and, with a sudden surge of excitement, I needed both my hands to tell her that my batting efforts were worthy of the English team's.

'It's not to the good balls that I got out. No. It was to high full tosses or double bouncers, when I bent low, played a perfect straight drive, and held the pose as I heard the death rattle.'

She laughed along with me.

'But at least I could go back to my father and tell him all about the beauty of my shot. That I'd been bowled was a minor detail.'

'My father played too,' she said.

I waited for her to say more, perhaps that he was a batsman or a bowler, but she pursed her lips, as though she were caught in a recollection. A girl who'd grown up in the Oxfordshire countryside and who liked cricket enough to bring it up – a good thing could only go so far. I couldn't expect her to ask me whether I knew how to bowl a slider.

'The problem with my father was that he was Hornsbury's star batsman. A hard act to follow…' I trailed off.

Her face had changed, as if she were fighting a cramp. Puzzled, I thought back over what I'd said.

'Are you alright?' I asked.

She nodded tightly. 'Just remembered something,' she let out.

'Well, I guess I won't talk about cricket then.' I smiled broadly. 'That's all I thought about when I was a kid. That and girls.' She didn't smile. I felt like I'd poked a long needle in her thigh, and that I was pumping blood out with every one of my jokes. 'But now I haven't watched a game for eight years. Proof that men can change!'

She rose, nodding curtly at the bathroom. I'd done something, and now she was going to leave without saying goodbye. It had to be the cricket chat. But she'd looked interested. Hard to read a woman, I consoled myself. A minute later, she walked out of the bathroom, her arms swinging freely, the colour back in her face.

'So tell me about France,' she said as she sat down.

France fascinated her. She wanted to know why I'd moved there, what my first job was, whether the mountain glare hurt my eyes, the reasons behind my Antibes boss's barbed comments, how I'd felt when she'd been fired.

'How can you care about people when you move so much?' she asked, leaning towards me, genuinely interested in my answer.

I answered her questions as best I could, watering down my justified cynicism to match her rosier vision of the country.

Her lips clasped into a pensive pout.

'Do you smoke? Everyone smokes there.'

'I tried but I don't like it.'

'Me neither,' she smiled and I felt like I'd passed a test. 'Ah well, you'll have to tell more another day. Do you speak French?'

The question made me chuckle. 'Well, I tried. Most locals didn't speak any English, so I had to.' I thought back to my first few attempts at French slang and smiled. 'Do you speak French?'

'Tu es un peu mystérieux,' she said, sounding delighted.

'Oui, il faut bien.'

She seemed happy in French. If sometimes she emphasised the wrong vowel, I liked the charm she lent the words. For the first time, I was seeing her a little self-conscious. Looking at her smile even more than before, I felt like I had a say in where we were going.

'Allons prendre une glace,' I said.

We never made it to the ice cream shop. My laces having come undone, I kneeled and she didn't wait. I stared at her arse, the cloth of her dress fondling a cheek at a time, until I caught up to her. At the corner of Temple Street and Cowley Road, I grabbed her arm and she turned towards me, her eyes large with seriousness and curiosity. This time, I pushed my fears aside and our noses brushed and our eyes stared at each other's mouths. I paused. From above, I saw her bite her lower lip, teeth breaking the arc, and I desired them more. Her hands laced around my shoulders; my fingers rode down the wave of her back. I would have waited and built on that last ounce of doubt, but she crossed the gap, and my tongue tickled her upper lip. My world narrowed to the softness of her cheeks, the strand of hair following the line of her nose, her lips, sometimes dry, sometimes wet, and to my suddenly sensitive cock, twitching every time her stomach came too close to mine. For a nineteen-year-old, she knew what she was doing.

We must have stood there, next to one of Oxford's busiest roads, clogging the pavement as lips met lips, and hands bundled flesh, for close to ten minutes. When it got too much, I held out my hand and she took it. I didn't know where I was going, but I knew we had to go somewhere, or my balls would ache all night. My own room wasn't far, but my parents were home. As we crossed the Cherwell, I remembered sneaking into the Botanic Gardens when I was fourteen. We walked down Rose Lane and into the rose garden by the day entrance.

'I love white roses,' she said.

'Follow me.'

There were two cameras fixed to the residential building overseeing the gardens. I took her straight through their beam, out of their sight, and stopped by the shed abutting the main door. With my fingers, I mimed what we had to do. I went first, raising myself onto the shed's low roof, and, crouching down, I helped her up. Peering over the garden's wall, I saw that the bench was still there. I scrambled over the wall and lowered myself onto it first, and then helped her down. I looked at her dress, at the bench, at the wall.

'You might...' I mimicked a tear.

'It's only a dress,' she beamed, her voice growing louder.

'Shh... Security does rounds here and...' I pointed at three dark buildings giving onto the gardens.

Again, I took her hand, and on the little memory I had of the place, I made my way towards some dense shrubs next to Rose Lane. Action sharpened my focus, and the damp warmth of her fingers elated me. Skipping over a flower bed, we slipped behind waist-high ferns, and found an enclave of clear earth between the wall and the ferns.

We were on the ground kissing, and she was pushing me down, and there was a rock poking me between the ribs, and it was gone, and her hips were grinding through denim and cotton, and my hands were soft and my hands were tight. They explored, groped, scratched, caressed, and I was delighted with everything they found. I reached for a condom inside my jacket and struggled with the buttons of my jeans, while she looked on as if she were caught in a dream. While I fumbled, she sat on my thighs, cutting off the circulation to my legs, a hazy smile on her lips, a crackly silence in the air. And then I had the condom on, and she lined her hips with mine as if there hadn't been an interruption. Such flow, I thought. She still had her underwear on, but I ripped the elastic and it felt right. As she bore down on me, I felt a certain resistance, as though I hadn't positioned myself right. I tried again and the same thing happened. The third time, she laid one hand on my chest, the other on my cock, and pushed, and pushed, until she was down and her pupils were dilated. The fingers on my chest were clawing through my t-shirt.

I could hear something, maybe a voice, maybe someone singing, but it didn't matter. The only thing that mattered was the feel of her sliding up and down. 'There's a bit of noise coming from that wall.' This time I could make out the words: it was a voice and there was also the beam of a torchlight. I pulled Leona against me and hushed in her ear. She kept moving her hips.

'Look at you, checking everything tonight. What did the missus slip in your tea?' a gruffer voice said.

I could hear their footsteps on the other side of the ferns, and I could feel Leona's flesh parting around mine. I tried to force her hips still, but she was too strong for me. Light reflected off their jackets and pierced through the leaves. I held my breath and covered her groans with my hand. Wet and hard, her tongue dug into my palm. I looked through a gap in the leaves, and for a second, I was looking right into the grey eyes of a bald man. He had a boxer's broken nose. And then he'd moved towards me, into the ferns, and I couldn't see him anymore.

Just as I was racking up excuses – deny or appeal for privacy, I'd choose on the spot – a chorus of boastful voices drowned the sound of their shuffling steps. They were all speaking, laughing, shouting at the same time, but what was important was that they were on the other side of the wall.

'Oh mate, you've got no idea!' one boasted loud enough that I could hear him.

'Not after what Cecilia told everyone about your little… habits,' a different voice, with something like a German accent, shouted back so strongly that his words drowned out our wet slurps and slaps, and the ensuing laughter overpowered the security men's chuckle. I was certain that that boxer of a security guard had seen me, but now both groups were moving away from us, one further into the gardens, the other along the road, and I relaxed. The ground felt soft and we were proud and we giggled. Although I stayed in her for a while, it was no longer about the sex.

Later, as we had our clothes back on, as we lay with our backs to the soil's dew, and I had my jacket over us, I noticed her tearing petals out of a white rose. Every time she flicked one onto the ground, she brought the flower close and inhaled deeply. Propped on my elbows, I looked at my crotch. I lay down and stared at a gap between the clouds.

'Was it your...' I asked.

She nudged her head between my arm and chest. I gathered her closer and felt glad she hadn't told me. I would have fretted and she would have obliged my worries. Instead, she kissed my neck, I burrowed my nose into her hair, and I wanted to laugh in awe. At that moment, I felt like I could say anything, like I didn't need to say anything.

* * *

That night, I had my best sleep since my return: seven solid, dreamless hours. In the morning, I spurted half-formed plans as water broke over my back and sheathed my body. But thoughts of Leona kept on surfacing, wiping away my best designs and leaving me with a contented, perplexed smile. Her stifled moans as the warmth of her breath condensed against my palm, the shape of her straightened arm when she sat and rested her hand by her thigh, the few rebellious hairs stroking my forehead as she pressed on me, the tempo and steadiness of her voice as she told me about her sister, and her quivering upper lip as the security guards walked away from our hiding place. There were doubts too but they didn't stick. So that by the time I walked down to the kitchen, my emotions had settled and I felt as though nothing could move me from my high: life back home was taking a good turn.

My mother walked into the kitchen and started making herself a cup of tea, while I was sitting on the knotted kitchen table, halfway through my porridge.

'I'm making you one too,' she said. Her hand stopped inside a bag of loose leaves, and she looked at me. 'Do you want one?'

There was a hint of deference in her question, as if she expected me to say no. The mother I'd left would have thrust a cup of tea underneath my nose, and she would have looked on sternly until I had some. Now, she was striving to bring her maternal authority in check.

Seeing her changed moved me. Even if I appreciated the spirit behind her efforts, I felt uneasy at the thought that the mother I'd left wasn't the one I'd come back to. A voice within told me that I was responsible for this. Her firstborn disappears and avoids her for eight years – how else was she supposed to react? I was trying to make amends by giving more of myself, but my attempts always seemed forced, as if, by making them, I were acknowledging that there was something wrong.

She'd told me about the problems she'd had with my father on my third day back. 'They're over now, but it was hard while it lasted.' Her confessional tones made me instantly uncomfortable. I listened, split between turning away as I would have done, and gently asking her for more as I wished I could have done. In the end, I fought with my face and said: 'Oh, really.' When she added more, I looked at a book on a shelf, and I said: 'Oh, that must have been tough.' And just as I uttered the word 'tough', she went silent, suddenly looking embarrassed.

But this time, when she asked me whether I wanted tea, I felt a strong instinct building inside of my relaxed self, and I asked for Earl Grey as kindly as I could before I went back to my newspaper. The article I was reading had anecdotes about a Southern Governor who sang songs and read from the Bible at town hall meetings. A man who could play a role in a Republican administration. There was a photo of him, guitar in hand, wearing jeans and a chequered shirt, surrounded by a cheerful crowd.

'How was your meeting yesterday?'

I looked up, as she sat and laid a spotty mug down by my left hand. It had an uneven rim and a lip halfway around its handle – the last surviving member of a set she'd shaped herself before I was born.

'He thinks I have a good chance to get into the summer programme.'

'Oh.' She looked like she was going to say more, but she blew her tea cold instead.

'I'm thinking about it. It's not a big commitment.'

She smiled, and I saw how tense her face had been.

'Oh, I'm proud of you. Do you have everything you need to apply? If… you decide to apply.'

'Let me think,' I said and she stood up.

She paced as I listed what I needed, nodding with every item, whispering to herself loud enough that I could hear her, that she had that document upstairs, she just had to find it, or that she'd call her colleague and work something out. 'Don't worry,' she told me as she frowned and pinched her chin between her thumb and forefinger, and the words seemed more aimed at her than at me.

Up to that point, I felt that my mother and I had reached a new, steady sort of understanding. And then, just as she was about to walk out with a straight back, I made a passing comment which had her sitting down. Of course, I should have coated it in niceties, but I was caught in logistics, and this was one integral element.

'I'll have to find a place to live,' I said.

It was as if those words unplugged a leak, and her entire resolve drained down her spine. Her jaw sunk and the skin of her cheeks seemed to sag down to her neck.

'A place to stay, yes…' she said, tapping her finger on the table. It was the only thing I could see, that finger. 'You know you can stay here, if you want.'

A single image of Leona flashed through my mind – a receptive turn of her eyes, bare shoulders, bare chest – and I was back in my high.

'Thanks.' I reached across the table and grabbed her hand. 'But I'm used to living by myself.'

'Yes, of course you are,' she said and smiled a brave smile. 'You're used to it, that's only normal at your age. I und—'

I interrupted her: 'I don't have to live far.'

'No, you don't,' she said, and her eyes brightened. Once again, she started murmuring, to herself at first, but then the murmurs grew, and I recognised the names of colleagues, of friends. 'Let me make a few phone calls,' she said. Her voice was strong.

* * *

That night, Leona wanted to go for an evening stroll in Port Meadow. She was in a contemplative mood, the previous night's passion replaced by a quiet calm. We crossed the expanse of grass and she unfurled a blanket halfway between the path and the river. There were three horses ruminating to our right. While the clouds held together, the horses were dingy silhouettes against the faraway trees. But they came into our lives when the moon broke through. Then, we could see their piebald patterns, their tails swinging gently, their mouths skimming the grass. When the light first shone on their coats, Leona went silent and pointed at them, a delighted look on her face.

By 11 p.m., the temperature had dropped and I suggested going to my parents' house. They'd gone out for a romantic getaway, a night out in a bed and breakfast down in Somerset. That was how my mother put it while I'd smiled in what I hoped was an encouraging fashion. Leona nodded with a calm smile, and we gathered our things.

We didn't linger in the common parts of the house – it was too soon for that. My hand on her lower back, I guided her straight to my room. Once inside, we piled our things over my desk chair. She went to turn the light on, but I caught her hand at the switch, and I took her in my arms. The sex was different the second time around. It was a more serious affair, and I was the older lover. The ease she'd had the night before was gone. She kept her top on and lay down on the bed, waiting for my next move. I obliged her, whispering instructions, unclasping her bra, helping clothes off, but all the while I was waiting for the sort of impulses that had pinned me to the earth and left a red mark on my side.

I guided her hands, ran a finger over her lips, nibbled her ear in the way that had her almost throwing me off the previous night, all the time prepared to feel her fingers dig into my flesh. But Leona smiled, groaned. She followed my instructions, all of them, dutifully, asking me whether what she was doing was right, and soon I was taking my role more seriously. I slipped a pillow under her waist and, with thoughtful pleasure, she said she liked it better that way.

When we were finished – I was lying on my back, and she had her arm over my chest – I thought over the Leona I'd just encountered. Brain-spun ideas were telling me that I ought to be disappointed, but deep down, I felt that I liked this other Leona very much. A bottle of wine, skipping a wall – she'd gone headlong into the previous night's rush. Tonight, we'd spent an evening alone in an open field, and an inquisitive calm had taken hold of her. It was pure, the way she followed the moment.

Her sleepy voice diverted my musings:

'When you walked into my café yesterday, I thought you were French.'

I ran my fingers through her hair and asked her why.

'I don't know, I just thought you looked French. You had a French accent at first.'

'Did I?' I asked, worried. Having an English accent in France was hard enough. I didn't want an accent in my own language.

'When you gave me euros, you counted them in a French way.'

'Do I 'ave a Frrench accent?' I whispered.

She laughed a quiet laugh, and I rearranged the sheets for she was cold and I was hot. The air was just right for my exposed skin, and I felt myself drifting off to sleep. Leona's breath was slowing. I could smell sweat and sex; I could feel her arm weigh gently across my chest.

'What are you thinking about?' she asked.

I was about to say 'nothing', as I usually do when the question comes up, but I felt like talking despite sleep's pull. So I told her about the course I was going to start.

'My mother's found me a flat in Cowley. I think it belongs to a colleague who's on sabbatical in Australia. Apparently, I can have it.'

'What's it like?' she murmured.

'I haven't seen it yet. She told me it was on Stockmore Street, very close to the ice cream shop we didn't go to last night.' I felt her eyelashes brushing the skin around my nipple. 'It sounded big enough.'

'Oh, that's good,' she said, her voice distant as if she were in the flat already. 'We'll be able to live together.'

It happened just like that, without a trace of hesitation, with nothing but a contented sort of tiredness. The feeling was contagious – as soon as I heard her say it, I wanted to have her every night, her naked body covered with a single sheet, the same tree-sap smell permeating the air.

It was that night that she started telling me about her past, the words low and gentle. She told me about her first boyfriend, at the age of fourteen. He went to the same school, two years ahead, and he spent all his money on a Gibson electric. He was the first man she'd kissed, which she'd liked. He was also the first man to touch her breasts, which she'd found rather painful. He wrote her four grungy love songs. The fifth one had a line about her naked and dead, and, despite his artistic disclaimers, she broke up with him.

Among her soothing words, I remember her mentioning another girl. It was the only girl she ever felt attracted to: tall, with a black father and a white mother, luscious lips and curly black hair. She blew out smoke rings, bit her lips, and watched them dissipate. Leona tried to kiss her once, but the girl turned away and reached for another cigarette.

I told her about Rebecca, my tempestuous first girlfriend, who I'd kissed properly twice, on our first day, and a month later, on our last day, when I finally managed to slip my tongue past her braces. Besides that, I didn't say much. My thoughts were as lazy as her words, still spent from the stresses of the day, still calmed by the sex. Her fingers ran circles around my thigh, sending a gentle tingle all over my body. I felt comfortable next to her. A strong image came to mind, in which she stood clear against a warm background, leaning against the railing of a Mediterranean veranda, inviting me up the stairs. The picture was hazy, but I knew that I could let go and trust her. With time, my confusions would clear, and I would reconcile the nympho in the Botanic Gardens with the pupil on my unmade bed.

The only time she spoke of her family was when she mentioned her grandmother's death. We'd been speaking of love – death was only a natural extension.

'She said she didn't want to die bound to a hospital bed. She made sure we were all with her, at her house in Fontaine-le-Bourg. I helped her put the mixture together in the afternoon, when everyone was having a drink in the garden. We had a great big dinner, with her favourite dishes, her favourite wines, and then she took it.'

There was enough beauty in her words that I asked her more, and she told me about the herbs she added: 'Thyme, coriander, and dill,' she said. 'Her favourites. To mask the bitterness.'

I nodded, for it made sense. After a few minutes of silence, my hand became more adventurous, and it was right to ask her how the sex had felt.

'Soft,' she said. 'And hard. It felt hard and soft at the same time.'

*　*　*

Another good night: almost seven hours. In the morning, I asked her not to have a shower until we had breakfast. I wanted to see her hair ruffled for a little longer. My fingers had worked all night, hand in hand with sleep, to bring it into that most private of looks. She wore one of my old t-shirts, one that had always been too big for me but which I'd bought when big and baggy was the fashion. It reached to the middle of her bare thighs. While her tea was cooling down, she unfolded her legs and went to look at the pictures by the counter. She picked up an old frame, studied it, and moved to a newer one.

'Oh, yes,' she said, 'James is your brother.'

It was a matter-of-fact statement, as if she'd thought about it already, and the picture only confirmed the obvious. The quiet joy that had me smiling out of the corners of my mouth suddenly dimmed, becoming almost silly in its new light.

I should have realised it: a girl growing up so close to Hornsbury would have at least seen my brother a few times. But it only dawned on me then, and with it, I understood that if she knew my brother, she knew who I was. I remembered how tight her face had gone when I'd mentioned Hornsbury on our first date; eight years on, it was still raw enough that it had caused her pain.

Ever since Sally, whom I couldn't have told because that would have been telling the whole cruise ship, all of my girlfriends had known, and not one of them had made it an issue. But now that I had trouble sleeping, I felt something around my chest shrink and gather dust. As her index finger traced the inlay of the wooden frame, I realised that there had been a pure kind of hope swelling inside of me, and it was gone already, before I had time to cup it in the fleshy parts of my hand.

'How is he?' she asked me, in the same tones she'd used all along. I looked up to make sure she wasn't judging me.

'He's alright,' I said automatically.

'Oh, that's good,' she said, and I heard genuine relief in her voice. Her tones puzzled me: 'The last time I saw him, he looked very pale. Nothing but skin on his bones. I don't know if you know, but he used to go out with Debby, one of my school friends. You haven't met any of my friends yet! We must do something with them one day.' Her voice went distant for a few words, before coming back to its usual earnestness: 'Yes, Debby and James. I haven't seen her for at least a year, but we used to spend a lot of time together a few years ago. Especially two years ago. They'd go and do their thing. I wasn't into that, so I guess that's why we drifted apart... Oh, I'm glad to hear he's better.'

'He's a little better,' I said with more feeling. Listening to her clear voice, so full of relief at first, turning wistful at the mention of Debby, and then coming back to the same genuine relief as she concluded he was better, I saw her again on her veranda, an orange, ivy-clad wall behind her. I put my sense of loss aside and focused on my brother: 'He's back in London now.'

She was still holding the picture frame, rotating it between her hands. The morning light shone through the messy strands of her hair, framing the invitation in her eyes, in her mouth as it drifted open. And I told her more. At one point, out of habit, I hesitated. I looked into her face, our gazes crossed, and I realised how strong she seemed at that moment, half naked, her hair ruffled, her eyebrows raised in concern. As if she realised it too, she looked down at our hands and, squeezing mine, urged me on.

I told her the way he'd cut his potatoes, till they were nothing but mash, the way he'd slammed his bedroom door on my outstretched hand, the way he'd sneaked back to London. Saying it all, I realised that it'd been bothering me, and I started to feel lucky.

An hour after she'd left, I was still smiling. There was a girl who'd been born good and, for some strange reason, she liked spending time with me.

* * *

That afternoon, I rode my bike into town and went past a college sports ground full of men in white. I stopped by the midwicket boundary, just as a stocky man bowled a lob to a watchful Indian batsman.

I hadn't played cricket since I'd left England, except for a few street games in India, where it was impossible to avoid the game but where I never spent more than a few days at a time, and one pick-up game when I worked in the Alps. The expat community had huddled, and from one man's trunk, from another's garage, we'd managed to find two bats and a plastic ball. Then, amongst peaks and cliffs, in a park a few hundred metres below the snowline, we'd played the sixth test of that year's Ashes. It was a matter of making the most our limited resources: the wicket was a track, which was still hard enough for the ball to bounce. One of the set of stumps was made of three sticks hammered into the ground, while the other was made of a stack of beer boxes. And it wasn't about the cricket either: three of the Australians decided they were more interested in David Boon's record – fifty-two beer cans over a twenty-four-hour period – than in the cricket itself. They passed out a long way before their half-century.

Putting my bike on the ground, I stood on the boundary, reacquainting myself with the game as it was meant to be played. I watched the batsman bend a long way forward to each innocuous delivery, as if there were some hidden danger in them, while his partner urged him to give him the strike. Their banter carried clearly across the field, and the rest of the batting team, safely sitting on the pavilion steps, sniggered quietly. On the penultimate ball of the over, he stepped out of his crease, reached the ball on the full, and swatted it high and fast in my direction. There was a fielder at deep midwicket, but it eluded him and came right for me. Shuffling, I stretched out one hand and felt it slam into the heel of my thumb, and my fingers curl around it.

The batting team cheered. Some in the bowling did too, but theirs sounded more ironic. I returned the ball, while the umpire signalled a six by raising both his arms so far behind his head that he looked as though he might fall down. There was one more ball in the over: the batsman blocked it, just as he'd blocked the first four, but this time he called for a single. His partner already had his back turned, clearly waiting for his turn facing. 'Yes, yes!' said the Indian, running towards his partner. By the time the non-striker realised what was happening, he was halfway down the pitch, and the keeper was breaking the stumps. Looking at the pavilion, I noticed that the batting team was no longer smiling mockingly, but seemed a little worried now. They all averted their eyes as the non-striker walked in.

'He can't fucking call!' I heard, together with another string of 'fucks' while his teammates stayed quiet. I didn't stay to see how the new batsman would do.

Taking a catch off a six, seeing a farcical run-out, these should have had me yearning to play again, but instead they just made me realise how much I'd changed over the years I'd spent away. As a seventeen-year-old, I would have stayed up all night to watch England take on Australia on Boxing Day, while now, I smiled at the contest but didn't feel the urge to go and join a team.

* * *

Leona was helping me sleep. A few hours with her, and I worried less. Her body next to mine, matching my breath to hers, I slept even better. There was something comforting in her steady presence, in her deep unbroken sleep. She had a way of moving when she slept, of touching me just when I needed it.

But alone and sexless, I could only manage three good hours before I started drifting. In and out of a sort of sleep, of a sort of dream. Lucid hallucinations, memories congealing, evolving into something between the real and the mad.

By the fifth hour, I was gun in hand, surveying the field. Eric was on the ground, dead, unconscious. And everyone else was fighting between red and black. Or red and white. I pointed the gun at my foot: I could see skin, muscles and bones through the leather of my shoe. And I aimed for the nail of my big toe.

Before I could pull the trigger and watch a hole form itself between concrete and leather, my heavy eyes flicked open, and there was no chance I could go back to sleep. And I waited in bed, or I rose and wrote.

One morning, my mother pointed at the pot of coffee I was brewing myself.

'Is that just for you?' she asked.

I eyed the pot.

'I drank a lot of coffee in France.'

She traced lines under her eyes:

'You look a little tired.' She sat down at the kitchen table.

'It's normal. I'm not a big sleeper. I've been this way for a long time,' I said, looking directly into her eyes. I saw real concern.

'Have you been to a doctor?'

'No, I don't want to. I don't like shrinks.'

'Not a shrink, no one is speaking about shrinks,' she said. 'Just a GP. There are things you can do, you know, and if they don't work, they'll prescribe you sleeping pills.'

I said I'd look into it, for I could see that my mother wouldn't let go until she felt I'd listened to her, but I'd already browsed the internet for advice, and I'd tried their relaxation techniques. My case was different. That memories were mingling with dreams was the cost of coming home. A few more weeks, I told myself, and I'd be fine.

* * *

I moved in to the Stockmore Street apartment the day after my first class. The car was full of everything I thought I needed, comfortably stored in the boot, together with everything my mother thought I needed, which extended all over the back seat.

'You have to feel at home,' my mother said as she added lamps, sheets, duvets ('Two, just in case, and you can always store the other one under the bed'), cutlery, plates, two pots and a Teflon pan ('You'll be able to cook with less oil').

When we first reached the house, the third in a row of eight identical 1950s townhouses, and she pulled out its key, she told me there was a spare and I could leave it with her if I wanted. I gave a non-committal answer, imagining instead Leona's reaction as I handed her a key. Would she be delighted, or take it in her stride, I asked myself, and I imagined both scenarios. I liked not knowing: whatever she did – I pictured a plethora of smiles and weighed it against a thoughtful cock of her head – I'd discover more of her. But then, as we climbed to the upstairs floor, which the flat occupied, I told myself that I was being silly: it had only been a few days. Surely, I should hand the extra key to my mother.

I listened to what my mother was telling me. The house, divided into two flats, was empty for the summer. Both of their children had been offered jobs in London within a week of each other, and her colleague being away, hadn't had time to rent them out yet.

The upstairs apartment had a put-together feel, as if some architect had decided to add each room independently of the others, and the furniture had followed the same logic. The main bedroom stood four steps above the rest of the flat, as if it needed the extra height, while the other bedroom, empty but for a desk and a exercise ball, was almost too small to be lived in. The kitchen, with its purples and bright greens, looked as though the architect had decided to turn a corridor into a psychedelic statement. And the living area, with its flowery sofa and its transparent plastic table, had a window facing the garden so high up the wall that I had to stand on a chair to see the top of the garden's shrubbery.

'We didn't bring anything to put on the walls,' my mother said, and before I had time to say that I'd only be living there for a few months, she told me that I must come and take some posters and paintings from the garage. 'Do you remember the big one with the church your grandmother did? It would fit well on this wall. But of course, you can take whatever you want.'

After I agreed, she left me and I called Leona. While I waited, I noticed that my mother had left the spare set of keys on the kitchen counter. Don't rush into anything, I told myself. But the scene I'd already constructed came to my mind, and this time I pictured a gentle, naïve smile as I handed her the keys. This expression felt so right that I forgot all the other scenarios, and I winced. Such innocence, and me, dirt peeling from my arms!

Rather than keep on thinking, I made myself busy, unpacking a few boxes, making the bed. When Leona arrived, I walked down to open the door feeling only slightly uneasy. But even that vanished when I saw her, the strap of her light blue bra toying with the strap of her green summer dress, and my hands, my nose, my lips followed impulses of their own. Feeling giddy, I made a show of covering her eyes until she was inside the flat.

When I took my hands from her eyes in the living area, she swivelled even slower than I'd ever seen her do before, her gaze taking in everything from the floor to the ceiling: 'Do you think that chimney works? It'd be nice in winter... I like the polka dots on those curtains... How would you close the ones on that high window? ... Nathan, there's even a washing machine. Oh, look at this vase!'

I listened, sharing in her delight.

'Nathan, this is perfect.' Running her fingers along the wall, she found a door I'd glanced over, and peeked in. 'There's even a hoover.' Opening the bedroom, she told me how much she liked the bedding.

'That's my mother's,' I said.

'She has a lovely eye for detail. I'd really like to meet her. You must come and meet my parents too. We have a little vegetable garden. I can pick some tomatoes, and soon I'll be able to pick blackberries, and that'll make a great salad.'

Her voice, light and happy, suddenly became urgent: 'There's a spider,' she said and before I had time to react, she added: 'I'll get it.' Bemused, I watched her as she took off one shoe, held it by the toe, climbed on a chair, and swung her weapon into the web. 'Missed it.' She coiled her arm back again, pointing at the spider with her other hand, one foot balancing on the chair, the other on the kitchen counter, and she swung.

'Here we go. Dead.' She came down from her chair, beaming. She showed me the flattened spider glued to the sole of her shoe.

'How about next week? Could you come then?' she asked.

As we haggled over a date, I thought back to the way she'd wedged the chair against the kitchen counter, to her glee at the small spider's crushed body, and I felt oddly comforted.

* * *

While tomato sauce simmered in one pot, and pasta boiled in another, Leona remembered that she'd brought me a book.

She handed it to me with a worried fold between her eyebrows. 'I hope you'll like it,' she said. It was a well-worn paperback with a black cover. In its centre was a white star that looked like a Star of David gone curvy. *Thoughts on Thought*, I read, and hid a wince. The author's name, Kuraetsokov, only made me more worried.

'He led a very interesting life,' she said enthusiastically. 'He was born a prince in nineteenth-century Russia, but when he was in his twenties, he had a revelation, and he gave all he had to an orphanage. He started teaching all over Europe, and then in America.'

Having spent the afternoon shifting boxes, I was far more interested in her inviting, exposed skin than in meta-thoughts. But I must have hidden my reticence well, for she spent half an hour telling me more about the Russian's brand of philosophy, while I stole glances at the curves her green dress hugged. I don't know what it is, they didn't use to bother me, but now these sorts of semi-occult, semi-existential dwellings on life and the universe always make me suspicious. Years ago, when I was at sea, I used to seek out the esoteric. Like when I was in Pondicherry at the same time as the hugging guru and her white-clad posse of white faces with disposable income, and I was ushered to the front of a fifteen-thousand-strong crowd, so that I could better witness a miracle in progress. I sat with my legs crossed humming along with her fan-base, grasping at a strand floating under the tent, until I became so tired and dehydrated that I was ready for my own hug. For months afterwards, I told strangers this story, and they asked me what the guru had whispered in my ear. At first, I played it up – I wanted them to believe she'd known me personally. Me amongst fifteen thousand. But as the months passed, I stopped pretending – I hadn't heard what she'd told me, and I didn't want to know either.

Yet, seeing how easily Leona pronounced his name, I curbed my impulses and looked at the book more closely.

At that time, she seemed to have his ideas divided into two. On the one side, Kuraetsokov preached forgiveness as a state of being. 'Forgiveness is here,' Leona told me, and for a second I grew more attentive, for she was situating forgiveness around her heart, pressing down on her left breast so that her cleavage swelled. 'When you embrace forgiveness, you start to love. It can't work otherwise, don't you see? And love hides the ego.'

And this is how she linked it to his second concept: 'To do that, you must stop thinking.' When she mentioned thinking, she tapped her skull, which didn't have the same effect as forgiveness. 'Because, if you think, it always comes back to you. Me, me, me! How can you forgive, how can you love that way? Can you imagine, he came up with all of that a hundred and fifty years ago!'

I browsed through the book until we finished dinner. Then, stating that the book was interesting in as convincing a way as I could, I smiled mischievously, and to my relief, she answered in kind. Rising, I looked at her green dress, at all the furniture we still hadn't made our own, and I pushed her down on the sofa. When she started pulling her dress up, I stopped her hands at her hips and bundled the cloth on her warm stomach.

Later that long evening, when we were lying down on the bed, and I had a bare leg dangling down its side, I asked her whether she liked champagne.

'I love it,' she said. She turned towards me and studied my face. 'Why?'

'It'd be nice to have champagne right now. We'll have it next time we celebrate something.'

'Like this flat.'

'Yeah,' I said.

'Our anniversary.'

'That's a long way away.'

'Our six-month anniversary,' she said.

'That's a long way away.'

'Four-month anniversary.'

I turned towards her and kissed her.

'Yes, our four-month anniversary,' I said.

'Nos quatre mois,' she said.

She had to leave by nine the next morning to get to work on time. She woke up too late to do anything. After she said goodbye, while she was still gathering her things, I lay on my stomach, put a pillow over my head, and called out to her:

'Leona!'

'Yes,' she said, sounding fresh.

'There's a key in the top drawer under the stove.'

'Alright,' she said. And I fancied I heard a note of awe in that word, but I didn't look up until I heard her leave the flat. Then I turned on my back, threw the blanket off my body, and smiled at the ceiling.

* * *

Halfway through the morning, while I was trying to tame the hot and cold tap combination so that I could do the dishes, she sent me a text message saying her parents were cooking for all three sisters that night, and that I was welcome to come along.

I'd only met two girlfriends' parents. First, Anna's: her mother had made me hot chocolates and discussed people from school as if they were mutual friends, but her father, with his red bald head, had grabbed my shoulder and told me that whatever his wife said, his daughter was his daughter, and I couldn't stay past dinnertime. And then, years later, Marie's: I'd spent weeks in between seasons at Marie's mother's house, near Lyons, nodding to everything she said even though I only understood half. I thought she liked me until Marie, in between two cigarettes, smiling sardonically, told me that her mother had decided that I was too quiet.

Still, in my imagination, Leona's parents were loving, affable people, who would eventually warm to me. And yes, I thought that having survived the shooting might earn me a few pity points.

Just as the water reached the right temperature, I heard a brief ring. I plugged my sink and fetched my phone.

Great. They are excited! The address is: 18 Churchill Street…

I read the address once and frowned. I read it again and my insides sunk while my body somehow remained upright. The bicycles locked to the fence on Churchill Street, the dark wooden floor in the TV room, the yellow-brick wall we used to kick a ball against, they flashed and then my mind went blank.

There was a tingling feeling in my chest, and the phone in my hand was a strange object. It had a screen and a keypad. For the first time, I noticed that the number nine had four letters under it.

I stood there until I heard a strange noise. I turned to look at the sink: water whooshed out of the tap and fell into a moving mass, making a rich, hollow sound. The sink seemed to swell and breathe, and the strange noise kept on reaching my ears. Following the edges of the sink, I noticed water on the counter. There was a thick lip over the drying rack flowing into a narrow stream and falling. Falling, and splashing on the kitchen tiles. Breaking into islands. Joining islands. All of a sudden, the haze cleared.

'You fucking idiot!'

The words came out strained by the tension in my throat. I repeated them again and again as I turned the tap off, plunged my hand in the burning water, unplugged the sink, and mopped the floor.

When I finished, I walked around the flat looking for something to hit. I swung at the exercise ball in the small bedroom. The ball bobbed through the air, hit the wall with a deep sound, and came back exactly where it started. There was something about that ball that pissed me off. I kicked it again. And again, for three times was better than two. Then, fetching a knife from the kitchen, I tried to stab it. The blade bounced off the surface.

'It's just a fucking ball!' I shouted so loud that I realised I had a knife in my hand. Dropping it on the bedroom floor, I left the flat.

The world outside seemed different. There were cracks all over the bitumen. Here was a dented line going across the road, and there was another one, barely twenty yards down. And here was a different type of crack, a sort of necklace following the line of the road – just where a car tyre would roll, I told myself. A bit further down the road, the necklace became a rut, and then it lightened again. Around a traffic light. But why weren't there any cracks on this road, I asked myself, looking at the darker colour of a new road. New roads don't have cracks, I thought, and I nodded to myself.

By the time I noticed my surroundings, I'd walked all the way to the top of South Park. Falling on the grass, I felt my phone in my back pocket, and remembered that Leona expected an answer. I called her.

'Oh, I have so much work. I just realised. I know it's rude…'

'Are you alright? You sound a little strange.'

'Oh, yes, don't worry. Just had a look at an assignment.'

'Ah, alright.' She sounded sad. 'Well, I guess I'll call my mother. I don't think she'll mind.'

'Good, that's good,' I said.

'Are you outside? I can't hear you very well.'

'Yes, outside. Just taking a break. I'll get back to it in a minute.'

'We can do it another night. I can ask my parents if you want.'

'Yes, you do that. We'll talk about it some other time.'

She strung some more words together: something about work, I think, and we hung up. And then, staring at the Magdalen tower, at the Radcliffe Camera, I punched the ground.

'You fucking idiot! She even looks like him... Go back to raking sand.'

The gothic towers stared back serenely. A hint of mist and a thin cloud cover softened the warm June light. The colleges' quads and gardens seemed to float happily over the vast red-brick expanse surrounding them.

More softly this time, I asked myself why I hadn't realised that she was Jeffrey's sister. I pictured both of them next to each other: her voice had the same happy tones, and her nose, it was so obvious now that I knew, her nose was a miniature copy of his. Compare her to her mother and it was even clearer: same hair, just about the same height.

And in this calmer state, I felt resigned to the inevitable – there could be no future. I saw her, I saw him, and I shivered. Compared to him, I was the bastard who'd survived, all luck and no merit. But then I thought of the way she'd kissed my back before she left for work, and my head dropped.

With a deep breath, I went over all the times I could have worked it out. When she served me at Georgina's, when she spoke to me, when she gave me her name, when she said which area she lived in, when she told me she knew my brother. The list was damning. Then, with a hint of pride, I answered myself. There was a big difference between an eleven-year-old child and a nineteen-year-old woman. Plus, I'd never really looked at her when she was little. And I could think of at least three other Baker families I knew, who lived, as she did, in the Oxford suburbs. And it was up to her to tell me, I told myself, raising my head and looking at the deep green leaves of a vast, strange tree.

On that thought, I went home and buried myself in my work, forcing my head back into my books whenever I caught myself staring into space.

*   *   *

As Jeffrey forced his way back into my mind, Leona as a growing child took her rightful place alongside him. He'd doted on her when she was a baby. I could picture her as a toddler ogling us while we assembled Lego blocks into a pirate fleet. He'd spent days teaching her to respect our edifices, and unlike my little brother, who would take pleasure in seeing me upset, she kept her dangerously jerky baby limbs far from our fortresses.

Until she turned five, she spent every waking hour trying to get close to her brother. So much so that he'd hide under his bed and ask me to tell her he was gone to school when she knocked on his door.

'School?' I remember her asking me one Sunday, sticking a strand of platinum hair into her quivering mouth so that she wouldn't sob, because her brother had told her that big girls didn't cry in front of boys. And I told her it was a special sort of school that she'd also have to go to when she'd turn eleven.

Jeffrey was more aloof with his other sisters, who were only a little younger than Leona. Being the first, she got all of his attention – the cruel love of a growing boy – and she wanted more. For a whole year, the year my mother drove us to every cricket game because my father was too busy to play and Jeffrey's parents were struggling to keep their flower business afloat, Jeffrey played master to Leona's maid. Ever eager, she made his bed until there wasn't a crease on his sheets, and then asked him to check that everything was to his liking. Most times I witnessed their game, he adopted a critical air, and walked through his room with his chest puffed up and his hands crossed behind his back, nodding and humming his approval at the bed, the toy boxes, the desk, but always finding one detail to bring to her attention – a pillow that wasn't set straight, dust on a shelf. *So that she improves*, he explained to me. At other times, power made him sadistic: like the times he started dropping fruits so she'd clean them up, and he told her that if she didn't pick them up quickly enough, she'd have to lick them clean with her tongue. I'd like to think that I came to her protection once or twice, that I didn't laugh along with him, but she was a child, and I doubt I spent much time talking to her or thinking about her.

By the time we were seventeen, she was ten and he'd settled into paternal kindness, lavishing her with dashes of his attention, which she lapped up with more dignity than when she was a toddler asking for his hand, his arms, his bed.

The more I recalled her then, the more I grew puzzled. We'd spent ten days together, ten intense days, whispering into the nights, skins sharing warmth, and never did I think that something stood between us. Something as big as Jeffrey, my best friend, her beloved brother.

Something had to show. I rummaged through my memories. Of course, I could attribute every twitch to her dead brother, just as I could say that the postcard on her notebook was really meant to be her sitting over her dead brother. But most likely, twitches were just twitches, and the postcard was nothing but a painting. Short on evidence, my mind sought theories. It was always possible that she'd never thought about him once, that she'd reached a chilly balance with her grief – a deal in which she'd never think of him again and, in return, she'd never feel that half-formed surge of tears that often stopped in my throat when Anna, Jeffrey or Eric flashed forth in a potent light.

The idea was too foreign. I dismissed it and thought about the one time she'd met Eric. I was sixteen and Eric had only been at our school for a few months. After repeatedly trying to sell each one to the other, I wanted my two closest friends to move past their passive mistrust. On a crisp winter day, when the winter sun had us ignoring the snot dripping from the tips of our noses, I called Jeffrey to tell him I was dropping by, omitting the fact that Eric was with me. That was perhaps a mistake. Jeffrey had privately told me he didn't understand why

Tom and Paul disliked Eric so much, but Eric had his oddities. It'd taken me a while to get used to his cold unfocused stares, his unexpected moody silences (best ignored), and even longer to pay no attention to the way he'd be caught in his own thoughts one minute, and expounding an opinion as much with his voice as with his hands the next.

Jeffrey wasn't prepared for any of that. He welcomed Eric with a veneer of formality – may I offer you something to drink? Would you mind turning that switch on? I kept on hoping that it would pass, that he'd show him one of his fun-loving smiles. And then, we were in the garden by the apple tree trying to juggle oranges, and Leona came to watch her brother in action. Jeffrey and I, well practised, started with four each and tried to add a fifth. But Eric had never juggled before, and trying to imitate us, he tossed four in the air and ended with three on the floor. Making sure we weren't leering, he put one down behind his back and tried again.

'Eric,' Jeffrey said, while he was tossing his own set ever higher, 'perhaps you'd do better if you started with two.'

His tones were slightly condescending, but I'm certain Jeffrey meant well. And I'm sure Eric would have listened if it hadn't been for Leona picking up on her brother's tones and snickering cruelly.

'Even I can do three,' she said. 'I could do two with my eyes closed.'

Without saying a word, Eric put down the fruits in an evenly spaced line and charged inside. When I went to look for him, he'd already left Jeffrey's house, intent on walking all the way home if he couldn't find a bus. I managed to calm him and coax him back to Jeffrey's, but from that point on, he never listened to anything Jeffrey told him without thinking that Jeffrey was trying to make fun of him.

'Why does he even say hello to me?' he asked me two weeks later.

As I struggled to focus on my work, I found it easy to think back to that episode and toy with its significance: it was a turning point, the last time I tried to bring Eric into our crowd, the last time Eric thought he could become friends with the others. If only Leona had stayed quiet, events would have turned out differently. But I was tired, and I was thinking silly thoughts. I knew it instinctively: Leona had struck Eric out of her memories. It was the right thing to do. That way, she wasn't spending her days doubting. That way, she was sleeping soundly.

* * *

After a patchy night, agitation fighting with my dreams, I woke up recalling a discussion we'd had on our third night together.

'How many children do you want?' she'd asked me.

Marie had never been the sort to ask me these questions. With her, sperm remained sperm. But with Leona, I immediately asked myself whether there was a future between us, marriage even, and just as I was starting to see her surrounded by our children, I cut my imagination short.

'Two,' I said. 'And you?'

'Three.'

'How many siblings do you have?'

'I have two younger sisters,' she said.

With all the clarity of an active mind in a resting body, I asked myself whether she'd lied to me then, recalling the way she'd spoken, the way she'd moved, and oddly, even though it would have been natural for her to tell me that she'd lost a brother, I concluded that what she'd told me was her version of the truth.

I flipped my phone open and found a new text, in which Leona suggested dinner that night. I waited until I'd had breakfast, showered, and done an hour of work, before I texted her that I still had too much work. In a way, it was true: there weren't enough hours in the day to parse through my course's over-generous reading lists.

That day, I didn't blame myself so much. Instead, there lurked a deep resignation near the bottom of my lungs, so that whenever I sighed fully, I became mournful. It was a conceptual kind of mourning: the death of a promise, a spark, a relationship. I didn't spend much time thinking about it; I didn't have to. It was just there, with me, surging occasionally.

An imaginary experiment, much like many my mother had signed me up for, came to mind: one of my mother's colleagues had Leona and another girl in a room. My task was to go in, talk about anything but the shooting, and then fill out a questionnaire. However I ran the scenario, when I read that one of them had lost a brother, I guessed that it was the other girl simply because Leona looked so untouched by the worries of life.

Her uninterrupted grin on our first evening, or the time she asked me whether I was ticklish, her fingers between my shirt and my summer jacket; they popped into my mind while I searched for other signs: ready tears, prolonged silences, or perhaps some sort of emotional bravado. But instead, I saw her smile and the squashed spider, the way she pivoted on her toes whenever she walked into a new space.

I didn't get her. I'd spent eight years in a different world and my hands still went damp whenever a conversation neared the shooting. But she could fuck her dead brother's best friend, the one living person who'd seen him die, and curl into his arms as if he'd protect her. All of this without ever acknowledging that blood and death had seared a natural chain between us, each inch-thick stainless steel link welded to our skins.

It happened the day she asked me what school I'd gone to:

'Hornsbury School,' I said, looking away, my eyes feeling shifty all of a sudden.

'Oh, were you there when it was still called that?'

'Yes.'

'They built a new building at the back,' she said, her voice holding her usual rolling cadence. 'It's made of glass, with one tall spire. When you climb it, you can see through the whole building. Like if you were inside a stomach. And they renovated the old façade too. It looks really nice.'

'Do you like glass buildings?'

'It depends. I like it when they look like they're moving,' she said, and we started talking about modern architecture.

* * *

At noon the next day, Leona called me. I let the phone ring while I readied myself for the conversation I knew I had to have. Endings were never easy but I had to face things as they were.

I picked it up on the fourth ring, put the receiver to my ear, and inhaled deeply. There was a short silence on her side of the line, but then, as she heard me breathe out, she said 'hello' with her usual ebullience and I felt something shift, as though it were slotting into a different set of tracks.

'I think I've read enough equations for the next month,' I answered her with some of her enthusiasm.

'I know what you mean. I had two full day shifts, and then I did a catering shift last night too. At a sweet Frenchman's big house, not two streets away from yours. I think he likes having me, he always asks for me.'

The picture of a sweet French man wanting her at his house pushed me further into the moment. I couldn't remember what I'd been thinking before she called.

'Listen, I want to catch up with a friend in London tomorrow. She lives in Angel, five minutes from your brother. Let's go see him! And then we could go see a show. Do you like musicals, or would you rather see a play?'

If the conversation had started differently, I'd have grown serious at that point, but as it was, my thoughts were running ahead, focused on the choice she'd given me – I didn't want to give her the impression that I was a theatre sort of man.

* * *

I stood under the Oxford train station's awning, while a cold breeze blew straight through the wool of my jumper, and a line of buses shook the air with their rambling engines. When I saw her emerge from a sea of bikes (in her vintage flower-print summer dress) and wave happily as soon as she saw me, I put the station's asphalt and concrete to the side, and replaced it with the two of us: her scent, the smoothness of her skin, the lightness in her voice, and the flow of our conversation, the warmth of my hand in hers. It went to my head like a field of flowers in bloom. My fingers traced the line of her hips and I kissed the point of her cheekbone. Our hands parted once, when she went to the counter to get her ticket. From a distance, I watched her bare calves, her dress hang from her hips, her plaited hair brush the nape of her neck, and I looked around me, wanting to share my delight. At least two men were looking at her, I noticed and smiled.

And then she turned to glance at me – for half a second, I saw the line of her nose on her opened face, and I remembered Jeffrey's profile when we were eleven. We were playing football in his garden, he was shielding the ball with his body, and he glanced at me over his shoulder. It only lasted an instant – then she was walking towards me, brandishing her ticket, and Jeffrey's image was cast out of my mind.

Halfway through the train journey, while she was resting her head against my shoulder, I remembered my doubts. I turned my nose away from her hair, stuck it in my seat, and inhaled deeply. Then, turning back towards her, my eyes followed a power cable that ran between the trains and the green hills.

'Eight years ago,' I said, squeezing her hand, 'do you remember? I was with my mother and you were with yours, at Tesco. Do you remember?'

'The one in Summertown?'

'No, the one in Witney. You were doing something with your leg. Some ballet.'

'Oh, I used to practise everywhere. Mum says that I was trying pirouettes in the dentist's waiting room when I was five.'

'Why did you stop?'

'I grew up, I guess, but I haven't stopped… Sometimes in the garden, I take my shoes off, and…' She slipped one shoe off and raised her leg with her toes pointed.

I chuckled. 'I can definitely see you doing that… But do you not remember that day in the supermarket?'

'Ah, no… We often went there. I don't remember seeing you.'

Lest I fall back into our momentum, I tried the name we'd never mentioned:

'It was right after Jeffrey died,' I said.

For three seconds, her body stiffened. Her neck straightened, her fingers were crushing my hand, and her elbow was poking hard into my ribs.

'Oh. Yes, I see,' she said slowly, her voice harsh. 'But no, I don't remember.'

On those words, her body loosened again, suddenly resting as comfortably on mine as it had done before.

'I remember the time you came skiing with us,' she said, in her vagabonding voice, 'and you fell off a slope, and ski patrol had to rescue you. How many times did that happen when you were living in Chamonix?'

And so the conversation righted itself, held up by its speed, like a motorbike swerving around a pothole.

* * *

Her mother called her just as we were reaching my brother's. Mouthing 'two minutes', she waved me inside while she stayed on the street. Alone, I suddenly felt reticent. I rang the bell and waited. No one answered. Pulling out a piece of paper, I checked the number of the house against the one I'd jotted down. I rang again, and pushed the door at the same time.

I walked into a dark vestibule. Green wallpaper was peeling off bare walls. There was a pile of shoes behind the door. I put mine next to them, and trod on the once-grey carpet. A loud beat pulsed down the corridor. Following the sound, I reached a room with a sofa, its cushions scattered all over the floor. An eyeball changed colour to the rhythm of the music on a flat TV screen. And amongst the cushions, my brother lay on his back, his body spread into an X. His eyes were open.

'Hey, James,' I said.

He glanced at me, before he looked at the ceiling once again.

'Oh, it's you,' he said. 'Mum said you'd be coming.'

'I tried to call myself, but I couldn't get through.'

'I don't answer unknown numbers.'

He glanced at me again and, for a second, I saw him as he must see me: a creased-up twenty-six-year-old clinging to the way things were when I was seventeen.

'I couldn't leave a message either,' I said. 'Your box was full.'

'I don't listen to my messages.'

'Can I sit down?'

'Yeah, sure.'

I sat on a cushion, my back against the sofa.

'Nice music. What is it?'

He kept silent, his eyes still on the ceiling. There was a damp smell of skunk in the air. A minute after my question, he spoke:

'Fat Freddy's Drop,' he said. 'They're pretty good.'

We stayed silent for another minute, listening to the singer repeat the same line over and over again.

'You like them?' he asked.

'Yeah.' Through the music, I heard a shrill noise. 'Someone's ringing the bell,' I said.

'Okay.'

'Should I get it?'

'No, they'll work it out.'

A few seconds later, I saw Leona come into the room beaming. She looked at me, ignoring the plea on my face. Her smile grew when she saw my brother.

'James!'

His eyes shifted slowly towards her, but as soon as he saw her, his whole demeanour changed.

'Leona!' He smiled and stood up.

He wasn't quite steady on his feet by the time she ran into his arms, but he managed to hold on. They seemed to ask and answer a dozen questions at once.

'It's been so long. How long? How are you? I'm expecting stories—'

'—Why? Yes, good. Why, what? What are you doing here?' he said.

'I came with Nathan. I wanted to surprise you! How are you?'

'You surprised me alright. Good. Day off today. How's uni?'

I looked at them enviously. With Leona, my brother seemed less foreign. She came to sit next to me, resting her hand on my thigh, while they caught up with each other. From her questions, I glimpsed a side of my brother I didn't know. I saw my father's dry humour and my mother's cheeky smile, the one she kept for her friends.

'So, are you out of rehab for good?' she asked, and I wanted to be able to ask that question in the same easy tones.

'Yeah, I think so. Just smoking a little grass, but that never hurt anybody.'

I nodded thoughtfully, while she answered:

'Depends how much you smoke!'

He laughed:

'I'm still standing. It's not a little grass that's going to knock me down.'

She smiled at him:

'I'm so glad to see you.'

At that moment, looking at her cocked head and sweet smile, at his grateful eyes, I felt like I could add my own:

'Me too,' I said.

He barely looked at me, but I was glad I'd been able to say it. We stayed chatting until I noticed a game console, and asked him whether we could play something.

'Sure,' he said. 'Do you know how to play, Leona?'

'No,' she said, 'but I want to see the two of you play.'

An hour later, Leona looked at her watch and said that if we wanted to get cheap tickets, we ought to go. While Leona slipped her boots on, James grabbed my arm.

'What is she doing with you?'

'I don't know... Just met her.'

'But you're taking care of her, right?'

'Yeah, of course.'

He let go of my arm. Looking at the field of cushions on the floor, he whispered:

'You're one lucky bloke.'

* * *

We came home late, still tipsy from the three bottles of wine we'd shared around the show. In bed, we fumbled and then we slept. After an initial slump, my mind flared around the paste lining my mouth. I woke up. It was five in the morning, and the sun was announcing its presence by the far edge. I drank some water and I lay down again. Just as sleep nudged aside to let me in, the person next to me turned and snorted, and the darkness of sleep lightened, and I was thrust into a new lucid dream, a new vivid memory.

There is Eric and there is Jeffrey coming from opposite lawns and meeting under the outdoor archway, where I stand with my opened bag perched on my knee, looking for my physics notebook. Jeffrey, taller than he's ever been, taller in his long limbs and his stretched face than Eric, who himself stands like one of the archway's thin columns, skimming the floor, rooted to the ceiling. Jeffrey extends his long arm and his thin hand for his newest handshake: clasp, two-finger pullback, knuckle graze. And he notices Eric, turns towards him, and offers him his hand like he's offered it to me. I can count the hairs on the back of their palms. Eric takes it and squeezes the clasp, misses the pullback, punches the graze. When Jeffrey leaves us for the lure of Tom's latest joke, Eric follows him with all of the chill in his eyes.

'Why does he bother pretending?' Eric says.

'He likes you, he's like that.'

'That's even worse.'

And I look at Jeffrey's back the same way Eric does: with the sort of hate that burns through raw flesh.

I heard another nasal grunt, and I held my eyes open until the freshness in the air had stung me to tears. From Leona's blurry shape came an uneven snore, chipping away at my calm with every snort. A girl who snored. Irritated by my lack of sleep, I made a list of all the things I didn't like about her.

One. That she'd asked me whether I snored before we'd spent our first night together, but that she'd neglected to tell me it happened to greater mortals.

Two. The way she looked at me sometimes, as if there were a zip starting just above my solar plexus that stretched all the way to my balls, and she was the only one who knew about it.

She squirmed under the sheets, and I stopped my list for a second to watch her. An arm first, she turned onto her side, a new snort followed by a precarious silence.

Three. The time I took her on my morning walk, and we came across the lady with the black hat in Holywell Cemetery. She was, as she'd been every morning of my walk, standing with her hat in hand, her head bent over a grave that stood two yards behind Kenneth Grahame's. Everything she wore was black, from her shoes to her turtleneck. Black long sleeves and black tights covered every inch of wrinkled skin but that of her hands and face. That skin was spotty but smooth, glossy around her eyes. At five past ten, as she always did without ever looking at her watch, she put her hat back on her head and left the cemetery through the church gate.

Leona scampered towards the grave, squinted and then nodded thoughtfully. She came back to me and told me the most recent name was from 1985.

'And she's here every day?' she asked.

'All of last week.'

'Do you know where she goes after here?'

I shook my head, and she grabbed my hand. It was her who started it. I was reticent at first, but she seemed so interested that I fell into her game. We found the woman turning into Jowett Walk. For her frail frame, she walked at a good pace. As fast as a loving couple. Her back only a fraction less bent than it had been over the grave, she went past the King's Arms, crossed to the Bodleian side, and stopped at the café in front of Balliol. Leona pulled me inside behind the old lady, who'd taken her hat into her hands.

'English Breakfast, buttered toast?' the waiter asked her.

'Thank you, Sam,' she said in a voice half her age.

'I'll bring it out.'

'Thank you, Sam.'

She turned her back to the counter, and walking right past us without seeming to see us, she went to the café's terrace. While Leona ordered us a pot of green tea, and eyed the café's scones, I observed the old woman: she pulled out an aluminium chair and settled down. Seated, there was something haughty about the way she scanned over her fellow customers. When she finished her inspection, she pursed her lips, reached inside her bag and pulled out a notebook. Leona and I peered at it once we were closer, on a table of our own, a few yards away from the old lady's. Its burgundy leather had cracks splitting it front and back. Even though there was no chance the lady with the black hat would have heard us, Leona leaned close to whisper. 1985, she said. It was possible.

The old lady's face remained very still, her eyes brittle as she focused on the notebook. She took a finger to her mouth, licked it, and lowered it to a page. After ten minutes, Leona suddenly squirmed in her chair.

'Where do you normally go after the cemetery?' she said.

'The Parks, but wait...'

I held a hand up, still watching the old woman.

'Let's go now. There's rain coming,' she said.

'Wait.'

The old lady sipped her tea one last time, stood up slowly, the chair catching on the terrace's asphalt. Her white hands brushed crumbs off her black dress. She grabbed her bag and left. We watched her, between mouthfuls of scone, cream and jam, until she came to the bus stop outside Sainsbury's.

'She forgot her notebook,' Leona said.

It was spread open on the table, and I couldn't see the old lady anymore. I stood up.

'Don't!'

Leona tried to pull me down by my shirt. She asked me to sit down, to leave the notebook alone, but I pushed her hand aside.

It was her idea, I told her and I went to look it over. A dull and dirty white page flickered with the breeze. There was nothing written on it, nothing written anywhere in the notebook. But in between two pages, there was a lump. It was a bright magazine: a beautiful blonde with two necklaces and a black frock, her face too airbrushed to be real; and headlines about the rich and famous, about a new sex position. I held it up to Leona, challenging her with it, and then I went to give the notebook and its content to the waiter.

'What did you have to do that for?' she asked me, but I could have asked her the same.

By the time we reached the Parks, we were talking about something else, but I felt it for the rest of the day. And I remembered it as I made my list: you can't start something like that and not finish it.

She stirred, and she was lying on her back again, her breathing thickening and catching halfway up her throat. More fodder for my list.

Four. Her Russian philosopher and the time she spent talking about him. There was something wrong with it but I couldn't quite work out what that was.

Like on the bus ride from my brother's place to Leicester Square, when images from the day mingled with thoughts from the past. She was looking out of the window. I grabbed her hand, put it on my thigh, and covered her cold fingertips with my palm. Breaking out of her reverie, she smiled at me.

'James is nice,' she said.

'In a way. What was it you were saying about forgiveness?'

'Forgiveness?' She became serious. 'It's not something you do once and forget. No, it's a state of being. You see' – she put her hand on my heart – 'when you stop thinking, when you stop judging, you embrace everything, and forgiveness embraces you.'

'Like a kind sort of love?'

'Yes, exactly,' she said, looking delighted. 'That's forgiveness. Isn't it wonderful?'

I went quiet for a minute. Then I asked her whether that was what she felt towards my brother.

'Of course. He doesn't deserve anything less, don't you think?'

'He hurt people,' I said.

'He hurt himself more. But that doesn't matter. What matters is him today.'

I raised her hand to my lips and kissed it. I admired her then, and yet I wished it had come out of her naturally, rather than out of that black book, its white symbol, and the foreign name on its cover.

Five. The way I couldn't tell her certain things. Like the time she'd talked about skiing, and I wanted to tell her of my first time off-piste, when her brother had taken me between two trees for a short chute, but we'd ended up in a flat bowl, and had to trek two hundred yards through two feet of fresh powder. Or later, on the train back from London, when she asked me what I thought the problem was with my brother, and I skirted around my departure, unable to tell her exactly why I'd had to leave. Or this dream, of her brother and Eric, which I had to deal with by myself.

I imagined myself waking her up and telling her everything, and for a second I had my hand on her shoulder, ready to shake her awake, but then I seethed, forgot my list, and I went to the little bedroom. There, I pulled out a sheet of paper, and I started drawing a spaceship.

* * *

For the rest of our first month together, Leona spent four nights a week at mine. The first few days, she rang the bell before she entered, but soon she learned to let herself in. It first happened when one of my course's group meetings lasted until the library closed. I came home to find her sleeping on the couch, curled up into a ball, a light blanket thrown over her, and a lukewarm curry in a pot. As it happened again, I learned to recognise the sound of the first door opening, her steps skimming the stairs, her key clattering on the edge of the lock, sliding in with a quick rattle, and the door's late creak while it swung open. She would walk in and tell me about a funny customer, unrequited love between two of her colleagues, or the French lady she'd served, and how much she was looking forward to starting classes again in late September.

When she spent the night, I had much time to watch her sleep: the early hours, when she lay very still and nothing moved but her chest; the four o'clock toilet run; and then the agitated slump, when I kept on thinking that she'd wake up, but when, in fact, I could breathe in her ear, poke her ribs, only to see her change side and sleep some more. On good nights, the ones when food and sex came together, I slept six, seven hours. One night, I managed nine. On other nights, when we had a drink too many, or when a little rust seeped into my sleep, I had to leave my bed by five in the morning, or risk the caprices of memories and dreams. Then, I went to the little bedroom, and I drew or pretended to draw. And I always made sure I was back in bed by eight, for Leona liked me next to her when she woke up.

On one occasion, after a big night with Mike the South African, after Leona had convinced both of us that we had to drink a pint and a shot for every one of her half-pints, I worked on my spaceship from three until eight in the morning. I was convinced of it: with my design, NASA could send astronauts to Mars in under a month, and that was a reasonable timeframe for trained professionals. Minutes after I snuck back into bed, Leona opened her eyes and, in her quiet morning voice, asked me why I hadn't been in bed around six.

'I was drawing,' I said.

'At six in the morning?'

I had to lie, but I turned my head away so she wouldn't see it.

'I don't need to sleep much.'

After that day, she started to refer to the little bedroom as my studio, and she never entered it without asking my permission first.

* * *

Three days after we visited my brother, my mother dropped in for tea while Leona was at work. A conference poster rolled up under one arm, her laptop in her other hand, she put her things down on the coffee table, and studied her surroundings. I unfurled her poster and looked at its pictures of brains, its stylised experimental designs.

'You look smug.' My mother looked at me with a smile.

'Do I?' I said, putting the poster down. 'The course is interesting, I guess. And I like this place.'

She gazed around the living room, her eyes fastening on a bunch of wild flowers Leona had picked on one of her walks.

'Have you met someone?'

'Yeah, I guess.' I picked up the poster again and pretended to delve into it.

'Oh! What's she like?'

'She's nice. Just a girl, I guess.'

My mother looked at me for a second, her lips silently reaching for words, but then, seeing my averted eyes, she pointed at the poster and started explaining her student's experiment. When I told Leona that my mother had worked out I'd met someone, she told me that after all she'd heard about her, she wanted to meet her.

'I didn't talk about her, did I?'

'No, but James did.'

'He's been fighting with her,' I said.

'She sounded…' she looked for the right word '…formidable.'

'Yeah, I guess she is. She used to be anyway.'

'Well, I'd love to meet her! And you must meet my parents. It didn't work out last time, but when you have less work, they want to meet you.'

With those words, I realised she hadn't told them who I was, but I didn't pick up on it. Ever since I'd mentioned Jeffrey on the train, I'd been careful to keep our common past from the surface. Sometimes, when work made me particularly stressed and I was yearning for my fifth cup of coffee, I told myself I had to bring it up, but whenever an opportunity presented itself, I shied away, both glad and frustrated that I'd avoided it.

Two days after my mother came to see me, I went to have dinner with both of my parents. It was a hot night, and for once my father had left his sports jacket in his room. In his tieless shirt, with the sleeves rolled up, he looked like he was enjoying the summer.

'Liz tells me you have a girlfriend. Is that true?'

'Yes,' I said and I attacked my mother's staple dish, a potato gratin, with more vigour than usual.

'Who is she?'

My father's eyes were looking directly into mine, his eating hand lying still, waiting for my answer.

'Leona.'

'Leona who?'

I cringed inside, but I spoke on because I didn't want to mark a pause.

'Baker. Leona Baker.'

My mother's fork clattered on her plate.

'Leona Baker,' she said. 'Which Baker? Jeffrey's sister?'

My eyes looking anywhere but at my mother, I said in a small voice:

'Is it that bad?'

I heard her gulping some water.

'No, no, of course not. But Jeffrey's sister…' She closed her eyes. 'It's just that there are so many other girls out there. Couldn't you have chosen someone else?'

'Maybe. But it just happened. I didn't know who she was when it happened. And then…'

'Oh, Nate. It's just going to make it more difficult. Can you—'

My father interrupted her:

'Liz, you told me yourself, everyone copes differently. Let him cope how he wants to cope.'

'What do you mean?' I asked, seeing an opening. 'How did others cope?'

'Your mother knows better. Tell him, Liz.'

My mother looked shaken, but with every word, she seemed to regain her colour. She told me about some of my classmates. Harry who'd moved to Australia as soon as he finished university, and who was doing very well, according to his mother. Worked in the mines near Perth, and he had a surfboard strapped to his Landcruiser. Beth who had gone to spend a year in Africa, and had come back five years later with a black girlfriend – long-limbed with a queenly profile. They were still together and I laughed, for I'd been right all along, and Jeffrey had nothing to blame himself about: it's hard for a man to compete with a woman. My mother smiled with me, and then she averted her eyes. It was about John, who'd become so depressed he'd tried, and failed, to take his own life twice. Cheerful daring John who'd terrorised and delighted the teachers with his pranks. He'd changed, I guessed. Everyone had changed.

'He hasn't done anything like that for years now, thank God. But it was too much for his parents. They split up last year,' she said.

And there was Josh, who'd gone to Cambridge, got a first, and found a job in the City, or Jeremy who was now working for the Foreign Office.

'Like nothing happened,' she said, and she looked at my father. 'Very different, aren't they?'

The more we talked about the others and their turnabouts, their failures, their unnatural rectitude, the more we, the Dillinghams, felt like a normal family. I'd gone away for a while, James had done a lot of drugs, my parents had nearly split up, but all in all, we were alright.

My mother kept on speaking: Eric's mother had moved to New Zealand, and she'd stopped answering her emails months after she'd arrived. And Jayvanti's family had moved to India at the end of the 1999–2000 school year, but they were back in England now. 'That's what Charlotte told me anyway. Do you remember Charlotte?'

When I said I ought to go home, my mother escorted me out. She walked with me all the way to Banbury Road.

'Leona…' she started. We took a few more steps. 'Do you think that Leona is a wise choice?' she said, her voice taking on her tutorial tones.

'I didn't choose her because she's Jeffrey's sister, Mum. She's just really nice.'

She nodded thoughtfully. We crossed a road and she started again:

'With her, will you be able to leave what happened behind?'

'I've done that already, Mum. It's been eight years.'

She nodded again, and walked silently with me for a few minutes. Then she grabbed my arm, and said she was going to go back home.

'Give your mother a hug. You've grown so much. Not my little boy anymore.' She reached up and flicked a strand of my hair into place. Then she turned back.

* * *

Three days before our one-month anniversary, I bought a bottle of Cava and put it in the Cowley flat fridge.

'Champagne!' Leona said, when she found it.

I put my brush down and came out of the smaller bedroom, the room Leona had labelled my studio.

'You bought champagne! What for?' she asked with a smile.

'For our first month.'

'But we said we'd only get champagne for nos quatre mois.'

'It's not champagne, it's Cava.'

She studied the label and smiled. But then a worried expression came over her face.

'Oh no, we have to keep it for some other occasion.'

'Why?' I asked.

'I thought we'd go to my house for dinner that night.'

I could hear it in her words, I could see it in her frown – this time, there was no point in changing the topic. So, as though I'd yearned to see her parents all along, I told her that I could skip class for one night. There was an uneasy lump stopping me from smiling fully. It stayed with me as the date approached – the Bakers were nice people, I knew, but I hadn't spoken to them since Jeffrey had died, and I could feel it deep inside: that had changed everything. To them, I was the one who'd seen him last. To me, I was the one who'd failed their darling, my best friend.

The day before our one-month anniversary, when we were sitting on the sofa, her head on my lap, my hand in her hair, I asked her whether her mother knew who I was.

'Yes, I told her.'

'What did you tell her?'

'That you were funny, good-looking, that you were called Nathan, that you were doing a bridging course. Everything!'

I shook my head.

'Tell her my full name, Leona. Please.'

The next day, hours before the dinner, we spoke on the phone and I asked her the same question.

'Don't worry, she knows.'

'Leona,' I said, enunciating every syllable, 'let me know when you've told her.'

'Yes, yes, she knows.'

'You're at home now, aren't you?'

'I am.' She sounded cornered.

'Then do it now, and let me know what she says.'

Forty-five minutes later, I received a text: Done. Come at 7, x.

* * *

Amanda Baker was a young mother. She was twenty-two when she had Jeffrey, twenty-seven when I first met her, and thirty-one when I came across her bare-breasted in the Churchill Street sunroom. I pretended not to stare, but I still see her reclining, wearing only a bikini bottom, the rest of her body offered to my lust. She saw me through half-opened eyelids, she asked me how I was, and she went back to the sun.

I loved her breasts. They were still big with milk, sitting on her ribcage with a life of their own. They seemed to spread every time she breathed out, to perk up every time she breathed in. I don't know which I liked best. All I know is that I wanted to touch them, to put my mouth on their broad nipples. I imagined them dangling in front of my wagging tongue, and I blushed. For almost a year, until I came across my first *Playboy*, I stole glances at her breasts, clad in a simple t-shirt, blouse, white button-up shirt, in the grey-blue shirt that fitted her so well, or underneath a winter jacket, and I remembered them as I'd once seen them in the sunroom.

I remember David, her husband, flattening her breasts against his chest once, and me, little me, not listening to what Jeffrey had to tell me, but asking myself whether she felt any pain. Years later, when I first kissed a girl, I brought her to me in that same embrace. And an instant before our lips touched, I asked myself whether I was hurting her breasts.

Three or four times, Amanda told me how shy and quiet I'd been when I first came to their house. I must have been five. 'But one day, I was making raspberry jam, and you came into the kitchen all wide-eyed. I asked you what you wanted, and you just stayed there, all quiet, looking at me stirring my jam.' She laughed her slow laugh. 'So I went to the fridge, and I took out a jar of blackberry jam I'd made the previous night. When I turned around, you didn't know what to look at: the jam in my hand, or the one on the stove. I opened the jar, and I waved you closer. Smell it, I said, smell it. And your eyes! "Do you want some?" I said, and your eyes went even bigger. Half your face, they were. You were very cute, tall as that, you were.' She chuckled. 'You couldn't say yes, you were so shy. So I handed you a big spoonful. You took it with both hands, you did, and you were all serious, licking every last bit off the spoon. Then you handed it back to me, and I said "Do you want more?", and you nodded, and I said "Do you want more?", and this time you spoke. You said "Yes, please".'

Amanda was a stay-at-home mother. For a few years, while David was persisting with his flower shop, she worked behind the counter in the afternoons. But then, as his organic restaurant took off, she went back to minding house and children. When I was six, I asked my mother why she wasn't at home more.

'Jeffrey's mum is always at home,' I said.

'But Jeffrey's mum doesn't work. Mummy works.'

'Why?'

'Because working is important.'

'But Jeffrey's mum doesn't work!'

'Of course, she works. She cleans, she makes meals. Who makes you food when you go to see Jeffrey?'

'You do that too. I don't want you to work! I want you to be like her.'

For many years afterwards, before administrative duties forced her back into her office, my mother came home in the afternoons, and, keeping an eye on James and me, she worked in the corner room until dinner time.

Even though we had a bigger house, a bigger garden, and a ping-pong table, Jeffrey and I still spent most of our time at his house. There was something about the place and it wasn't just his mother. Something about its age: an old farmhouse that Oxford had swallowed as it grew. Everything in it seemed right. The mattress on the floor, which we could easily stand upright to play Lego. The high yellow-brick wall at the back, around which we must have invented fifty games. The apple tree in the corner and its waist-high branches, which we could use to climb the wall and retrieve the ball. The sunroom to play Uno in winter. And the plastic table in the garden, when we were older and we had to talk girls and cricket over a ginger ale.

When I rang the bell for the first time since Jeffrey's death, Leona greeted me in her green summer dress, the one which left her tanned shoulders bare, a handful of silver bracelets tinging from her wrist to the heel of her palm. She kissed me on the porch, took my hand, and dragged me into the house. I listened to her with one ear – her sixteen-year-old sister was spending the night at her boyfriend's – while I looked around. At first, nothing seemed to have changed: there were still the dog's basket, shelves crammed full of multi-coloured books, magazines, pamphlets, and a door-less cabinet full of shoes, with four pairs of wellies overspilling on its side. But then, some details stood out: there never used to be a fish bowl on that console in the living room; that blue sofa was new, yes, it'd replaced that patched-up orange divan I'd found so disquieting; and that Labrador sniffing my leg wasn't Robyn.

'Come!' Leona said. 'Mum's in the kitchen, Dad's outside. Let's go say hi.'

Amanda Baker was busy chopping an onion, her back turned to me. With that first glimpse, I asked myself whether I should call her Amanda, as I used to, or Mrs Baker. She turned around and wiped her hands on her apron. There were obvious signs of age: wrinkles around her mouth, the pink in her skin gone grey, a stone around her waist. Yet, she was the woman I'd known: thick blonde hair stood an inch above her skull; the curves of my boyish fantasies had become bigger. I didn't know why, but that made them more comforting.

'Nate, glad to see you. Come in, come in. Give me a second, I'll wash my hands first, and then I'll come and give you a kiss.' After a cursory rinse, she took hold of my elbows and studied my face. 'You'd look better shaved. You have a nice chin, don't you hide it. Well, how are you?'

'Fine, and you, Amanda?'

'Fine. Splendid. Sit down, sit down. You've become quite the man now, Nate. Not the boy I knew. Isn't he handsome, Leona?'

Standing on an arched leg, Leona smiled at her mother.

'Yes, she told me that you go by Nathan now. But old habits, you know how it is.'

'It doesn't matter. Nate, Nathan, it's all the same… The house looks nice.'

Leona grabbed my hand:

'Do you want a tour?'

I looked at her awkwardly. Then I turned towards her mother, unsure of what I should say.

'Nothing's changed,' said Amanda. 'You can show him later, darling. Why don't you take him to see your father instead? And tell your sister we'll be eating in a few minutes. She still hasn't set the table.'

Leona rolled her eyes and shook her head. I followed her to the bottom of the stairs. 'Vicki! Mum wants you!' she had to shout three times before we heard an answer. In the meantime,

I looked at the family photos by the staircase. There was a haphazard progression going left to right, as time added more and more frames: at first, the wedding picture, black and white grandparents shots. Then a St-Maxime holiday with friends and no children. And further right, baby shots, family reunions, the girls dancing, a picture of Leona in a ball gown, the three sisters hugging each other. I looked more attentively: there was a picture of a baby in a young Amanda's arms. And a group shot of the family in the Alps, Jeffrey to the right of the frame, buried beneath a bright green ski parka and a red hat. Besides these two pictures, there was no other sign left of my friend.

'Is she coming down?' I asked.

'She'll come down when she feels like it. Let's go see Dad,' she said and she loped away.

There was a new hedge against the garden's back wall – the yellow bricks only broke through in glimpses. David was busy watering plants in a little patch where the apple tree had stood. When he saw me, he squinted hard.

'Dad, come and say hi!'

He poured a little water into his palms, rubbed them together vigorously, flicked the water off, and offered me his large hand. It was our first handshake. Before, he'd always taken my presence for granted. If anything, he'd pat me on the shoulder and hurry away. By the time I was old enough to form my own impression of the man, he'd become too busy to play cricket: there was his shop, his employees, tax returns, his restaurant, a problem with his suppliers. But, from the titbits Leona had divulged, I understood that his organic business had taken off, and that the family had finally come into a stable financial situation.

'The garden's changed a lot,' I said.

He frowned.

'Yes.' He went silent. 'So you're having dinner with us tonight?'

I glanced at Leona. She was bending down by the tomato plants.

'Yes.'

'Good.' He turned to his daughter. 'How long until dinner's ready?'

We went back to the kitchen. Looking for something to do, I set the table. At first, Leona grumbled it was her sister's duty, but then she helped me, and soon we were exchanging smiles over forks and knifes. Vicki came down just as we were finishing. 'Typical,' Leona whispered. There was something in her statement. I had almost no memory of Vicki, but on seeing her, I recalled how she used to make me feel.

'I remember you,' Vicki said just before dinner. 'You had big pimples on your nose. They're gone now. How did you get rid of them?'

She sounded like she really wanted to know – perhaps out of mere curiosity, or perhaps so that she could deal with the clusters on her own temples. It took me a second to react.

It happened again over dinner, when Amanda left the table to fetch more wine, and Vicki asked me what I was doing. I told her about my summer course.

'But why haven't you finished school?' she asked, just as her mother was walking back into the dining room.

'Darling, the sort of questions you ask!' Amanda said.

'Was I being insensitive?'

'No,' I rushed in. 'No, of course not. You know…' I could see Amanda's face growing more worried. 'I really felt like I had to leave. After all that happened, I couldn't stay. Does that make sense?'

'Not really,' she said.

Her father cut in:

'Vicki, don't be thick.'

She shut her mouth, stared at her plate for ten seconds, and jumped to her feet. Her chair toppled and hit the floor. After exchanging a look with his wife, her father went after her.

'Have some vegetables,' Amanda told me. 'Go ahead, serve yourself.'

I felt Leona's hand brush my thigh under the table. The first time felt accidental, but then I felt her knuckles run against my trousers. Her lips were pursed mischievously, as if the whole outburst hadn't happened. Her mother was recounting a scandal about a local councillor, looking as if she expected me to listen, or contribute even, while Leona's hand was brushing, poking, squeezing, and most of all, eluding my grasp. The fifth time I tried to grab her hand, Vicki came back with her father, her cheeks damp but her face otherwise composed, and I once again felt that I was to blame for the awkwardness in the air.

'Leona tells me you were living in the Alps,' Amanda said.

'Yeah, I worked a few seasons there.'

'Oh, and were you falling off cliffs then too?'

'I remember that,' David said. 'I tried to rescue you. If that tree hadn't caught me, I would have landed on you,' he chuckled.

Vicki stayed quiet while we compared ski slopes and mountain shapes. Leona chirped in once or twice, but for the most part, she seemed happy to watch me immersed in her family. Her hand squeezed mine whenever her parents laughed. After snow, it was sand, and then, as the meal neared its end, I asked David about his business. I could see it in the three women's faces – it was the right question at the right time. Even Vicki nodded. Warmed by half a bottle of wine, mellowed by an apple and rhubarb pie, his voice went low, and softly, he recounted his original vision and its happy realisation.

* * *

Dinner ended when Amanda laid both hands on the table and stood up. While I fretted over a drying rack with a damp towel, she asked me what I wanted for breakfast. Then she asked Leona whether we needed another mattress. Leona shook her head, a half-smile on her lips. And so, to my surprise, I realised that I was expected to spend the night at their house, with Leona, in her single bed.

'Give him a towel,' Amanda said.

Her bare shoulders pointing proudly forward, Leona led me past the picture frames and up the stairs. I had my right hand in hers; the other trailed over the dark wood handrail.

'The bathroom's at the end of the corridor. Come, I'll give you a towel.'

While she looked through a drawer by the bath, I turned and looked at the four doors, two on either side, giving onto the corridor. The close one on the left used to be her parents' room; the three girls used to share the room on the right.

'Which one's your room?'

'The one by the stairs.'

'That used to be your father's office.'

'Not that one. That's Vicki's room. The other one.'

She grabbed my hips and whispered in my ear:

'I have your towel. Let's go to bed.'

She laced her arms around my stomach and pressed her breasts against my back. Her hair tickling my ear, she pushed me, step by step, towards the door. When she reached for the doorknob, I expected blue walls covered with Led Zeppelin posters, a mattress on the floor, and dusty Lego boxes next to the window. Instead, the corridor light shone on a narrow futon, traced shadows around hung picture frames.

We reached for the shoulder-high light switch at the same time.

'How did you know it was there?'

'Just guessed... That's where they always are, right?'

The walls were pinkish now; the fluffy carpet was gone, stripped off to the original wooden floor, a brown rug covering half the strips; there was a small desk with a computer where the Lego boxes used to be.

She put her things down, turned on a weak desk light and flicked the ceiling light off.

'I've slept on this bed most of my life, but I've never had a boy here before,' she said, her lips inches from mine.

I smiled and she kissed me. Tugging my belt, she pulled me down onto her. While I was on top, I smelled her hair, tasted apples on her lips, blew hot air on the side of her neck. But when we tumbled over, I lay flat on my back, a hand and a leg propping our two bodies back onto the bed. She laid her head on my chest, and I looked up at the slanted ceiling, on which I'd bumped my head many times before. The top three buttons of my shirt were undone, and her lips were edging towards my nipple. The paint on the walls was mauve – perhaps they'd tried to paint it pink, and it'd become this colour because of Jeffrey's blue.

I crossed my arms over her shoulders and pinned her against my chest.

'I don't understand,' I said.

She sighed, and I felt her breath under my shirt.

'What?'

'This is Jeffrey's room.'

She instantly stiffened; the point of her chin pressed hard into my ribcage.

'It was,' she said.

'Yeah, it was. And you haven't said anything about it.'

Her hand found my navel under my shirt. She scratched her nail against its contour until I felt a deep burn, and with the pain came the feeling that I wasn't holding the girl I'd met in the Covered Market. The Leona scraping the top layer off my stomach wasn't trying to tease me. She was trying to hurt me.

'No,' she said tightly. 'Why would I?'

The hostility in her voice stopped me for a second. But I had a right to speak.

'I don't know,' I started. 'It's not a small thing. It's like you've forgotten him.' Her finger started digging into my navel. 'Easy there!' I tried to move her finger but she didn't budge. Now that I'd started speaking, I had to finish: 'You're in his room and… No pictures of him anywhere. We didn't talk about him at dinner either. It feels strange. When I used to come here, I spent all of my time with your brother. Now, nothing…'

'So what, you expected a shrine?'

She took her finger out of my navel, and started kneading my stomach, as if she were trying to pull my intestines out through my abdomen wall.

'No, no, I don't know what I expected. Stop, you're hurting me!' I reached for her hand, but she was too strong for me. This meant more to her than it did to me. All I could do was move her hand to my back. When the pain stopped, I added: 'Each to their own, I guess.'

'There's not going to be a shrine! I haven't forgotten him. He's with all of us, alright?'

Her nail cleaved a path into the small of my back.

'Yes, he is. Of course, he is,' I whispered. 'It's alright. Just a random thought, that's all. Nothing to worry about.'

'I don't have to apologise.'

'No, you don't. Don't worry. Here, give me your hand. Softly now, don't hold so hard, that hurts. Softly.'

She propped herself on her elbow, let go of my hand, and stared at my crotch.

'Are you hard?' she said, and she reached for my crotch. 'Why aren't you hard?' She turned towards me, her hair dishevelled, strands shrouding her eyes. 'Take your shirt off.'

I undid a button.

'That's too slow.' She grabbed a button and pulled. When it didn't give, she used both hands and yanked hard. The shirt opened, and two buttons landed on the wooden floor.

'You're getting hard. Hurry up,' she said.

I didn't have time to react. It's a testament to denim that she didn't rip my jeans off. She straddled me without worrying about a condom. When I tried to take her top off, she pushed me back on the bed. She raised her hand and curled it into a fist. I tracked it as it rose high and fell in a sure arc towards my face. I caught it not a foot away. Her hand yanked back up immediately. This time, I put my arms up in a shield, but her fist followed a different arc, and she beat her chest three times, just between her collar-bones. The third time, she dropped her hand to her side and grabbed hold of my thigh, clawing her nails into my flesh. With that gesture, I stopped being afraid, and the pain ruffled me in a nice way. Her eyelids half closed, she looked at the ceiling while her hips swivelled. We changed position once, when she asked me to take her from behind. 'Slower, slower,' she said. 'In circles, yes, that's it.' And a minute later: 'Faster! Faster!'

I obeyed until she collapsed. I put my arms around her: the tension in her body stayed for a few minutes, and then it was gone, and she was as soft as she'd always been. She cried quietly and fell asleep.

* * *

David and Amanda were whispering in the corridor and the sun was beating on the curtains. It was 6 a.m. I could make out what they were saying through the door. I remembered Leona's yelping, grunting, screeching only hours earlier. Readjusting the pillow under my head, I closed my eyes and hoped the darkness would absolve me. Time passed, but sleep stayed a step away.

To avoid the dreams, I tried to think. In his room, as hot in the morning as it used to be, I couldn't help but think of him.

There was a dent in a beam above me that I recognised. His oldest cricket bat in hand, the one with the chopped toe, he'd been tossing a tennis ball and I'd been hitting him catches. But as the memory sharpened, I felt a ghost spread from my oesophagus. And it flashed to life: his leg twitching its last, all the more powerful for the grunt that he couldn't hold back. I forced it down, and my bat smashed into the beam.

'Shit!' I said, but Jeffrey laughed, and his laugh became increasingly guttural. It took a sudden rush of will, and the moment was gone. The dark shook, and a tree propped me high, its leaves shielding me from the sun, its branches ready to catch me if I jumped. Eric was talking, but no, I would not listen! Once was enough. I knew better now. I distorted his voice until it was nonsense, until it became two voices.

David and Amanda were in their room again, speaking in low tones. Moving Leona's arm from my chest, I spread the sweat beads down to my stomach and closed my eyes. When the front door clicked shut, I couldn't do it anymore. I rose softly so as not to wake Leona up, and put on a jumper over my ruffled shirt to hide the missing buttons.

Amanda was alone downstairs, wiping a kitchen counter.

'Nate, quite the lark, now? You used to sleep until eleven.'

'I wish I still did, but now I'm up before nine even if I went to bed at five. Work habits and all that… I guess that's why I'm going back to my studies,' I said, willing myself into a lighter mood.

'Yes, regular hours do that to people. And that room gets a lot of sun in the mornings. So, you told me you like fruits for breakfast? Well…' She put the kettle on, pulled out a chopping board, and reached for an array of colours: gala apples, strawberries, a kiwi fruit, a pineapple. Her hands got busy, and the fruits were peeled, diced, mixed. 'How about some mint in there?' she said, and I laughed.

'Normally, I just have a couple of bananas,' I said.

'You should be eating a varied diet. And don't you think this is a normal day! It's been a long time since you've been sitting in that chair asking me for more jam.'

I smiled.

'This is better than anything I'd make myself,' I said. Then I remembered seeing her in the supermarket. 'I thought that you wouldn't want...'

I looked at her, hoping I wouldn't have to say more, wishing I hadn't said anything.

'You know I like to cook,' she said, still smiling.

'It's just that last time I saw you...' I started, despite myself.

'When?' she frowned, and then she remembered: 'Oh, Nate, don't be thinking anything like that. It was your mother I was angry with. Never you, now, how could I? You'd just been shot. But Liz...' She hesitated for a second. 'How are you supposed to react when someone asks you how you feel, and then goes and repeats everything you said to some journalist half an hour later? You never saw her, bedbound as you were, but she was always on the phone, and I guess she was worried about you, but... But I guess you know all that now, don't you?'

Apprehension mingling with curiosity, I ignored my unease and kept the conversation on the subject:

'Just that she was on the phone, as you said, but she never made phone calls in front of me. Thought she had to shield me from all that, I suppose.'

'Protect you, yes. Can't fault her there.' She grabbed an apple and studied it. 'I shouldn't be telling you this... But look, I know it was her who told George Hume your story, and I just wish she'd let the police do that. It was their job after all.' She shook her head and put the apple down on the table. 'She was everywhere, Nate, everywhere, and she was the only one who still had her baby breathing.' She paused, and her face opened up. 'Thank God for that.'

I smiled and for a moment, everything was as it used to be. Then she frowned and rose to her feet.

'You know, Leona tells me everything, and what I can tell you is that she's never liked anyone like you before. Now you know what I think of you.' She leaned against the counter, facing me. 'But you see, I'm a little worried. Leona…' She glanced down briefly. 'In my mind, you're Jeffrey's friend first. In David's mind too. The other girls were a bit young. They might not remember. But Leona…'

'She doesn't want to remember,' I said.

'No, it's not that. She cried non-stop for three weeks after he died, she did. And then, one day, her father went to speak to her. Told her she had to make a choice. And she came down and she said she wouldn't cry anymore. And she stopped, didn't shed another tear. You see?'

'I guess.'

'Then, one month after he died, I asked everyone to follow me outside. A few seconds of silence, joining hands around the apple tree. Didn't expect anything, I just thought it was important. Well, Leona, she started yelping, an awful sound! Like a stray dog with a broken leg. We thought the neighbours would call the police. I took her back inside, but she lashed out.' She tapped her stark-white front tooth. 'Fractured. Didn't mean to, of course, and it wasn't hard to fix, standard procedure and all that. Anyway, she calmed down. Took her a few minutes, but she was calm as normal.' Amanda looked straight at me. 'Do you see what I'm getting at?'

I thought I did, but I couldn't quite put it into the right words.

'Leona doesn't like it when Jeffrey comes up,' I tried, 'and I'm… Well, I'm me.'

'No, it's not that. Not just that. But yes,' she said and she smiled strangely. It was a sad yet affectionate smile. 'But she's been so sweet about everything else. Think of it, Nate, all of a sudden, she was the responsible one. And the girls love her. Of course they fight, who doesn't, but they'd give their right arm for her. You should have seen her just before the flower business folded. She wanted to give us all of her savings, all eighty-nine pounds of them! What, she was twelve, and she'd spent years putting every spare coin into her little box. We said no, of course, but she wouldn't hear it. One night, she snuck it under our pillow. That's the sort of heart she has, my little girl.'

She pulled a chair and sat across from me. 'With you, though… What's she like with you?'

'She's fine,' I said, and I went quiet, thinking about what I should say. Then I remembered the previous night's screams.

She chuckled in that slow way of hers: 'You're blushing. Are you in love then?' She stood up and smiled her strange smile. 'I'm happy, I am. Eat as much as you want, I can make you more. It only takes a minute.' She got up and went to her cutting board. Then she turned to me, a thoughtful look over her face:

'Was Leona getting up? She might like some fruits in her muesli. I tell you, children can be complicated sometimes. You'll see when yours start dating.'

* * *

My nights deteriorated until Leona's warmth no longer helped. My pattern was always the same: I watched Leona sleep, until her slow breath became mine, my eyes fell dark, and three hours had gone. Three solid hours before I started to feel my body, hear my thoughts. It was half past two, and dread was building in the gum below my lower teeth. It was four, my mind was too close to that grey heat, and I had to get up. Until daybreak, I sat hunched over my exercise ball in my grand atelier, staring at my A3-sized sketches, hesitating over every stroke. When one proved particularly difficult, I thought half-formed thoughts. Fancy toyed with facts, and Hillary Clinton had won Super Tuesday, Obama was rousing a crowd, and Mike had completed our group's entire assignment, and he was asking me the same question, again and again, and there was Amanda too, in the background, holding a basket of fruit, while she spoke and spoke, a stream of well-formed sentences, each rejoining the other.

I always understood her. After all, she'd only concretised what I'd thought before. But at the same time, there was Leona's raised fist, my fear one second, and my excitement the next, and I was telling myself off. Whenever someone heard my name, saw me as the hero-boy who survived, and twisted me into a five-legged lab rat, my every movement became a mechanical sort of squirm. And there I was, burdening Leona with the same rubbish. Let her be, I thought, and I clung on to the words until they became slick as glass and my fears slid off them.

By daybreak, I was in control but Leona slept on. So I worked and fretted and time passed in its slow swings. In those twilight hours, I was idle and I thought too much – curtailed movements, abstract summaries, sweeping judgements. More than anything, I thought about myself and I came up short. Eight loose years, an atrophied mind, a sagging body... At twenty-six, I had a deep crease across my forehead, a forest drawing its boundaries around my eyes, and a handful of flab around my hips.

Two weeks after I first visited the Bakers, when I'd resigned myself to the drone and drops of many sleepless nights, I decided that I'd use the most wakeful of my pre-Leona day to tackle the one problem I could fix. A pair of shiny yellow running shoes on, my feet thudded and skimmed and thudded Oxford's streets, swerving around the early morning traffic, threading down the white lines splitting one row of houses from another, until my breath ran out and rushed back, and my mouth ballooned into a smile. I came home and showered, and Leona was awake ready to leave for work.

Of course, I should have known how she'd feel. But running was making me happy and blind. She waited until the morning of my sixth run before she put her foot down and asked for a bit of her own. Now, with the benefit of hindsight, I can put two and two together and come close to four.

In our first week, she'd seen the best of me – a happy man gone bold with passion, tickling and teasing like there never was a dull moment. With that man, she'd shared body and late-night murmurs. She'd kneeled to his side so he could talk of his brother, and gently, with a caress and a loving word, she'd helped him talk past a stutter, until his emotions aligned themselves with his confessions. How quickly that all changed! The day she invited me to meet her parents was when it started slipping away. She noticed the silences, she heard the distress in my voice, but she read me right – push and I'd flee. She started to wait. She was good at waiting. Her parents had gone through hard times – they could never fully hide them from her – and she'd seen their trust, their love in each other, in the belief that things would improve. To wait was to build. I wasn't answering her calls, but that was alright: it was her duty to walk alongside me until her love had smoothed my hurts. So she walked and we went to London, and she was happy to see me happy. I never said it out loud (I never had to) but every time I held her in my arms, tightly so I could feel her breasts push against my chest with each of my breaths, I was thanking her, I was rewarding her, and she kept on putting up with my irritable mornings, my sudden vacant stares.

Such moments mattered. Opening her eyes in the mornings and finding me lying next to her, or sitting on the pile of cushions we'd stacked on top of the flat's gardening books, eyes adoringly resting on her shapes (she was getting up, finally!). With her slow smile, pulling me into bed alongside her. Even I knew that of all our little rituals, this was the most important – sleep almost overtaking me while it left her, her possessive hand resting on my groin, close but far from my subdued arousal, her limbs gradually stretching, her lips moaning with the last of their haze, until the little hand ticked over the I and the X and she had to go to work. It was like a hinted vow, those mornings, and right after the past had come closest to the surface, in Jeffrey's old room, when she needed it most, I'd taken it away from her just so that I could indulge in a runner's high.

On the morning of my first run, sweat dripping down my temples, I'd thrust my chest out and, with a dominant laugh, told her to look at the time. There was life to be lived, and she was moping around in bed. I was being bullish, oafish, all in the name of a better night's sleep.

* * *

I was so good at ignoring the signs that when she grabbed my freshly showered wrist on the morning of my sixth run, I felt nothing but blind worry. There was the girl who'd forgiven me everything finally telling me that something was wrong (in me, I knew, even if she was too diplomatic to say it), and all of my self-preserving thoughts were probing into the dark.

'What is it?' I said.

'We haven't…' She hesitated.

I thought about sex, which we certainly had.

'What haven't we done?' I sat on the bed.

'We don't talk as much as before.'

She looked away, only furtively glancing at me, as if there were shame to her concern. I winced. It was serious. And to make it worse, it wasn't the first time a girlfriend had made that complaint. Marie had said the same thing the first time we'd followed the seasons, and moved from mountains to sea. Then, I'd tried talking work – my boss fighting with the manager he couldn't fire. I'd tried talking ex-girlfriends – Sally and the rosy catalogue in which she documented the torsos of all the men she'd slept with. But nothing worked: Marie's reproach hung in the air for a whole month, until she took a day off and dropped in on me unannounced at work. In a flimsy summer dress, the sort I wanted her to wear all the time, she strolled between two rows of Russian models tanning topless, grabbed my arse and stuck her tongue in my mouth. After that day, I put my English sensibilities to the side and embraced public displays of affection.

But with Leona, it was different. She wasn't the jealous type. All of the friends she'd presented to me had been girls. When we were at the White Horse one evening and a colleague called to see whether Leona could cover her shift, she'd left me with a full pint and the prettiest of her friends.

I was sitting on the bed, a sock on my left foot, the other in my hands. She was lying down behind me. Casually, I threw my legs on the bed.

'Have we run out of things to say?' I said playfully. Playful was best. 'Because you know, if you want, I can read you my books to sleep. Plenty of things to say in there.' I grabbed one by the bedside and, lying next to her, I opened it. 'You ready?'

She smiled feebly.

'No,' she said.

'What, you don't want to hear about World War II Britain?'

'Not right now,' she said.

I threw one arm over her and brought her closer.

'Well then, what shall we talk about?'

She smiled with tight lips and laughed through her nose. A little wistfully, it seemed.

'I don't know,' she whispered, looking at me. Now I was certain of it, the buried wistfulness.

She reached for my other arm, placing it pillow-flat under her head. Her hair safely disentangled, she turned to face the ceiling.

'How about I tell you a story?' I said. 'I'll make one up. Are you ready?' I cleared my throat. 'Once upon a time, there was a princess. All over the world, people talked of her beauty and intelligence. Every little girl dreamed of having her rich blonde hair and kind blue eyes. Every father dreamed of hearing her advice. But her heart was already taken. By a great prince, mind you, very handsome, and also pretty funny, in case you hadn't guessed. So, I forgot to tell you, but this story is pretty short. Beautiful princess, very, let me repeat, very handsome prince. No need for a happy ending, I've given you a happy beginning.'

To my relief, her muted smile seemed to loosen. A few seconds into my story, my mind had gone back to my post-run blank, and I'd had to wriggle away with more warmth than wit. Now, it would take another minute of play, and I'd be able to start my day.

'Is Brian working today?' I asked her. The question didn't seem to register. 'Or is it just the two of you?'

'Yes.' She glanced at me. 'The two of us,' she said and she went back to her thoughts. Her head, with its spoiled contentment, kept on nailing me to the bed.

'I think that's my phone,' I said, and I pulled free to fetch it. As I bent down and felt for it on the bedside table, I noticed that I had only one sock on. I'd been awake for hours, and I didn't even have my socks on.

'It's my mother,' I said, and read the text out loud: James is in town. Give him a call. I know he'd like to see you. Mum. I turned towards the bed. 'Can you believe it?'

'What?' Leona suddenly sounded more interested.

'She knows how to send texts. I spent a good hour last month teaching her.'

'That's so nice of you...'

My sock was next to my shoes, where it should be. I sat down on the gardening books and put it on. I'd taken off my right shoe, white leather gone dirty with too many dusty walks, without undoing the laces, and they needed some picking.

'What about your brother?'

I looked up. Eyebrows barely lifted, Leona had shifted closer and turned one ear towards me, as if she expected me to whisper. We weren't talking as much as before.

'What? He's the one coming to town. He should be contacting me.'

'He sent me a message,' she said.

'When? You didn't say anything.'

'I haven't had time to say anything. Here...' she grabbed her phone, thumbed through her messages: '... 2.17 a.m.'

My fingers strained, my nails picked, but the laces resisted. I looked up:

'Well, he didn't send me one,' and I picked harder, smarter. This end was probably feeding into this loop. I just needed a moment of leverage, and then it would all come undone.

'Don't you want to know what he said?'

'Not really,' I said too quickly. Her eyes had widened. 'Oh, alright, tell me.'

She hesitated.

'What did he say?' I asked. My nail was mindlessly searching for purchase.

She looked at me for another second. 'Just that he wanted to see us.'

'Us? What did he actually say, Leona?'

She looked at the message. 'That he's in town and it'd be nice to see us.'

'He said you. He meant just you, not me.'

'Why do you say that?'

There it was, the catch I was after. Suddenly, I was pulling and the knot was loosening, and an instant later, I had my foot well shod.

'It's obvious. You saw the way he's with you and the way he's with me.'

I stood up and picked up my history book. It was well past nine. I hadn't walked two steps before Leona called out:

'Don't you want to see him?'

I turned around. She was sitting cross-legged on the bed, her British Telecom t-shirt folding around her thighs, her elbows resting on her knees.

'You're going to be late.' I made a show of looking at my watch.

'It's alright, I'll call work. He won't mind. I'm always early anyway.'

I studied my watch again.

'Come and sit here.' She tapped the bed in front of her. 'Come, I'll give you a massage. After your run, you need one.'

I could hardly walk out of the room now. Churlishly, I followed her instructions. Her fingers soon found their own knots. In circles, jabs, and gentle thrusts, she set to loosen them. Her hands adding to my debt, she remained patiently silent, in her airy humming way.

'You saw the way he treated me in London.' I let my voice trail off, imbuing it with meaning.

'Hmm, hmm.'

Her fingers worked on.

'He didn't want to see me,' I said.

She started on my shoulder blades, and my head swam with pleasure. James was a distant presence.

'Why do you think that is?' she said.

James sprang back to the forefront of my mind: I'd bloody abandoned him for eight years, and now what, I wanted it to be just like before? Please…

'You are tense,' she said. 'You see, it's good we're doing this now.'

I couldn't say anything. Start on James and it'd lead somewhere, everywhere. And there was Amanda to consider.

'What are you thinking?' she asked.

'Nothing.' I could feel her waiting; she could wait and wait, always kindly, lovingly. 'It doesn't have to be big,' I let out. 'Even a small thing is enough sometimes, to drift apart.'

'Yeah.' She sounded thoughtful. 'What do you think that was?'

I shrugged, lifting her hands with my shoulders.

'Take a guess.'

The initial bout of pleasure was gone. Now, I was all resolve.

'I don't know,' I said. 'What do you think?'

She rested her chin on my collar-bone, and I could feel her voice gathering, vibrations spreading with her thoughts. She leaned back and her hands went back to massaging me.

'I think he wants to see you. You know him, he's not good at talking, but inside he's got so much heart.'

Her fingers were soothing. They were working up and down my spine, threading and pinching, up to my neck, brushing my hair.

'What do you think I should do?' I asked her.

She answered straightaway, and I could hear how happy my question had made her.

'Let's invite him for lunch. I'll call Brian. He'll cover for me. Can we? Please?'

* * *

Darkened by the sun, I couldn't make out his face. All I could see was a shape, somewhat like my own, on the other side of the doorsill. We'd never hugged when we were little, but that's what loving brothers were meant to do. That, or like the French, a kiss on both cheeks.

'Hello!' I smiled and extended my arm. I could barely reach him.

'Nate, thanks.' He came closer, and my hand had something to latch on to. An elbow, and then, for I wasn't a politician, it hovered in the air. He glanced at it and, as if it were the last thing standing between him and upstairs, he shook it with three damp fingers. 'Where's Leona?' he said.

'Upstairs, come. Close the door behind you.'

Leona was wiping her hands with a tea towel as I walked in, giving them a final rub on her apron as James followed. She saw him, and she was on tiptoes, smiling, already laughing, her arms outstretched. For a minute, there was their London chatter, a host of questions gone unanswered, until she took a step back, and looked around to see where I was. She'd forgotten me.

She looped her arm in mine.

'I'm almost done. Just finishing the salad. You two talk. You must have so much to say to each other. Give me five minutes and I'll be with you.'

In the indoor light, I could see him better. He stood in my kitchen, one bent knee poking through a hole in his faded jeans, Zola's '*J'accuse*' printed all over a blue t-shirt. Except for his eyes, he looked just like my father. Like me too, I guessed. But there was something foreign in the blurred outline around them, in the lazy way he looked around.

'Nice place,' he said. 'Your stuff?'

I shook my head:

'It came furnished.'

'Leona,' he called, 'did you help him decorate?'

She turned around and grinned at him.

'No, no, it was all here, except for your grandma's paintings.'

He chuckled.

'Give me five minutes and I'll be with you,' she said. 'I'm not good with knives.'

She turned around, and it was once again just the two of us.

'So you're in town just for the day?' I asked.

'Yeah.'

'Oh, how come?'

'I had to pick up some stuff.'

He looked around the room as if he were casting for something more interesting.

'Have you seen Mum and Dad?' I asked.

'No.'

'Are you going to see them?'

'Mum said she has a lecture until three.' He spoke slowly, with plenty of careless pauses. 'If I'm still here, I might say hello.'

He pulled out a cigarette and lit it.

'Do you mind if I smoke here?' he asked me.

'Well, I don't mind, but it's not my place, you see…'

He looked at me, smoke rising to the ceiling.

'It might leave a smell,' I said. He looked at me still. Leona was chopping cucumbers, her back to us. 'It'd be better if you went outside.'

'Fair enough,' he said, and he left the flat, a trail of smoke following him.

When he closed the door, I felt the same burst of anger I used to feel when he'd pretend he'd nicked the ball onto his legs, and that he therefore wasn't out. I turned towards Leona like I'd turned towards my mother, wanting her to be both witness and jury. She looked so cheerful that I ignored her sympathy:

'Oh, come on, I'm trying,' I said.

'You are, I didn't say anything.'

'It's not like he's making it easy.'

'He's shy around you.'

'Forgiveness and all that, does that mean I'm meant to have him smoke up the place?' I asked.

She left her chopping board and shuffled towards me until she was close enough that I couldn't take in both her eyes and her mouth at once.

'Try to talk to him. Go see him outside now.'

'You saw him,' I said. 'He's not going to say anything to me.'

'Talk first then. Tell him things.'

I yanked my head back. My body followed and I could see the whole of her:

'Like what? I haven't seen you for eight years, sorry, but now I think we ought to act like nothing happened.'

'Don't make fun!' she said, hurt.

'I'm not.'

She stepped closer – there was the bedroom wall to my back – and her nose was brushing my lips.

'Don't think, just open up.'

'Open up,' I repeated with a mocking smile. The irony of it! Open up…

'Yes, open up first. You'll see. Come on, go and see him.' She ushered me towards the door. 'When you come back, lunch will be ready.'

Open up. It was the first time she put it into words and it cut straight to the heart of my worries: immediately, I understood that it was what she wanted from me, and that it was what Amanda and common sense forbade me.

James was on the street, looking decidedly dodgy, as if the years he'd spent making Oxford his own had rubbed away with London and his drugs. I thought of Leona's Russian philosopher, and I tried to clear my mind, to embrace forgiveness.

'Leona's almost finished,' I told him. 'She told me to keep you company for a few minutes. She likes being alone in the kitchen, you know?'

He took another puff of his cigarette. Another minute, and it'd be finished.

'She's special, Leona,' I said. 'Always trying to help everyone, don't you think?'

'I don't know,' he said. 'She came to most of our gigs.' He trailed off, and looked at a car driving past.

I sensed an opening:

'Are you still in a band?'

He turned to me and shook his head.

'Oh, actually, I am in one,' he corrected. 'But I haven't seen the guys for a couple of months.'

'What are you called?' I said.

'Gabriel's Drones, I think. That or Suffolk Stoneheads. Can't remember what we agreed on.'

I laughed but he didn't seem to find it funny. He studied the cigarette butt in his fingers, twisting it this way and that, before he flicked it towards a gutter. We went upstairs. I didn't speak much after that. Leona managed the conversation well enough: a laugh, a serious look, even an admonishment, James accepted them all. I did the dishes.

When he left us, she gave me her understanding look. It was almost appreciative, certainly condescending.

'For fuck's sake!' I said. 'It's not my fault!'

'What do you mean?'

'Spare me the rubbish about taking him in my heart!'

Her eyes went moist, and my anger was gone.

'Don't...' I put my hand out but she didn't take it. My fingers hung in the air for a second. Then I blotted the tears off her cheeks.

'It's just...' she sobbed, and I hugged her. 'It's just that you could... Sometimes... just a little... open up.'

'For fuck's sake...'

'Sorry,' she said. 'Not often, but sometimes I want to ...' she hesitated, '... know more.'

'I'm a quiet bloke,' I said.

'I know.'

***

One morning at her parents' house, after I'd spent three hours trying to go back to sleep, I got up quietly and found Amanda busy in the kitchen. When she saw me, she pulled out a fruit salad she'd already made me.

'I found you some raspberries this morning. I hope you like raspberries.' Her proud smile waned as she searched my face. 'You look tired, Nate. That mattress is too small for the two of you. I need to speak to David. Leona needs a double bed now.'

While she spoke, I made myself a pot of coffee, and thought of how I could get her talking.

'That'd be nice,' I answered. With a deep breath, I decided to ask her outright: 'What you were telling me the other day, you know, about Leona not liking to talk about Jeffrey, don't you think that's changed now? That was a long time ago.'

She frowned and clasped her hands together.

'Nate, that was a very hard time for us. Jeffrey... well, you knew him. He was my son. My only son, and there's not a day I don't think of him...' She brought her hands to her heart, and blinked hard. 'But everyone grieves their own way, don't they?'

She studied me and her expression became all kindness.

'Oh, Nate, it's not hurting you, is it? But we have to respect everyone, don't we? And Leona, she's put the whole episode behind her. That's how she dealt with it, and look at her, isn't she a beautiful girl? So we have to help her, don't we?' She shook her head as if she were coming out of a daze, and smiled in her no-nonsense way. 'You know what you need? Vitamins. I'll make you some fresh juice. You like beetroot?'

* * *

There were two women in my life, and I could only keep them away from each other for so long. If it had to happen, I wanted it to be over lunch. It would be more manageable that way: my father would be at work, my mother would only have an hour to spare. And something could always come up: a last-minute appointment, an emergency phone call.

A waft of cookies came from the High Street side of the Covered Market. I waited for Leona in the same aisle in which I'd first asked her out, by the café's sign, in its flaking reds and blues. An old man was bundling tulips in the flower shop. When she came out, folding her apron into her bag, she smiled too – that broad smile that grew until I could see nothing else.

I spoke, I laughed, she smiled. Smiled as we talked, smiled as we rode our bikes, past Exeter and Jesus, and Balliol and St John's, and all the other saints that crowded around the Banbury Road, past the renovated neo-gothic façades and the 1960s concrete blocks they'd tried to conceal behind them. We were in front of the house, and I hadn't found a way to put the lunch off.

Too late: my mother had come out to greet us. I noticed make-up around her eyes for the first time since I'd come back. Leona extended a hand.

'You don't remember me, do you?' my mother said. 'I guess you were only small. You came once or twice with your mother to pick your brother up.'

'She doesn't have the best of memories,' I said.

'No, I remember,' Leona said.

As we walked in, Leona wandered down the corridor, her eyes on the family pictures above my grandmother's cabinet. With a sign, I took my mother aside.

'Don't mention Jeffrey…'

I laid a hand on the wool of her brown jumper: my palm, my fingers seemed too large, too strong for her shoulders.

'Oh, of course,' she said. When I let go of her, she added softly: 'That must be hard for you.'

I winced and turned away.

Lunch was already on the kitchen table: a salad bowl full of greens, a closed pot letting out a hint of steam, poppy seeds lining the bread basket, all neatly arranged in the middle of three place settings.

'So this is where you grew up?' Leona asked me.

'No,' I said, embarrassed.

'Oh,' she said.

My mother gave me a sharp glance.

'In Hornsbury, Leona,' she said. 'You know that.'

'Ah, yes, of course.' Leona's brow aimed at the cupboards above the kitchen counters or at the crown moulding, I couldn't be sure. She pivoted on the balls of her feet and took the whole of the room in. 'Mrs Dillingham?'

'Liz, please, dear.'

'Liz, can I help with anything?'

'Thank you, dear, but it's all ready. Here, sit, sit. Let's eat while it's still hot.'

My mother took the seat at the head of the table, and gestured Leona to her left. With a serving spoon, she reached into the pot until we were all served, each with a slice of bread resting against our split-peas mash. Leona held her fork in hand, with a merry, hopeful expression, waiting for my mother, mirroring her movements. Their forks swooped, gathered and rose an instant from each other.

'Nate tells me you're at university,' my mother said to Leona. 'What are you studying?'

'French. I just finished my first year.'

'She's very good,' I hastened to add.

My mother glanced at me, a fleeting acknowledgement, and then turned her green eyes towards Leona.

'Do you like it?'

Leona's cheeks creased with the smile she was keeping back. 'I absolutely love it,' she said, and she gave way to her happiness.

It made her vulnerable, to show so much so quickly. My mother was nodding, thoughts lengthening her long face. I imagined her in her college office: Leona, her student, formulating answers on the spot, and my mother, the tutor, nudging Leona closer to the right answer with every question.

'That's important. What do you want to do with it?'

'I'm not sure yet.' Leona's voice went small with the possibilities. 'I was thinking of the Foreign Office. But I'd also like to live in France for a few years. Maybe I can do both.' And then her voice perked up: 'But I'll get an idea when the time comes.'

'That's wise,' my mother said. 'It's good to know your options, but it's even more important to know that things won't stay the way they are today.'

Leona, in her own way, was passing my mother's test. Sitting back, eating more than the two of them combined, I watched my mother's questions run out and Leona's start – career choices, life in academia, women in science, she was probing into my mother's secret world, the one she'd kept hidden behind stacks of dry papers and the decorum of obligations.

'Are you interested in academia?'

'I like teaching,' Leona answered.

'If you like teaching, become a teacher. To be a professor, you have to like research.'

'Ah, yes.' Leona stopped to think for a moment. 'But you have students, you said, in your lab.'

'That's in the sciences,' my mother started, and she was telling Leona about the humanities and the loneliness of theses, the toil of publishing, the importance of tagging on to a school of thought, and Leona was agreeing, commenting, exploring.

It was five to two and my mother wouldn't let Leona help her clean up.

'You go back to work, I'll tidy up. It's nothing, I said. Go! Nate will help me, won't you, Nate?'

I walked Leona out, all the way to her bike, sensing her excitement. She grabbed the bike's handle and let it go just as quickly.

'Oh, Nathan, thank you.' She looked over at the house, as if to judge whether her voice would carry. 'After all I heard, I thought she was amazing, Nathan…' she started, and she went thoughtful:

'She looks like an important woman,' she finally said.

Despite myself, I breathed in, proud. My mother's calmness, the evenness in her voice, yes, Leona was right. A soothing breeze carried a leaf into the spokes of Leona's front wheel.

'You know,' Leona said, 'I wish Mum had been a bit more demanding when we were little. Like with the piano. I just wish I'd stuck to it.'

I chuckled: 'I wish my mother had left me alone.'

Leona looked at me seriously:

'What do you mean?' she said.

'I don't know, I was just joking.'

Reproach marred the remnants of her joy.

'It must have been hard for her,' she said. 'You know. Your brother was getting high and you were overseas, don't you think?'

'Yeah.' I grabbed her hips and brought her to me until all I could see was the line of her neck. In the moment it took to make her think about something else, I knew that I ought to give her all that she asked for.

Back inside, my mother was wiping the table. The sink was clean, the dishwasher was purring, the salt and pepper shakers were back on their shelves.

'Let me do that, Mum.'

She pushed a cluster of breadcrumbs into the hollow of her hand, and, leaving the sponge on the table so I could feel like I'd contributed, she opened the kitchen window to feed her summer birds.

'She's a nice girl,' she said.

I wiped the table waiting for the rest. She washed her hands.

'That's all?' I said.

She dried her hands, and hung the tea towel on the oven handle.

'Lovely girl. Such a sweet smile… Yes, she is nice. And it looks like she's got her head on her shoulders. When a girl's as pretty as that, I don't imagine that's something you think about. But believe me, Nate, that's the most important thing.' She closed her eyes and frowned. 'Can't do anything about her family.' Her face smoothening out, she gave me a sad smile. 'I'm happy for you.'

It was buried in the words, but I could hear the same warning that Amanda had given me twice. Coming from both of them, it was easier to dismiss – it was a mother's protective instinct, not a real insight into Leona's character. My doubts, our mothers' doubts, it wasn't my job to put them above Leona's wishes.

* * *

I laid the last of my fears aside on a day that had all that I loved her for. I'd waited for her on a bench in Christchurch Meadow. For the first time that summer, there wasn't a cloud in the sky. Between me and the water, there was the path, its stream of amblers, and a dozen little ducklings circling their mother. Then there was the sun glittering on patches of the river, and a cry of 'Catch it!' coming from the Queens sports ground beyond the water.

I didn't need to look to know that it was her sitting next to me. She put her hand in mine.

'It's been three months,' she said, a gentle glee in her voice.

I smiled.

'One more month and it's nos quatre mois,' she said.

'We should celebrate.' I looked at her.

'No, that's just for nos quatre mois.' She smiled at the river.

'We have to do something,' I said, but I liked where we were.

We watched a punt struggling upriver, a young man in shorts and a boat hat dropping his pole to the deep bottom, bending to his knees to push the punt a few yards, while two girls sat in the back, nibbling on jammed-up scones.

'Let's go punting,' I said.

We stood up.

'Can you come up with a poem?' I asked her. 'A punting poem?'

We spent the rest of the afternoon between our punt and the banks of the Cherwell. An afternoon in the sun, my fingers stroking her forearms, my hand sliding over the fabric of her dress, and above all, her perpetual smile – not the one she had in pictures, but the one she had in bed, when her mouth approached mine, when her upper lip lifted above her gum, when her teeth looked small, her eyes became long, and her pupils shone.

I took a picture of her, at the back of the punt, dripping pole sliding between her fingers, her eyes on the river ahead. And, despite the focus on her face, she couldn't hide the smile she'd had for me a second before.

Later, when clouds appeared and the sun quietened, we walked to the George Street cinema, turning into Cornmarket from the High Street. We pushed our way through a Saturday crowd: teenagers in twos and tens, a busker singing 'Hallelujah!' to the sky, couples drifting in and out of chain stores.

Halfway down, in between the two music outlets, my eyes passed over a man and a young girl. I looked at the man again. A large forehead, a ponderous walk, thick square glasses, and underneath these glasses, dark eyes darting left, darting right, over me, at me. They stopped for a second, his eyes in mine, and then they were looking at something ahead. For that second,

I felt like I'd been thrown into a gigantic copper pot on a slow boil, filled to the brim with eight years of fears. I remembered when he'd come to my house to taunt me, and I remembered his challenge. Oh, I knew what he'd wanted to do: poke the folds of my brain with his dirty fingers, so that he could show everyone else how much tar I'd concealed.

I caught up to Leona. When we were in the cinema, sitting around a bucket of popcorn, she cocked her head and studied me:

'Are you alright? You're a little pale.' She stroked my cheek with the back of her fingers.

'Yeah, it's just…' I looked at her.

'What? You can tell me.'

'Just saw someone, that's all. In the street, I mean.'

'Oh,' she said.

'No, not an ex.'

'Who?'

'Just someone…'

She reached for some popcorn and turned to face the screen.

'Don't take it like that,' I said.

'I'm not. If you want to talk about it, I'm here.'

'Leona,' I sighed, building up courage. 'Andrew Hill, do you know who he is?'

She shook her head.

'He was in charge of the investigation when… When I got shot. He was the one who came to ask me a lot of questions. It wasn't easy, that's all.'

She looped her arm in mine, kissed my shoulder, and rested her warm head against me.

'Yeah, that must have been hard,' she said.

My eyes on the top of her head, I expected her nails to dig into my arms, but instead I watched her crown fall and rise slowly, steadily. A cuddle to thank me – I'd opened up. When the first preview ended, an action thriller full of testosterone and helicopters, she looked at me with a big smile:

'Let's go see that! Do you want to see it?'

The movie flashed and banged, and I saw actors kiss and kill, but I didn't follow the story. My mind was all about the inspector, his challenge echoing within the confines of my skull. And I thought of Leona's easy reaction, I watched her enjoy the movie, as if I'd said nothing out of the ordinary. With a girl like that, I could say anything.

* * *

Three weeks ago, it started raining that soft Oxford rain. Never much more than a dampness in the air; clouds never fully open, never fully closed; the water table steadily rising. Most of the time, we pretended it wasn't there, our umbrella either in my pocket or in her bag. My clothes became wet and then they dried. It never took long. By Saturday, thirteen days ago to the day, the soles of my shoes squelched on the grass at the front of the house, and water seeped through the sides. It started raining harder, and there was standing water on the path to Iffley. The river swelled and rippled, its bottom following the current, its surface following the winds.

That evening, Leona came home with water dripping from her hair. I grabbed a towel and asked her why she hadn't used her umbrella. She said she didn't know.

I laid the towel over her head, covered her skull with my hands, and, in slow circles, I felt the masses of her hair through the cloth. She stood, her arms hanging limp, like a daughter with her father. 'Don't stop,' she said. I kissed where I thought her forehead was. Then I dried her hair some more. And I kissed where I thought her nose was – it was her nose; I knew that bump, even through fluff and threads. Are you dry? I said. I don't know, she said. I put a hand under the towel, through her hair. Then I took my damp fingers to my lips, to my nose. You're not dry, I said. I rubbed harder, and she laughed. Your shirt is wet, I said. What are you going to do? she said. I'm afraid you'll have to take it off, I said.

I took the towel off her head and pulled her shirt up. For a second I held my breath: she stood with her hair ruffled and wet, her eyes closed, leaning back, and the skin of her stomach stretched warm and taut, swelling with her slow breaths, from the hem of her skirt to the frill of her crimson bra. Then she opened her eyes and she turned the lights off.

'You're so dry, so warm,' she said. 'That's not fair.'

She opened the bedroom door and a draught swept past our feet. The door slammed closed behind us. The only light in the room came from the moon through clouds, water, and night. I lay on my back, and I watched water rustle a new path down the window. We moved in a slow, purposeful way. I understood what she was doing when she rubbed her bra against my bare skin, and she understood me when I ran my teeth along her sides. We didn't come the first time. It didn't matter. She had Sunday and Monday off and it was raining.

'I feel like I'm floating,' she said.

'Yeah.'

We floated together, our bed carrying us above the rains.

'What's the thing you feel worst about in your life?' she said.

'My whole life?'

'Yes.'

I studied her. She lay on her back, the sheet covering most of her legs: the one raised knee, the other foot brushing my calf. Her eyes were hazy with dreams. From the first pubic hairs to the hand softly tapping the window, she was naked, all mine.

'What about you?' I asked.

'Me? Let me think about it...' She started singing in that soothing way of hers; in her own language, to her own melody.

She'd only sung that way once before, when our natural distance had crumbled into a pretty heap. Afterwards, while she'd been getting ready for work, I'd replayed her voice and the beauty of her flat notes in my head.

'Vicki,' she said. 'The way I am with her. I can't help it, I try, but sometimes I'm a bitch to her…'

'Bitch how?'

'Well, I don't know how to explain it. When she doesn't do something my mother asks her to do, like watering the herb garden.' Her words focused in a gentle, forgiving way. 'That's her job, you know, but she forgets, or she pretends to forget, and then my father comes home, and it's eleven at night, but he's not going to bed, no, he's watering the plants instead. She doesn't mean any harm, she really doesn't. It's just the way she is. And when my mother asks her, and she doesn't even turn her music down to listen, then I shouldn't, but I do. I get really upset, like she was doing something to me, personally. And I shouldn't, but I did it the other day. I went to her room and… And I asked her what was wrong with her, why she didn't just get it like others do.'

She went quiet.

'That's not so bad.'

'I said it in a really mean way. Like I was just repeating what everyone else says. And you know, the worst is, people do say that. She's never quite with it. She doesn't have many friends, and I know she finds it hard.'

I grimaced as I thought of how much I disliked Vicki.

'Sometimes, it's good to be tough.'

'Yeah, but she's… fragile. All of last year, she wasn't eating properly. Scary how thin she was! But now that that's over, she doesn't need me bringing her down.'

'Oh,' I said, and I glanced at her, looking for a counterweight to the conversation's flow. But nothing had moved except for her eyes. They were looking at her fingers against the window.

'And you?' she said.

'I don't know,' I said. It sounded true when I said it. But in our silence, cushioned by the rain's murmur, a face came to mind. Leona's finger started drawing lines in the fog. First a figure of eight, then a house. Reaching up, I drew a tree next to the house. 'A friend,' I said. 'You don't know him. He's dead. I should...'

'What?' she said, and I detected nothing but quiet curiosity.

'I should have done more.'

She didn't say anything. I drew a square and a cross in its middle, and I rubbed it out. My fingers lingered by hers for a minute. Then our fingers met, and she held hers still while I followed the line of her arm to the goosebumps around her nipple. I turned onto my hip, and I reached for her legs with my other hand. It started with her mischievous smile – her languor broke and we moved faster the second time, each following muted signs, perhaps in the way she shifted her hips, or in the pitch of my breaths, in unison, from position to position. And that dialogue, unseen and unheard, was enough. We didn't talk. There was the sound of wet flesh on wet flesh, and there was the sound of the rain on the glass panels. She came twice; the second time with me, her body heavy on mine, mine heavy on the bed. It was the first time we'd come together.

The smell of sex in the air, she lay on her back with one arm over my stomach. I looked at her and I thought of the way Marie used to smoke after sex. She would lie on her back much like Leona, bringing cigarette to lips, blowing smoke. And yet, they were nothing alike; on the one side, Marie's perfectly composed features, her breasts hanging in the way that suited them best; and on the other, Leona's contentment, the skin folding between breast and stomach. I didn't know how I'd managed to stay with Marie for so long.

'The friend you talked about earlier.' She spoke as if she were asking a question.

'Yeah,' I said.

'What was his story?'

I hesitated, but I was too relaxed to think.

'He was messed up,' I said.

Her arm was warm on my stomach, so I kept on speaking:

'He had a lot of anger inside of him, and he didn't have much luck. With his family, with friends. It's complicated. He…' I wanted to do him justice but a part of me held on tight. 'You know,' I said, 'he had too many ideas. About what was right, what was wrong. But he forgot what mattered.'

'What's that?'

'People. You, me, everyone else. The bloke was brilliant. Probably the smartest person I ever met.'

'What did he do?' she asked, and all of a sudden, I realised that I'd drifted far into the forbidden. I panicked:

'Something stupid.' I could turn the conversation around. It wasn't too late. All I had to do was find someone else who fitted the description. Or invent someone. I could kill Denret. He was probably dead anyway.

'You're talking about Eric Knight, aren't you?'

I froze, expecting her hands to plough into my stomach, to curl into fists. She barely moved. The back of her hand was still warm, still resting against my hip. Her head tilted a fraction towards me, and on it I could detect nothing but an avid sort of curiosity.

'Have you forgiven him?' I said.

'Yes,' she answered immediately.

'Like you forgive everyone?'

'Yes.'

I didn't know what else to add. She didn't seem to mind. I relaxed. She'd just worked six days straight. Perhaps she was too tired to react, I thought, and the gloom lightened for an instant. She got up to go to the bathroom. I listened to the door close, to the door open, and then I heard nothing. I waited for ten minutes before I called out. I didn't hear a response.

She was running home in the rain, naked.

The door opened. It was her, a tray of food in hand.

'Your stomach was rumbling,' she said.

We ate, and it was 10 p.m. and I was hard again. Three times in the one evening, it was unusual. But it was raining and she looked beautiful. This time it was about her. For once, she listened to her urges and she told me exactly what she wanted.

'What was he like?' she asked me when the sex had drained the last of her body, and she covered my body with a leg and an arm.

'You don't remember him?' I asked, thinking of the time we'd juggled fruits in the Bakers' garden.

'No,' she said and I believed her. If she didn't think of her brother, there was no reason she'd remember Eric's visit.

Her initial question in the air, I took a deep breath and remembered the inspector's words on the day of my eighteenth birthday, Leona's easy reaction when I'd mentioned seeing him on the street. Mothers' misgivings, my early doubts, it was easy to stoke fears. What mattered was Leona now: she wanted to know and the words wanted to come out.

'Well, he was tall, taller than me. Curly dark hair and piercing blue eyes. You haven't seen any pictures?'

'Yeah.'

'Alright. I guess he was a bit strange. That's what a lot of people said. Not everyone.' I couldn't tell her that her brother was nice to him. 'But most people thought he was strange.'

'But what was he like with you?'

Eric was in his shed fixing my bat until one in the morning; in his room, showing me how to differentiate logs; high in his tree-house late one afternoon, telling me about his old football team, about his primary school, until the sun had set and it'd grown cold; and before any other image pushed through, I bit my lip till it leaked blood.

'With me,' I said, calmer, 'he was different. He was nice, he liked me. I don't know why, that's how it was.' I sighed and my body felt light. 'He was very kind to me. I think he could have been that way with everyone, if only…' I stopped myself, but the words were gathering a dangerous momentum.

'But you were his friend. That's got to be enough, no?'

The moment of his death flashed very bright: his body collapsing, and frozen on his face, the hint of a betrayed expression stopped short by death. For the first time in six years, it occupied the whole of my mind, the image truer for I was awake, and I opened my mouth because I had to. Nothing came out. What had I done? I was a bloody traitor, a selfish twat, and next to that, Eric, he… All of a sudden, there was too much to feel, too much to say, and the words, the space didn't exist. My lips were loose, my tongue thick, and I blabbered.

'I could have…' I repeated the words three times, each time seeing another thing I could have done. 'I could have done something. For him, for everyone else. I could have known. I should have…' and I couldn't speak anymore.

Leona enclosed my head in her arms, in the way I'd held her head so many times before. I smelled the skin around her collar-bone and I closed my eyes, caught in between two rushes: the words, pervasive, accruing behind the images, violent. Both were moving too fast to comprehend.

I woke up at four in the morning with a hard-on and an urgent need to go to the bathroom. When I came back, she was awake, smiling. A new urge pulsed through my limbs, and I put my cock by her mouth. Her lips opened and closed around it, and I realised she was still asleep. Seeing her dutiful in sleep, persistent as she woke up, aroused me more than I'd ever been. When I came, I felt a deep pain spreading from my loins to my chest, and I shivered as it echoed through my guts. I curled into a ball by her side, until I felt I could breathe comfortably. She grabbed my arms and pulled, until I stretched out a little, and she snuck in, blanketing my body with hers. She was so close that I could feel her every breath but I couldn't see her face. It felt like a blind sort of acceptance, her embrace. I rested my chin on her head, tasted her smell, and surrendered.

'There were so many shootings back then,' my mouth spoke through her hair. 'It was always on the news. In America, of course, but we heard about every single one of them.' My thoughts couldn't explain the dull pain, the feverish pleasure that words and images were bringing forth. But why was I resisting the glow of release? Open up.

'Eric, he liked to talk about them, but only when we were up in his tree-house. He'd built this bridge, and there was this platform…' The bridge and the platform captured me for a few instants. She was rubbing my back with her damp hands, and my feet were dangling over the great oaks. The crown of her head was hiding her from my eyes, and yet I knew it: her body loved me. We were already sharing skin, mouth, nose. We were ready to share everything. I spoke faster: 'He smoked whenever he talked about them. There was Columbine, but there were others too. Heritage, and I forget the names of the others. I should remember. The first time he said he understood them, and I… well, I agreed. He had that effect on me. Yes, I said it made sense. But I didn't really think about it, while he… well, he spoke about them often. And I guess I was interested. It's morbid, but it's interesting. That's why they're on the news so much, right?' Her grip was getting tighter, but I didn't wait for her answer. 'Well, I was! So I wanted to know why they did it, how, what happened to them, pretty much everything! But I shouldn't have done that, should I? I should have disagreed, I should have thrown his little pack of cigarettes overboard.' The pain in my chest lessened as I raised my voice. 'I should have pushed him off the platform!' Hearing myself shout, I went silent and I listened to the sound of the rain on the window, to Leona's breathing. 'That's what I should have done, right?' I said.

I felt something warm tickle down my chest, leaving a cold, salty trail behind.

'Don't cry,' I said. 'You're too sweet.'

I tried to look at her but she shrivelled into herself, masking her face with her hair. Kind as always, she didn't seem to mind me holding her. Every time she exhaled, she whispered something to herself, but soon it was lost in her breath and she sounded better. Her skin felt cool to the touch, while, every few seconds, a new wave of heat started in my skull and coursed down to my toes. I wanted to give her all of my heat but she stayed cool, and I sweated. Naked, I climbed out of bed, pulled the second duvet from beneath the bed, and covered her with it. Then, lying around her, I rubbed her body through the down until she fell asleep.

* * *

It was ten in the morning when I woke up. It was still raining and I was hungry. I went to the fridge and found a few bananas. When I brought them back, Leona was starting to stir. I sat with my pillow against the window, and I ate slowly.

With the dull light, she looked like a black and white movie, her hair big with sleep. Silent, I watched her for half an hour. Her eyes eventually betrayed her: they turned from the rain to my grounded eyes, and the connection brought her down from her dreamland. She stretched and held a hand out for me.

'Are you hungry?' I said.

'Shh.'

She pulled me closer and laid a silencing finger over my lips. I kneeled up and looked out the window.

'I'll get the paper,' I said.

There was no one in the streets. Nothing but water on the ground, water in the sky. In the corner store on Iffley Road, the shopkeeper, a Bangladeshi, had his radio on. I handed him the *Observer* with my two pounds. He pointed to a stool and asked me what I was doing out on a morning like this.

'Wait five minutes,' he said, 'it's raining hard.'

I sat on the stool, and listened to the voice on the radio. Inshallah, the rain will stop.

'Big night out?' he said, waving at my face.

'Big night in,' I said.

We spoke cricket – his afternoon game was cancelled already, and Bangladesh were rubbish.

'Coke?' he said, miming the lines around my eyes.

'No,' I said, and I looked closer. He had a beard that wisped down his neck, a pianist's fingers.

'You want some weed?' he said.

I said no, and we sat in silence until the rain thinned. Then I stood up, he put my coin through the till, and bid me goodbye.

* * *

'Come to the kitchen, you won't believe what he told me.'

Leona was still in bed, lying on her back, her eyes jumping all over the room. She was holding the sheet between her fists, pressing it tightly against the skin above her breasts. Yes, she'd barely said a word all morning, but I didn't have time to think about it. I could feel it deep inside: I had to get us back to the previous night's space.

It took my Bangladeshi story and the promise of a brunch to drag her out of bed. Blade in hand, she slit the paper's plastic wrapping open and found Obama on the front page. Ever since he'd wrestled control of the party from Hillary Clinton's hands, Leona had become interested in the American election. His picture, thumb and middle finger touching, an index finger raised at the camera, woke her up and her voice rose hoarse. It smoothened as she expanded on his problems with Hispanic voters. Once she started speaking, words rushed out of her so fast that I hardly had time to answer, and she took control of the moment. While I pressed oranges and chopped chives for the omelette, she summarised each article for me: a problem with mortgages; Bush said something silly; Brown looked sullen. Whenever I tried to string two sentences together, she threw another story at me. Our plates were empty by the time she came to the sports section. Reaching for one of the supplements, she asked me whether I knew a five-letter word for a springy wood.

'Isn't this nice?' she said. 'Spending a Sunday doing the crosswords?'

A muscle running down my back started a slow ache.

'Should we go back to bed?' I said.

'No, it's nice here.'

'It'd be nicer in bed.'

'No,' she said, and she focused on the next word. When we finished the crossword, she found the Sudoku, and the muscle down my back tensed up some more.

'I thought you didn't like Sudokus,' I said.

'But you do,' she said.

'Alright, one Sudoku.'

I focused on the paper, on the grid and nothing else. Nine rows, nine columns, nine boxes, eighty-one numbers. Ones, twos and nines, I ordered them around. No, you can't go there! Only a three in here. A foreign object (a yellow pencil, hardly more than a stub) appeared on my page, and started to scribble a two where there could only be a six or an eight. I flicked it away: its point broke as it hit the floor.

'Voilà,' I said, and I realised I'd just interrupted her.

She looked at me like I'd said something strange.

'That was quick,' she said. 'Let's try this other one.'

'Let's try it in bed,' I said, and I bundled all the sections of the paper under my arm. She picked up a bowl and held it at arm's length, staring at it, seemingly frozen. Just as I opened the bedroom door, I heard it shatter behind me. Leona looked shocked: her fingers still open, her eyes on the cheap white china shards littering the ground.

'Don't worry about it,' I said, and gathered her into my arms. Her body went loose. 'Accidents happen,' I said.

'No, they don't,' she said.

'Come, we'll clean it up later.'

She stumbled heavily behind me.

'Have you sorted out the recycling?' she asked me as I pulled her into the room.

'We'll do it later,' I said. I propped myself against the window, and I beamed at her. The duvet covering my feet, I felt liberated all of a sudden. I wanted to laugh, cry, and most of all, I wanted to talk. Through watering eyes, she stared at the point of my chin. Lest she became caught in a dumb silence, I poked her, I tickled her. A faint smile played with the edges of her lips.

'Last night… Are you happy we talked?' I said.

'Of course,' she answered immediately. Her face grew firm and I realised how slack it'd been. Her whole demeanour sharpened, as if she'd finally stopped daydreaming, and her hands reached for my side, tickling me as I'd been tickling her, but more insistently, her fingers clumsy enough that they hurt me. Pushing my t-shirt up to my chest, she laid her head and her warm hair on the skin of my stomach, and tapped my crotch through my jeans.

'No, wait,' I said, embarrassed and limp. There were a hundred impatient images going through my mind – they'd waited long enough, now they wanted out – and not one of them involved sex. She undid my buttons and stroked it.

'No,' I whispered.

'Yes,' she said. She took me small in her mouth, and I blushed. She worked on me, while I told myself to shut up and enjoy. Then, constricting the base of my cock with one hand, she positioned herself over me, lined me up, and pushed me inside her. By the third stroke, I was limp and crying.

'Let's...' I started, but I didn't know how to finish.

Her face turned to the ceiling, she pivoted on top of me for a whole minute, before her head came down and her hair followed. Our gazes crossed and I had her back with me. Lying down, she burrowed her face into my armpit.

She groaned softly, questioningly, I thought.

'No...' I said, 'sorry...'

'No,' she repeated, her voice trailing off.

'It's here,' I said, jabbing my chest with the point of my fingers. 'And, it needs to...' I threw my hand at the air, as if I were tossing away a rib and a fistful of flesh. I didn't know what she could have said but I waited anyway. Then I added:

'Are you judging me?'

'No, of course not.' Her voice came out sanitised through my armpit.

'You're allowed to.'

She started to say something but all that emerged was a weak groan.

'You think I'm a monster,' I said.

'No!' she said immediately this time, tilting her head so that I could hear her. 'I don't. I'm not judging you.'

'Do you love me?'

She paused.

'Yes, I really do.'

It was the first we'd mentioned love. Up to now, I'd thought it too obvious to tell her.

'I need you,' I said. 'As long as you love me, you're allowed to hate me.'

'I really do.'

'Can I tell you more?'

'Yes,' she said, her voice ashen with the rain. I tried to look at her face but she tilted it down again so that all I could see was the point of her jaw. I hesitated, but then, with a deep breath, she added: 'Yes, I want to know.'

That was all I needed. I turned on my side and enclosed her in my arms until I could feel parts of her comforting me from my toes to my chin. Tilting my head just so, I could see her as I'd seen her the night before. I inhaled: yes, she even smelled the same. And I was relieved, for I was back in the previous night's space, that guilty refuge.

'I'm a bad man, I'm a terrible man. That's what it is. You can't be friends with everyone. My father always told me so, and he's a compass on those things. You see, I should have done more. So much more! But there I was, talking one day to Tom, the next to Eric, like there was a bridge between them as big as that space between my eyes. You see, if I hadn't been there, what would Eric have done? Nothing, that's what. He couldn't, he wouldn't have had a clue. He'd have been on his own planet, consumed as he was with his own problems, and he'd have never thought of them. But with me telling him how bitchy Anna was, with me repeating Tom's latest prank, with me telling him how Jeffrey fancied Beth' – the words came out so fast that I didn't think about them, that I noticed Leona getting tenser but I ignored her all the same; to do justice to the past, I had to hound her with my words – 'with me telling him how we were all fascinated by Jayvanti's rack, well, with all of that, how could he not relate? How could he not hate? It's not that he wasn't in, no, it's that he was excluded from a world he knew everything about. Because he was curious in his own way. Of course, he always had more to say about the latest advance in nanotechnology, or whatever it was back then, but when I told him that Anna hadn't let me sign Josh's birthday card, oh, he listened alright. Are you beginning to see how bad I was?' I paused. 'Are you?'

Except for the word 'no', I couldn't make out what she answered. She shifted, her forehead slipping down my torso, catching my chest hair between our skins, until all I could see of her was the back of her head. I preferred her that way: it was easier to believe what she said if I didn't see her.

'I'm terrible, but that's the least of it. It gets worse, and you can judge me, you should judge me. Someone should... All that everyone cared about is what happened that one morning. Rubbish that. Why does it matter? It's out! Everyone's dead, except for me, fuck justice, and that's the end of it. Isn't it? And you tell me, what about the evenings when he was thinking about it, the nights when he was planning every step? You see, there were days he talked about it, and I was there, in that ankle-high bean bag, or in his tree-house, looking at the next hill like I was its long-gone master. And you know what, I listened to what he said, I nodded my head, I asked the odd question like I did for everything else he said. Except that this wasn't everything else. Two fourteen-year-olds open fire in some far-gone American state, that's not quite the same as talking about the best way of tying three ropes into a bridge, now, is it?

'But look, after Columbine, what else were we going to speak about? And when he said he understood them, of course I said I understood them too. It's never hard to understand anger. Especially when I was sharing his three days a week.'

A picture of the two of us talking, scheming even, came to mind and the words grew heavier. But I needed to finish what I'd started:

'After the first shooting, he told me he understood why. He explained it to me – fairness, respect, he had every right to expect both. But a month later, he'd forgotten about it. That energy of his, that power he had, it was focused on smaller things, better things. And then there was another shooting, and this time he talked about it in a different way. It wasn't so much the why that interested him – it was like he'd already established it was right, and he didn't need to prove it again. Mathematical mind, he had – he wanted to be an engineer, and he would have been a great one, but you need to be dull to study. He was never that. Too intense, too strong. Yes, this time it wasn't the why that interested him, but the how. How they did it: what they needed, how they planned it, how they carried it out, where they failed. And on every item, he told me how he'd improve it. Sometimes, it was like we were talking about it together: in Arkansas, they pulled the fire alarm, watched their classmates file out, and took aim at the whole school from a row of trees, he said, and we analysed the pros and cons of doing that. Pro: confusion. People don't know what's going on. Con: inefficiency. You'd get more people if you were closer. But some other times, he'd thought everything out beforehand, and he was merely presenting me with an executive summary. Like guns: given how easy it was to get guns in the US, he found it disappointing that they only used what their parents already had. He'd read reports of sixteen-year-olds buying assault rifles with no ID checks. Assault rifles, he told me. Nate, assault rifles. Can you imagine what we could do with assault rifles, he told me.

'And then I don't know exactly what happened. He didn't tell me much, you know. In some ways, he told me everything, but in others, he said almost nothing. I think he had a fight with his mother or with his stepfather. That wasn't unusual. And that was also when he had his second fight with Paul. This time, it was Eric's fault, from what I could put together. He told me that I should have seen the way Paul looked at him. Like he wouldn't even piss on his foot, he said. So he punched him. Hardly worth calling it a fight, when Paul didn't have time to fight back. Still, it was decent of Paul, and decent of Tom too who saw everything, to keep their mouths shut when teachers started asking questions. After that, though, people kept well clear of Eric.'

Leona shifted for the first time since I'd started speaking. She squirmed, one hand rising until it covered her ear. But her fingers were open: she could still hear me.

'And there was another shooting, or people started talking about one of the old ones. Whatever it was, the subject came back, and this time Eric started to wonder how one could do it in the UK. Very general at first. I told him you couldn't find a gun out here, and he said that if some random gang up North had them, he could get them too. If you put your mind to it, he said, you can get anything. I told him that there were so many CCTV cameras that the police would know right away. He just laughed. And then he saw that I was serious so he explained it to me – no one watches the tapes live, he said, and besides, what does it matter if they do? I'm not going to be alive to face them, he said. And you know what, I just kept on asking questions, bouncing off his energy, like he hadn't said anything wrong. Not alive? He was adamant about that: there was no way he could do something like that and still be alive afterwards. It'd be a travesty, he said. Travesty, that's the word he used.

'That's when he leaned towards me, very quiet all of a sudden. It was pretty cold so we'd left the tree-house, and we were in his shed. Two bodies in there, and after ten minutes it was warm enough to take our jackets off. So he said that he couldn't kill himself. Couldn't live, but couldn't kill himself. Can you imagine what that would do to my mother, he said. Her son commits suicide. It would break her. So he leaned towards me, and with all that intensity of his, he asked me whether I'd kill him in that case. He asked me whether I could look at him and pull the trigger. He'd do the same, don't worry. At the same time, count down from three. Three, two, one, bang, and his mother doesn't have to suffer so much.

'I told you I was a terrible man. Terrible. I guess I thought it was all academic. No, that's not even true. I have no idea what I thought. All I know is that I said yes, and that he seemed relieved, and that I was happy to be doing him and his mother a favour.' I paused. 'Do you think I'm a bad man?' I asked Leona.

She didn't answer. In fact, I couldn't even hear her breathing.

'Do you think I'm a bad man?'

I grabbed her tighter and shook her. Her head bobbed twice against my chest.

'Do you think I'm a bad man?'

'No,' she said weakly.

'Tell me the truth, I'm a terrible man.' I shook her again. This time her body went rigid and she tried to push herself off me. My arms like a clamp, I held her close.

'No,' she said louder this time, 'you didn't realise,' and she stopped struggling. For a moment, I compared my brutish arms and her limp body and I hated my own strength. I couldn't go on, I was hurting her. But then I heard her clearly:

'It's not your fault,' she said, and I forgot my doubts.

'You don't believe that. I did realise. I'm not sure what I realised, but I realised something. And when he walked into the classroom with his chains, I realised I'd realised. That's how bad I am. And you know what, he looked at me, and he realised that I'd realised. Yes, he did. Because he didn't shoot me. It's hard not to shoot someone. In a small space like that, when you're shooting everyone else, it's very hard. And then – oh, for fuck's sake – no, I'll say it. Yes, he called my name. I was hiding. When he called me, that's when the adrenaline really kicked in, that's when my mind sharpened until all I could see was the two of us. Before that, and isn't that the worst of it, before that, I'd watched it all as if we were throwing paint at a canvas. Here's a little blue, and here's a whole bunch of red! But when he called me, I forgot everyone else, all of my friends screaming, spilling their guts on the floor, and I thought of me, me and me. Fuck, I was afraid. Nate, he said, hurry up. He was still businesslike then' – Leona pushed her elbows deep into my stomach, and it stopped me short for a second, but I knew it: she wanted to hear more. I held her tighter, and her body became loose again – 'I went to him, he handed me one of his guns, carefully and everything, handle first, careful where you point it, and then I saw it in him. He was afraid too. It caught up to him, but there was no point in trying to stop it. You don't start something like that and not finish it. Before, he'd looked like a prophet, the sort of man who would have stood in the middle of a crowd, and everyone would have gone to their knees. But now, he looked like a little boy. And that's what saved me. With a prophet, I'd be dead like him. You can't resist that sort of charisma. But with a little boy, I became very angry, oh so fucking angry. Angry like I'd never been before. Not thoughts-swimming hazy angry. No! Very, very, sharp angry, like I could see the muscles around his eyes twitch, and I wanted to cut them up with my nails. Gritting my teeth, how am I going to smash your face to pulp angry. You ready, he said, and oh boy, I didn't know what I was going to do then, but I was thinking hard. He raised it, I raised it, and he started counting. Three, it was weak the way he said it, maybe he was thinking about his mother, maybe he was imagining the police knocking on her door, but then he said two, and he said it with more strength, like he was thinking about his stepfather, like he imagined all the people he hated, like he'd shown them what justice was really about, and I could see it in him, he was in it, deep in the mechanics of his death, and just when he said two, I knew what I was going to do. He said one, and I'd already pulled the trigger, right at his head. We were so close it was hard to miss. His hand was already falling when he shot me. He missed my head, got me in the stomach, but he was already dead... You're allowed to miss when you're dead.'

With those words, I realised I'd finished speaking. I felt spent. My brain was a long blank, and every single one of my muscles felt like it was melting into the sheets. Leona was still in my arms, a lump my limbs folded over. She could have been jabbing me in the gut and I wouldn't have felt it. For a while, I stared at one of my grandmother's paintings – at least, that's what I think I did, for all I can remember is that my eyes wouldn't move, and that they were looking at a shape on the wall.

* * *

I woke up at four in the morning, when the rain beat hard against the glass panes. I'd slept ten dreamless hours. Ten hours gone and not a smudge on my mind. Leona was lying on the edge of the bed, cocooned inside her duvet. I drifted out of bed into my studio. The street lamp outside mixed in with the low clouds to give the room a metallic tinge. My spaceship looked like a pigeon: the cabin dominating the hull like a pigeon's head dominates its body. Even my revolutionary piecemeal design, with its disposable elements, looked like simple feathers. Still, my pigeon was white, and my pigeon was big.

Armed with this insight, I went back to bed, and I lay on my back, focusing on deep slow breaths, the sort that stretched my lungs into my stomach, the sort that made me as light as the last of my breath, and I felt myself rock from side to side, as if I were on a pirate's board, ready to be tossed to the sharks. I slipped and I was standing in the room, dark while Leona was asleep and blue. I decided to visit my old school, to see whether I'd recognised the stones under the gigantic glass belly, and I was there, walking over the clean sports ground, towards the Kemp Annexe they had razed, and the glass structure they had erected in its stead. The place was silent. There was no light but a dim pulse that came from me. I walked through the glass, towards my old physics classroom. When I reached it, I stood tall, and looked at the darkness around me. And then I saw a pair of shiny white scissors on the ground, the only other bit of light in space. I bent down to pick them up, but before I could curl my fingers through their handle, I left my new reality and its soothing calm, and I slept some more.

At one stage, just before the sun rose, I thought that I saw Leona in the doorway, a long object in hand. My mind captured her shape, nothing more than a shadow, decided she was holding a sword, lumped it into my sleep and accepted its sentence.

When I opened my eyes next, it was nine in the morning, and Leona was no longer in bed. I went looking for her, shouting her name.

Six

That was when it all changed. After what I told her, it had to change, and yet, the coward within kept on hoping. I hoped until I tried her mobile and it went directly to voicemail. Until I thought of calling her parents, and I didn't dare, because I didn't want to have to tell Amanda that I was looking for her daughter, for the same daughter who'd slept naked in my bed for over three months, when she'd warned me, when she'd spelt out the issues as far as a mother could condemn a child.

It must have been noon when I picked up the receiver and started dialling Amanda's number, when I let it ring once, and when I hung up, disgusted with myself. What would I do, speaking to Amanda? I couldn't influence the jury while it was deliberating. No, I had to wait. It had been my choice, and now I had to wait for her verdict.

I made myself a tidy lunch: two slices of brown bread, one buttered, the other coated with onion chutney, two leaves of lettuce, a square of spiced Gouda, and half a tomato. Then I wasn't hungry anymore, but I had half a tomato left, so I made myself the same sandwich again. There was a lettuce leaf black with wrinkles on my plate. I traced one of its creases with my fingers and found it sticky. Like Leona must find me. And suddenly I wanted to rinse my hands, to scrub them clean.

Before I tried her mobile a fourth time, I asked myself whether she'd get a missed call for all of my attempts. Surely not. Not when it didn't even ring. The eighth time, I let the message run until it beeped, and then, faced with the crackly silence, I left her three hurried words: call me back.

She didn't call. Not that day, nor the next. It was Monday and thankfully I had an assignment to hand in the following morning. She might come back, I thought, and I waited. It was 11 a.m. by the time I'd become too disgusted with myself to remain alone. I went to the library. There, I met a few friends going for lunch and I took them, as if by chance, to Georgina's, where Leona was meant to work. But she wasn't there and there were no free tables. Every time a vibration travelled to my thigh, every time I heard someone else receive a message, I pulled out my phone and checked it. It remained resolutely message-free.

She'd found me guilty and this waiting, like a cold vice pressing and twisting into my chest, was the start of my punishment.

* * *

On Tuesday morning, I clutched at her side of the bed and found it cold. Before my thoughts could thicken into a vile paste, I heard the house crackle, and I told myself that it could be her in the living room being considerate, unaware that I was already awake. Or that she could have come back during the night, seen me in bed, remembered how much I disgusted her, and opted for the sofa instead. These images were too inviting. I walked to the living room, a morbid sort of hope hanging from my lip. It was despairingly empty, except for three darkened banana skins: remnants of the previous night's dinner.

To shake myself awake, I went to hand in my assignment. When I came back, I looked at my empty flat, I listened to my steps resonate, and I sat down on the sofa. There was a cushion tilting my hips, hurting my lower back, but it didn't matter. My mind was thinking over questions it couldn't answer, all variants of the one worry: how would Leona react to my story? The more

I thought about it, the more I saw signs of repulsion in her behaviour, in the way she hid her face, in her tears, in the way she tried to push herself off me. Repulsion silenced by compassion. And I asked myself what she would do, how she would judge me, whether she'd see me one more time, whether she'd wait until I fell asleep before she cut my cock off. Thinking did no good but I couldn't stop it.

There were noises coming from outside, noises on the steps, more tricks I was playing on myself. The noises sharpened, defying my fears: the sound of a key sliding into a lock. The door opened and Leona appeared.

She shuffled into the flat and the light cast harsh shadows, the sound of my pen tapping on the coffee table rang hollow. From my sofa, I turned to look at her. She looked the same, and yet she didn't. Her usual daintiness had made way for an aggressive lean. For the first time since I'd met her, she was wearing a pair of old jeans and trainers. I couldn't be sure, but it looked like her nose and eyes had tightened, as if she'd brooded so much they'd folded on themselves. And yet, her cheeks, her forehead had become slack, as if shock had grappled with only half her face. It was a frightful contrast: all I could do was stare and wait.

'Fix your tyre. Let's go for a ride,' she said, and I didn't argue. Twenty minutes later, I was following her around South Parks Road, as her calves and her thighs pushed her narrow-tyred, aluminium-framed bike ever further away from mine. I caught her just as we came off Banbury Road, when she rode through another red light. She was laughing.

'Where are we going?' I said.

She looked at me as if I'd asked her whether the moon had a sister, and she pushed hard against her pedal, speeding away, laughing at the road ahead.

It should have been a stormy morning. Instead, the skies had whisked together three lonely clouds. I wanted them to gather, darken, and break, so that Leona would slip and stop. I'd pick her up and nurse her grazed elbow, kiss the wound, lap her blood. But the clouds weren't even capable of covering us with their shadows for more than two minutes.

We reached Wytham and Leona rode around the pub, up the narrow lane that leads to Wytham Woods. Seeing her lock her bike to the outside gate relaxed me for some reason – the way she looped her lock through both her front and back wheels especially. When we'd walked to the top of the hill, after twenty minutes of the lonely sound of feet on gravel, twenty minutes of questions I couldn't answer by myself, I ignored the curious focus etched over her face and grabbed her wrist. I had to pull hard to bring her to a halt.

'What is it?' I asked.

'What's what?' She looked confused.

'Why are we here?'

'Can't you just enjoy the woods? Look,' she pointed at one side of the ridge, 'on this side, there's still dew on the spider webs, and on that side, the grass is dry. How beautiful is that?'

'Don't you have work today?'

She turned her face away:

'It doesn't matter.'

'It doesn't?'

'No, but this' – she waved her arm around her – 'this matters.'

She turned around, and I grabbed her wrist before she could walk away. I had to know what it would be.

'After what I said the other night…'

'Yes?' She looked at me defiantly.

'You left so… abruptly. That's it, isn't it? You hate me.'

For a second, she looked truly annoyed.

'I don't, didn't I say that already? Why do you keep on asking?'

'I thought…' and I didn't know what I thought anymore.

I studied her face as if it held the answer I needed. And her expression changed, its rightful disdain making way for the artifice of virtue.

'Don't think,' she tapped her temple, 'in here, all I have is forgiveness. You didn't know, that's alright. You didn't know...' Her voice trailed off, and her eyes were on the path ahead.

At that moment, I wanted to tell her that I did, but I knew that it wouldn't matter, that she'd talk forgiveness just the same, and I hated her for it. But then I looked at her closer, and I saw the fold between her eyes, that new fold, lush with youth, deep with anger, and I stopped believing her: she'd judged me and she'd found me guilty on all counts: treachery, deceit, cowardice, I listed word after word in my head as I walked behind her – duplicity, pretence, passivity – and I felt better for every new label.

She walked on until the path curled left and down. Then she left the path and strolled towards a knoll in the meadow, an athletic sort of beauty taking hold of her – her legs hardened through the denim with every stride, her bare arms tightened at the triceps with every swing – a beauty so different to the softness that had pulled me towards her in the first place that I both wanted to be ordered to the ground, and to seek asylum in the gothic manor at the bottom of the hill. She took a blanket out of her bag and tossed it open.

'This is my favourite spot in the world,' she said.

I looked around. We stood in a green field, a hedge of trees masking the path on the hill's crest, grass flowing down to a creek and a sun-kissed manor, and in the distance, Oxford and its colleges, its halls, its chapels. We were alone, and yet behind those trees, there could be a class of eight-year-olds scrutinising the different types of weed endemic to Oxfordshire. I turned back to Leona. She was unbuttoning her jeans.

'What are you doing?' I said.

She pulled her trousers down.

'Lie down here.' She pointed at the ground. 'Your head this way, I want to see the view.'

Her arm stretched imperious, her knuckle sharp against the trees in the distance. Against my will, I moved to where she wanted me to be. She took her pants off. Just as they reached her ankles, her knees barely bent, her back almost flat, I looked at the soft flesh of her arse, that flesh I'd caressed, fondled, slapped, and I saw a hard muscle I'd never noticed before. It started halfway up her thigh and rose up the one buttock like a wave crashing against a wall. That moment, that strength she'd hidden from me, that single image of Leona squatting, a band bulging out of the back of her thigh, changed the way I saw her, and I became afraid of her. She was no longer my Leona. I didn't think about singing her a lullaby while she nursed an imaginary wound, but I looked at her bare legs, those legs I'd kissed most nights, and I saw how they could grab my neck and twist until my skull popped out of my spine.

And there was still that lone finger pointing at the blanket on the ground, that order I couldn't rebel against, despite my one clear thought, the word 'no', murmured, and then shouted, and then whispered, but only ever within the confines of my head because my mouth wouldn't do what a mouth is supposed to do. I lay down and she reached for my jeans. Nothing but that finger, nothing but the promise of those muscles, and I was hard. It made me cry. She never saw those tears. When her head bent towards me, her eyes were closed. They only opened when she looked at the view, ecstatic. I didn't want to like the feel of her wet flesh on my taut skin. I didn't want to like the way her bones ground into my pelvis. And yet, pleasure and pain, they all felt acutely wonderful. There was a stick with a pointy knob driving into my kidney every time she pressed down, and another where my head could have rested. I liked those pains: I deserved them. But I hated my body for enjoying itself – I didn't want to stay erect, I didn't want to feel the start of an orgasm gathering my guts into a knot.

I saw something move on the path. I couldn't be sure, but I thought it was two men running. It didn't matter. We weren't five minutes into it before I came so hard that my legs twitched. Then she put her clothes back on and lay alongside my body to catch her breath, her eyes closed. To the runners, to the class of eight-year-olds, we were once again nothing but a loving couple taking in the view. Her eyes finally fell on me, and I hated the genuine concern that spread over her.

'I'll make you that pumpkin curry you like so much when we get home,' she said.

Despite myself, I looked forward to that curry for the whole journey back. If I couldn't speak now, I'd be able to say what I felt with that medley of spices. Such was the power of food.

While we ate, every time I chewed through a cumin seed, every time a dice of pumpkin melted on my tongue, I thought about talking – telling her that I needed to know what she thought, telling her that I hadn't wanted her in Wytham Woods, telling her that there was a weight dragging me down as surely as if two hands were pulling my shoulders down to the ground, and that she, her and no one else, only had to say the word and I'd be free – but then I remembered the power in her legs, and I noticed the confused intensity in her face, as if she were struggling with a knife and its blunt side, and I told myself that I'd wait until we were in the bedroom, that I'd give her a massage and kiss her neck in that way she liked, until she sang to her own melody, to her own language, and that then, I'd be brave because she'd look weak.

I chewed and chewed, but there was only a plateful of curry, and I'd finished it. She grabbed her things and told me she had to go home.

'You don't want to stay here tonight?' I asked.

'No,' she said, and she left.

* * *

Two days later, a week before nos quatre mois, when I was becoming resigned to the idea that I would never understand her, I came home one afternoon to find her huddled on the sofa, her arms enclosing her legs, her chin resting on her knees, and a trail of her things (tissues, keys, a notepad, two inch-high pencils dented with teeth marks) tracing a path between her and her bag on the coffee table. When I first saw her, I felt myself lift, but then, before I had time to dwell on my happiness, a trickle of apprehension tainted my pleasure. She was intently watching television. It took me a second to think it through: we didn't have a television. She was watching it so intently that she barely noticed me, her attention on an insurance man with a cheerful voice.

Slumped on the sofa, she looked withdrawn enough that I dared walk towards her and kiss her on the cheek.

'Hey,' she said and she went back to the screen.

For a second I thought of sitting next to her, but the second lapsed and I went to the fridge instead, as if that were what I'd intended to do all along.

'Where did you get the TV?' I asked. I hadn't seen one in the flat before, but I hadn't looked through the mess in the staircase cupboard. There hadn't been one at Leona's either. In fact, we'd had a few conversations talking about how we didn't like television – Leona because it excited her too much, and me because I never cared enough.

'Did you find it somewhere?' I said.

'Bought it.' She glanced at me.

I looked closer: medium sized, flat screen, expensive.

'You bought that... today?'

She gave me a dismissive nod, her eyes still on the screen.

'Why?' I asked.

'The fish,' she said so matter-of-factly that I pictured a fish bowl built into the plain grey television frame.

The television's speakers now let out a New York accent interrogating a black man who said 'Sir' and 'Ma'am' every three words. Leona seemed even more interested in them than in the ads people.

'No work today?'

She shook her head absentmindedly, and I sat at the table, pretending to read an academic article I'd printed the day before. As I watched her watch the screen, her face slacker than I'd ever seen it, TV shading her face with faded blues, I forgot my circus of thoughts, the ever-fresh images speculating on my doubts, and I saw her: a nineteen-year-old girl who'd heard something so repulsive that she'd missed work at least twice, so repulsive that she didn't mind blowing her savings so that she could dive into another world. The same Leona who'd, for months, made sure she was ten minutes early so that she could help her boss open up, was now sitting dumb on my sofa. And in front of her, broadcasting a world of crime and sex, was another product of her confusion – I couldn't imagine her buying a TV any other way. She was confused, struggling even, and it was my fault.

I was glad to see her suffer. It was easier than if she'd been a stern judge, dozing through my plea, only waking to raise her hammer and pronounce her verdict. Pain had pulled us together.

Still, I wanted to hear her speak, to divulge her thoughts as she'd always done. When, in between two shows, she went to use the bathroom, I looked at her bag, spilling its guts on the coffee table, offering her secrets to me, and I pinched her phone. What mattered was that we understood each other, and if she wasn't going to speak to me, then reading her messages was perfectly justified.

I heard her open the toilet door and I jumped up. But I needn't have worried: she walked right past me and slumped on the sofa in exactly the same position as before. Guiltily, I grabbed a textbook and went to the small bedroom, as if I were doing work. There, I flipped the phone open and I parsed through her inbox. A message from me asking her whether she was coming home, another telling her I'd made her some dinner if she was hungry. And then, between two more of my messages, the last of which was dated before our rainy weekend, a message from her friend Jenny, the school friend I'd never met. 'Love sucks. Chocolate and ice cream tonight?'

I switched to her sent messages. There were very few – she only ever responded to half of mine. At the top of the list, I found the one addressed to Jenny: 'Cried all day. I think I'm going to do something crazy.'

Something crazy. The words flashed so hard they burned themselves onto my retinas. For the rest of the evening, when I sneaked her phone back into her bag, when I watched her stare blankly at the television, when I stared into space, when I tried to sleep, I saw them, holding court over my mind. Something crazy. Perhaps she'd forgive me, perhaps she'd choose love. Or perhaps she'd stab me, store my body in a freezer, and eat me one limb at a time. But she was merely thinking of doing something crazy. She hadn't made her mind up, I thought, and I clung to that hope.

* * *

My nights had changed. I'd shed my Pavlovian 5 a.m. drugged-with-sleep start to the day, and embraced a seven hours' stretch, oscillating between oblivion and flying dreams, sandwiched between two crusts of gut-rattling brain twists.

When Leona turned the television off and snuck into bed for the first time since she'd disappeared, I noticed how she lay right against the edge of the mattress, how she had her back turned to me, and I briefly emerged from my dark pool to silently torture myself – to ask and stab, to fearfully deduce. Something crazy. The next morning, when I woke up alone in bed, I felt like I'd slept in a hot room after drinking too much the night before and

I couldn't go to the toilet. And then I started listening to myself: if she wanted me to call up the BBC and tell my story, I'd do it for her, and I'd crawl to Santiago, and I'd climb the Himalayas barefoot, and I'd chart the spread of man-eating ants through the Amazon.

My morning guilt ran its course: it was the price for replacing a rotten core for a rotten conscience. A price worth paying. My past and its iguana tongue had slowly but surely drained me into half of myself, and I only realised it now that I could once again sprint up Shotover Hill.

I appreciated my newfound energy when I was in the library later that day, and I tore through a schematic understanding of supply and demand, or when James, the only other student to have worked at sea, started discussing the merits of Obama's foreign policy, and I attacked his interpretation with nine examples, two of which concerned Indonesia's role in the Muslim world. As long as I kept myself clear of Leona, my mind added and associated faster than it had in months.

* * *

That evening, as I was working on the flat's only table, Leona walked in with lines under her eyes, and three opaque plastic bags in her hands. A shapeless navy blue hoodie, with Oxford written big across her belly, masked her as surely as any disguise – she looked like an American exchange student who'd spent the last five nights exercising her right to buy alcohol. After a curt greeting, she put the bags where I couldn't see them, and tossed a vampire novel on top of my notes.

'It's for you,' she said, her eyes focused a foot beyond my face.

Puzzled, I studied the sensual blood etched on the black cover. She had to know my tastes better than that.

'For me?' I said. 'Thanks.' I put it down on the table and pretended to read the back cover. 'What else did you buy?'

She stood awkwardly, glancing first at me then at her bags.

'A DVD player?' I said.

'No. Read the first chapter,' she said, and she mimed me reading the book.

I opened it, expecting to find a handwritten note breaking us off, but the pages were crisp and clean. I started the first chapter – an evil vampire posse chasing our presumed male lead. After two pages, I looked up to see whether Leona could give me a clue. She was hunched over in the kitchen so that I could only see the top of her head.

'What are you doing?' I asked.

'Tidying up,' she chirped.

I stared at her unusual straight parting splitting her hair right down the middle, and I went back to the man-vampire jumping out of a building. Just as he was backing into a dark alley, Leona appeared next to me. She stood with a hand on the table, as if she needed to steady herself. I looked up. She was so pale that I felt afraid. Something crazy, I remembered. Her eyes had stopped floating: they were now focused on my lips.

'I want to ask you a question.' She spoke in a grave voice, her face solemn.

'Anything,' I said.

'When Eric called you to him that day,' she said, and my back straightened, stiffened, 'was Jeffrey still alive?'

'I didn't—' I started, but I was back in that room, and I was standing up, and Eric was calling me – Nate, come on, Nate! – and there was Grace and Tom and Mr Johnson all down, and there was a group forcing the door, and another voice, I couldn't remember who, telling Eric that he didn't have to do this, and I was moving towards Eric, like a moth to a flame, a step at a time, while he was shooting past me, over me, around me, or perhaps he wasn't, and there was silence, and I was next to him, inspecting the room, my limbs drained of blood, my mind blank, and he handed me a gun, carefully and everything

– So easy, Nate! – and he levelled his gun at Jeffrey, who was standing straight looking at both of us, and I wanted to shout but I couldn't move, and Eric reloaded his gun, and he shot three more times, crack, crack, crack, I couldn't look, and he turned to me, for there was nothing but a hoarse silence in the room now, and he looked afraid.

Next to that moment, I was insignificant. Even if I'd wanted to tell her, I wouldn't have been able to explain it: sometimes, a man does nothing, and it's the wrong thing to do. That couldn't be enough of an explanation, even when it was all I had.

'When Eric gave you a gun,' she pushed through my silence, 'was Jeffrey still alive?'

'He grunted,' I said.

I saw it for an instant. A great pain in her face – she'd loved her brother, she'd loved me, and I'd done nothing. And then it was gone. She pulled a chair and sat opposite me, her wide-open eyes searching for mine.

'It's nos quatre mois next Friday,' she spoke very carefully.

'Yes,' I whimpered. 'We should do something.'

'I want to make you a special dinner. A watercress soup. A strawberry risotto. A coconut flan. And then, when the moon is high, we'll go to the river. There's a wild spot before Donnington Bridge. That's where we'll have our final drink.'

'Final?' The word scared me.

'Champagne,' she stated. 'For nos quatre mois.' My eyes met her stern eyes. She looked directly into me until I turned away.

'Alright,' I said.

She nodded slowly, her head rising and falling, and we'd sealed a deal. Only the corner of her mouth, with a simple twitch, betrayed the expression. And I saw it. It wasn't a hangover on her face, but the calm after a storm – a face that emotions had torn apart and that had finally come back together, tired and decided. I watched her stand, as she laid both hands on the table and pushed up, and I understood that what I'd been waiting for had happened. She'd made her choice. Now I'd get to find out what it was.

'I'm going home,' she said, and her voice was suddenly distant, devoid of her earlier gravitas.

'But you said you were staying tonight.'

She shrugged.

'I feel like going home.'

She grabbed her bag, slung it over her shoulder, and I spoke again, because I needed to know, and this was my chance:

'Have you forgiven me?' and I cringed over the word 'forgive'.

'No,' she said immediately, with none of the anger she'd had the last time I'd asked her that. She laid her cold fingers on my arm and squeezed it affectionately. 'Why do you keep on thinking about that?'

'Well.' I felt stumped. 'What about Kuraetsokov?'

'Exactly. Stop thinking,' she said. 'Thoughts get in the way.'

When she was almost through the door, she gazed back at me, two creases drawn across her neck, a wild look glistening in her eyes. Her hazy voice, her wild gaze, she didn't seem all there. And I realised that she'd just done something important for herself too, and she was going to leave without telling me what it was.

'My mother's the same. She keeps on asking me strange questions. Why can't you all see it? Your heads, they just get in the way.' She pointed at her head, then at her heart, and she smiled harrowingly.

As she left, her smile kept me rooted to my chair. It had none of her usual joy, none of the glee that used to take over her face when her lips were inches from mine – cheeks lifted to her eyes, nothing but teeth and gum – a smile that demanded my lips surrender their control and answer in kind, even if teeth were going to smash into teeth, for all of the joy in the air was making hurts and burns as right as a mother's caress. No, this smile was tight-lipped. It stopped where tears trailed. It was her pain.

I needed to know what she'd decided. I remembered her bags and went into the kitchen. In the fridge, I found three bunches of herbs. I recognised one: coriander. There had to be something else. She'd been hunched over behind the counter while I'd delved into her vampires. I looked into the three cupboards she could reach from her position but nothing seemed out of the ordinary – just plates, pots and biscuit tins. There was something about coriander, but I couldn't remember what. I knew that she never used it in her cooking. I went to my computer and, perched on the green exercise ball, in between two of my larger graphite sketches, I searched the internet for herbs. It took three clicks and I'd found the right picture: yellowish green, like a miniature pine tree. One of the herbs was dill. 'Thyme, coriander and dill,' she'd said. And I recalled her grandmother's quiet death.

A surge of adrenaline sent me back to the cupboards. There had to be more than just those three herbs. While she'd had me in that book, she'd been plotting my downfall. I just needed proof. I took out the pots, the tins, and patted the shelves, running my hand over all the surfaces, looking for a bulge. There was nothing. She'd hidden it somewhere and I needed to find it. While the adrenaline ran high, I was all action. She'd repeatedly glanced back at her bags – she'd been so obvious about it all, tossing me the first novel she'd found at the till, like she'd toss a dog a bone while she readied his last needle. I opened the tins. The first one was still full of stale biscuits. The second had two new medicine bottles. My heart started pounding. A pink bottle with the picture of a flat and tanned stomach; a green bottle with Spanish words, and a label pasted over it: 'Vet Supplies.'

Fear took over. My breath shortening, I went to my computer with the two bottles, and searched for their names. Nembutal and Pepto Bismol. Pepto Bismol, the pastel pink bottle, was an antiemetic. To stop my body from vomiting the other drug. Nembutal was a sleeping pill, banned in the UK. Taken together with an antiemetic, my browser was spurting Dr Death articles, assisted suicide, euthanasia. This was how Leona had helped her grandmother die. And now, this was how she planned on killing me.

A few pills dissolved into a watercress soup, crushed into a strawberry risotto, or even concealed in a flute of champagne, and I was a dead man floating down to London. I wouldn't go far. With the Iffley Lock three hundred yards past Donnington Bridge, my body would hardly have time to bloat before a man and his dog found it, and the police asked my mother to identify my half-distended deformity, my cheeks gone brown with silt, my lips a bloodless white, and my eyes bulging out of my head with water, only so she could better see how vacant they were.

No, I was letting my fears override my reason. She'd realised I had trouble sleeping and now she wanted to help me. And the antiemetic – well, perhaps she had heartburn. There I was making everything out of nothing, forgetting the times she'd spontaneously asked me whether I wanted a massage, the plethora of dishes she'd cooked after a long day waiting at tables just so I could try to integrate another logarithm, the picnic she'd made me three weeks earlier, and the sandwiches she ran home to make so that two of my friends could invite themselves along. I was forgetting the ease behind her smile, the light tingle of her forefinger running back and forth over my wrist, and the way she kissed my neck, with lips, tongue and hot breath, each ingredient added after another week together, until she had me just right. And three herbs; I was remembering her story wrong. It could have just as well been basil or parsley. The drugs were a mere coincidence.

I needed to wash my hands, to douse them in soap, and to rub until I'd erased the last of my fingerprints. The sink wouldn't do: I went into the bathroom and had a shower, turning the tap into the red until it burned my skin. I was big enough to stand it. When I became used to the heat, I turned it hotter still, and then I made it as cold as possible.

The contrast made me groan, and the groan became a shout. And I loved the release, the way it started in my gut, the way I clenched my fists and thrust my chest out, the way its echo broke through the sheets of water. I shouted until I ran out of breath. Then I turned the shower off and, naked, I went to sit in the living room. Water pooled in the sofa's creases.

Someone had to die to make up for her brother's death. That much was clear. Ever since she'd hit her mother, she'd started to repress the violent side of her grief. That was what Amanda had meant. And now that she'd waited so long, now that I'd drawn a target on my neck, she was preparing to execute me. She had a rope around my throat, and she'd pulled her noose tighter with every hour we'd spent together. I'd started to feel it in Wytham Woods, when it was still loose enough that it rested heavy on my shoulders. But a day watching television, and worst of all, the hours she'd spent away from me, when I was nothing but a faceless prisoner, and she'd pulled the rope tighter, inch after inch, until I could feel the imprint of its grooves on my jugular.

I pictured her sitting across from me, my papers strewn all over the table, her vampire novel split open over my notebook earning its first crease, and I understood the expression on her face as she spoke of our final dinner: its length, its paleness, and the extreme stillness of her eyes. A judge handing out her first death sentence, hiding behind a wig and a grave face. And I remembered her standing up, both hands flat on the table, her single nod like a scythe to my heart, and that singular twitch in the corner of her mouth. I couldn't argue with that twitch; it was my crowning proof. As damning as if she'd shed a tear. A dash of pain, compassion, doubt to justify the rest.

But it was only a dash. The part that wanted to see my fingers crisp and drop my champagne flute under Donnington Bridge ruled her. I'd been punched on the back of the head. My brain had squeezed through my eyeballs and splattered on the wall. I started to shiver, but I didn't move. After a long time, I found a blanket, draped it over my shoulders, and lay down on the sofa until night fell and sleep came.

* * *

I woke up in bed with a vague feeling of guilt and fear, as if I'd set myself an alarm but couldn't remember what I was getting up for, only that I couldn't be late. Wading through my schedule, I asked myself whether it was my turn to prepare the Saturday picnic, and I felt a sharp surge of adrenaline. I swung out of bed, looking for something to do, to act so that I wouldn't think: correct the wobble of the three kitchen chairs, remove the vinegar stain on the coffee table, see whether I could unwarp my front wheel – the bicycle, resting against the lower flat's veranda, the wind brushing its spokes, held a message addressed to me. I went into the garden, unclasped the wheel, and laid it flat on the garden's only patch of grass. When I looked right down the axle, I could see the back of the wheel rise into a crescent. Hammer in hand, I hit it once. The wheel spun, rubber burning my fingers. I turned it back to where it'd been, eyed the flatness of the plane, and hit it harder. The feel of the heavy hammer clanging against the light aluminium frame satisfied me, but I couldn't see whether it was straightening the wheel. I needed a level. There was one in the kitchen under the sink.

As I walked up the steps, the seams between the stairs' bricks tried to tell me something, but I couldn't make out the secret locked in their pattern. The kitchen tiles listened to the bricks and waved too. I stopped in the middle of the kitchen, wondering why I'd gone up in the first place. And then, where I'd left them the night before, I saw the two medicine packs on the counter: the green bottle promising sleepless sleep, and the pastel pink bottle that would quieten my body's doubts. The last of the adrenaline stored in my glands came up. Without thinking, I reached for my phone and called Leona. It rang and it rang and it went to voicemail. Standing in the middle of the kitchen, I tried again.

'Good morning, Nathan,' she said in a sluggish voice.

Surprised, I looked at my watch: it was 8 a.m. She was probably asleep in her room, in Jeffrey's old room.

'Are you going to work today?' I said.

'Maybe,' she groaned.

She was still missing work because of me.

'Only ten days left before your classes start again.'

'They think I'm sick,' she said.

'Oh.'

'I'm not sick.'

'I don't think you are.'

I grabbed hold of the kitchen counter. I was losing control of the conversation.

'Mum thinks I'm sick too. But I'm not, alright!'

'You're not sick. You just needed time,' I said and winced. I couldn't take her side when she'd planned my death. I clenched my fist. I needed certainty, and I needed it now. 'Listen, I just saw you had some herbs in the fridge…' I trailed off, hoping she'd confess. A word, a sob, she didn't have to say it outright. But all I could make out was her breath, sounding heavier than usual. 'Thyme, coriander and dill,' I pushed on. 'What am I meant to do with them?'

'They bother you?' she barked, the line crackled, and I had my sign. Immediately, I felt my fears confirmed and a need to calm her down.

'No—' I started. But why should I calm her when I was a finger away from yelling myself? The answer came vividly: she'd cried in my arms while the rain beat relentlessly on the windows, while a turbid smog travelled from my lips to her ears, while every puff had made my lungs and mind swell, and had withered her limbs into her gut.

And with that image, my anger choked on its stillborn carcass. I was guilty and she had a right to be angry. I'd been selfish to unburden myself on her. Now that she was suffering, I had to pay for what I'd done, for the pain I'd caused her.

'No,' I said, 'they'll stay fresher if I put them in the bottom drawer. Are they for Friday?'

She stayed quiet.

'For the soup?' I said.

'No, for after,' she whispered.

'The risotto?'

'No,' she said, her voice seeming as distant as mine, as if a part of us had moved to a different plane, and every word was just another wink to answers we already knew. 'It's for the surprise.'

I smiled against the receiver.

'On the river?'

'Maybe,' she said. 'It's a surprise.'

'Go back to sleep,' I said and I hung up.

The medicine bottles stared at me serenely. They were hovering on the white counter like two buoys in a harbour, the green gate freshly painted, the red marker faded to pink with the sun, and I felt myself rush between them, down a sea of white towards a weeping willow. I grabbed the green bottle and studied its Spanish writing – México, D. F. written along the bottom ring. There was a plastic seal along the top ring. If I broke it, I could try a pill and see how I felt, and then I could try two, and then three, until my body became immune. There I'd be under Donnington Bridge, pretending to float dead, but really laughing at the stars.

But if I broke the seals, she would notice. We would have to sit down, look each other in the eye, and talk about it. My hands went damp – I forced myself to consider it: she was blowing cold air on her cup of tea, while mine cooled down on the coffee table. (I had to do something about that vinegar stain.) I looked for the right words, stuttering, humming and hamming, struggling to bring it to the surface, where it would only harden into a shell, when we both knew, when we both knew we knew. No, silence was a better option – that way at least, we could pretend that everything was fine. I placed the two bottles back where I'd found them, in the 1920s French cake tin Leona had bought at La Rochelle – the metal one in shades of brown with the picture of a little girl holding a doll.

I held on to that resigned decisiveness while I took a shower. When I turned the tap off, I realised I'd left the door open and steamed up the whole flat. I'd be dead in a week; a little moisture on the walls didn't matter. But I was still annoyed. My mind was pacing, racing, and my eyes followed, jumping all over the room, fastening on every vivid detail. The full-length mirror on the bathroom wall cleared with a fresh draught, and I could see myself. There was a furrow across my brow. My mind latched on. Such a unique expression: four half-moons spreading from the corner of my eyes, with a single white unbroken line spanning from one temple to the other – no one else's brow creased in just that pattern. The beauty of the expression, so true to everything I was, moved me. And soon my forehead would be as smooth as a sheet of wax. I'd spent three years at the Chamonix gym working on my triceps until I could see them sharpening the back of my arms, and there they were, poking through freckles and moles, bulging when I flexed them. In a week, they'd be bark starting their slow wither. Not even a week: five days. Five short days, and September would be almost over, and Leona would be getting ready for her second year of university.

It wasn't possible. The world couldn't go on without me, that bee buzzing over my face included. If I weren't there to see them fly, bees wouldn't bother. They'd die with me gracefully, like a pharaoh's retinue, shutting their eyes when I shut mine.

I needed to move. Naked, I ran down the stairs, skipped the little gate into the garden, and lay on the grass. The grass would die because it only existed for me, just like that wall and the people looking at me behind the curtains of that window. I laughed. They didn't know it, but they were about to die. Enjoy the view while you can. Those triceps, the rebellious tuft of hair on my chest, and my cock, enjoy them. That cock, which had led me like a ship's rudder, that cock which had hosed piss over Europe's highest mountains, into the Pacific's warmest currents, that cock which had shot sperm on a redhead's thigh and smeared it down to her knee, as if it were my brush and her thigh my canvas – Fuck! – that cock would remain forever placid, and shrink until it was as long as the tip of my little finger. The man behind the curtains showed his face and knocked loudly on the window, but I didn't care about him. I wanted to hit a fast bowler back over his head, and to stay in that moment when only I knew the ball was going for six. I wanted to put on a pair of 188s, climb over a ridge, and plunge over unbroken snow. The ground to slip rugged under my skis, a tree rushing to embrace me, and with my strongest push, to graze past it, laugh, and charge a bigger trunk.

I jumped up, standing tall with my arms on my hips and my chest ready to flatten anyone who dared challenge me, and I stared down everything around me. That measly tree, nothing more than a bush stretching a foot higher than it should; that concrete slab, dark with cancerous cracks, crumbling with next year's rains; and the paint peeling off the gate, three blue leaves hanging from another blister.

Fuck them all.

I would never meet another girl. A blonde with cropped hair, a ring in her nose, who could tickle me wild with the stud in her tongue. A scowling brunette, who'd hold out a soft hand just when I thought I'd screwed it up. I wouldn't hear a new voice quietening to a whisper and pulling me in as surely as if there were a cord fastened to my heart. Stealing glances, delighting in the impossible, and yearning for flesh, flesh and more flesh (round, smooth and firm), I wanted it all and I could have none.

My shoulders slumped and I sat back down, folding my legs so the neighbours wouldn't see my shrinking cock. There might be more muscles hiding my body, more hair covering my arse, but I was still the boy who'd feasted on Eric's madness and backtracked come payday. The same killer who'd spurted bullets at Leona. I could fight it all night but the facts were there: one, I was guilty, two, I deserved to die. It was time for the blindfold.

I surrendered. My mind was the centre of a storm, and images, ideas, memories all flapped with the winds. Time passed. I did things, time did things to me – I can't remember. And the bike was fixed, I was dressed, I was cycling in the middle of the road, and I was avoided by cars, taxis, and buses full of men in football shirts and tracksuits. By a grandmother who kept on sounding her horn, wanting to claim the centre of the road back for her kind, who pulled up next to me when she finally overtook me, asked me whether I was crazy, and who drove off when I gave her the finger.

The September sun had finally vanquished all of the summer's clouds. I squinted to see through the asphalt's glare, and recognised a ditch on the side of the road. There used to be flowers pinned to a telephone pole by this ditch – because an eighteen-year-old boy had killed himself driving too fast, my mother had told me – but the telephone pole was gone, and with it the flowers. And there, it felt closer in a car, was a turn I'd taken thousands of times, with a harvested field waving yellows and greens.

I stopped by a new sign: 'Hornsbury Sutton School'.

They'd changed the name. It made sense, I nodded to myself. I hadn't planned on going to my old school – I wasn't capable of planning anything – but I'd ridden on the windy road escaping

Headington Hill, and now, there it was – it'd changed its name but I'd found it anyway. I turned my bike into the lane leading up to the school. The road had been freshly relaid; new white lines shone on its sides. My wheels glided silently over the dark bitumen. I heard nothing but the tyres' gentle hum and the deaf sound of the wind pressing on my ears, until I reached the crest where the side hedge turned into a woven-wire fence and my old red bricks rose from the hillside. Just before the bus circle stood a discreet sign: 'Hornsbury Memorial' and an arrow pointing down a path once only used for June Jamborees.

I put my bike on my old rack, the closest one to the stairs – since it was half-hidden by a hedge, there was always a free spot – and I stood at the bottom of the main steps, longing for a pair of heavy doors I could blast open. Hornsbury School's master was returning home, I laughed at the renovated façade. They'd removed the black crust that used to pile on the bottom of each brick, so that the white bricks interlaced in between the red bricks finally showed their pattern. Getting it pretty for my return; that was even funnier. I felt like a madman thrown into his dream world. If only I had two guns on my hips, I could kick the doors open and swagger my way home.

Instead, I walked up the steps and two automatic panes silently slid open. A woman with a ponytail glared at me. It was 2.30 p.m. If I remembered the timetable right, students would finish their current period in five minutes. I walked down the lino-lined corridors and came out exactly the same door Jeffrey and I used to take to go down to our physics class on Thursday mornings. The neo-gothic archway still left the building to finish abruptly halfway down the hill. I followed it until there was a gap between the trees and I saw the glass spire Leona had talked about. It spanned twenty yards above the ground, and at its end, it opened into a glass flower, as if its nectar could attract dead souls back to Earth.

I turned around. Students in their green blazers, the boys' ties tighter than I used to wear mine, girls still pushing the rules a button at a time, swarmed out of the main building's back doors. Yes, with two guns, I could spray bullets until thirty were down, march to the memorial, pray, and die a fitting death. A group of sixth-formers strolled down the archway, looking at me funnily. I'd show them. Perhaps it was because I wasn't wearing a uniform, I thought, and for the first time, I took a second to notice what I'd put on. Brown sandals, paint-stained jeans, a business shirt opened to my breastbone, plus a five-day beard. I would have stared too. If I lingered any longer, a teacher would come and ask me to leave the premises. Impulsively, I made my way towards the spire: as I came closer, I saw its fat round base, also made of glass. All together, it looked like a pimple shooting pus at the sky. It was probably meant to symbolise something, perhaps hope. I skirted around the flower beds that surrounded it and went right to the centre of the sports ground.

The football posts were already up, the white lines already painted, but a wicket the groundsman must have used in August still looked playable. I took guard at the crease and pulled a long hop, cut a throat tickler over the slips for four, backfoot drove like I'd never backfoot driven before.

'Oye!' I heard behind me. A black dog was running towards me, its nose tickling the grass. The groundsman followed in his green sleeveless jacket. His two gardening gloves in one hand, he was waving me off with his other hand.

'You're not allowed to be here. I can report you to the Dean.' He stopped a few yards away. His dog came to smell my hand. 'Are you a student? This is private property.'

'Mr Rivers?' I asked, smiling at the normality of the moment. He'd shouted me off his field just the same way before.

He squinted: 'Yeah?'

'Nate. Nate Dillingham.'

He pursed his lips and eyed me up and down.

'So you are. You've got hair all over your face now. Hard to recognise you.' He fidgeted with his gloves, his eyes on the grass, on his dog. 'What are you doing here?'

'I don't know,' I said with a wide big smile.

He looked at me like I'd said something strange.

'Are you on something? Acid, LSD?'

'No.' I couldn't stop smiling.

His eyes on his hands, he put his gloves on and took them off again.

'What have you been doing since… since you left school?'

I looked at the green field around me, at the grass stubble poking through the square's mud. It was all so simple, all so real.

'None of it matters,' I said. 'I've been living in a dream.'

He nodded, his lips pursed. He didn't understand me, he couldn't understand me – for eight years, he'd been cutting grass, painting lines, rolling pitches, while his dog trotted around him. He'd stayed firm while I'd ran away. His life had flowed from his past, and now he could stand on his field, and he could say that he belonged. In the meantime, I'd reneged on what I'd done, what had happened to me. And I'd fled, I'd grasped at air, I'd come back a shell of a man.

Mr Rivers put his hands on his hips.

'Well, don't stay there, you'll mark my pitch and the grass won't have time to grow before winter.'

'Are you still playing?' I said, bending down so I could pet his dog.

'As much as the body will let me play. My knees aren't what they were.'

'You were never one to steal a quick single,' I chuckled.

'No, no, but now I have a bionic knee, and this one's about to go.'

His voice hadn't changed: the same stout chat I'd heard behind the stumps when we used to play him in the OCA. In those days, everyone knew him as Johnny Cricket – the man who played four games a week, and who'd happily have played seven if it weren't for his wife.

'Do you still keep?'

'If the captain's smart, I stand at slip and that does me fine.' He smiled and looked around his field. 'It's changed a bit since you left, hasn't it? They built the memorial—'

'A monstrosity.'

'Well, they consulted everyone. Three years of consultations. You could have told them. And they finally built a proper pavilion.' He pointed his thumb at a building I hadn't noticed, a modern take on a traditional pavilion, slick concrete walls rendered to look more like wood.

'Looks nice, doesn't it?' I said.

He sniggered.

'Typical of them, isn't it? The space I have in there, the tractor hardly fits anymore. Always trying to save money. That hasn't changed.'

Nodding, I wrestled a ball from his dog's jaw and threw it far. She ran after it.

'Listen,' I said. 'Do you mind if I stay here for a bit?'

'On the square?'

'No.' I moved off the square. The dog came back with the ball. 'Just here.' I waved my arm at the field, at the trees.

He studied my face, and then he nodded.

'Just don't get in the way when I'm mowing the lawn.'

As he turned around, I snatched the tennis ball out of the dog's jaw, and threw it the other way. She looked at the green ball travelling through the air, at her master ambling in the opposite direction, at the ball, at her master, and pounced after the ball, her thin legs heaving her big belly and its white under-fur across the grass. The ball dipped and bounced, and it dipped again, and her body flew angled across the ball's path, until they were travelling together, and she was turning around in a slow circle. She dropped the ball, heavy with her drool, by my feet and this time she didn't look at her master. A gentle breeze carrying the smell of freshly cut grass, the sun resolutely shaking off all troublesome clouds, I played with her while Mr Rivers cut the lawn. After what felt like a hundred throws, she brought the ball back and slumped to the ground, keeping the ball in her teeth. We were both tired. I sat next to her and petted her, my eyes closed, enjoying the singular beauty of the moment. Her whimpers, her uneven breath, they were all part of it. When Mr Rivers turned his tractor off, she rose replenished and ran his way. I lay still, facing the trees down the hill – the ones I used to fetch cricket balls from whenever the wicket was too close to the downhill boundary and a burly right-hander got stuck into our friendly spinners – but I didn't think of the past. An appreciative calm had taken hold of me – my view, the smell, the temperature, they were all perfect, and it was only now, when I had hours left, that I realised it. I breathed deeply, air swelling into my gut, and I floated happy in the moment.

At one stage, I heard two voices, getting nearer, shouting, perhaps at me. When I turned around, Mr Rivers was walking towards them. It was two young men, teachers I guessed, coming to investigate, to kick me off the school grounds. The three of them, pointing at me, spoke halfway between the memorial and my patch of grass. Then the teachers walked back towards the school, and Mr Rivers came by.

'I'm going home,' he said.

'Do you mind if I stay a bit longer?'

He took a second to answer:

'As long as you don't vandalise my pitch.'

'Thanks,' I said, and he called his dog to him.

I lay on my back and watched the clouds. With them, the beauty continued. They were thickening, cooling down the air, drawing patterns in the sky. If I'd worked at it, I could have learned to draw clouds. It was all about their shadows – easy enough for the eye to discern, hard to render with a pencil, with a brush. An enormous canvas of a cloudy sky, capturing its volume, its movement, the shades of blues and whites. There couldn't be a better picture than that. I didn't have the time to work on it now, but it didn't matter; a young man would stare at the sky one day, and dedicate his life to capturing that single beauty. It would be a life well spent. And it struck me as obvious: to capture beauty and give it to someone else was the only way to spend a life.

I remained there for hours, for soon it was dark, and I couldn't discern one cloud from another. My body was damp with dew and stiff with cold, but that was incidental. The field looked different at night, and so did the memorial. Dimly lit, its tip darker than the trees around it, it had a foreboding beauty. It stood exactly where the Kemp Annexe had stood. There was a ramp approaching it from the field and another from the school. I took the one from the field. Lights low on the walls lit the path like a plane's aisle. The flower beds sitting on the parapets were prettier for the half-light. I could make out handprints moulded into the wall, and small plaques beneath them. I bent down to inspect the one right by my foot: 'I learned that nothing was for granted.' And the student's name: Harry Williams. The one student I'd disliked, for his petulant mouth, his spanky hair, and the way he'd always tried harder than he should. And in an instant, that image disappeared, replaced by one of a boy (a man now, I guessed) who had never fitted in, and who, when he'd lost people who hadn't cared about him, had still lost it all. I placed my hand over his handprint – his fingers were surprisingly long – and went inside the memorial.

Leona had described it as like being inside a stomach made of glass. At night, with the few lights making the glass walls a cavernous boundary, I understood her. The walls curved high towards the start of the spire, meeting it at least four times my height from the ground, so that the reflected light barely brushed the ceiling. Instead the spare lighting focused on a low wall, made of a damp yellow stone and angled like a lectern, which formed most of a circle and occupied the centre of the monument. I followed its inside, my fingers running over the stone: Graham Johnson, Tom Davies, Laura Clarkson, Jayvanti Patel, Jeffrey Baker, Satish Choudary, Edward Moss, Paul Cumnor, Grace Li, Anna Walker. They each had a simple gold-plated plaque with their name in a bare font, and underneath each plaque, I could feel it with my fingers, were a few handwritten words engraved into the stone. 'No one will make us laugh like you' was written under Anna's name, and 'The cats always sleep on your bed' underneath Laura's. The writing under Jeffrey's name was Amanda's. It said, 'We think of you every day'. Ironic, I thought: Leona never thought of her brother. But there was beauty in her way too, I corrected myself, and I saw it clearly for the first time: her life had never been anchored by grief, and that was perhaps the freest of lives.

There was no plaque with Eric's name on the wall. Searching for one around the monument, I came across another yellow-stoned wall near the exit. It had the names of all those who'd come to our help. Batterthew, Elizabeth Batterthew, that was the name of the kind paramedic who'd taken me to hospital. I didn't know the other names, but I remembered the uniforms busying themselves around us in the room, and outside, in the sharp light. And, centred, alone, on the far edge of the wall, under its own heading – Wounded – a plaque with my name. If I had to have one, I preferred it where it was, isolated.

The space, cosy where I stood, but soaring at its centre, invited me to follow its contours. Walking along the glass wall, I almost missed it. It looked like dirt smeared on the ground, but there it was, on a small slab, like a saint's tomb in a cathedral: Eric Knight. Nothing but those two words. I was glad to see them, and I remembered the groundsman: three years of consultations. If anything had needed consultation, it must have been that name, which should have stood on the round wall, but which some would have never wanted in the memorial at all. I kneeled next to it and prayed, to no god in particular, but to the enclosed space, to the memory of those I'd let die, to Eric and his mother, and most of all, to a kindness that was spreading from my solar plexus like it would encompass all.

Then I went to the room's centre, and I sat on the yellow-stoned bench that lay in between the circle of plaques. The stone was porous yet smooth. From that point in the memorial, every line seemed to funnel my gaze up towards the spire, and further towards a small window that crowned the spire. Through it, I could see a corner of the sky: two ex-centred stars in a black disk. I closed my eyes and I let my thoughts glide down to the stone dais and my crossed legs, like a Buddhist monk in between chants. I saw myself; with distance, it all made sense. I was going to die because I deserved to, because Leona needed me to.

It was when my thoughts quietened that I realised that I was hungry. It was half past nine, and I hadn't had any food all day. But I wanted to flow with the beauty around me. I called Leona. She answered on the first ring, her voice as hazy as mine.

'What are you doing?' I said.

'I'm in bed,' she said, murmuring, and I could almost touch her detached kindness. She sounded like she'd spent the day agitated too. Immediately, I felt like anything I could say would be right:

'Sleeping?'

'Maybe. I don't know yet. I'm just in bed. Maybe I'll fall asleep, maybe I'll stay like I am.'

I don't know why, she never said so, but I knew she was at her parents', in her green flannel pyjamas, the same duvet cover she'd had since she was eight, a uniform red with three embroidered yellow flowers, covering her up to her midriff, her left hand resting on the duvet right above her hip-bone.

'Tell me about your day,' I said.

'I went for a long walk along the Thames and then I made jam,' she said. 'What do you want to know?'

'The walk, the jam, everything. I want to hear you speak.'

'Well, you know Farmoor Reservoir' – she started, and I listened to her voice narrate her day, and I delighted with her when she told me of the trees overrunning the path, when she described the sweetness of her pears. We spoke until I ran out of credit. She called me back but it was half past ten and she needed to sleep.

Happy, I meditated. Had I years rather than five days left, I would have spent my life striving for the state I was in now. I felt it deep inside: it was time to let go of my hysteria, to see death as an opportunity. My thoughts felt free. They brushed and circled and caressed the Leona I'd known. The flow I'd noticed on our first date. The ease with which she'd moved, with which she'd spoken. Yes, our first few careless days had been something special. And then Jeffrey's ghost came in between us, for I needed to lay him to rest and she needed to keep him at bay.

I remembered a spot I'd hiked to alone in the Alps, the one summer I'd spent in the mountains, when I was trying to spend a day away from Denret. A farmer's dam in a secluded valley: above it, two rugged slopes meeting in a narrow stream. Below it, a rapid drop to a cosy plateau caught in between the peaks, dotted with green pastures and yellowing cornfields. On a whim, I'd veered off the main path, following a goat's trail instead, and I'd reached a crest. From my vantage point, I could see the vastness of the mountains in the distance, and right by my feet, this little valley folded on itself, with its dark pool carved into the rock, the water so still that I could see its high walls reflected on the surface. I walked to the top of a small knoll that formed one of the pool's walls, and I stared down at it: it was late in the summer, and the water was so low, the walls so slick, that a man falling in would have drowned while trying to climb out. From the distance of memory, I flew above my spot and thought of Leona: such wild beauty in the scene, from the jagged rocks forming a spine on the mountain ridge, the high grass darkening the gully, the haze softening the yellows and greens of the plateau, to the waterhole itself, deep, simple and threatening. The view was different from within the dam – from there, all I could see was the brown clay smudging the dark walls, and above, between sky and rock, the top of the knoll and the grass on the crest. From that view, I was a man drowning. And there I'd been, taking a walk in this little valley with Leona, guiding us to the waterhole, while she preferred the view from the crest, nudging her closer despite her resistance, and then at the edge of the hole, when she looked at me with a compassionate smile, I'd pushed her in.

My thoughts lined themselves around the scene: I'd pushed Leona into the darkest part of herself, some sort of angry grief she'd repressed, when she'd lived in a world as beautiful as that valley. And I pictured her standing in her green summer dress, her skin lightly tanned, a rebellious strand of her hair slowly falling towards her other cheek, while inside, she ignored her swirls of anger and resolutely clung on to everything that was beautiful within. I felt a deep, awed love towards the girl who'd listened to her father three weeks after her brother's death and chose everything that was noble within, to the girl who'd fought all her life to stay that way and who'd kept on trying when she'd realised who I was, when I had, selfish and clumsy, repeatedly mentioned her brother.

And suddenly, jarring me out of my amazement, I understood that I was leaving her drowning in a waterhole. I'd be floating under Donnington Bridge and the police would be knocking on her door. I couldn't have her in chains, locked up when she was innocent at heart. I opened my eyes and looked at the memorial around me.

I needed to move. There was so much to do. Five days to help Leona. Five days to parse through the surge of feelings throbbing through my veins. Five days to capture beauty. I was outside, striding by the archway to nowhere, looking through my pocket for my bike key, pacing around the main building. I'd been a good enough sketcher when I was twelve, but after my years in the wilderness, I could feel it with my spaceships, my lines were good but five days weren't enough to get them right. I'd have needed five years. In five days, all I could do was write my story, starting where I'd left off, and hope that amongst stacks and piles, in the four months I'd put down on paper, I'd capture at least one moment in all its beauty. One would do: a fraction of a sky, the edge of a cloud, splitting glare and shadow, and my life would be well spent. A simple anecdote, the way Leona scratched her temples when she thought – to watch her fingers tap-dance across her brow one more time!

I pulled my bike off the rack and started riding on the unlit roads, down the hill towards the main road, cool air playing through my hair, the smooth asphalt smoother still at night. I felt ecstatic, full of purpose. The feeling had to be contagious – I had to share it with my parents, with my brother. If only he felt the way I did, he wouldn't need drugs and he'd stop his silent war with my mother. Five days; I made it into a refrain, and I sung all the way home.

* * *

Fuck. Three hours until Leona arrives. She'll have dinner pre-made, safely locked up in a bag full of Tupperwares. A travelling pharmacist travelling for me and only for me. She told me to throw away the herbs she bought when she was here last Saturday. She had a new dish in mind – she wanted to use basil instead, and there was some in her garden at home. And now, I have three hours to write what happened in the last five days. Three manic hours until we celebrate nos quatre mois, until this spirit rallies for one last hurray, until this grace comes across the simplest of fears. Here it comes, the first shot of adrenaline, and my fingers are shaking.

Four days ago, I woke up full of a thinning purpose. Before my feet touched the floor, I'd counted it: four days, and a pang of fear started in my heart's lowest chamber, tightened the muscles across my shoulders. Four days. But I had a purpose – that much was clear. When I asked myself what it was, all I could come up with was a single, meaningless word: beauty. Hissing, I forced my mind back into the memorial, to the stone dais under the spire, in between the plaques, until I felt some of the previous day's calm. Then I started my computer and opened a new document.

After I'd spent twelve hours writing, after I felt my gut drop for tiredness, after I thought I'd collapse through my green exercise ball, that I'd waver and roll with it until I slammed through the ground, I stood up, shook the stiffness out of my muscles, and went to my mother's. I had no food left in my fridge. My vision, so long narrowed to a white screen, broadened on the walk over. When I saw her sitting at the dining table, her laptop on the one side, a pile of papers on the other, her careful eyes shifting from one to the other, her hands fingering the paper softly, I felt a pang of regret. This is what she'd done every night throughout my childhood, what had earned her the respect of her world, and there she was again, years later, my mother doing what she was best at. I was seeing it for one last time.

'Nate,' she said, standing up, forgetting her all-important work. 'You haven't been answering your phone.'

'I guess I haven't.'

'Are you hungry?' she said, already walking towards the kitchen.

'I haven't eaten for two days.'

She came close, grabbed my wrists and studied me. And then, with a mother's certainty, she hugged me like she'd hugged me when I was little and tearful. In her clasp, I recalled the smell of my tears on her woollen jumpers, the weight of her long arms enclosing me when I'd fallen off my bicycle. When she made as if to let go, I hugged her tighter in turn, snugly, consoling her for what was to come. We stayed in each other's arms for a whole minute. There was everything in that hug: my apologies, hers, my goodbyes. Everything but an outright explanation – but I couldn't tell her what she'd want to know without compromising Leona.

'Your father's out of town,' she said when I finally released her. 'It's just the two of us then.' She opened the fridge. 'What do you feel like?'

I smiled a son's smile and kept on playing my part throughout the evening. It was my parting gift. When she prodded me, I offered no resistance and went along with her wishes at the merest of hints. I told her everything she wanted to hear – my thoughts on life after my course, a research project on the ethics of internet subscription plans, how nice Leona was – and none of it felt like a lie. I was proud of the subtle change that came over her. It was in the way she spoke that I noticed it best: her voice's timbre became thoughtful and her ideas grew more and more open to discussion. For one precious evening, I was seeing my mother as she'd always wanted me to see her: a determined mother and a close friend. A woman who would do all to protect me, who wanted me to call her at four in the morning because I needed to cry. A mother who felt like she was getting closer to her son. Before I left, I hugged her again. It was different this time: my arms found her aged – it was a precious feeling, to see my mother in full and to find her a diminished woman. I rocked her from side to side, happy to know her so. She sobbed in my arms.

On my walk back, I tried to call Leona but I had no credit left. Funny, I thought, that something as insignificant as money could get in the way of a man's last wish. Funny that so much was made of a man's last wish, when it was the one wish in a man's life that had the least bearing upon the rest of his life. The young man with long hair walking towards me would lend me his phone if I explained my story. But if, a week earlier, I'd told him that my girlfriend and I were going through a rocky patch, he'd have told me that he had no credit left. And yet, a week ago, I could have still saved myself from this fate.

Just as I opened the Cowley flat's door, I knew what I was going to do for Leona. The plan came to me unannounced, fully formed, flawless. It was so easy: look at the labels on the medicine bottles and place an express order for the same ones on the internet. It took less than an hour, and the two same drugs I'd found in my cake tin were flying across the world to meet me. A green and a pink gate, and I'd be floating guiltless under Donnington Bridge, a satisfied smile marring my death rictus, and she'd be crying in her mother's arms, safe from those who ask too many questions.

Emboldened by the time I'd spent with my mother, I caught a train to London the next day and dropped in on my brother. I walked up his street with a decided step, by its blackened red-brick houses, its small front yards, its withering trees. When I rang the bell, I expected no response – I'd walk in, he'd be stoned in his living room, and we'd talk like we'd never talked before. But there was no music escaping the front porch, and I heard footsteps coming to the door. James opened the door and looked at me with bloodshot eyes.

'Oh, it's you,' he said. He poked his head out to look at the street.

'What, are you expecting someone else?'

He stood straight:

'What are you doing here?'

I smiled awkwardly.

'Can I come in?'

'Sure,' he sighed.

I followed him inside, past the peeling green wallpaper. I didn't know what was missing, but the corridor felt barer this time. He went into the living room. The sofa's cushions were still scattered all over the floor. There was a man I didn't know hunched with his back to the wall. He was so thin that veins bulged blue and green all over his exposed skin, thick on his temples, forming a web over his bald skull. He looked at me suspiciously.

'Hi, I'm James' brother,' I said.

He looked away, suddenly uninterested, and I sat on the cushion next to my brother.

'What are you doing here?' James asked.

I took a deep breath:

'I was hoping to spend a little time with you.'

'Have you broken up with Leona?'

'No, no, why are you saying this?'

He sneered: 'Why didn't she come with you then?'

I didn't know what to answer. I shouldn't have come like this, without letting him know first.

'What time is it?' the other man in the room said.

'Oh, for fuck's sake!' James shouted at the wall, and then turned angrily towards me: 'What?'

I looked at his friend.

'Can I speak to you alone?' I asked.

'Fuck, fucking hell!' James shouted.

'Please, James. Please.'

'Alright.' He stood up and sniggered. 'Here will do right,' he said in the corridor. There was no point in arguing, in pushing for more privacy. 'What do you want?' he said.

'Well,' I started, looking at him, thinking that if I didn't do it now, it would never happen. 'I wanted to say that you're very important to me.'

He rolled his eyes.

'You're my brother,' I said.

'Fucking hell, Nate.'

We stood looking at each other, me trying to convey sincerity, him sweating impatient disdain until the bell rang. He rushed to open the door, shielding his guest from my eyes, and negotiated in whispers.

'Hold on,' I heard him say. Patting his pockets, he walked towards me. 'You care for me, right? Then give me ten pounds.'

I felt like running away, last chance or not. I only had a twenty.

'Twenty will do,' he said.

Half a minute later, he was back in the corridor, hiding his fix from me, exuding a relaxed charm.

'Thanks Nate, I heard you. I'm on edge sometimes. It hasn't been easy, you know. But I'm feeling better after rehab. Slowly climbing the slope, you know. One step at a time,' he smiled.

I smiled back, trying to hide my pain.

'Alright, I need to spend some time alone with Julian,' he said. 'I'll call you when I come to Oxford, alright?'

'Yeah,' I said, and we stood with our arms hanging awkwardly.

'Hug?' I asked.

'Yeah.' He tapped my back three times, and he was moving into the next room.

'Enjoy London, Nate,' he said over his shoulder, 'it's a nice city. Plenty to do if you have a few hours to spare.'

Hours to spare. I bit my lips to stop a grimace, said goodbye to both of them, and left my brother for the streets, their blackened bricks, their leafless trees, all whooshing in unison with the wave of despair that took hold of me. Where was the beauty gone now? Even the cloudless sky couldn't reach a decent blue. I had three days left and I was walking through London, bloody London, choked with cars, sprawling wherever it could clone another row of bland houses, spewing its smog into lungs, leaves, and that flock of silly birds acting like it was spring. Where was the memorial now? The grace that had inspired me felt as pale as a London sky. Still, mechanically, for I had no alternative, I made my way to Paddington station and caught the next express train to Oxford, back to my computer and my schedule.

After an hour of watching city dissolving into fields, I felt like I could once again rationalise my path. It was how society worked: do something wrong, pay for it. The only difference between me and the child killers splattered over the *Daily Mail* was that I hadn't been caught.

I unpacked my guilt, each element strengthening my resolve. I'd become Eric's friend; I'd made him care about people so he could better hate them; I'd nodded along to everything he'd said and I'd kept quiet when I should have spoken out; and the list continued, more satisfying for the pain it caused me: I'd followed his words when he was firing his guns; I'd frozen when I had a chance to help Jeffrey and Anna and Grace, and then, in the epitome of a deep-seated selfishness, I'd finally come into my own when it'd become about my own life; and I'd betrayed the one who'd put his whole faith into me. But it didn't stop there. That couple, sitting across from me, a happy toddler smiling and laughing on their lap, wouldn't let me tickle his feet if I told them the half of it. I'd survived when everyone else had died, and I'd let my mother shape my memories with every one of her well-meaning prods, and I hadn't told the truth when I'd been given the chance, and I'd lounged on Chris and Mary's sofa like a man without a care in the world. And then I'd fled, and I'd come back to corrupt a good girl, ignoring every sign, pushing and pushing until she cracked, just so that I could sleep better at night. Yes, the list was long.

But above all – I dried the sweat off my palms on my seat's chequered felt – my crime was a passive suggestibility. It had dogged me my whole life, from the days I'd followed Tom and Paul around the streets of Oxford; to my fascination with Eric and that moment when, gun in hand, I could have done so much more; to my weeks in hospital and the hours I'd let my mother reshape my story; to my years travelling and the months I'd spent following Denret. It had made me into a criminal. But now I was going to follow Leona, and for once my crime was going to prove my redemption.

By the time I rode home from the train station, I was remembering parts of what I'd felt, the hours I'd spent on the field in the sun, the silence inside the memorial, the freedom of my thoughts. I couldn't stop something I'd started, no. I'd decided to capture it all – now I had to write quickly and finish my story before nos quatre mois. I was following no one this time: writing was my own pursuit. But I still wanted to share it, someone to read this text, someone to like it, even when I was dead. The more I imagined a reader, the more I remembered the inspector's visit on my eighteenth birthday, the more I addressed my words to him. He'd laid claim to my story when he'd asked me for the facts and nothing but the facts, when he said he wouldn't judge me, when all he sought was the truth. I would find his email address and I'd send him these two files, the one I'm typing now and the one I finished before I met Leona, and one man would know all. One man would be able to understand me. It crossed my mind that what I'd done lay so close to the edge of the law that, if I were to come clean today, he might opt not to charge me. But that just proved that there was something wrong with the law – the thought of my arms swinging merrily, free of the shackles they deserved, repulsed me. If there was even the smallest of chances that I'd walk free, then I was right to seek my own punishment.

I stopped at the corner store – it was the young Bangladeshi's day off – and I bought three loaves of bread. One per day. Once in the flat, I filled two empty bottles full of water, found an empty jug in case I needed to piss, and I locked myself into my studio, piling three chairs and two boards I'd found in a cupboard, kitchen table extensions I gathered, in front of the door until it looked as though I would die were a fire to start in the kitchen. For forty-one hours, I stayed locked in my bunker, on my green exercise ball, dozing an hour here, an hour there with my head between my arms, and most of all typing – typing when I felt good, typing when I had cramps, typing when I had doubts.

There was a point yesterday when I pictured OJ, the sailor from the Home Counties I'd met onboard *Hunter*, and I recalled my first storm. A ship as big as ours, and she was rocking, creaking, heaving, water and wind trying to throw me overboard. The thrill of it! All I had to do was leave England and I could face another storm – my passport still had twelve months on it, my bank account 11,000 pounds. Another bottle of whisky with OJ and he'd tell me to find myself a fresh cunt. 'She's got you locked in with those lips of hers, my boy. A new girl and you'll be right as daybreak,' I heard him say. Picturing him, I looked at the barricade I'd built myself and stood up. But I hadn't been on my feet for hours, and I was hungry, dehydrated, tired. I sat back down. There was no escape.

Hours later, when I was dozing next to my computer, I felt vibrations travelling through the concrete slabs up to my bones. I woke up and tried to listen. The sound of footsteps. It was Leona pacing around the flat, her steps heavy when they used to be light. I rushed to my feet, pushed the chairs aside, and opened the door. Her hand on the main door, her bag over her shoulder, she looked surprised to see me. Guilty, I thought.

'Are you leaving?' I said.

She let go of the handle and walked towards me, concern fighting off the guilt on her face.

'I didn't know you were here,' she said. 'But yes, I have to meet a friend in town.'

Extending a hand, she stroked my cheek. There were tears in her eyes.

'You look terrible, and you smell too,' she said.

'I'll look good tomorrow, don't worry.'

She bent her head and stifled a sob.

'Don't cry,' I said. 'You don't have to.'

She looked up and gave me a brave smile. Then, her fingers finding the back of my head, she leaned in and kissed me, salty tears on her lips. Our foreheads touched and our kiss stopped, each resting on the other, catching our breath. After a few moments, she leaned back and looked at me:

'Don't cry,' she said.

'I'm not.'

She smiled sadly and kissed me again.

'Thank you,' she whispered, leaning back, clutching her bag to her chest.

'I should be thanking—' I started, but she laid her hand over my mouth.

'No,' she said. 'I'm going to be late otherwise.'

'Alright,' I said.

She pulled out a tissue and wiped her eyes.

'Leona?'

'Yes?' She looked up, her eyes moist.

'Term's about to start. Are you ready?'

She tried to smile me away.

'Have you bought your books?' I insisted.

'No.'

'Why not? You have money.'

'I… I haven't thought about it.'

'But you will, right?'

'I don't know,' she said.

I needed more. There was no point otherwise.

'Term starts soon, and you need to do well if you want to go to Paris, remember? Promise me you'll buy your books. You'll buy them tomorrow.'

'Yes,' she said, looking at my feet.

I grabbed her by the shoulder.

'Promise me,' I said with more force.

'Yes.' She looked at me, blinking a tear away.

'Say it!'

'I promise I'll buy the books,' she said slowly.

'And you'll study hard,' I added.

'Yes.'

My grip loosened. And it became a caress.

'Okay,' I said. 'Thank you.'

For a few instants, my thumb traced the contour of her shoulder, while we both looked at the ground.

'I put the herbs in the bin,' she said. 'They'd gone bad.'

'You did?' I said, suddenly hoping.

'Yes, I told you, I have a new dish in mind. I'll cook at home and bring it tomorrow. See you at seven?'

'Seven, yes,' I said, conjuring benign ingredients, searching her face for something that would confirm that hope. But she still looked caught in between sadness and relief.

As soon as she left the flat, I went to the La Rochelle cake tin. The medicine bottles were gone. In that bag she'd clutched to her breast, I thought. My hopes soared further, giddy with possibility, and crashed, cruel as they hit the ground. There was no point in hoping, I knew, and yet, despite my best efforts, my mind kept on looking for a way out. I didn't remember putting them there, but both of my credit cards were now resting on top of my passport, inches from my left hand, so that it need only take a moment of weakness, and I could put on my jacket and be back at what I do best: flee. And this morning, just as I was writing about the moment I discovered the medicine bottles, I told myself that perhaps she wouldn't be able to feed me the drugs when it came to it. The happy Leona I'd fallen for would resurface and put a stop to the whole masquerade. In which case

I had to be careful: of course, I'd open the bottles I ordered the other day (they arrived this morning), but I shouldn't take the drugs until I was sure she was going to poison me.

I punched my thigh hard, the pain clearing my mind. Hope was torture. I'd accepted her decision. Now, I had to take the pills before she gave them to me. That way, like the one man shooting a blank in a firing squadron, she'd be left clean. Police would confirm it, I'd make sure of it – yes, I'd leave a suicide note, the drugs' receipt, such evidence that no one could ever accuse her – and in a few years, she'd once again live as if nothing had happened.

Twenty minutes to seven, and I need to shave, to put on some perfume, to iron my shirt. Don't hesitate! Tonight, first here in this flat, and then later on the river, I will make up for everything I've done. I must be proud of myself. Many lesser men would have fled already. Just like I did when I turned eighteen. It's simple: I should have stopped Eric or I should have died with him, and I did neither. I shouldn't have talked to Leona about her brother, and I spent two nights confessing. Tonight, I'm a man in control of my own heart, of my own mind, and tonight, pills in my pocket, I'm a man in control of my own death. Surely, a man's final act can atone for the rest. Yes, I see it again, the beauty. It's there, my redemption, the beauty of a graceful death.

Acknowledgments

I wrote this book in Paris over a twelve-month period. Many people helped me to make it what it has become and deserve to be acknowledged.

First, my parents, who not only wilfully suspended any disbelief they may have had in a novelist's prospects, but also did their all so that I could write a decent book.

Then, the Anglophone literary community in Paris: that eclectic mix of poets, novelists, and musicians hovering around Shakespeare and Company and spilling into breakaway groups; meeting over coffees, cakes, beer, or at one of David Barnes' creations. Special thanks to the Montmartre Thursday-nighters: Rafael Herrero, Wendell Steavenson, Sophie Hardach, and Helen O'Keeffe. Bloody hell, we helped each other!

And the people who read and commented on full drafts of this book: Dane Austin, Sarah Hancock, Gina Hanrahan, Anita Koester, Barbara Lauriat, Emily McLaughlin, Chris Newens, Valentina Olivastri, Alberto Rigettini, Laura Silver. I asked a lot of you, and you delivered.

And finally, the people who turned this book into a solid object. My agent, Peter Straus, who never seems to waste a word. His wonderfully efficient assistant, Felicia von Keyserlingk. And the people at Garnet: Arash Hejazi, Marie Hanson, Pam Park, and the rest of the team.

Thank you.